Savvy Summers and the Sweet Potato Crimes

Savvy Summers
and the
Sweet Potato Crimes

A MYSTERY

Sandra Jackson-Opoku

MINOTAUR BOOKS
NEW YORK

First published in the United States by Minotaur Books, an imprint of St. Martin's Publishing Group

SAVVY SUMMERS AND THE SWEET POTATO CRIMES. Copyright © 2025 by Sandra Jackson-Opoku. All rights reserved. Printed in the United States of America. For information, address St. Martin's Publishing Group, 120 Broadway, New York, NY 10271.

www.minotaurbooks.com

Design by Meryl Sussman Levavi

The Library of Congress Cataloging-in-Publication Data is available upon request.

ISBN 978-1-250-35190-6 (hardcover)
ISBN 978-1-250-35191-3 (ebook)

Our books may be purchased in bulk for promotional, educational, or business use. Please contact your local bookseller or the Macmillan Corporate and Premium Sales Department at 1-800-221-7945, extension 5442, or by email at MacmillanSpecialMarkets@macmillan.com.

First Edition: 2025

10 9 8 7 6 5 4 3 2 1

*In memory of Great Aunt Oceal Ennols
Patterson, 1903–1984 . . .*

*Who journeyed the Great Migration from
Mississippi to Memphis to Chicago . . .*

*Who ran several West Side eateries and helped
raise us with stern, steady love . . .*

*And taught her nieces to appreciate and cook
hearty soul food dishes.*

Savvy Summers

and the

Sweet Potato Crimes

CHAPTER 1

"Help Me, Obi-Wan Kenobi"

"Oh, Miss Savvy. I'm about at the end of my rope!" Matilda Jaspers stood there with curlers in her hair, slippers on her feet, a robe wrapping her body, and a stricken expression on her face.

My sous-chef, Penny, had commandeered the catering cart, I was staggering under the weight of a jumbo-sized pan of smothered chicken, and Mattie was blocking the doorway. I glanced at the frosting-smeared cake topper she held aloft like the sword of Damocles.

"Move away, Miss Mattie," I said calmly, but firmly. "This thing's as hot as hell and heavy as deep-fried sin. We don't want another accident."

Before an unfortunate mishap arose, Parker Welbon managed to ease his grandmother aside, take the pan from me, and carry it into the kitchen.

"What am I going to do?" Mattie moaned. "We can't have a wedding without a cake."

The poor dear was acting like anybody's stressed-out Bridezilla, though she'd obviously forgotten this was her fiftieth-anniversary celebration, not her nuptials. Even if it had been, there was no law on the books that you needed a wedding cake to tie the knot.

I put my arm around her shoulder. "Don't fret yourself, Miss Mattie. These things happen."

She didn't have to tell me what the problem was. I'd just watched it happen from across the kitchen—slow enough to see it, too fast to prevent it. The deliveryman from Annabelle's Sweet Stuff Bakery had tripped coming through the very same kitchen doorway we now stood in. Just four hours before party time, a triple-tiered coconut cake went tumbling to the floor. He should have wheeled it in on a cart. That was the professional way to transport a tiered custom cake.

Mattie had fallen to her knees, weeping over the ruins. I had to drag her away so the delivery guy could clean up the mess he'd made. It's the only way my helper Parker, my sous-chef Penny, and I would be able to safely bring in the rest of our food and catering supplies.

"Don't worry, Miss Mattie. I'm sure the bakery will refund your money."

"You don't understand," Mattie fretted. "Annabelle gave me that cake as . . . I don't know what to call it."

"An anniversary gift?"

"You could say that. She didn't want to do it in the first place. I had to call in a big ol' favor." She clutched the cake topper so tightly, I feared it might crumble. Beneath a thin coating of frosting, I could make out a young blond couple in formal wedding dress.

Help me, Obi-Wan Kenobi. You're my only hope.

Okay, she didn't *say* it, but that was what Mattie meant. Like she couldn't have come to me from Jump Street instead of Annabelle Beasley's place way out in Dolton. At Essie's we don't drop our food, okay?

Well, you know me, Jane Dandy to the rescue. I left Penny and Parker to carry on without me and zoomed back to the café to whip up a batch of fresh desserts. In short order, I had baked ten sweet potato pies and four pans of peach cobbler. I loaded them into the catering racks in the hatchback of Red Rover, my candy-apple-red RAV4, returning in record time with everything still warm. Emergency averted!

I wish I could say that was the last mishap of the evening. If you thought that cake crash was a disaster, what happened later was an outright catastrophe. In fact, all the crap that hit the fan at Granderson and Matilda Jaspers's fiftieth-anniversary party made me utter my Great-Aunt Essie's favorite epithet. *Lord have mercy on their naked souls!* If you catch Savvy Summers acting the fool way up into my seventies, please slap some sense into me.

My three-person staff worked the Majestic Ballroom in our signature white shirts and black slacks, our crisp white aprons boldly emblazoned in red. The image of two hands upholding a steaming platter still bore the initials SSS-CCC, though no one called us that anymore. Beneath our logo, the motto read: "A pinch of bacon grease and a pound of love."

It had been clear from day one that this was a Mattie Jaspers production. Granderson Jaspers was just along for the ride. His wife had set the theme, picked the menu, invited the guests, and recruited her tribe of kids and grandkids to decorate the ballroom with gold streamers and balloons.

"Does Grandy have any menu preferences?" I asked, trying to include her husband in the planning.

"I'm the one throwing this party, Miss Savvy," Mattie scolded. "Grandy don't know nothing from nothing."

As long as I'd known Mattie Jaspers, she'd never worked outside the home. How she was going to finance those catering costs was none of my business. It wouldn't be long before it became so.

Mattie wasn't quite as cheap as Grandy, though she did believe in getting her dollars' worth. She ordered a budget-friendly banquet "without service," meaning heated trays of food set out for folks to help themselves. No way that was going to work with the rowdy Jaspers clan and company.

I shouldn't even offer that no-frills option, since I'd seen my share of sedate, churchgoing grown folks going full beast mode at unstaffed banquets—overloading plates to the tipping point, butting ahead of people in line, picking through trays for the choicest morsel, even whipping out to-go containers to dish up grub and carry it home.

Annabelle's Sweet Stuff Bakery wasn't the only business giving a pro bono contribution. As an anniversary gift to the couple, I threw in myself and Penny Lopés, Essie's two-person staff. Parker Welbon, a handsome college student with dental braces, rounded it out to three. I'd been hiring him regularly for weekend work at the café and the occasional catering job, though this time his Grandma Mattie had bullied him into volunteering. While I appreciated the extra set of hands, I was relieved his fee wouldn't be coming from my whisper-thin profits.

I took Mattie's guest list, doubled the numbers, and adjusted the price accordingly. I would have done well to triple it. Only forty-two folks confirmed their attendance though over a hundred turned up that evening to feast on baked macaroni and cheese, smothered chicken, fried perch, mixed green salad, coleslaw, squash casserole, green beans and red potatoes, buttermilk biscuits, and cornbread. I wasn't contracted to provide desserts, but of course that changed at the last minute.

Our community of people does not respect the RSVP, it pains me to report. Instead of clicking off a thirty-second email or making a one-minute phone call, they expect the Magic 8

Ball to send their confirmation by ESP. Then they just show up. These are the very ones who howl with righteous indignation when there isn't enough for all the hungry mouths you weren't expecting to feed.

"It might taste good," they'd grudgingly admit, "but Essie's ain't hardly going to fill you up."

In a backless cocktail dress displaying ample curves, Winifred Mae Jaspers Welbon strolled over to the DJ stand and promptly hijacked the playlist.

"Enough with all these done-to-death dusties," she ordered. "Let's get this party started!"

A loud rap song soon blasted from the speakers and Winnie leapt onto the dance floor.

"*Ain't no party like a hip-hop party,* 'cause what?" She chanted the call and placed a hand to her ear, waiting for the response. Nobody answered so she did herself. "*'Cause a hip-hop party don't stop.* Dang, y'all some lames up in this piece."

Her two older sons sighed in embarrassment while the grandkids snickered and pointed. The husband Penny dubbed "Henpecked Henry" smiled with bemused tolerance. Their youngest son, Parker Welbon, shook his head at his mother's antics as he replenished the spread with fresh trays from the kitchen.

Grandy glanced over and did a double take. "Winnie Mae Welbon, sit your yella ass down. Don't nobody want to see all that back fat jiggling. Folks liable to catch their death of motion sickness."

"Don't hate on the thickness, Daddy." Winnie waved dismissively. "This party is dead as a dodo bird. Let us young folks have some fun."

In her mid-forties, she was hardly the ingenue she made herself out to be. In fact, Winnie Mae was already a grandmother three times over.

"Don't write no checks that your ass can't cash." Grandy shook a warning finger. "You ain't too big and bad to turn across my knee."

The girl had the nerve to match her father's finger with one of her own! I'd known the Family Jaspers long enough to realize there were reasons for her misbehavior. For one thing, Winnie had been freely imbibing at the bar. For another, people said she'd always been a problem child. The father blamed the mother.

Grandy swore that when his wife finally birthed a plump daughter after six slim sons, "Mattie turned the child into a mama's girl and spoiled her fat ass rotten."

"This is a grown folks' party!" An enraged Granderson Sr. stalked over to the DJ station. "Take that hippety-hop off the box right now. I pay the cost to be the damned boss."

Which wasn't exactly true, if Mattie was actually bankrolling the event. The DJ deftly segued from rap music into King Floyd's "Groove Me." I did a quick solo step to the tune. It was our song, the one my first husband and I had picked for our wedding dance.

A scene soon erupted between father and daughter. Terms like "demented old goat" and "wretched little she-demon" were generously bandied about. It ended with father inviting daughter down south where Satan lived and daughter promising father she would send him there first. People watched the fracas in half-bored amusement. Between the eldest Jaspers and his youngest child, these disputes were prone to blow up on a regular basis.

Winnie gathered her husband, two sons, and three grands. She tried to scoop up her youngest son, Parker, on the way out, reminding him that "I'm the one paying for all that metal in your mouth." That's when I had to intervene. Parker Welbon was on the job and I desperately needed the extra set of hands.

"You won't have Winnie Mae Welbon to kick around, Daddy. Come on, kids. Henry, we're outta here."

It wouldn't do to disagree or there'd be hell to pay. The Welbon family minus its youngest son dutifully followed their matriarch down the stairs and out the door. Though they'd come at different times from three separate directions, Winnie had the Welbons leaving in a caravan.

However regrettable their departure, it had a fortunate side effect. Mattie had only ordered food enough for forty. Even though I had doubled it to eighty, it still wasn't quite enough. With the seven Welbons gone, there'd be more to spread around. We'd still have to limit serving sizes and second helpings, but not quite so drastically as before.

Penny commanded the buffet line, carefully portioning out one salad, one meat, one vegetable, one bread, and one starch per person. No second helpings under any circumstances!

Parker helped me unload the truck and carry the pans to the empty dessert table. Mattie had wiped off the rescued cake topper and placed it high atop a candleholder. I tried to ignore the frozen couple looking down on my humble desserts with a piercing blue-eyed gaze. Didn't they make these things in the dark-skinned, senior-citizen variety?

I started slicing pie and plating cobbler servings. Stationed in an alcove between the bar and the head table, I had a sidelong view of the ballroom and all its goings-on.

The couple of honor didn't have to line up with everybody else. Parker served his grandparents' meals on real china, silverware, and crystal, not the paper and plastic everyone else was using. I took two generous helpings of sweet potato pie, topped them with whipped cream and a sprig of mint, and asked Parker to take them to the head table.

A busty young woman in a scruffy blond wig stepped into his path and firmly maneuvered the dessert plates from his hands. Of all the greedy gut moves! I was just about to intercede when I saw her sashay over to the head table, adjust her cleavage, lean over, and present the plates to Mattie and Grandy with a flourish.

Now, what was the point of all that brownnosing? It may have just been my imagination but Mattie seemed to cut the girl a sharp side-eye.

A muscle-bound bartender with arms straining the seams of his shirtsleeves grabbed two bottles of champagne. He went from table to table, pouring into people's plastic flutes.

"Y'all better make it last 'cause it ain't but one glass apiece," he kept repeating. For all his bulk and brawn, the man had a squeaky, Mike Tyson type of speaking voice. "Save it for the toast."

Did I say champagne? I was sadly mistaken. When the bartender scooted past the dessert alcove, I could see that the sparkling wine he served was a dubious brand. It was of a variety that Penny derisively referred to as "headache champagne."

As I continued carving sweet potato pie into slices that weren't too small to be miserly nor big enough to be extravagant, I watched the party shift into speechifying mode.

Mattie sure got her money's worth with the DJ, who was also her MC, photographer, and videographer. The socializing, music, and dancing halted as the DJ-MC-photo-videographer announced the next part of the program.

"Dessert will soon be served, good people," he promised, "and along with it, a series of champagne toasts. Hold on to your glasses!"

Well, that was unfortunate timing. He must not have gotten

the memo. That cake disaster and rescue mission had pushed the schedule back at least forty-five minutes. I hadn't even finished plating the desserts and people were still lined up at the buffet table. As a perfectionist and borderline type A personality, I hated it when my plans didn't go as expected. I frantically beckoned Parker over, and he began loading servings of pie and cobbler onto trays and taking them around to the tables.

Meanwhile, the guy who'd made the premature announcement propped a videocam onto his shoulder and pulled out a handheld microphone. He headed straight for me and thrust the mic into my face.

"What's cooking, catering lady?" He grinned. "Omar Saladin at your service."

"I'm busy, Omar Saladin. Keep it moving, please."

Ignoring my request, he took down the camera and panned the dessert table, focusing in on an elaborate cake topper of the young blond couple in wedding dress.

"Well, what do we have here, Barbie and Ken?" Omar joked. "Becky and Chad? The Missy and Massa of desserts?"

I didn't dignify his remarks with a comment although I'd been wondering the same thing myself. My silence didn't deter the overeager videographer. He eyed the array of pie and cobbler servings. "I hope it's as good as it looks."

"Believe me, it is."

"Well, the proof of the pudding is in the tasting."

He laid down the mic, snatched a slice of sweet potato pie with his bare hand, and crammed almost half of it into his mouth. Then the rude dude swung the camera around and aimed at his own chewing mouth.

"Mm-*mm*. That's a thumbs-up for taste and a thumbs-down for size. In fact, skimpy seems to be the theme for tonight's refreshments. Why so stingy, catering lady?"

Just what I needed, a critic and wannabe comic. So, Mattie underestimated the turnout and people didn't bother to RSVP. What business was it of his? I beckoned him closer and grabbed the mic from his hand. Then I clicked it off and covered the camera lens with my hand.

"What the hell, catering lady?" he protested. "I'm working here."

"Well, guess what? I'm working, too. And the name isn't catering lady, it's Savvy Summers. Now, you see that guy over there, grinning like a mule eating briars?"

Since both my hands were busy, I inclined my head toward a beaming, balding, brown-skinned fellow on the other side of the room. He looked like a chubbier version of the actor Mark Sinclair, AKA Vin Diesel. His signature black lollipop dangling from his mouth, the man held court amid a throng of admirers shaking his hand and posing for selfies.

"Well, I'll be damned." Omar peered across the room. "If that isn't . . . ?"

"None other." I nodded. "And you know he's itching to chew the fat. Go ahead, Omar. Make his day."

It was our celebrity guest of the night. Delbert "Do-Right" Dailey represented our corner of Woodlawn in Chicago City Council. Rumor had it he was the out-of-wedlock, biracial son of a prominent political family. The gossip circulated as an open secret though he coyly denied it whenever questioned. However amusing the story might be, we all knew it to be a big ol' whopping lie.

Penny Lopés, who had a nickname for everything and everybody, had christened the man Delbert *Do-Wrong*. "The man is a sho 'nuff bastard all right, just not of that particular pedigree. Does he really think people don't notice that flask he carries around in his back pocket? How he thinks he can be a mover and shaker nipping at the sauce is beyond me."

Dropping them like they had the pox, Delbert Dailey ditched his fans for the microphone. As he spoke into it, he prowled the room like a plump brown panther, stopping at tables and shaking hands, greeting everyone as "sweetheart" or "dear brother," as was his inclination.

As he congratulated the anniversary couple, Delbert also gave a thinly disguised campaign speech. Aldermanic elections were coming up, and he was shamelessly hustling votes. When he finally paused for air, Omar gave him the "cut" signal and reclaimed the mic.

"May I have a word?" A hand went up at a rear table and Omar scurried over to it.

The speaker was a paunchy, double-chinned white gentleman with a suspiciously dark flattop 'do. I couldn't tell if it was a tint or toupee. A shiny purple shirt buttoned halfway down showed off a coarse carpet of gray. I guess Clairol doesn't make chest hair dye.

"Greetings, folks." He grinned into the mic, showing impossibly even teeth. "I flew in all the way from Glencoe and boy, are my arms tired. Ba-dum-bump."

"Uncle Tuck is so corny," Parker leaned over and whispered to me. "Nobody ever laughs at his jokes."

The kid had a point.

"Granderson and me, we go way back in the Wayback Machine," Tuck continued. "I used to manage the Soul Serenaders during gospel music's Jurassic period. You know, back when dinosaurs roamed the earth?"

He paused again for laughter that didn't arrive.

"Aw, c'mon, folks. You're killing me." Tuck turned toward

the head table, lifting his glass in a toast. "Between Grandy and the boys—James, wherever he might be, Junebug, and Theobald—may they rest in peace, not pieces—we helped put Chicago gospel on the music map."

"Is that who I think it is?" the man of honor suddenly shouted. "Oh, hell no! It ain't going down like that."

"Grandy, please." Mattie grabbed his arm. "Don't you start no mess."

Ignoring his wife, Grandy hoisted himself up and stalked over on his walking stick.

"It ain't that kind of party, Tuck Pfeiffer," Grandy spat. The hand without the cane drew back into a fist. "You're not welcome here, so make like the ass you are and split."

Tuck flashed his dentures again. "Hey, I've been thrown out of better places than this. Congratulations, Grandy, Miss Matt. I'll see you folks around."

"Damn right, you will. In court!" Grandy snatched the mic away. "Now get your crooked ass up outta this piece."

Grandy had been claiming for years that Tuchman Pfeiffer had ripped him off of lucrative songwriting credits. I knew about the alleged lawsuit, since Grandy claimed the millions would be rolling in any day now. The Soul Serenaders' time in the sun came and went decades ago. Wouldn't the statute of limitations be expired by now?

As Tuck made for the exit, I saw the back of his head. A few strings of wispy gray peeked out from the bouffant black at his neck. Yes, definitely a toupee.

Grumbling under his breath, Grandy huffed back to his seat, the microphone still in hand.

CHAPTER 2

Love Takes Time

I felt a moist murmur at my right ear. Penny Porter Lopés, Mouth of the South (and the greater Chicago metropolitan area), sidetracked me on her way from lugging in a box of Sterno cans from the kitchen.

"That Tuchman Pfeiffer used to be way up into R&B. You know he hosted *Rhythm and Blues Chicago,* that old TV show."

"I'm surprised you remember that."

"Well, it was on about a million years. I used to watch reruns with my grandma. And, everybody on the South Side knows the story. Old boy went down to Hattiesburg, Mississippi, found a singer in a juke joint, and brought the sweet young thang up to Chicago."

"What, Grandy used to sing R&B?"

Penny rolled her eyes in mock horror. "Mr. Holy Roller? Perish the thought! It was Matilda Montgomery. Once they got back to Chicago, Grandy met Mattie and scooped her up. Bippety, boppety, boo! Like the fairy godmother in *Cinderella,* all he had to do was wave his magic wand."

"His magic wand?"

"His dragon tail, his pork sword, his heat-seeking missile."

"All right, that's enough," I sighed. "You sure can take a metaphor and run with it. Get on back to work."

Penny ignored me. "And Grandy's still out there catting around, or doing the best he can with a little assistance."

"What, he brings somebody with him?"

"Better living through chemistry." Penny winked. "If you get my drift."

"How can you possibly know that, Nosy Lopés?"

"I have my sources. See that chick at the bar guzzling headache champagne? The one in that scary wig, lurking like a predator?"

I glanced over at a young lady with blond hairpiece askew, the one who'd intercepted those pie servings earlier. The bewigged beauty seemed around twenty, twenty-five at most. In the skimpiest of midriff tops and skintight jeans ripped at the knees, she was severely underdressed for the occasion. And she apparently hadn't gotten the one-glass-per-person memo. In the bartender's absence she was pouring out her own. She filled her plastic flute to the brim, drank it dry, and poured again.

I was confused. "And that would be one of your sources? Careless attire for a semiformal affair, wouldn't you say?"

"Affair?" Penny giggled. "You got that right."

"Talk sense, Penny Lopés. Some of us have been crisis baking. I am too tired for your riddles."

"That's Shysteen Shackleford but you can call her Shystie. The girl puts the 'ho' in home-wrecker. An uninvited and very unwelcome guest, if Mattie Jaspers has a say in it. One of her husband's latest, um . . . acquisitions, shall we say?"

"What would a girl that age want with gray-headed Grandy Jaspers?"

"I know, right?" she agreed. "With his asthma, gout, lumbago, and gas."

"So now you have access to his medical record?"

"Of course not, girl. You know they got those pesky HIPAA laws. No, it's that song from *A Funny Thing Happened on the Way to the Forum*. Shysteen must be gunning for Grandy's Social Security check, that's all I can think of."

"You watch too many musicals and pass too much gossip, Penny. It's not a good look on you."

"Hey, don't kill the messenger. I got it all on good authority."

She always had her news "on good authority." Penny made it her business to be up on all the latest scuttlebutt. Hell, she was even up on the vintage scuttlebutt. When Grandy and Mattie got together in the last quarter of the last millennium, her own parents probably weren't even born.

"Oh, well," I sighed. "Three sides to every story. Now get your butt back to work. People are abusing the refreshments."

I pointed to the buffet table, where the baker, Annabelle Beasley, was making her way to the front of a long line. The woman actually had the nerve to show up as a guest without having RSVP'd, and after her anniversary cake had blessed the kitchen floor.

"Oh, hell no," Penny growled. "Miss Thang has already gobbled her plate of food and she's coming back for seconds? Some people haven't even been served."

I turned my attention to my own work and left Penny to deal with hers. I continued arranging individual servings of pie and cobbler on tiered trays and topping them off with dollops of fresh whipped cream and sprigs of chocolate mint.

Meanwhile at the head table, Omar was posing the couple for pictures and video shots. Mattie lifted her champagne flute. The bartender brought out an ice bucket with two bottles. He popped one open and filled Mattie's glass to the brim.

Don't fill it all the way up! I wanted to yell. *Wine needs air to breathe.* As a bartender, he should have known that. I hoped it was a better brand than that headache champagne everyone else was drinking.

Grandy put a hand over his wineglass, pointing to his bottle of beer. "I'll stick with my Genuine Draft."

Mattie raised her glass and Grandy his beer bottle. They clicked them together and tried to drink in the classic "arms-linked" wedding pose. A dribble of champagne splashed against Mattie's bosom and she drew back. "Don't be messing up my dress now, Grandy!"

"Let's try it this way," the photographer instructed. "Offer your drinks to each other. She'll take a taste from your beer and you sip from her champagne."

"That bubbly stuff is too rich for my blood," Grandy protested.

"It's just for the camera," Omar promised. "We want to get a nice shot."

They dutifully leaned in toward each other. Mattie took a delicate sip from his beer.

Grandy guzzled Mattie's entire glass of champagne then made a face.

"Almost perfect." Omar moved in closer with his videocam. "Do it again, this time without the grimace."

The bartender shook his head in irritation, but the videographer insisted that he pour out another glass. After drinking it, Grandy sneezed. At the end of the next one he shook his head. "It tastes like flavored air."

They had to repeat the pose four times in all—Mattie sipping at Grandy's bottle, Grandy guzzling from Mattie's champagne flute. Four champagne flutes were refilled and finished. The entire bottle of wine was empty before the photographer/ videographer finally got his footage.

"Baby, I'm still thirsty." Grandy leaned toward his wife, pretending to lick the droplets that had spilled down her neckline. It was a move meant for the crowd and the camera. His racy gesture was greeted with a few elbow nudges, a chorus of wolf whistles, an "aw, sookie-sookie now."

"Y'all need to quit it." Mattie took the mic and scolded, gently pushing Grandy away.

She stood, smoothing down a gold lamé mermaid gown with a deep plunge of cleavage. For a woman pushing seventy, she still had a good body. Mattie took her champagne flute, found the glass was empty, and raised her water goblet instead.

Don't do it! I wanted to warn her. Aunt Essie always said it was bad luck to toast with water. *You're better off using the empty glass.*

I frantically signaled the bartender. He scrambled over and drew another bottle from the ice bucket. Too late. Mattie had already started her toast.

"Let me take this occasion to tell my husband, Grandy, just how I feel about him. Thank you, sweetheart . . ." Mattie turned and placed a hand on his shoulder.

Grandy sat there grinning like a possum, guzzling his bottle of beer.

". . . for the last fifty years of pure-dee misery. Fifty years of cheating, fifty years of lying, fifty years of whoremongering. I held out for my golden anniversary hoping you would change your cheating ways, but you ain't got it in you."

"Mattie, no," Grandy pleaded. "Don't do this to yourself."

"Just doing unto you what you've done unto me. I'm fed up and finished, Granderson Jaspers. Now sit on it and rotate."

She blew him a kiss and handed him the mic. Grandy stared down at it accusingly, like it had delivered those insults of its own accord. In an Oscar-worthy exit, Mattie pivoted on a stiletto heel and sashayed toward the exit.

The crowd's reaction was a beat delayed. Whispers and gasps of salacious disbelief rippled throughout the ballroom as we watched her shapely behind wiggling down the marble staircase. Then all eyes joggled back Grandy's way to see what would happen next.

"Er, uh." His eyes darted around the room, brown face glowing red. "Thanks for coming but the party's over. Y'all ain't got to go home, but you do got to get out of here."

With that he scrambled up from his seat, grabbed his walking stick, snatched the remaining bottle from the ice bucket, and stumbled after his wife. He passed close enough for me to read the label: *Fizz 56 Sparkling Red.*

The DJ rushed to fill the void with an ironic, though oddly appropriate, choice of songs. Mariah Carey's "Love Takes Time."

In the subsequent hubbub and sudden departures, a good deal of the carefully portioned desserts went uneaten. Annabelle Beasley pulled out the Tupperware containers she was known to travel with. Shysteen and several others gathered paper plates to pile up the remains.

With emergency desserts added on, a sizable catering bill was left unpaid. No one was around to settle the balance, so we packed up around 11 p.m. and got out of Dodge.

CHAPTER 3

Cat Burglar Lurking

Who knew that last night's trouble would revisit us the next morning?

It started out like any other Saturday morning in the kitchen of Essie's Place. Yes, this place is "Essie's," no matter what it says out front. I've been meaning to file a corporate name change, redesign my logo and business cards, and repaint that sign in the storefront window.

What was I thinking, saddling my business with a name like "Sapphire Summers Soulfood Café and Catering Company"? It wasn't long before folks were calling it SSS-CCC's, then slurring that to "Essie's." Which is what I should have named it in the first place, considering the menu was built around my Great-Aunt Essie's treasured recipes.

I turned the sound system to the 1970s oldies channel and warbled along like no one was listening, unless you counted Jesus, President Obama, and my late great-aunt. Not in person, of course. Aunt Essie seemed to wince from the gallery of portraits on the wall above my work desk.

You got a nerve, Aunt Essie, I thought. *You're singing impaired your own self.*

I fell into the rhythm I knew so well. Within the next two

hours I had perfect circles of biscuit dough resting on buttered baking sheets, ready for the oven. Salmon croquettes were mixed and measured into shape, waiting for the griddle. The perch fillets were lemon-peppered. Seasoned chicken parts marinated in Perry, my commercial fridge named for the former Chicago Bears defensive lineman. Raw vegetables steeped in apple cider vinegar wash, waited to be rinsed and chopped.

And Penny Porter Lopés was twenty minutes late and counting.

As baked sweet potato pies cooled on wire racks, I assembled two peach cobblers in industrial-sized baking pans and set them to rest in Perry. My dessert menu was simple but classic. Sweet potato pie, peach cobbler, and pineapple upside-down cake, all from Great-Aunt Essie's unwritten cookbook.

Occasionally I'd venture a Nana's 'Nana. I gussied up my maternal grandmother's banana pudding recipe with a gingersnap crust and lemon-scented custard layered with cinnamon-sprinkled banana slices. A fluffy meringue topping would be lightly browned beneath my kitchen blowtorch, Sweatt, named for an infamous arsonist. I only made Nana's 'Nana on special occasions, since the perishable nature of bananas made the dessert too delicate to go a day's distance.

Those emergency desserts I'd made last night had nearly exhausted my supply of Beauregard sweet potatoes. I reminded myself I would need to place an order from my wholesale produce supplier.

Though I'm faithful to the food I grew up on, sometimes my customers enjoyed something a bit more elevated. My out-of-town daughter-in-law, a chef specializing in vegan "nouvelle soul food," often urged me to try out her dishes. In the downtime before the café's opening, I decided to take a crack at her recipe for vegan sweet potato pie.

I cooked and mashed the last batch of sweet potatoes. There was none of the "vegan butter" she insisted on, so I used coconut oil instead.

I pulsed the grinder and deeply inhaled the scent of fresh nutmeg, then added honey, vanilla, coconut milk, nutmeg, and cinnamon to the potato mash and examined it. The mixture was too loose. Though the recipe was supposed to be vegan, I added an egg for binding (instead of the usual two), gave it a generous squeeze of lemon and another pulse of the mixer. I tasted the pie filling. It still needed something. Fat, definitely more fat. I stirred in another quarter-cup of coconut oil.

Then I poured the batter into a pie shell and slid it into Bessie, the industrial batch oven that cost nearly as much as Red Rover, my truck. As I set the timer and crossed my fingers, I heard a key turn in the front door lock.

Penny rushed through the dining room and scurried into the kitchen. She grabbed a clean apron and wrapped it over her black leggings and tank top. "Don't say a mumbling word, Savvy Summers. I know I'm late."

"Again," I reminded her.

"Girl, if you knew the night I had."

"We were out until almost midnight, Penny. I had the same night."

"No, I'm talking afterward."

Penny left the unsaid floating like aromatic nutmeg sprinkles. She slipped out of her strappy heels and into the rubber-soled kitchen shoes she despised. Her pretty brown face bunched into a scowl as she grabbed the vegetable bin, dumped the rinse, and ran clear water over stalks of carrots and heads of cabbage.

"What's eating you? Looks like you've been sucking on a lemon."

"Yeah, a lemon named Sergio Benjamim Lopés."

I shook my head lest she begin to regale me with details of their overactive love life. It was like trying to stick to a diet while people told stories about all the food they're eating. If I wasn't getting any myself—which I wasn't after a year widowed—I sure didn't want to hear about anybody else's.

"TMI, Penny."

"Seventy damn dollars," she muttered. Her knife flashed like silver lightning as she expertly chopped cabbage into cole-slaw shreds. "Can you believe it? The man went out and spent seventy dollars on fishing equipment."

"Did he, now?"

"Oh, he certainly did. I swear, I feel like washing that man out of my hair and sending him back to Brazil."

I asked if that was from the musical *Oklahoma!*

"Try a little farther west. It's from the movie version of *South Pacific.*"

In contrast to her urban chic persona, I knew the nerdy side of Penny. She was a pop culture junkie with a special fondness for movie musicals.

"How could Sergio be so selfish, as broke as we've been lately? You know how close we came to losing the house last year."

I couldn't help the nagging question that inserted itself into my thoughts. *Wonder what his side of the story is?* My Great-Aunt Essie, rest her soul, always said *there were three sides to every story: her side, his side, and the dad-gum truth.*

"That doesn't even sound like Sergio," I mused. "He's not so much the spendthrift, is he, Penny?"

Sergio was the cheapskate of the family, with his thread-bare clothing and broken-down collection of old cars. In fact, when he first came to Chicago from Salvador, Brazil, he used to walk two miles to the El station just to save a quarter on a bus transfer.

"Girl, he's talking about catching fish in the lake to keep us from going to the grocery store."

"You're kidding."

"No, I'm not. He put the fishing rods and tackle on the Walmart card, thinking I wouldn't find out. You know I never shop at Walmart, not if I can help it."

"How dare he try to save you some money? The nerve of that man!"

"Cut the sarcasm, Savvy. It's not even cute."

I knew well my sous-chef's spending habits. I had to restrain myself from pointing out that some of the fuel that had driven them to the poorhouse was Penny's predilection for designer shoes and handbags. It was a penchant she tried to justify by shopping the consignment shops, Poshmark, and eBay. But even secondhand Louboutins weren't cheap.

The oven timer dinged. The "veganish" sweet potato pie had browned but didn't completely set. Though it rose around the edges after baking for forty-five minutes, it was spongy in the center.

After it cooled, I cut two small slices and tasted one. I was decidedly underwhelmed. "Care to try some, Penny? Let me know what you think."

"Hm." She chewed thoughtfully. "Good flavor, nice spice balance. But a little too heavy on the custard and there's an oily aftertaste. This isn't your regular recipe. What's in this thing?"

"Sweet potatoes, of course. Some coconut oil, lemon, coconut milk, spices."

"What, no butter? No sugar, no dairy, no eggs?"

"Just one egg. It's supposed to be vegan but I doctored the recipe."

Penny shook her head. "Bad idea. Your Aunt Essie's sweet potato pie is a crowd-pleaser. If it ain't broke, don't fix it. You want me to throw the rest of this away?"

"No, I'll hand them out as samples for the lunch crowd. Waste not, want not. That last crumb might be the one that fills you up."

Penny rolled her eyes. "Only from the mind of Great-Aunt Essie."

I cut the remaining pie into tenths and plated the slices on paper doilies atop one of Great-Aunt Essie's antique silver trays.

That's when I heard an unnerving scratching sound coming from the dining room. I almost dropped the tray of pie slices. "What on God's green earth . . . ?"

"Sounds like Freddy Krueger playing 'Chopsticks' on a chalkboard."

Penny and I cautiously approached the front door. Grand-erson Jaspers stood on the other side, running his bone-handled walking stick up and down the window. It was 7:38 a.m., twenty-two minutes before opening. He usually didn't turn up until well after ten.

I'd splurged on that window glass when I had the space re-modeled, a fancy crackled design with lines fractured into a circular spiderweb. Through the distorted pattern I could see a hooded figure peering over Grandy's shoulder. I couldn't make out exactly who it was, though the silhouette was much too tall and lean to be his wife.

An odd slant of sunlight through the warped glass seemed to graft Grandy's upraised cane onto the figure behind him. I had the momentary illusion that the hooded shape held a lifted sickle. Had Grandy brought the grim reaper along for a break-fast date?

I shook my head to dislodge the crazy notion. The sun

shifted and a sickle turned back into a cane, scratching persistently at the window.

I flinched at the grating sound. "He'd better not be leaving any marks on my glass."

"How could you tell with that funhouse window?" Penny was not a fan of the crackled pane effect. "I'm surprised that geezer's got the nerve to show his face in daylight. Don't let him in."

"Now, Penny," I scolded. "He's an old man."

"An old lech. Need I remind you that just last night . . ."

"I know, Penny. I was there. Such a sad situation."

"More power to Mattie, I say. It's about damned time. I have it on good authority that Grandy's been prowling Woodlawn in his ancient Cadillac, hitting on girls his grandkids' age. You saw Miss Thang at the party last night. I swear, Savvy. Viagra is the worst thing going."

"Viagra?" I heard Grandy's cane scraping the window again. The pane was thick and reinforced, so I knew he couldn't hear us. "What does Viagra have to do with it?"

"I already told you. That little blue pill has these old fools out here trying to keep up with the young fools."

Grandy now had his nose pressed against the glass, his face fractured into a dozen jagged angles.

"You'd think it was summertime instead of October. We shouldn't leave him standing there, Penny. It's hot outside."

"Hotter in hell," she grumbled. "Which is where old boy is headed, sooner or later."

Who could have known how that prediction would come to pass?

"Well, I'm not letting him in." I walked over to the beverage stand and measured out scoops of fresh roasted Arusha. I poured two pitchers of filtered water into my Bunn coffee maker. "Opening the restaurant is your responsibility, Ms. Lopés."

Penny sighed, fished out her key, unlocked the double-sided dead bolt and held the door open a crack. The door chime jingled in response.

"Are you here to settle the catering bill? Otherwise, we're not open. And pass the message to your friend back there."

"Who, me?" The person standing behind Grandy spoke, a man's voice. He stood on tiptoe, trying to peer around him. "I don't owe any catering bill."

"Is that how you treat your good-paying customers?" Grandy fumed. "Leaving us on the sidewalk out here in the burning heat?"

"Good-paying customer, that's rich!" Penny snorted. "Savvy's been good to you, Grandy Jaspers. Are you and your wife just gonna walk out on what you owe her?"

"You take that up with Mattie. When are *you* gonna give me what I got coming?"

I turned around and frowned. "What on earth is he talking about, Penny?"

"Girl, I don't even know. Maybe he's still drunk from last night." Penny began closing the door in his face. "Come back later, Grandy. We don't open until eight."

"Let him in, Penny."

She sighed, held the door open, and stepped aside. Grandy stumbled into the café, the other person emerging from behind him. It was neither Mattie Jaspers nor the Angel of Death.

In a skullcap and shades, a black hoodie and sweats, the man seemed to be sporting some sort of disguise. The artist $tevie $tevenson could have used him as the model for an urban folk art portrait, *Cat Burglar Lurking Outside the Café.*

The hooded figure was none other than Noble McPherson,

a man with whom I'd had several less-than-pleasant dealings. The last time he came I had asked him to leave and not return. He sauntered in on Grandy's heels and parked his behind at a seat at the counter.

Why was Grandy here so early on a Saturday morning? Why was Noble here at all?

CHAPTER 4

Don't Take No Wooden Nickels

"Whew, Lord! Thank God for air-conditioning." Grandy fanned himself, leaning on his cane. "Is it hot out there or what? I'm feeling like ol' Robert Johnson today. Got a hellhound on my trail."

"What do you know about the blues?" I teased. "A gospel-singing gentleman like yourself?"

"Baby, I don't need to sing the blues. I done live them a-plenty."

And passed them around, I thought, but didn't say it.

He headed for his customary seat, humming as he hobbled along. His cane tapping out the rhythm. I recognized an old gospel song Great-Aunt Essie used to sing in church.

I been 'buked and I been scorned
I'm gonna tell my Lord when I get home
Just how long you've been treating me wrong.

Grandy wasn't looking quite himself this morning. He'd always been a snazzy, if a somewhat dated, dresser. Summer and early autumn, he'd be sporting one of his crisp panama hats. In cooler seasons he wore a felt fedora. His shoes were always spit-shined Florsheims or Stacy Adams. He wore shirt-sleeves and bow ties nearly every day of the year. I'd never seen a hair out of place, and he had a headful of it.

This morning his eyes were baggy and bloodshot. His salt-and-pepper Afro was dented and linted, squashed to the side like a cake that rose lopsided. The plum-colored tuxedo he'd worn last night looked like he had slept in it. And he was sweating like a racehorse.

Penny sidled over to Grandy's throne beside the potted fern. "Well, look what the rat dragged in. You look like death on roller skates."

"Ain't nobody studying you, Pennylopes." Grandy always pronounced her name to rhyme with "antelopes."

"For the umpty-millionth time, it's Lopés. The letter L. The letter O. The letter P. Accent on the 'e.' The letter S. Low-PEZ."

Grandy ignored her. "I ain't feeling so hot, Pennylopes. Need to get some food in my stomach real quick."

Penny pointed to a bulge at his waistband. "Is that a lead pipe in your pocket or you're happy to see me?"

Grandy looked down at his lap like he'd never seen it before. "Good Lord, who done this?"

If he wasn't looking so confused and distressed, the exclamation would have been comical.

Penny snorted in derision. "I know you're not expecting that thing to answer. And the Good Lord had nothing to do with it. How you gonna come out in public pitching a trouser tent?"

Grandy blushed and bristled at the same time. His feebleness vanished in a flash of irritation. "So why you looking way down south? If you wanted some of this, all you had to do was ask. Now quit your yapping and get me some food."

Penny smirked and whipped out her order pad. "And what

can I bring you? Salmon croquettes and breakfast potatoes? Bacon and eggs? Grits and gravy?"

It was a trick question, of course. Granderson Jaspers Sr. had been a regular practically since we'd opened our doors. He always ordered the same thing, morning or afternoon. Two buttermilk biscuits and a cup of coffee.

In homage to Great-Aunt Essie, I offered a seniors' special to patrons over sixty-five. Two biscuits and a bottomless cup of coffee for a dollar fifty each. Grandy took full advantage of what Penny called "the bleeding heart that'll sink your ship one day."

Grandy would order his two biscuits and wasn't shy about sending them back if they weren't fresh and piping hot. He'd slather them liberally with butter and maple syrup then tell the server to pour his coffee cup two-thirds full. This wasn't because he was watching his caffeine intake. It was to make room for a generous dose of cream and four or five sugars. He'd guzzle down his coffee and demand a refill two, three, four times over.

"Next time don't fill it up so high," he'd often complain.

Grandy could run through nearly a pot of Arusha on any given day. Thanks to Grandy, I would probably have to change the refill policy.

When he wasn't flirting with female customers, Grandy would pester anyone who listened with tales of his gravy days as lead singer and songwriter with the Soul Serenaders Gospel Quartet. To hear him tell it, he'd be swimming in cash by now if he hadn't been shafted by Tuchman Pfeiffer, that no-good manager who had stolen his songwriting credits. Any day now Grandy would win his case and the cash register would start ringing, or so he believed.

When Grandy reached capacity and had to answer the call

of nature—or we finally put him out, whichever came first—he'd count out three-seventy-five for the bill and tax, then leave it on the table, sometimes all in coins. Granderson Jaspers was never known to tip unless you counted his usual parting quip, "Don't take no wooden nickels, now."

Penny put the order pad in her pocket and flounced away. "The biscuits are still in the oven and the coffee's brewing. You're gonna have to wait, old man."

Grandy hunched miserably in his seat, sighing with more dejection than the announcement seemed to call for.

"Look, you're sweating up a storm," I told him. "Some orange blossom lemonade might hit the spot."

"Lemonade, my left boot," Grandy snorted. "I want my coffee."

"Make that two," the man at the counter added. "And they're both on me."

Grandy inclined his head in Noble's direction and doffed an imaginary hat. "Mighty decent of you, young man."

Lord forgive me, but "decent" was hardly the word I'd have chosen.

Grandy shifted around to face him. "Most folks like to sleep in on a Saturday. That ol' empty belly blues got you out of bed this morning?"

Noble looked perplexed. "I beg your pardon?"

I rolled my eyes. "He's asking if you woke up hungry."

Though I preached the virtues of Standard English, I didn't trust a Black man who couldn't comprehend the native tongue. You didn't have to speak Ebonics, just understand a little. It wasn't all that hard. Penny's husband Sergio managed, and he was born in Brazil.

"Hungry?" Noble asked. "Oh, I'm not much of a breakfast person."

"No?" Grandy asked. "Then what you doing here?"

The man had a very good point.

Realizing his strategic error, Noble tried to cover himself. "Um, well. I don't usually eat this early but I decided to come in . . ."

"For what?" I asked him.

He looked around aimlessly, like the artwork on the walls might give him an answer. "Oh, just a little something."

I had an excellent idea what that "something" might be. Noble was as predictable in his way as Grandy was in his. He'd been harassing me for months about buying out my business, and didn't seem to comprehend the simple word "no."

I rolled my eyes, filled two mugs with coffee, and handed them to Noble. Since the man was playing big spender, he could damn well carry the old man his cup of joe. And he better not be looking for the seniors' discount!

No sooner had Noble handed it to him than Grandy gulped down the coffee and waved to me for a refill. He hadn't even doused it with his usual cream and sugar. I came over with the pot.

"Y'all hurry up with those biscuits," he complained. "I'm feeling right pea-ked, kind of sick to my stomach. Seems like everything has a blue haze around it."

"How about a test sample of sweet potato pie? It's a new recipe."

Grandy snorted. "Don't nobody want sweet potato pie at eight in the blessed morning. I had my fill last night."

"It's on the house."

I took his grunt for assent and went to the kitchen. As I returned with the tray of samples, Noble made a move to grab one.

"Sitting up here starving," Grandy called across the room. "And you offered me first."

"He's right." I lifted the platter above Noble's reaching hand. "First come, first served, and you don't eat breakfast, according to you. I'll be right back."

I went to Table Two and set a slice on a dessert plate. Greedy Grandy didn't bother with it. He grabbed two of them directly from the tray and wolfed each down, barely stopping to chew.

"Wow, you must really be hungry. You liked that, huh?"

Grandy grunted again, but it wasn't in assent. His eyes bugged out in sudden alarm. His pecan-colored face flushed a dull crimson shade, then the color drained out into a pallid gray. He clutched at his chest, pointed to me, then slumped sideways in his seat.

"Grandy Jaspers," Penny warned, bringing his biscuits from the kitchen. "That's so not funny!"

I set the tray on the next table and peered into his face. His grizzled head had lolled over onto his right shoulder. I lifted it up and it wobbled to the left.

"Lord, do remember me!" I cried out in panic. "Penny, I don't think he's joking."

We got busy Heimliching and CPRing. We lowered him to the floor and gave him mouth-to-mouth. Or rather, I gave him mouth-to-mouth. Penny adamantly refused. "Nobody knows where those nasty lips have been."

I'm sure she wouldn't have been so flippant if she'd known how it would end.

Although Grandy seemed to have fallen unconscious, the protuberance in his pants did not subside. We smelled of "eau de old man" before we were through, equal parts Altoids, Bengay, and Old Spice.

Then there was the panicked 911 call, the wailing ambulance pulling up to my door, a pair of EMTs rushing into my dining room. Noble inched closer in morbid curiosity. Paramedics shooed him away then got to work on Grandy.

They pounded his chest and breathed into his mouth. The paddles of a portable defibrillator sent shock waves to his heart. After a while, they closed poor Grandy's eyes, covered his contorted face, and zipped him into a body bag.

"Oh, no," I breathed. "You're giving up already?"

"We tried our best, ma'am. Sorry, he's gone."

Grandy can't be gone, I foolishly thought. *He just celebrated his fiftieth wedding anniversary.*

After they left, I suddenly registered a certain absence.

"What happened to that tray of sweet potato pie? I distinctly remember setting it down at Table Three."

"Really, Savvy?" Penny frowned. "You're obsessing over pie at a time like this?"

I shrugged. "Yeah, I guess I'm in shock."

But I couldn't let it go. Had Noble McPherson taken advantage of a tragedy to steal my pie samples, silver tray and all?

The front door opened, but it wasn't Noble bringing back my silver tray. A scruffy old man stood in the doorway with his scruffier dog. He doffed his hat in an old-fashioned gesture I might have found charming if I hadn't been so traumatized. "I beg your pardon, ladies. That wouldn't be Granderson Jaspers they carried out?"

"Oh, for crying out loud," Penny shouted back. "You know good and darn well who that was!"

"My condolences." The man touched his hat again, grabbed his dog by the collar, and backed away.

"I know you're upset, but wasn't that a bit harsh?" I scolded.

"No, it wasn't. Some of these people are straight-up ghouls. Look at them out there crowding the sidewalk."

Penny locked the door and lowered the blinds against all the lookie-loos trying to peek through the picture window. She headed back across the dining room, then came to a sudden stop at Table Two. Frowning, she bent over and picked up something from the floor.

"What's that?" I asked dully. "Did something fall?"

"Yeah. You could say that." Penny slipped the object into her pocket then got busy cleaning up pie crumbs that were all that was left of Grandy's presence.

CHAPTER 5

Sole Serenade

The sound system set to the oldies channel played "The Crossroads." Bone Thugs-N-Harmony's anthem to fallen comrades struck a little too close to home. I switched it to another channel. Earth, Wind & Fire's "I Think About Lovin' You" streamed into the kitchen.

I sat at my desk, looking back from the intersection of Hindsight and Regret, sorting out my feelings about Granderson Jaspers. "Love" might be an oversell, but I'd always had a certain fondness for the old gent.

Native American warriors may have said, "It's a good day to die," but this shouldn't have been one of those days. Not on such an unseasonably warm October Saturday when the sky was bright, birds were chirpy, and inner-city Woodlawn was as serene as any suburb.

Yet this hadn't kept Granderson Parker Jaspers Sr. from toppling like a fallen timber pine, face-planted in a plate of sweet potato pie. Not even Grandy deserved to go like that, mug twisted in a scowl, greasy crumbs in his goatee.

So what, he was an insufferable womanizer who had wrecked the lives of women and maybe a man or two? Yes, he was also a confirmed cheapskate, always trying to get something for nothing, or at least for very little. What's more, he'd become Essie's one-man loitering problem.

Grandy was one of our oldest customers. The café had been his second home practically since we opened our doors. He'd come hitching in on his walking stick and commandeer his regular spot. If Table Two was occupied, he'd lean on his cane, shifting from one foot to the other and side-eyeing whomever had the nerve to be sitting there. If no one intervened on the customer's behalf, the poor soul might be guilt-tripped or aggravated into leaving early or changing seats.

Once parked at Table Two, he always requested the special he ordered so often Penny nicknamed it "the Grandy." Then he'd angle himself around to face the door, eyeballing any random woman coming in and out.

Did I say "random"? I stand corrected. Granderson Parker Jaspers would hit on any human female between sixteen and sixty who gave him the time of day—sometimes even younger, but never any older.

"What do I look like talking to somebody my age? Seventy-five and seventy-five make one hundred and fifty. And Lord knows, I can't do nothing with that."

"Grandy, why're you always in here flirting," I once asked him, "with a fine woman like Mattie at home?"

"You know I love me some Mattie. I also love me some hamburger. But as much as a man loves hamburger, don't nobody want to eat it twenty-four seven." Yet he never had a problem scarfing down my buttermilk biscuits on almost a daily basis.

Shaken as I was in the aftermath of his demise, I couldn't face Grandy's family. I had Penny call Mattie and deliver the sorrowful news, then told her she could take the rest of the day off.

Grandy Jaspers was what I called a COG. He could sometimes be a "congenial old gent." More often than not, he was a "cantankerous old goat." I wasn't the only one he managed to infuriate. Penny shook her head as she changed out of her kitchen shoes, fished something from her apron pocket, turned her back to me, and transferred the unseen thing to her purse.

"Saturday's the second busiest day of the week, Savvy. I wonder how much money we're losing."

"Don't worry about it. I'll pay you for the day. It just didn't seem right to be serving food where a man just died. It's a matter of respect."

"You gotta give respect to get it. Just like that musical *The Civil War.* 'You live or you die by the sword.' I'm not saying he deserved it, but chickens do come home to roost."

"Now, that's cold," I scolded. "Even for you."

Penny gave a deep sigh. "You ever had to sell your soul to the devil?"

Roused from my funk, I sat up in my seat and stared at her. "You're talking out of your head. What does selling your soul have to do with anything?"

"Rest in peace, Granderson Jaspers, not that you gave it to anyone else." Penny blew an air-kiss toward Table Two. "Still . . . what's that your old auntie used to say? *The devil you know is better than the angel you don't.*"

"Don't take Aunt Essie's name in vain and don't speak ill of the dead," I ordered her. "You're delirious, Penny. Go home."

People had different ways of grieving, I decided. Sometimes sorrow can masquerade as rage. *How dare you up and die on me!*

Yet all this was beside the point. Something terminal had happened here.

A man *keeled over* while wolfing down a double test sample of sweet potato pie.

He'd *met his demise* in a cheery urban eatery filled with lush green plants, urban folk art by struggling painters, and smooth jazz filtering through the speakers.

He *expired* at Table Two beside an overgrown fern that needed pruning.

He *passed away* beneath the image by a local artist with the nom de guerre $tevie $tevenson. The work was satirically titled *Grim Reaper on the* Soul Train *Line*. People had always thought it was a hoot. Now I'd have to take it down.

"*A dead corpse here in the eat shop, Savvy?*" Great-Aunt Essie would have shaken her head and *ump, ump, ump*ped. "*Ain't no way that's going to be good for business.*"

The café was finally still, the turmoil subsided. Yet a cloud of distress lingered in the air. After Penny left, I put a sign on the café's front door: CLOSED FOR A PERSONAL EMERGENCY. Then I returned to the kitchen, turned up the music, sat at my desk, and stared at the wall.

It wasn't every day you witnessed someone perish before your eyes. Although truth be told, I'd seen more than my fair share of dead bodies.

There was a meme on social media: "If you can't understand why someone is grieving for so long, consider yourself fortunate you do not understand." My grief was still fresh. Just last year, I'd experienced a loss I still hadn't recovered from. I didn't think I'd ever recover. No, this wasn't something I was ready to think about, much less talk about.

Yet it wasn't much easier reliving the pain of many years past. One winter morning when I was ten, my mother forgot to awaken me. I'd gotten up all by myself, dressed up in my Sunday best, and came downstairs for the breakfast of Canadian bacon, biscuits and syrup, grits, and redeye gravy we always had before church.

No cooking smells greeted me, no sounds percolating from the old coffeepot. I found my parents under the covers, huddled together in their first-floor bedroom.

"Mama, Daddy. Wake up!"

I shook them but they didn't respond. My father didn't say, "What's shaking, bacon?" My mother didn't gather me in her arms and cover my face with kisses. Their eyes were open and bloodshot, their lips red, their bodies cold beneath the blankets.

Invisible carbon monoxide fumes from the basement furnace below their room had seeped into their dreams, freezing them in forever slumber. The only thing that had saved me was a bedroom on a higher floor on the opposite side of the house.

I stayed with my pastor's family while the grownups figured out what to do with me, the fatherless and motherless child. I felt like a plate of leftovers no one wanted to claim.

Most of my family still lived in the Mississippi Delta. There was talk of me going down south to live with my grandparents or staying with Uncle Harry in Benton Harbor, Michigan. He was the younger brother that Mama never got along with. I didn't want to go to either place, I just wanted my parents back.

Foster care was discussed in harsh whispers that I couldn't help overhearing. Then one evening my father's maiden aunt Essie Mae Slidell called Reverend Harding's house. Those were the days of landlines. I was doing a lot of eavesdropping and listening in on extensions, so I heard the whole conversation.

"Ain't nobody putting that baby in foster care. Savvy already lost her parents. She ain't fixing to lose her home."

Rather than uproot me, she'd chosen to transplant herself from a temperate southern city to the cold and frozen northlands. Great-Aunt Essie had already relocated once. She'd moved from Mississippi to care for an older brother up in Memphis. When Abel finally died from lung cancer, she was free to move again.

Aunt Essie always said that in her seventy years of life she'd been slowly, steadily moving northward. "I wonder where I'm headed next? What comes after Chicago, Savvy?"

I pictured the map in my head. "There's Wisconsin, Upper Michigan, and Canada. Then I think it's Greenland and the top of the world, which is the North Pole."

"I'll get up there one day, God willing."

"Which one, Aunt Essie?"

"Whatever God spares me to see."

My first husband, Fanon, and I had worn matching outfits made of blue Nigerian *adire* cloth for our African-style wedding in the Perennial Garden at Jackson Park almost forty years ago. We both liked the idea of an outdoor ceremony and the symbolism of a place called "perennial."

Our union hadn't lasted in the end, but two years later something perennial was planted, our precious baby son. And the same plants and flowers continued to grow year after year in that patch of parkland between Cornell Drive and Stony Island Avenue until the land was reclaimed to build the Obama Presidential Center.

As guests watched from their folding chairs, I inched along the path with Great-Aunt Essie hobbling beside me on a cane. She had insisted on ditching her walker for the occasion and held tightly to my elbow, as much for stability as ceremony. I'd been leaning on my aunt for almost a decade. Now it was her turn to lean on me.

When we got to the center of the circle, she reached out and gripped my fiancé's hand. "I'm giving you Savvy and you better take good care of her. If you don't, I'm taking back my baby. I ain't playing with you, boy."

A titter of laughter arose from the congregation. Fanon managed to keep a straight face as he meekly nodded. "Yes, ma'am, Miss Essie. I'll do my best."

Afterward our guests walked the three blocks to a reception at Tre's Banquet Hall. Aunt Essie had been cooking for a week. She wouldn't hear of us paying a caterer, but insisted on preparing the whole spread herself, right down to the wedding cake. I'd never know if the exertion had pushed her over the edge.

Fanon and I were headed back from Saint Lucia when we got the news. Aunt Essie had gone into the hospital three days after our wedding, though Fanon and I didn't know it at the time. She'd bullied and badgered everyone into keeping it a secret until our honeymoon was over. Either she thought she'd recover and put it all behind her, or she was trying to hold on until we got back. She almost made it, too.

I was a newlywed with a husband who loved me and tried to help me through the grief. I wasn't distraught or hysterical. I was eerily calm, my eyes as dry as dust.

"Your heart is broken, Savvy Franklin," Fanon told me time and again. "Go ahead and cry, girl. Get it out of your system."

Perhaps I'd gotten accustomed to death too early on. Maybe it was the PTSD of so many losses. I felt sadness, pain, and regret like a cold knot in my gut. But I never seemed able to summon any tears. Not for my mother or father, my second husband or Grandy, not even my Great-Aunt Essie.

I sat there in my café kitchen feeling all the accumulated losses around my shoulders like a necklace of boulders. Staring at her portrait above my desk, I asked: "Aunt Essie, why can't I cry?"

The streaming music stopped, a sad silence echoing throughout the café. The strangest thought went skittering through my mind as I relived Grandy's collapse.

Mattie's going to be sorry now after shaming Grandy last night.

The music kicked back on. Another oldie set the mood for another sorrowful reminiscence. Aretha Franklin, may she rest in power, lamented a man whose absence left a lonely sound in her soul serenade.

I realized Grandy's demise was the dead end of the Soul Serenaders, no pun intended.

Funeral Fund in a Pickle Jar

Despite his annoying habits, Grandy Jaspers had his own brand of charm. His presence at the café had grown on me over the years. And now a day after his passing, the emptiness at Table Two screamed his absence.

I found myself struggling with memories of all the people who'd perished on my watch. I seemed to carry the invisible burden of the departed everywhere I went.

I knew it was my imagination, but sometimes I could hear my Great-Aunt Essie whispering into my right ear. *Tomorrow isn't promised, Savvy. Get all your living did while you're here to enjoy it.*

I regarded the hand-lettered sign over the cash register. *A pinch of bacon grease and a pound of love.*

"Penny, do you think we should change our motto? That bacon grease reference might be sending the wrong message. People might really think we douse their food in animal fat."

Penny shook her head. "Girl, don't underestimate your customers. People know a metaphor when they see one. Nobody takes it literally."

We loaded the portable steam table with salmon croquettes, turkey sausage, scrambled eggs, blueberry waffles, buttermilk biscuits, breakfast potatoes, and tropical ambrosia of pineapple, mango, and shredded coconut dressed with vanilla yogurt.

Out of respect for the deceased, the café had stayed closed all day Saturday. We had reopened Sunday morning, the busiest day of the week with the after-church crowd descending on us in droves. Today the turnout was even higher than expected, what with all the curiosity-seekers sniffing out gossip about Grandy's untimely passing right here at Essie's Place.

Though some people left when they saw the line, we were able to accommodate the overflow by roping off chairs and tables just outside the front door. Those who waited could dine al fresco on this unseasonably balmy Sunday.

I had both hands on deck, and God knows I needed them. I prepared pan after pan of brunch dishes. Penny helped with prep and kept the beverage bar stocked with coffee, tea, and fresh-squeezed OJ. Parker Welbon bussed tables and monitored food pans. Though I'd given him the day off to mourn his grandfather's passing, he had turned up all the same.

"There's way too much drama going on at home." He shook his head. "I had to get out of there."

The three of us scurried back and forth from the kitchen, replenishing the dishes.

Grandy's death still nagged at me. There was a not-quite-settled sense about it, like a half-risen sweet potato pie. Penny showed an unexpected flash of compassion, considering there never seemed to be any love lost between her and Grandy.

She made the sign and taped it to a one-gallon pickle jar— *The Granderson Parker Jaspers Funeral Fund: All Donations Welcome*. Those who wanted to contribute inserted their coins, bills, and checks through a slot cut into the lid.

"You realize they still owe me for the anniversary party, right?"

"Yeah, I know." Penny sighed and tucked in a thick wad of bills. "But funerals are so expensive, and . . ."

"Whatever." I shrugged and let it go.

Some who'd known Grandy as a fixture around the café brought in flowers, cards, notes, and bow ties of every description. A makeshift shrine assembled itself at Table Two.

Someone had left an old 45 of a Soul Serenaders single. Another brought an Afro pick, its handle a fist clenched in the black power salute. Some joker had even left two blue pills, rolling loose on the table. Those I threw away. Offerings piled up as the day went on. I had to add another table to accommodate the overflow.

People came and left their mementos, bowed their heads, and paid their respects. Then they went about their business or took in the brunch buffet. Others who hadn't heard the news or didn't really know Grandy seemed confused by all the hubbub around Table Two. Others were clearly curiosity-seekers, Lord have mercy on their naked souls!

As I moved back and forth between the kitchen and dining room I overheard comments and whispers and salacious gossip. People piled up their plates and chewed on the news.

"Is that where it happened?"

"Yeah, the table over there with all that stuff piled on it."

"How does somebody choke to death on sweet potato pie? That's so soft and mushy, it's practically baby food."

"Girl, I don't know. Poisoned is what I heard but don't start me to lying."

"Well, ain't that something? *Ump, ump, ump.*"

Now how, I silently fretted, *are you going to sit up cramming your face at a place where you think someone was poisoned? My people, my people!*

We always closed by 4 p.m., except on Sundays when we stayed open until 6:30. The early dinner hour was just as busy, with just as many busybodies. Essie's stayed dark on Mondays, which was always a welcome relief after a busy six-day workweek. But I didn't expect to stay closed on Tuesday, too. Also Wednesday, Thursday, and who knew how much longer? The other shoe had dropped. The Department of Health came knocking at my front door.

A phalanx of white-gloved inspectors descended Monday afternoon to inform me there'd been a complaint—unpermitted outdoor dining, suspicions of tainted food. And no, they couldn't tell me who had filed it. They peered in every cupboard, looked into the refrigerator, and searched every cabinet, shelf, nook, and cranny. I even saw one of them pawing through the trash.

Finally, they took samples of my Arusha coffee beans and the ingredients used to make the sweet potato pie Grandy had eaten. They asked for the leftover vegan pie samples, but of course, they disappeared in all the hubbub after Grandy's death. I tried to explain that Penny and I had eaten that pie and suffered no ill effects. They just ignored me and kept on snooping.

Upon leaving, they taped a sign inside my crackle-paned window. They needed time to test ingredients to determine if they were implicated in Grandy's death. Until then we weren't safe to operate. The Department of Health had shut us down! We wouldn't even be able to fulfill catering orders, and I had a family reunion luncheon that weekend. I'd have to find someone else to service it.

I don't know which was worse, the lurid gossip drifting through Woodlawn or all the income we were losing.

As a one-day shutdown became two, then three and four, I took advantage of the downtime to organize my books, update my supply orders, and begin compiling Great-Aunt Essie's recipes. I intended one day to assemble them into a soul food cookbook I would call *Aunt Essie's Table*. I also left a message for my insurance agent to see if my policy would cover any of that week's losses.

I glanced at the portraits above my desk. Jesus, Obama, and Great-Aunt Essie stared down at me.

"Don't you forget, now, baby," Aunt Essie seemed to remind me. "*Trouble comes in threes.*"

CHAPTER 7

An Ignoble Proposition

That Friday morning there came a brisk rapping at the locked front door. I started to ignore it, I swear I did.

Who would come a-knocking with that notice plastered bold as sin in the window? Maybe it was the Health Department coming to remove it. I left the kitchen where I'd been refilling spice jars and cautiously made my way out front.

Oh, Lord. Not him again! I should have turned around and gone about my business. Unfortunately, my folks had raised me with manners. I sighed and opened the door.

There stood Noble McPherson holding a leather briefcase, wearing one of his endless varieties of disguises. This time it was blue jeans with a knife-sharp crease, shiny black shoes, bright white socks, and a U.S. Polo Assn. shirt. No self-respecting Black man I knew would be caught dead in a polo shirt with the emblem of a guy actually playing polo.

Back in his college militant days, my first husband, Fanon—an adopted name, not given—would have hollered right to his face, "COINTELPRO lackey!" Fanon had helped organize a New Black Panther Party chapter on campus. The old one targeted by J. Edgar Hoover's infamous infiltration campaign was no longer active by then, but the memory of it endured. You could tell them by their shoes, Fanon swore. Always black and brilliantly buffed, too shiny to be trusted.

This particular "agent" seemed to be playing the part of a laid-back buppie on his day off.

"Noble McPherson, what do you want? As you can see, we're closed."

"I do see." He squinted at the warning posted in the window. A faintly concealed sneer played around his lips. "Bad run of luck for you, huh, Sapphire?"

"My friends call me Savvy," I told him. "So you can call me Ms. Summers."

He threw back his head and brayed like a donkey. "Good one, Savvy."

"It's not a joke."

He pushed in past me.

"I don't recall inviting you in," I pointed out. "If my memory serves me right, I've asked you to leave and not come back."

Noble settled himself comfortably at Table Two. I had just taken down $tevie $tevenson's *Grim Reaper on the* Soul Train *Line* painting and removed all the Grandy memorabilia. No one had sat there since he expired. I wondered if Noble deliberately chose that spot just to rattle me.

He sat there grinning like a possum, hands folded atop his briefcase. "Oh, I think you'll be interested in what I have to say."

"I seriously doubt it." I perched warily across the table from him. "Whatever it is, get to the point. I've got a million things to do around here."

He looked around the empty room. "What with business booming and all."

"Okay, Mr. Smartass. You've got five minutes to say your

piece before I put you out. You don't want to see the West Side of my behind."

Don't get my Mississippi up! was one of Great-Aunt Essie's spirited warnings. She was sweet as pie and no bigger than a minute, but don't get on her bad side. Once her Mississippi was riled up, anything could happen. Crockery and skillets might be brandished, men twice her size silenced. I'd never actually seen her deliver a beatdown, but I never doubted she could do it.

I wasn't born in Mississippi but it was woven through my West Side Chicago upbringing. The side of the city where I'd grown up was part of the extended Southern kinship network. I felt the connection through blood and the blues.

Woodlawn, too, was a Southern community, transplanted "Up-South" to urban Chicago. Most of us were only one or two generations removed from our Arkansas, Tennessee, or Mississippi roots. You could hear it in our language and smell it in our cooking pots.

Noble reached into his briefcase and drew out a file. "My people are still willing to make you an offer. Not quite as generous as before. What with this Health Department shutdown and now the lawsuit, you're not the hot property you once were."

"Come again, McPherson. What lawsuit are you talking about?"

"Oh, you don't know?" He smirked. "It's my understanding that the Widow Jaspers has already filed, or will soon be filing, a wrongful-death lawsuit against your establishment."

"Hm. Now why do I think you might be lying through your silly teeth? Especially since I haven't heard anything about it and the matter has nothing to do with you."

"Oh, our legal eagles stay on top of these things. Business being business, you know."

He handed me the file and I leafed through the pages. It was essentially the same offer he'd presented to me before with a slightly lower figure.

The Jonesboro-Lee LLC was offering me a moderately low six-figure sum, not just for my café but to acquire my identity. They wanted to take Sapphire Summers Soulfood Café and Catering Company to franchise as a soul food brand. Apparently, they didn't know everyone was calling us Essie's Place.

Noble had come here on three separate occasions, each time clad in different wardrobe. The first time it was ill-fitting hip-hop attire he was too old and way too nerdy to even think of pulling off. Next time, the man was so suited up and buttoned down, I almost didn't recognize him. Then there was Saturday, his cat burglar costume.

Our first meeting had been cordial enough. He'd phoned me out of the blue, introducing himself as a potential investor with a business proposition. I was open to hearing what he had to say. In fact, I'd been flattered by the offer, though I quickly turned it down. The money would have covered the purchase price of the property but would barely reimburse me for my improvements. Besides, I wasn't interested in selling my business. Still, I gave him lunch on the house.

The next time he came with hard-sell tactics, as offensive as they were aggressive. My business acumen was called into question, my lack of culinary training. I'd asked him to leave and not come back. On the third visit, any scheming was forestalled by Grandy's untimely demise.

"Can't you just see it?" he wheedled. "A chain of restaurants across the nation, a Sapphire Summers Soulfood franchise.

That's something to be proud of, right? Your name up there with the Magic Johnsons and Oprah Winfreys."

"TV commercials, celebrity endorsements? Yes, I can see it now."

Noble McPherson whipped out a pen. "Then you're willing to deal. This is good, very good. I can promise, you won't be sorry."

I ignored the outstretched pen and handed him back his file.

"You're right, McPherson. I won't be sorry. Magic and Oprah own their brands and that's what I aim to do. If Sapphire Summers becomes a household name, it's because I make it happen. Not you or your damned franchise."

"The business of America is business," he lectured. "And identity is just another commodity. People sell it all the time. McDonald's, Wendy's, Starbucks. None would've grown into multibillion-dollar brands if they'd stayed in the hands of those who started them."

"So, because they sold out, I should follow suit?" I sneered. "If they jump off a bridge, I should go tumbling after. That makes a lot of sense."

"You're suffering from a terminal case of founder's syndrome." He rolled his eyes like he was trying to reason with a two-year-old. "You know the average lifespan of a food service business, don't you?"

"No, but I'm sure you'll tell me."

He pulled out a page and waved it in my face. "If you'd done a proper business plan before opening this place, you'd know that twenty-six percent close in the first year, another nineteen percent in the second year, and fourteen percent in the third. All told, fifty-nine percent of new restaurants will fail in the first three years."

"Business is more than percentages. We've been operating in the black since we opened doors almost seven years ago. We even made it through the pandemic on take-out orders and outdoor dining pods."

"Then you're living on borrowed time. Woodlawn's going through a renaissance with the university expanding, the demographic changing, the Obama Presidential Center opening."

"Good." I nodded. "More customers for me."

"No, more competition. It's just a matter of time before the tide turns. Look what happened to Gladys', Edna's, Soul Queen, Army and Lou's. All those soul food restaurants were in business for decades, now they're gone the way of the buffalo. I'm giving you a chance to avoid that fate. You might think your major asset is your food and your customers."

"What else would it be?"

"It's your corporate identity. That's the bottom line of any business."

"Well, why not start your own, Ignoble's *Mess* Hall? That's a good idea. You can have it, free of charge."

"It's not about starting from scratch," he pontificated, "but utilizing an undercapitalized asset. You have a modest reputation here for good soul food at reasonable prices. We'd like to take that reputation and expand it into a national brand. Maybe even global."

"How would I know what kind of food you'd be peddling under my name? Thanks, but no thanks. Just like I told you before."

"I'm authorized to offer a fifteen percent signing bonus but it's only good for today. We'll throw in this building for another ten percent, just to take it off your hands. Based on the commercial real estate comps in Woodlawn, it's not even worth half that much."

"What part of *thanks, but no thanks* do you not understand?"

McPherson frowned and shook his head, returning the file to his briefcase. "You're making a mistake, Savvy. A really big mistake."

I got up, walked to the door, and held it open. "Thanks for dropping by. Please don't hurry back."

He slowly rose and grabbed his briefcase. "Your profit margin is laughably narrow with salaries and supplies and overhead. With this bad publicity and legal action, this place will be history before the year is out."

As he pushed past me, I tapped his shoulder. "Why'd you take those pie samples, Noble McPherson?"

He flinched like I'd punched him. "I don't know what you mean."

"Oh, yes, you do. When Grandy collapsed, I set a platter of sweet potato pie on the table right next to his. By the time I looked around, they were gone and so were you. That silver tray was a family heirloom and I want it back."

"Poison served on a silver platter is still poison in the end. People are saying that pie was tainted. I can't help it, but that's what they say. Let's hope it didn't fall into the wrong hands. The police might be interested."

Well, now Noble had done it. He'd gone and struck a nerve. I'd bet dollars to doughnuts that he was the one who'd made that complaint with the city health department. My West Side surged as I grabbed him by his polo collar and looked him dead in the eye. "Is that some kind of threat, Mr. McPherson? I don't take kindly to threats."

He had the good sense to look frightened. "Cut it out, Savvy. Unhand me this instant."

"Savvy, you say?"

"Ms. Summers. I already told you, I didn't take your wretched pie."

Suddenly, I released my grip and dusted off his collar. I smoothed the wrinkles from his shirt, beaming my sunniest smile.

"I tell you what. Since you didn't get any the other day, I've got some pie just warm from the oven. The very same kind that Grandy ate. Hold up, I'll get you a slice."

Noble's eyes bugged out like those of a cartoon character. He bolted through the door, dashed across the street, and fumbled into his car.

Child, he went running out of here like a scalded haint, is how Great-Aunt Essie would have described it.

"Bring me back my silver platter," I called after him, "or I'm taking it out of your hide."

His ghost-gray BMW screeched off, burning rubber.

I could almost see my aunt shaking her head and *ump, ump, ump*ing. *That man is some kind of twisted mess. I bet his bowels ain't regular.*

CHAPTER 8

Nouvelle Soul

One of Noble's claims turned out to be true, Lord have mercy on his naked soul. A process server showed up not two hours after he left. Mattie Jaspers actually had the nerve to file a wrongful-death lawsuit against me.

My Great-Aunt Essie used to say that *fish stank starts from the head on down.* I couldn't help wondering if McPherson was the source of that odor.

Aunt Essie also said that trouble comes in threes. An elderly man had died on my watch. That was Trouble #1. Being shut down by the Department of Health made Trouble #2. The dead man's widow was suing me, Trouble #3. The way I figured, I was due a reprieve.

After we had gone a week without income, Penny called and mysteriously announced we'd be reopening soon. When I asked her where she got her crystal ball, she said she'd heard the news on "good authority."

Then we got the official word. The death certificate had been issued, the official cause of death determined. Granderson Parker Jaspers had died of a heart attack. Essie's Place was absolved of blame. We were finally able to reopen, then sit back and assess the damage.

∽

Hallelujah, praise the Lord! I had an actual, honest-to-God catering order, the first since the café's closing.

It wasn't full meal service, just passed hors d'oeuvres for a gallery opening on Friday evening in Bronzeville. But it was work, thank God. I was more than happy for it.

The client had requested Nouvelle Soul food, something a little more upscale than my usual fare. It was fun creating the special menu of crudités and cut fruit, collard green mini quiches, spicy black-eyed pea fritters, and salmon croquette sliders. Dessert was praline cheesecake squares and bite-sized sweet potato tartlets.

Grandy and Mattie's grandson, Parker, passed hors d'oeuvres in the front of the house while I worked the kitchen, cutting up fruit and veggies, heating the appetizers and arranging them on trays. At the end of the evening, my able young helper loaded equipment into my RAV4, Red Rover, while I finished with the cleanup.

Parker came back into the kitchen and stood there waiting.

"If everything's loaded up, you're done for the evening, Parker. How'd you get out here? Do you need a ride back to Woodlawn?"

"No, I have my car." He looked strangely embarrassed, shifting his weight from one foot to another.

"Is there something the matter?"

He looked off into a corner of the kitchen, like somebody might be standing there eavesdropping. I turned to follow his gaze, but didn't see a soul.

"Miss Savvy, you know that guy that's always coming into Essie's bothering you?"

"Noble McPherson?" That had to be who he meant. The only other man who made a regular nuisance of himself was his Granddaddy Grandy, dead and gone. "What about him?"

"He came to our house last week. I went down to my grandparents' apartment to get some food. There he was, sitting next to Grammy on the living room sofa. He had a bunch of important-looking papers spread out on the coffee table."

"I hope Mattie didn't sign anything. Please tell me she didn't."

Parker shrugged. "I don't know. When I went in the kitchen and got my plate, I could hear them talking. Something about witnesses for a definition."

"A definition? Hm. You think it might have been a 'deposition'?"

"Maybe. All I know is, he kept mentioning your name. I thought you might want to know."

I gave him a quick pat on the back. "Thanks, Parker. Good looking out."

"I don't trust that dude, Miss Savvy. He serves more shade than a monkey cigar tree."

"Parker Welbon, you sound just like your Grandma Mattie. Was anything said about some pie samples he may have taken?"

"No, but he left a serving tray with Grammy. I'd seen it before in the restaurant so I knew it belonged to you."

I mulled over the bit of news all through my cleanup, on my way out the door, and on the ride back to Essie's. It seemed Noble McPherson had been awfully busy, side-winding serpent that he was.

After wriggling his way into Mattie's life, he'd obviously manipulated her into filing that wrongful-death lawsuit. Trying to get what he wanted from me, that scoundrel had taken advantage of a man's tragic demise and a widow's grief. For Noble

McPherson, Grandy's untimely passing couldn't have come along at a more convenient time.

Unless . . . I considered a new idea as I pulled in front of Essie's, unloaded Red Rover, and carried the empty catering pans into the storage room off the kitchen.

Perhaps Grandy's death had been expected. Maybe even planned? I rolled that notion around in my mind.

CHAPTER 9

Trouble Don't Last

No disrespecting of the dead, but I call it like I see it. Between Grandy Jaspers, Noble McPherson, and the man sitting there with his atrocious table manners, a slime trail might have wound its way from the café's front door to Table Two.

"You know what the old folks say," Delbert assured me between open-mouthed bites of black-eyed peas, candied sweet potatoes, smothered chicken, and coleslaw. "Trouble don't last always."

Yeah, that was another thing they said about it, but I knew that trouble hadn't actually been banished. I could sense it lurking at our feet, nipping at our ankles like a rabid dog.

It was the lunchtime "rush," over a week since Grandy's death. We would normally have had a full house. Today there was exactly one patron—Delbert "Do-Right" Dailey, the infamous alderman of Woodlawn.

"That Department of Health closing and fallout over Grandy's passing has really hit us hard," I told him. "We've got to get back on our feet if we're going to weather this storm. What can you do to help us? You know everyone in town."

"Well, not everybody," he demurred, wiping his mouth on his sleeve. "But I do get around. I've always said it, sweetheart.

You've got the best little soul food restaurant not just in Wood-lawn, but Hyde Park, and South Shore combined."

"Along with Bronzeville, Grand Crossing, Chatham, and Park Manor," Penny added. "Make sure everyone knows the good news, Alderperson. Essie's is back with a clean bill of health."

"Sweetheart." That was the anonymous endearment Delbert used for any woman he met. Men, he called *my dear brother*. I suspected he was too lazy to remember names. "Public servants have a strict code of conduct. We can't show favoritism or support special interests. That would be unethical."

"And heaven forbid," Penny retorted. "We wouldn't want unethical."

The alderperson turned to her with a lifted eyebrow. He looked her thoroughly up and down, lingering at her full hips and shapely legs. Then he shook his head and turned back to me.

"Have you reached out to the grieving widow? I know she could use the support. She wouldn't even plan the funeral until she knew the cause of death. That poor woman's been through a lot."

"Poor woman?" Penny gasped. "Are you kidding me?"

I held up a warning finger and she flounced off to the kitchen.

"Mattie hasn't exactly been approachable these days." I tried to be diplomatic. "Now that she knows the cause of death, maybe she'll have some closure."

Delbert shook his head. "She's still not believing my dear brother died a natural death. She wants to get an inquest ordered."

"You can't call up the medical examiner and ask for an autopsy, can you? Doesn't there need to be cause?"

"There does. I feel obligated to help out. After all, Grandy and I were brothers in the same Masonic lodge. I referred him and Mattie to my heart specialist."

"All three of you have heart issues?"

"Well, the two of us now. We see a highly acclaimed Northwestern cardiologist, very exclusive, very hard to get an appointment. City Hall can move mountains and I can move City Hall, if I say so myself."

Penny peered into the dining room, tossing her head and clicking her tongue. "I must be hallucinating, Savvy. I thought I just heard the alderperson say he doesn't show favoritism."

Penny had her say and disappeared back in the kitchen, so Delbert directed his disapproval at me. "I'm just trying to help a grieving widow who believes her dear husband died by someone else's hand."

"I'm that someone, Delbert!" I cried out in exasperation. "Mattie is accusing me. Don't you know she tried to sue me?"

He didn't seem at all surprised to hear the news. "She'll come around, sweetheart. Just give her a chance. That good woman lost the love of her life. She's devastated."

Delbert Dailey had been right there at the Majestic Ballroom when "that good woman" delivered the very public kiss-off to her husband, Grandy. It was hard to buy that "love of her life" propaganda when their fifty-year marriage seemed headed for the skids.

"Why did Mattie think I was responsible for her husband's death?"

Delbert threw his hands up in the air. "Your guess is as good as mine."

After all, I continued the argument in my mind, *she* was the one who'd unceremoniously dumped her mate in front of family and friends. If Grandy's heart attack was anybody's fault, maybe she should look in the mirror.

"Please don't take this inquest request any further," I begged Delbert. "Reopening that can of worms won't do my business a bit of good. People don't want to eat where they think the food is killing people. I don't know how much more bad publicity we can take."

"Nothing lasts forever, sweetheart. You've had a good little run. Maybe it's time to call it a day and move on. Make some other plans."

"Call it a day? Move on?" I repeated. "But you just said our food is the best in Woodlawn and surrounding areas."

Delbert shrugged. "One door closes, another one opens."

Penny was obviously listening from the kitchen. She burst into the dining room like the Incredible Hulk, her thin chest quaking with rage. "So Savvy should roll over and play dead, just because somebody got sue-happy? Mattie's wrong for that, you know she is."

Delbert glanced at the bill, threw cash on the table, and got up to leave. "You can't take away a person's right to sue. It's protected in the First Amendment. Not that I'm on anyone's side in this. You're all my valued constituents."

"Not me," Penny muttered. "I don't even live in your ward."

He ignored her and turned to face me. "Don't be so hard on the widow, sweetheart. You know she's deep in mourning."

Penny held down her wrath until Delbert left. Then it spewed out like a geyser. "Deep in mourning, my ample derriere."

"I hate to rub it in, but you were the one who took up that collection for Grandy's funeral."

A strange look flashed across Penny's face. Was it regret or embarrassment? It couldn't be guilt.

"Well, that was before I knew Mattie was suing. She's just trying to weasel out of that catering bill. That woman's just as much of a cheapskate as Grandy, who put the *dead* in deadbeat."

"That's in poor taste, Penny."

"I tell it like I smell it," she insisted. "Mattie and Grandy are two of a kind."

"I'd never imagine she could be so vindictive. To think that she'd kick me while I'm down, well that just breaks my heart."

"Not to mention your pocketbook. If Mattie's the one doing the kicking, then dollars to doughnuts, Delbert is the one with his knee in your back. You notice he point-blank refused to help? *Let Mattie sue, it's her legal right. If you're being pushed then move on.* But he can bring his rusty butt in here to eat eight days a week, and half the time you don't even charge him."

"Didn't you see me give him a bill?"

"That's only because you were upset. And ethics? Humph. Don't make me laugh. Do-Wrong puts the *dick* in ridiculous. That worm shouldn't even be in office. You remember Soldiers of the Cross, that faith-based youth violence prevention program he was involved in?"

"The one where some government funds went missing? The media raked Delbert over the coals for that one. There was some kind of investigation."

"His people pocketed that money and you best believe he got his cut. When the crap hit the fan, he copped a plea and fingered all his cronies."

"It didn't do his career any good," I recalled. "He'll be lucky to get reelected."

"These lying, cheating, poot-butt politicians. Either they're screwing over women or they're screwing the public."

Or sometimes both, I thought. I was prone to questioning

Penny's judgment, but this time I knew it to be accurate. In addition to all his other failings, I suspected that Dailey frequented Essie's for other reasons than food.

He spent as much time eyeballing my bustline as he did my food. Delbert didn't even look women in the face when he spoke to them. Last year when my second husband, Francis died—no, I'm not ready to talk about that yet. It's only been a year and the pain is still fresh—Delbert had called with his condolences and offered to help with expenses. His offer was gracious and generous, or so I thought. When he walked into my upstairs loft apartment, I discovered his gift had strings attached.

"You're a grown, healthy woman, sweetheart. I know you have your needs."

"Francis isn't even in the ground, Delbert. How can you be such a weasel?"

I twisted from his grasping hands, walked to the door, and opened it. The nerve of him! Trying to hit on me, and the creep couldn't even recollect my name.

He made a surprise lunge and grabbed me from behind. "Girl, it's those tig ol' biddies of yours. They really turn me on."

The West Side of my behind came out like a full moon that night. I hit him so hard I fractured a bone in my little finger. The man barely got out by the skin of his teeth. I wonder how he explained the purple eye and scratches to his wife, Lynette.

By the day of my husband's funeral, most of Delbert's bruises had faded. He had the nerve to come to the pulpit and deliver a long-winded tribute. The man never met a speaking opportunity he could resist.

I wondered if he had made moves on Mattie, too. She was a decade and a half his senior but I wouldn't put it past him. The woman was blessed in abundance with the physical traits that Do-Wrong clearly admired.

As we cooked and served and cleaned the rest of that insolvent Saturday, something niggled at my consciousness. Beyond the regular annoyance that came with Delbert's presence, something about the conversation was strangely unsettling.

I couldn't figure out why Delbert wanted me to consider closing down. In that respect, he was reminding me of someone else who'd recently sat at Table Two. And it wasn't Grandy Jaspers.

It seemed like the alderperson and Noble McPherson were speaking the same language. Did both of them want to see me out of business? If so, then why? And what, if anything, might this have to do with Granderson Parker Jaspers's death?

CHAPTER 10

Going Up A-Yonder

Matilda Jaspers handed me my heirloom silver serving tray, the one that Great-Aunt Essie always said had been gifted to her family by the iconic Mississippi writer William Faulkner. When I handed her the pickle jar containing the Granderson Parker Jaspers Funeral Fund, it actually brought tears to her eyes.

"Penny's idea," I told her. "To help with expenses."

Mattie was from the generation of Southerners who believed grown folks shouldn't be called by their bare name. It was always Miss or Mister, regardless of marital status. "I am so sorry, Miss Savvy. I haven't been myself lately. But then, I've never had a husband die on me."

Mattie Jaspers had always struck me as the confident type. Style-conscious and carefully groomed, she seemed well put together for a woman her age. If anything, she'd always seemed a bit too classy for the likes of Grandy. Today her sixty-eight years were showing and then some. She'd lost weight since her husband's death. Clothing meant to be body-skimming hung loosely from her curves.

Mattie had come to the café early that morning with an

apology served on a silver platter. "It's over now, Miss Savvy. I've dropped the lawsuit."

"I appreciate that," I told her. "But how could you even think I'd harm Grandy or any one of my customers? I take my food and reputation very seriously."

"Child, I don't even know what I was thinking. I guess I've been letting other people do the thinking for me."

"People like Noble McPherson? Or was it Delbert Dailey?"

Mattie skillfully dodged the question. "Some of everybody's been in my ear lately. It's just so hard making decisions. You understand what I've been through."

"Yes, I lost a husband, too, but I didn't blame it on anyone else."

"Yeah? Well, the jury's still out on Grandy," Mattie muttered.

I tried to put it as gently as I could. "But how could someone have given Grandy a heart attack? Is that even possible?"

"Oh, they've got ways to do it, believe you me. He didn't do it to himself."

I suddenly remembered the man looking down at his lap with a pitiful cry of "who done this?" But Grandy had died from a heart attack. That's what his death certificate said.

"I don't know what anybody did to him, Mattie. All I know is, it wasn't me."

"I realize that now, Miss Savvy. Could you find it in your heart to forgive me?"

We hugged on it then she handed me the check. It was more than double what I'd been expecting.

"As soon as I got the insurance money, I paid all my bills," Mattie said. "I went to the funeral home then came straight over here. If that's not enough, you let me know."

"Enough? This is way more than what you owe on the catering bill."

"I'm settling my old bill and putting a deposit on the new one. I hope you're free on Saturday afternoon."

Mattie announced the upcoming funeral plans and hit me with a surprise request. She wanted me to cater the repast with the same menu as their fiftieth-anniversary party.

"Mattie, are you sure about this?"

"Your smothered chicken, buttermilk biscuits, macaroni and cheese. Those were Grandy's favorites."

"Even the desserts?" I asked, thinking of that Annabelle's Sweet Stuff Bakery cake fiasco.

"Just skip the sweet potato pie. Some folks might not understand."

"And Gawd has called his loyal servant home. We loved him dearly but Gawd loved him best. Praise the Lawd, chu'ch. Somebody say amen."

The congregation dutifully responded. Delbert was hijacking the pulpit, just as he had at my second husband's funeral. If anything, he was even more over the top. The pastor sat off to the side looking perturbed. He hadn't even got to preach his sermon yet. Delbert was stealing his thunder.

I spent most of the funeral with my crew down in the basement of the Cathedral of Holy Grace Missionary Baptist Church. Food pans were unpacked and warming over Sterno cans. Plates and cutlery were arranged, sweet tea and lemonade decanted. We set up the coffee urn and dressed the tables.

I stole a quick moment to go upstairs for one last look at Grandy before they closed the casket. I was too late to see him lying in state, but I did witness the end of Dailey's sermon, the beginning of Shysteen's command performance, and a few other things in between.

All the usual suspects were there, including those who'd been at the anniversary party. Grandy's children were in attendance, Winnie Mae Welbon and her six brothers, and most of their children and grandchildren. There was also Grandy's alleged lover, Shysteen Shackleford, and his former music manager Tuchman Pfeiffer. Noble McPherson was all decked out in a white shirt, shiny black suit, and fedora, looking like a retro penguin pimp.

I heard the musical selection about going up a-yonder to be with God, and the reverend's anticlimactic sermon from Romans 14. *For none of us liveth to himself, and no man dieth to himself.* I tried to slip away before the funeral procession but got caught up amid the exiting crowd.

As pallbearers led the coffin down the center aisle, a stone-faced Mattie followed behind it. A few steps to the rear stumbled Shysteen Shackleford in a loose-fitting black lace frock. A complicated church hat with a veil hiding her face was perched atop a blond wig, this one short and curly.

Just as dramatic as Mattie was restrained, Shysteen acted every bit the grieving widow. She strained toward the casket, hollering "Lord, don't take him." Delbert Dailey held her back with a sheepish smirk, a look that seemed equal parts shame and satisfaction. He half-supported and half-dragged the young woman down the center aisle.

It suddenly occurred to me that Shysteen was a younger, low-rent version of Mattie Jaspers. Both were short and shapely with bee-stung lips and flaring hips. They each wore similar hairstyles though Mattie's was dyed dark blond and Shysteen's seemed to be chosen from a collection of wigs.

So much for Grandy's infamous hamburger argument. *I like*

it but I don't want to eat it twenty-four seven. Why go to the trouble of cheating then pick a later model of your own wife?

In a brief instant that could be easily missed, Mattie glanced back at her rival with a murderous glare.

I pushed past the people in the pew behind me, ducked around the side aisle, and made it down to the repast two steps ahead of the crowd.

CHAPTER 11

The Fourth Trouble

"Annabelle Beasley!" I steadied myself from the impact. "What are you doing here?"

Rushing into the basement community room, I bumped headlong into my nemesis, the south suburban baker who fancied herself competition. Reeking of an oversweet floral perfume, Annabelle reared back dramatically, holding a bakery box high above her head.

"I didn't know I needed a personal invitation to attend a funeral, Safflower," she huffed in her screechy voice.

"It's Sapphire, as I've told you many times before."

"Tomatoes, tomahtoes. I brought Mattie's favorite coconut cake . . . which you almost crushed."

My attitude softened slightly. Maybe Annabelle wasn't quite so terrible after all.

"Well, that's thoughtful of you. I know Mattie was disappointed she didn't get to have any at the anniversary party. Here, I'll slice it up and plate it for you."

Yet when I reached for the box, she snatched it away. "This is for Mattie, not you. You'll probably just smash it again."

Correction. Annabelle Beasley was every bit as bad as I'd thought. Possibly worse.

"I know you're not blaming me for that cake incident the other night."

"Why not? You were the caterer on duty."

My West Side temper bubbled up. "We both know what happened to your dry, dusty cake and it was probably a blessing in disguise. Mattie's guests dodged a bullet on that one."

Her eyes glittered with malice as she cupped a hand to whisper in my ear. "So, it's true? Grandy Jasper got a dose of poison from your sweet potato pie. Mattie must be the soul of Christian charity to have you in here feeding folks."

Of all the wretched nerve! I was so taken aback, I couldn't even think of a quick retort.

Annabelle spotted Mattie in the crowd and waved the bakery box. "Hey, girl, it's me! Look what I brought you."

She went scurrying off to smother Mattie with perfumed hugs and sloppy kisses. I could hear her strident platitudes all the way across the room of Grandy "being in a better place." It was the absolute worst thing to say to a grieving widow. I knew because I'd been there.

Annabelle Beasley had once again proven herself to be a witch on wheels. And I didn't have time for her mess. I hustled off to check on the refreshments.

And that, by rights, should have been all she wrote.

Grandy's funeral should have been the end of the story, no pun intended. I should have fed the mourners, cleaned up behind them, returned to the café, began preparations for brunch the next day, and worked on getting my business back on its feet.

Maybe it was just my imagination, or the somberness of the occasion. Punctuated by the sounds of greeting and eating, strong undercurrents of suspicion seemed to gust around the room.

I hadn't gotten to see Grandy in his final rest, yet I kept remembering his face that last morning he turned up, feeble and disheveled, at my café's doorstep. It almost seemed he was running from something. *Got a hellhound on my trail.* Might that menace have been real?

I remembered Grandy's walk to Table Two, where he'd once held court and would come to die. Humming an old gospel song. *I'm gonna tell my Lord when I get home/Just how long you've been treating me wrong.* He had certainly mistreated others. Had someone returned the favor?

I couldn't get the image out of my mind of Grandy looking down at his own lap. Asking peevishly, almost accusingly, "Lord, who done this?"

I looked around at all the faces. Male, female. Young, old. Black, white. I got this prickly feeling at the back of my nose, the sensation that comes just before a sneeze. I call it my "lie-dar," a sixth sense I had when deception was afoot.

One Christmas season right after the pandemic, a supplier called A Fowl Affair was trying to unload a shipment of quail. A downstate poultry farm had gone under and was liquidating its stock. Quail was kind of highbrow for my modest establishment, but the supplier was selling it dirt cheap.

I thought about buying the entire stock. Aunt Essie prepared all kind of poultry back in the day, domesticated and game. She used to call it "bird meat." Turkey, goose, duck, chicken, Cornish hens. I could do a holiday special and give my patrons a rare treat. Marinate the birds in olive oil and citrus, do a dry rub with Montreal steak seasoning, then roast them with a wild rice and chestnut dressing.

The man opened up a box and let me look them over. I

leaned over and poked the plump, bumpy flesh. The carcasses huddled together in plastic seemed fresh enough to me. But then came that prickly sensation. I could almost hear my Great-Aunt Essie whisper. *How do you know they ain't plucked city pigeons?*

I turned down the offer, so I never found out if those quail were underhanded or aboveboard. My lie-dar at Grandy's repast was nowhere as intense as it had been in the Fowl Affair. Yet prickles of doubt tickled the back of my nose like pollen. It might have just been a beginning case of the sniffles or pepper dust from a spilled shaker.

I took a page from the book of my favorite celebrity crush. I had told my second husband, the one Penny dubbed St. Francis because he seemed so impossibly perfect—no, I'm still not ready to talk about him—that if I ever got a hall pass, Denzel Washington would definitely be the one. He played that crooked cop in *Training Day,* which was not my favorite role of his, though it won him an Oscar. In one iconic scene he threatened a bunch of thugs hanging out on the street—*I'm putting cases on all you bitches.*

Maybe I could do the same. I went around the room with a carafe of coffee, refilling cups and listening to scraps of conversations, eavesdropping on complaints and sullen mutterings. It's funny how quickly you become invisible when you're serving people their food and drink.

Could Mattie Jaspers be right? Was Granderson Jaspers helped to the grave? And if so, *who done this?* I tested out cases on the whole lot of them.

I spotted Annabelle Beasley at a corner table, all up in Mattie's face. The bakery box sat open on the table before them. Mattie frowned, toying with a slice of coconut cake on a plate. I wondered if her frown was from what she was tasting or what she was hearing. I sidled a little closer. Annabelle's stage whisper was so loud, it wasn't hard to hear.

"This could ruin me, Mattie. I need to know, just what did Grandy tell you?"

Whatever on earth that was about, it didn't seem quite kosher. Could Annabelle be the one who had done it?

What about Tuck Pfeiffer, the former manager that Grandy claimed had stolen his music? I overheard him gossiping with the pastor of the church. "The man had a vocal talent you can't deny, but he must have been smoking funny cigarettes. We both know who wrote those songs and it certainly wasn't Grandy."

Was it Winnie Mae Welbon, his spoiled only daughter with no love lost between them? Her grief seemed genuine, or was it? She sobbed on her husband's shoulder. "I kissed him so I wouldn't miss him. And Henry, his face was cold. Cold in life, cold in death. He never treated me right."

Was it Delbert "Do-Right" Dailey, the crooked politician with a weakness for wine, women, and dirty money? I saw him reach into his back pocket and look around to see if anyone noticed. He took a few swigs from his flask, then tucked it away.

Dailey was certainly sleazy enough to commit murder. I wasn't sure what his motive might be, but who knew what kind of history he and Grandy had. Dailey sat close to Shysteen, patting her shoulder and peering down her neckline.

"There now, sweetheart." He wiped at a tear with one of his thumbs, a gesture that seemed both sneaky and seductive. "A pretty young thing like you shouldn't be fretting herself."

"I don't know what to do, Alder Dailey."

"You know I'm a lawyer," Delbert murmured, "if you need any legal advice."

"But that's just it," Shysteen wailed. "I don't have money to pay."

"We'll work something out."

I shuddered to think what that something might be.

Was it Shysteen Shackleford herself, bawling and boo-hooing to beat the band? Didn't she know the protocol? You cried at the funeral and the burial, though the mistress should never outweep the widow. The repast was for snacking and socializing, not sitting around hollering at the top of your lungs. "God took that man too soon!"

Extricating herself from Annabelle's clutches, Mattie marched over and quietly demanded: "Turn down the noise. You're making a scene."

Shysteen's tears evaporated in a blast of fury. She leapt to her feet, snarling in the widow's face. "You can't shut me down, you hateful old bitch! I saw how you dissed Grandy in public that night. I bet you went and killed him, just so I couldn't have him."

Mattie gasped in disbelief. Trying to maintain the higher ground, she drew herself to her full five feet two inches, turned, and walked away. Hysterical and out of control, the younger woman scrambled after her and grabbed Mattie by the upper arm.

That's when Shysteen blurted out a newsflash that beat Mattie's anniversary exposé by a city mile. The fourth trouble exploded and scattered through the room like shrapnel.

"Where's that money he promised me?" Shysteen demanded. "He was getting his million dollars and setting something aside for me and this baby."

With a free hand Shysteen grabbed her dress and tented it into the shape of a full-term pregnancy. The netted veil flew back from her face. An angry bruise decorated her right eye. Now, who had given her that purple eye, and why had they done it?

Mattie snatched her arm from Shysteen's grasp and balled up a fist, ready to give the girl a matching shiner. Tuchman Pfeiffer rushed to her side and held her back. "It's Grandy's homegoing. Don't let that little tramp bring you down to the gutter."

"Why not?" Mattie asked bitterly. "Grandy lived in the gutter. He loved the gutter. That little slut ain't his first hoedown and sure won't be his last."

"Now, Miss Matt. You don't know what you're saying. Grandy won't be having any more hoedowns. He's in Heaven now."

"Oh no, he ain't. He's gone to the other place."

That's when the widow collapsed to her knees, shaking her fist at the floor. "Granderson Parker Jaspers, you been blinded by Satan. You never stopped sinning your whole wretched life. I know you're down there fornicating with all the brazen she-devils!"

Mattie began weeping and quaking like she herself was about to deliver a mess of demons. Melted makeup ran down her face. Tuck helped her up and led her to a chair.

I tried to erase the image that sprang to mind of the old man servicing a harem of horned and horny pointy-tailed Liliths. Considering the circumstances of his passing, he would have been ready for it.

Grandy had died in a state of extended arousal. That lead pipe in the old man's pants had outlasted him. If Penny, the Mouth of the South Side, was to be believed, he popped erectile dysfunction drugs like some men did Altoids. Had Grandy taken sexual aids the night before he died? If so, then who had he used them for?

After kissing him off at the anniversary party, did Mattie take Grandy home for some makeup sex? Or had he ended his evening in another woman's arms? Did he need the extra help to satisfy a lover exactly one-third his age? A lover that was now pregnant with his child, if Shysteen's story was to be believed.

Could Mattie Jaspers actually be the culprit? Had that wrongful-death lawsuit against me been a smoke screen to deflect attention away from her own guilt? The woman who, according to Penny Lopés, was now several hundred grand richer, thanks to her husband's life insurance policy. And she'd certainly had an axe to grind, what with Grandy's cheating ways.

Could it even be that shape-shifting snake that sidled over while I was clearing tables? "Miss Summers, may I have a moment?"

"You certainly may not, Noble McPherson. I can't believe the nerve of you."

Noble wasn't a legitimate mourner, since he hadn't met Grandy until moments before he passed. Noble couldn't care less about paying his respects. I knew what he was there for. He had crashed the funeral of a man he didn't know in order to hustle me. Nothing would make him happier than ruining my business and seizing it from me at fire-sale prices. But did Noble McPherson's manipulations hide a deeper, deadlier intent?

I found myself closely watching them all. The children and the grandchildren. The nieces and the nephews. The friends and play cousins and even, God help me, one of my own staff. Penny had made no bones about her aversion to Grandy Jaspers. Just how deep did that dislike run?

The deceased had always said, "Don't take no wooden nickels." Grandy meant that as "Watch out for shady people." Yet here I was now, in a room full of people with pockets full of wooden nickels.

Could any among them have hated Grandy enough to kill him?

CHAPTER 12

Free Is a Four-Letter Word

Shysteen Shackleford's antics at the funeral and repast guaranteed she'd be banned from the burial. The next morning at Oakwood Cemetery, we said our goodbyes in peace, tossed our flowers onto the casket, and watched it being lowered into the ground. Grandy had gone the way of all flesh, leaving confusion behind.

It should have been over and I should have been glad. Lord knows I had my own problems. Business at Essie's wasn't exactly booming almost three weeks out since Grandy Jasper's death.

A warm October eased into November and the weather turned chilly. It rained almost every day. Our business, which had never recovered from the shutdown, was further aggravated by the miserable weather. Even when I started offering midweek specials and daily deal vouchers, we struggled to get by.

My staff was under strict orders not to serve Noble McPherson under any circumstances.

Yet he continued to harass me by phone and email. His offer inched up several thousands, then tens of thousands. At times

I was almost tempted to cave. I could take his thirty pieces of silver, sign an agreement with the devil as Sapphire Summers Soulfood Café and Catering Company, then officially reopen under the Essie's brand.

Or I could leave this, my second career, and find something else to do. I'd retired seven years ago from my job as an English teacher and high school assistant principal. I'd reinvented myself once before. I could do it again.

I might even relax into full retirement. No more six-day weeks or ten-hour days. I would no longer be too tired to go out to dinner or the occasional nightclub, take in weekend trips to Lake Geneva like normal people. I could make regular visits to my out-of-town children, my daughter Nzinga Summers and my son Malik Franklin and his family.

The only problem was that I really loved my work. The clinking of silverware on china, the murmurs of conversation, the looks of gratification on satisfied faces, and the delectable smells that took me back to childhood.

I was happy cooking hearty, healthful, delicious food, creating a warm, comforting ambiance for my hungry visitors to eat, drink, and be merry. Sending them home full and satisfied. It was like throwing a party six days out of the week.

I even accepted the problems that came with the job. I delighted in winning over difficult customers, the ones who complained that the butter was too hard or the coffee too cool. I said a prayer for the cheapskates who never left a tip, knowing from Aunt Essie that *God loves a cheerful giver. You've got to give some to get some.*

Cooking wasn't as much a business as a ministry. I was following in my Great-Aunt Essie's footsteps. And running the café had helped me heal from the loss of my second husband.

What would I have done last year without Essie's to keep me going?

I don't even want to think about it . . . none of it.

"I told you before. Sweet potato pie is our signature dessert," Penny warned me. "It's Essie's golden egg. Don't fool around and kill the goose that laid it."

The goose unfortunately was on life support. Peach cobbler was selling like—well, peach cobbler. Our upside-down cake was right-side up in sales. I'd even had requests for Nana's 'Nana. Yet the few patrons we had left were avoiding sweet potato pie like the plague. They were hardly even ordering candied sweet potatoes.

What did somebody once sing about freedom? Oh, yes. I remember. It was, *just another word for nothing left to lose.*

Though innocent in Grandy's untimely demise, a successful vegan pie would vindicate itself. It would stand up, pound its chest, and declare—*I am sweet potato pie, hear me roar, in flavors too good to ignore!* I convinced myself that if I could come up with a better sweet potato pie recipe, our problems would be over. I knew it was magical thinking, but I couldn't give up on the notion.

I began experimenting again. It was almost a quest. I looked up recipes online, bought soul food and Southern cookbooks, asked friends and family to share their favorites. Nothing turned out well enough, but still I kept on trying.

My mission was a study in contradictions. I wanted to preserve Aunt Essie's legacy that had sustained generations, while continuing to evolve as a culinary artist.

"Slow your roll," Penny Porter Lopés warned me. "Don't

throw out the baby with the bathwater. Soul food is all about the flavor."

You would have thought I was the millennial, and Penny the boomer, the way she went on about me dragging people away from the comfort foods they knew and loved. But I knew better. Quite often those people were the very ones driving the train into Nouvelle Soul territory.

Today's soul foodies had a slightly different palate from what I indulged in as a child. Many had lost their taste for offal and organ meats like chitlins, hog maws, and mountain oysters, the pork intestines, stomachs, and testicles our enslaved ancestors learned to clean, tenderize, and make delicious. Much of the wild game Great-Aunt Essie used to cook—opossum, raccoon, rabbit, squirrel, and venison—was no longer readily available.

Sometimes tastes came down to timing. The breakfast clientele of older retired people might appreciate a heavy meal of grits with ham and sausage gravy or chicken-fried steak and rice. Our lunch bunch of working professionals was hardly the pork ear sandwich and souse on crackers kind of crowd.

Meanwhile, Nouvelle Soul gourmands were requesting dishes and ingredients my great-aunt had probably never worked with: Atlantic salmon, Maine lobster, jerk chicken, and shrimp and grits, which originated among Gullah Geechee people of the Carolina Low Country. Half the customers raved about it, the other half had to be convinced that grits weren't just a breakfast staple.

Despite Penny's arguments to the contrary, some customers did want lighter versions of classic desserts like banana pudding, peach cobbler, and sweet potato pie. Others enjoyed their meals with sophisticated wine pairings. Essie's didn't have a liquor license, but we offered bottle service for Sunday brunch and supper seatings.

People's tastes were changing and my food along with it. I was bound and determined to make their eating experience as elevated as it was soul satisfying. I tweaked Aunt Essie's old recipes with bright new flavor profiles. I kept a container garden out back with fresh herbs, tomatoes, and peppers. I sautéed my greens with olive oil instead of boiling them to mush. I simmered black-eyed peas and greens with smoked turkey instead of ham hocks or fatback, and no one seemed to notice the difference.

Yet some of the old-school gourmets could also be resistant to change. My son Malik once loved my vegan chili, prepared with a meat replacement made from wheat gluten.

"Nobody wants to eat something called seitan." Penny shook her head when I put it on the menu. "It sounds too much like Satan."

Even when I changed the wording to *wheat meat,* the vegan chili never really took off.

And when I tried to substitute oven-baked for Aunt Essie's famous smothered chicken, my patrons threatened a mutiny and I had to slip it back onto the menu.

CHAPTER 13

Leave Well Enough Alone

"No telling what kind of traffic I'll run into on DuSable Lake Shore Drive. Then I've got to find parking up there in Wrigleyville. I'll have to get going soon."

"No, you don't," I objected. "You'll park for free in District 19 Police Station lot, and I'm sure that Cubs game is at least two hours away from starting."

"Actually, three. How do you know me so well, Savvy Franklin?"

"Because I was married to you, remember? And the name is Summers, my having remarried twenty-five years ago, and all."

My ex-husband was always punctual to a fault, a faithful disciple of his Grandpa Charlie's wisdom: "Better an hour early than a minute too late."

Fanon sat sipping tea, his Cubs starter jacket draped across the back of my overstuffed easy chair. He watched me warily over the rim of his mug. I had invited him over for tea and pie. No doubt he was regretting having accepted the invitation.

I took the opportunity to share with him my suspicions about Grandy's sudden death. "There's more to it than meets the eye, Fanon. Somebody's lying about something."

"Yeah, I remember your lie-dar. It always sounded kind of kooky, I have to tell you."

"You can't deny my instinct for sniffing out the truth. And something about Grandy's death doesn't pass the smell test."

He shrugged noncommittally, turning the same logic against me that I had used on Mattie. "How could someone give the man a heart attack? Screw him to death? Tell 'yo mama' jokes and make him die laughing? Jump out of an alley and holler 'boo'?"

Fanon M. Franklin looked at me skeptically as he sipped from his cup of Constant Comment tea. He took a healthy bite of pie and chewed it thoughtfully. My ex must not have gotten the memo that my sweet potato pie was a killer.

Fanon was en route to participate in the wrongheaded foolishness of representing the wrong sports team. What could the man be thinking? He had lived in Chicago all his life. He really should have known better.

I'd reminded him of it time and again, before our marriage, during it, and after our divorce. Chicago was divided along baseball lines. North Siders always rooted for the Cubs, South Siders for the White Sox.

As a longtime resident of the Southwest Side neighborhood pretentiously known as Beverly Hills, Fanon should have learned his lesson from the infamous "Fubbies" incident.

One year with the Cubs and the Sox in an interleague matchup, he was sent out on a public nuisance call. A neighbor and fellow patrolman—Beverly was lousy with them—had spray-painted "Fuck the Cubbies" across his garage doors.

It wasn't actually an arrestable offense. Fanon informed the officer that the city would be citing and fining him for graffiti. Harsh words were exchanged. They almost came to blows.

When the dust settled, his neighbor in blue agreed to paint out the offending words, which he promptly replaced with "Cuff the Fubbies." Everyone knew what he meant.

"There are reasons someone may have wanted Grandy dead," I told him. "Just hear me out, Fanon."

He sighed. "This isn't exactly a game of Clue. It's police work, Savvy Franklin."

"Summers," I reminded him again. "And no, it's not. There was never a police investigation into Grandy's death. Zilch, zero, nada."

"Then call up the Department and file a complaint," Fanon suggested. "We're trained and paid to investigate. Leave it to the professionals."

Which you are not, I almost said. But I would never hurt him that way. I still cared about the father of my son, though we'd divorced three decades ago.

When I first met Fanon, he was a college junior minoring in Spanish, majoring in sociology, and active in the radical movement on campus. He came to activism naturally.

"It's kind of the family business," he always said.

His Grandpa Charles, a retired Pullman porter, was an organizer with the Brotherhood of Sleeping Car Porters. His father Charles Jr. had been a member of the Black Muslims before quitting in disaffection when Malcolm X was killed. "Little Charley Franklin III" remembers being taken as a very young child to a place where a hit ordered by the FBI was carried out by the Cook County Sheriff Department.

"The cops just left the door busted open, and anybody could walk in. The Panthers were giving tours of the murder scene. What the sheriff claimed were bullet holes from Panthers' guns turned out to be nail heads in the wall. I saw the bloodstained beds where two men were executed in their sleep. My dad said it was something I needed to see, and he was right. You might have thought it would mess up my head and turn me to the streets. Instead it radicalized me."

After his graduation he first worked as a community organizer. Then the activist hung up his black beret to wear the blue-visored cap of the Chicago Police Department. He'd now been on the police force nearly forty years and still hadn't made detective. Fanon hadn't learned to negotiate CPD politics or finesse the promotion he so desperately wanted. His frustration had been a nagging source of stress in our ten-year marriage.

Now he supervised a team of peace officers stationed in city high schools. They dismantled gang units, organized restorative justice programs, and mentored thousands of young men and women. Sometimes they had to arrest a kid. Mostly they tried keeping them out of trouble and away from the prison pipeline. The work they did was vitally important. But I knew disappointment still gnawed at Fanon's soul.

There he sat in front of me, the man with whom I joined my DNA to produce two generations of Franklin menfolk. He poked the dessert remains with his fork, still trying to change the subject. "This isn't your regular pie. What'd you do to it?"

"Vegan," I said shortly. "I'm revamping the menu."

"Bad idea." He shook his head. "Leave well enough alone."

"What harm will it do to look into the matter? Just to check and see what I find?"

Fanon smiled that gap-toothed grin I once found so irresistible. "Something tells me we're not talking about pie. Okay, what do you want from me?"

"Why do I have to want anything? I'm just talking to you, Fanon."

"Don't play the nut role with me. I know you too well."

"Well, okay," I admitted. "Do you have any favors to call

in at City Hall? I understand there's been a call for an inquest into Grandy's death. I'm wondering if that's happened and if so, what was found."

An alert sounded on his smartwatch, and Fanon instinctively reached for his starter jacket.

"Hang on, Carlos Villanueva," I teased, rechristening him as the former Cubs relief pitcher. "Not so fast."

Before my ex-husband became Fanon, his birth name had been Charles Merritt Franklin III. With his bright complexion and wavy hair, people often mistook him for Latino. Fanon didn't like knee-jerk assumptions and was quick to correct those who made them. He wasn't hating on anyone's background, he was just proud of his own.

"Oh, you got jokes. Hardy-har-har. Just what do you want from me, woman?"

I handed him a list I had jotted down earlier that day. "These people were around at the time of Grandy's death. His wife Mattie. His daughter Winnie. Tuchman Pfeiffer used to be Grandy's manager, and Shysteen Shackleford was apparently his mistress. Noble McPherson was in the café right before he died. Annabelle Beasley baked the Jasperses' fiftieth-anniversary cake, though nobody got to eat it. Delbert Dailey is our alderman . . ."

"I know who Dailey is."

"I'm wondering what you can find out about them."

"What, all of these people? Find out . . . like what?"

That was the problem. I didn't know what I was looking for. "Any kind of trouble with the law, I guess."

"Which could range from a parking ticket to a Class X felony. Go to Google and find a criminal background check. There're a million of them out there."

"Those things don't always work," I told him. "When I

hired that busboy year before last, his background came up clean. Only after he practically stole me broke did I learn the guy had a record."

"How'd you find that out? Wait, don't tell me."

"Penny Porter Lopés, who else? Anyway, there are seven people on this list. I just don't have the funds right now to do a search on all of them."

"I can't promise what I'll find." Fanon folded the list and stuffed it carelessly into his jacket pocket. I hoped to God he didn't lose it. "I can't really promise anything at all."

Fanon downed the dregs of his tea and stood to leave. At least he hadn't painted his face in white, black, and silver war paint, like some of the more diehard fans. Leave well enough alone, Fanon had warned. I decided to keep closemouthed about his attire. I'd bite my tongue and bide my time for now.

"I'd better get this show on the road, Savvy. That game isn't going to win itself."

I refrained from pointing out the obvious. Whether he got there on time or not at all, waving a foam finger and shouting "Go, Cubbies" wouldn't hand his team a victory. The Cubs would have to rise or fall on their own merit.

Probably they would fall.

CHAPTER 14

The Batter Thickens

"Blessings, Safflower. Just checking on you, girl."

"Annabelle Beasley. Good to hear from you," I lied, wishing I'd checked the number before answering the phone.

"I don't suppose you're bringing your sweet potato crimes to this year's In Your Face."

"Did you say *crimes*, Annabelle?"

"Of course not. I said *pies*. With everything going on, you probably want to sit this one out."

Oh, you wish, I silently fumed. *I won't give you the satisfaction.*

Annabelle Beasley was a big ol' fake. The last time I saw her, she practically spit in my face. Now butter didn't seem to melt in her mouth. Aunt Essie would have called her *nice-nasty*. Pretending to be all sympathetic when her every word was laced with toxic intent.

We could have been sisters in the cause, two Black women entrepreneurs in the unpredictable and sometimes unforgiving food service business. We weren't direct competitors, since I owned a café and she ran a bakery. My business was on the South Side, hers in the near-south suburbs. We didn't even serve the same clientele. So I don't know why she always acted like we were in competition. Actually, yes, I did.

It's because Essie's wins each year in the Sweet Potato Pie category of In Your Face, and Annabelle's Sweet Stuff Bakery doesn't even place. Professional jealousy's a bitch.

That's probably why she mispronounces my name, calling me "Safflower" instead of Sapphire. It might also explain her nasty attitude at Grandy's funeral repast. What it didn't account for was that whispered demand she made.

This could ruin me, Mattie. I need to know, just what did Grandy tell you?

There was definitely something going on there. I made a mental note to myself. *Just how did Annabelle know Mattie and Grandy? What kind of history did they have?* I hurried her off the phone with a noncommittal comment about In Your Face. Let her sit and stew on it awhile.

Annabelle actually did make a point. As preoccupied as I'd been after Grandy's death and as slow as business was now, not to mention the massive stress of Noble McPherson's harassment campaign, I really didn't have room for anything else on my plate. In Your Face should have been the last thing on my mind.

It was a lighthearted little charity event that took place every fall between Thanksgiving and Christmas. Chicago-area eateries entered the competition, bringing twelve freshly baked pies each. Four would be sliced and sold to patrons. One was taste-tested by a panel of judges. Two were held in reserve, and five entered into the games. A cast of local luminaries allowed bidders to hit them in the face with the contest's prize-winning entries.

This was all for a good cause, raising funds for local charities. I tried not to resent the fact that a dish I'd put so much into preparing wound up in the faces of minor celebrities, the floor beneath them, and the wall behind them. And in the end, would be swept up and dumped in the trash.

The crumb you throw away today might fill you up tomorrow, was one of my Great-Aunt Essie's mottoes.

On the plus side, the event got good television coverage, free publicity for the winners' businesses. And I could sure use some of that! I'd been entering my pies for the past five years and every year I'd won first or second place. Maybe by competition time, I'd have perfected a vegan recipe.

Too bad I couldn't enter Aunt Essie's crowd-pleasing peach cobbler. Contest rules were quite specific. Only open-faced, bottom-crusted, custard-filled pies were allowed. No fruit, no nuts, no chips or chunks. Even a coconut cream pie couldn't contain any actual coconut flakes.

Entrants competed in one of three categories. There was traditional—lemon meringues, pumpkins, key limes, French silks, and sweet potato pies competing in subcategories. There were heirloom pie varieties—the vinegar, buttermilk, shoofly, applesauce, and caramel (like pecan pie without the nuts). Then we had the catchall innovation category, which could be very much up for grabs.

"Taste this, Fanon." I handed him a fresh slice. "I think I finally cracked the code."

I'd been seeing much more of my ex-husband than I had in a great many years. Penny would tease me every time he showed up at Essie's. "You notice how he keeps calling you Savvy Franklin? Girl, he wants to re-wife you. Men are just like salmon. They always come home to spawn."

"Come home to spawn? Do you hear yourself, Penny?"

Fanon came by Essie's that Thursday afternoon, a slow day in a string of slow days.

"So how does it taste?" I asked, trusting Fanon to tell the truth. He was known to be brutally honest.

He tasted a forkful then took another bite.

"Hm. The crust tastes pretty much like your regular pie. The filling is definitely lighter, with a little more tartness and spice. Not bad." He smiled. "Not bad at all. In fact, it's pretty good."

"I'm hoping for another win at In Your Face."

Fanon made a face. "I hear 'my dear brother' will be making an appearance."

"You don't have a brother, Fanon."

"You know who I mean. That alder-thug of yours went and got himself cast as local talent. Anything to have his mug on TV. He's desperate to get reelected."

"They could raise big money with Delbert Dailey. Folks will wait around the block to deck that guy in the face with a pie."

Much to my delight, Fanon finished his slice and asked for more. Oh, now it was on. Watch out, Annabelle Beasley. Victory would be ours! I disappeared into the café kitchen and came back with one slice on a plate and a whole pie wrapped for Fanon to take home.

While I was gone he'd put on his reading glasses and taken out a legal pad that he was checking against another sheet of paper. I recognized it as the list I had given him last week, crumpled but still readable. A sheath of official-looking papers peeked from an accordion file he'd laid on the table.

"What have we here?" I asked. "Out with it, fella."

"Don't go getting excited. I've just been asking around."

"Well, what did you find out? Don't keep a sister waiting."

Fanon raised his hand like a traffic cop.

"First things first. Nothing I discovered screams evidence. But even if you think it does, I don't want you out there playing amateur detective." He handed me a business card. "It's an old colleague of mine."

"Your former beat partner?" I recognized the name, though I'd never actually met the person.

"Who is now Detective Sergeant Emerson Jacobs. A good person to bounce your—what should we call them? Theories against."

I lay the card on the table before us. "Fair enough. So, what do you have?"

"Except for the heart attack that killed him, Granderson Jaspers was in the kind of health you'd expect for a man his age. He was hospitalized last year for a hip joint replacement and spent some time in rehab. He's been under the care of a cardiologist for the last two years. A natural death by heart attack wouldn't have been surprising, except for one thing."

"And what's that?"

"Sildenafil citrate, otherwise known as Viagra. He had massive amounts of it in his system, enough to dose up a Brahman bull. His heart attack was caused by an overdose."

Fanon fished a stack of papers from the file and showed me the autopsy protocol and toxicology report from the medical examiner's office. The drug overdose was ruled accidental and could have occurred anywhere from six to twelve hours before his death.

"Which means," I mused, thinking aloud, "he could have taken them toward the end of the anniversary party, sometime overnight, or even the next morning."

"He had a lot of it in his system, that's for sure." He consulted the autopsy report again. "*The deceased's remains showed signs of priapism.*"

"I'm not up on my medical lingo, Fanon. What's priapism?"

"Too much of a good thing, an erection that won't go away. If he hadn't died, he'd have wound up in the ER. There was a ruptured artery and hematoma trauma to his genitals."

"Ouch! Poor Grandy."

Fanon nodded. "He must have been in agony. His stomach was also full of partially digested food, which might have reduced the Viagra's effectiveness. What was old boy thinking? Everyone knows you're supposed to take it on an empty stomach."

I lifted an eyebrow. "Oh, do they now?"

"Don't get it twisted, Savvy Franklin." He grinned. "That's from general knowledge, not personal experience. I don't need any help in that department, thank you."

Unless he was practicing self-gratification, this meant Fanon was still getting it on the regular. I stifled the question that popped into my head. *Wonder who he's kicking it with?*

Fanon never remarried after our divorce though I'm sure he had plenty of chances. He was a BMW, a "Black man working." A fit, attractive, middle-aged man like my ex certainly wouldn't want for company.

I picked up a page and pointed to a figure. "Is this what they found inside of him? The equivalent of fifteen to twenty 50-milligram pills? That must have been the whole bottle."

"Some men pop these things like candy. They'll share them with their buddies or use them recreationally, mixing them with booze and other party drugs. There are dangers with abusing these medications, as your man discovered."

I couldn't help glancing over at Table Two. I remembered Grandy hunched there next to that potted fern, sweating and disheveled.

"If Grandy deliberately took fifteen to twenty Viagra tablets, he sure was clueless about the results. He couldn't seem to understand why he was feeling weird. Could someone have overdosed him without his knowledge?"

Fanon shrugged. "I guess they could have crushed the pills to a powder and put it in his food, or dissolved them in water and mixed them in his drink. The ME ruled it an overdose but that doesn't prove that he took them himself."

"What do you think?"

"Look, the brother was old. Elderly men might have more reasons than others to use Viagra, but they're also more prone to the side effects. He might have forgotten just how much he had and kept on taking more."

"True," I admitted. "I've done that myself and I'm twenty years younger than Grandy. I'll look down at my multivitamins and wonder if I've had my daily dose."

Fanon continued. "Or maybe he just kept popping pills out of frustration that nothing was working."

"Not working because of all the food he ate?"

"Or all the liquor he drank. And what if his woman was lying there waiting? Man, that steps up the pressure. Trying to get it up and have a good time, old boy winds up taking himself out the game. Death by Viagra. What a way to go."

I pushed the documents aside. "Anything else?"

Fanon turned a page on his legal pad. "So, these people you had me run down in the record. Not exactly a rogue's gallery but a bunch of assorted characters."

He had discovered some interesting things about the Jaspers family finances. Grandy Jaspers had a mountain of unpaid bills on top of financial judgments from his various creditors. His home was in danger of foreclosure. If Shysteen was really after his money she would have been sadly disappointed. Or maybe she was the reason his finances were in the toilet. Had he depleted the family coffers playing sugar daddy?

As long as I'd known them, Mattie Jaspers had never worked outside the home. If Grandy had lived, both he and his wife would be in dire straits by now. That life insurance payout hadn't made Mattie rich. When supplemented with Grandy's Social Security, a half-pension from a foundry where he once worked, and dwindling proceeds from his record sales, the combined income might just keep her out of poverty. It depended on how she spent and how long she lived.

I was shocked at how deeply a man in his seventies had fallen into debt. With the financial shape they were in, I couldn't fathom why they'd splurged on a fiftieth-anniversary party—the venue, the staff, the food, the headache champagne. Though of course, the catering hadn't been settled until after Grandy died. If Mattie hadn't gotten that insurance check, how would she have paid the bill?

Fanon also found a discovery motion against Tuchman Pfeiffer filed by Project Respect, an advocacy group that helped Black musicians recover misappropriated publishing credits and royalties.

Winnie Mae Welbon had been arrested once on a charge of public drunkenness. Shysteen, on the other hand, had a rap sheet as long as my arm. She'd been booked several times for various offenses, from disorderly conduct to shoplifting. Just last year she had spent some time in the Cook County Jail awaiting court on elder abuse. The charges were eventually dropped. Interesting. Shysteen had some kind of criminal history involving the elderly.

Annabelle Beasley's record was a huge surprise, as big a born-again Christian as she made herself out to be. She had been arrested forty years ago in a drug sting at a Mississippi gentlemen's club. Had Annabelle worked as a stripper back then? Did Grandy know about it and hold it over her head? It seemed like the kind of thing he was capable of. If so, how far would Annabelle go to keep her past under wraps?

In addition to this, the week before his death, Grandy had been up to the Lake County Courthouse trying to get a restraining order against Tuchman Pfeiffer for harassment. The judge had denied his request and the order had not been granted.

"This is some kind of scoop, Fanon Franklin. After retirement you should think about being a private investigator."

He shrugged off the compliment. "Just called in some favors. What's up with this dude McPherson? He doesn't seem in the same league as your other people."

Noble McPherson had no criminal record that Fanon could find. He was squeaky clean, not so much as an outstanding traffic ticket. But what really floored me was the report on Jonesboro-Lee LLC, the outfit McPherson represented. They were big-time into the South Side real estate investment market, having gotten their hands on vast stretches of property in Woodlawn, Bronzeville, Washington Park, and South Shore. In fact, they held options on several parcels of vacant land right here on my block.

The truth was, this half-block where the café stood looked rather like a bomb had been dropped. Empty land stretched from my building almost to the next corner. It was like some new kind of physics; *vacant lots abhor a vacuum.*

Despite prominently displayed "No Dumping" signs, I was always calling the city to clear out garbage, old mattresses, car tires, and other refuse people discarded on a regular basis. This was more than just a nuisance and an eyesore. Sometimes it was downright dangerous.

Once night someone dumped an old refrigerator, doors intact. I was terrified some neighborhood kid would use it as a plaything, get trapped inside, and suffocate. I'd spent the whole morning on the phone to Delbert Dailey's aldermanic office, demanding they send someone out to haul the thing away.

It was true that Woodlawn had become a changing neighborhood, caught in the throes of rapid regentrification. My building was a half mile from the university, which probably made the land it sat on more valuable than the business itself.

Most of the structures on my half of the block had already been demolished. Only two buildings remained. There was my street-level storefront with two tiny upstairs apartments that I'd combined into one. Then there was a three-flat apartment building directly behind me across the alley. The rest were vacant lots on the tax delinquent rolls and Noble's company had acquired options on them all.

I stared at the document in stunned silence. "Those land-grabbing SOBs. I've been trying for years to get that piece of land next door. I wanted to expand my garden and build a parking lot for my customers. I even had Dailey's office look into it. They told me it was registered to an LLC and they couldn't pierce the corporate veil. That lot wasn't even supposed to be on the market."

"For the right price, anything's for sale. So, you'll have new neighbors. What's the big deal?"

"McPherson's been harassing me to sell out, that's the big deal. He's been at it for months and I believe he'll stop at nothing to get his hands on my property."

"What? I didn't know it was that serious, Savvy."

"As a heart attack," I muttered. "No pun intended."

"I'm afraid that's not all. I also learned some unsavory things about Delbert Dailey. Suffice it to say, he won't be winning Man of the Year anytime soon. You need to steer clear of that man. When the crap hits the fan, it won't be pretty."

I jumped up in excitement. "Did Delbert kill Grandy Jaspers?"

"Whoa, girl." Fanon held up a restraining hand. "You could be competing in the women's hurdles, the way you're jumping to conclusions right now."

I clicked my tongue in exasperation.

"If I'm jumping to conclusions," I told him, "then set me straight."

"I can't tell you much but I can say this. Delbert 'Do-Right' Dailey is not being investigated for murder."

"Oh no?"

"Absolutely not. Now leave it alone."

I let the news settle. "He's not being investigated for murder, but he is being investigated for something?"

"What don't you understand about *leave it alone*?" Fanon snatched off his glasses and pointed them at me. "Stay in your lane, Savvy Franklin. Fry your chicken and bake your pies."

My suspicions flared, fueled as much by what was hidden as what had been revealed. "If you won't tell me what's going on, I guess I'll have to have a little talk with Dailey."

"Oh, no you don't. Stay away from Delbert Dailey. I mean it, Savvy. The man is very bad news."

CHAPTER 15

Ice Maiden

My sous-chef went and did a Wonder Woman on me. Well, maybe it was more of a Superman. All Diana Prince had to do was twirl around and her costume would magically appear. Clark Kent needed a phone booth to get his superhero on.

Penny Lopés disappeared into the ladies' room as a sassy restaurant worker in an apron, hairnet, and rubber-soled shoes. She emerged from it a femme fatale, wafting Calvin Klein Obsession in her wake.

Her silk fuchsia minidress rose several inches above her knee, and her leather stiletto boots fit her long legs like gloves. Her jewelry was stylishly chunky and her makeup expertly applied. She and Sergio must have a hot date tonight.

"Watch out, world." She posed, poised for compliments. "Your girl is clean as a jelly bean."

Fanon applauded. "You look fabulous, Penny."

"Thank you kindly, sir."

"But I need a favor from you. Promise me you'll help keep my ex here out of trouble."

Penny glanced at me with a lifted eyebrow. "Why, what's she up to?"

"I think you know, young lady. I've already looked into the

matter, and to use an old cop expression—nothing to see here, move along. Savvy's trying to pull a Sherlock Holmes, when she's more of an Inspector Clouseau."

I cleared my throat. "You know, *she's* sitting right here. *She* can hear every word coming out of your mouth."

"You're a restaurateur, not a private investigator." Fanon turned and looked me in the eye. "Call Detective Jacobs sooner rather than later."

After Fanon left I asked her point-blank. "Penny, who pays your salary?"

She tossed her head, earrings jangling like chimes. "Why, that would be you, Miss Summers. I doubt if Sergeant Franklin has a place for little ol' me on the CPD."

"I have to give you your props, girl. You could have been a police dick if that's what you wanted."

"I prefer the term, private eye." She winked. "Police dick, that's your thing."

"Not *is* my thing, *was* my thing. Forward ever, backward never." Quoting Kwame Nkrumah, first Black president of Ghana, I held up my fist for some dap.

Penny bumped me back, but shook her head. "Never say never. One of these days you might decide to follow those breadcrumbs to the gingerbread house. Your baby's daddy been sniffing around here a lot."

"Only to help me look into Grandy's death. He's not after anything else."

"Well, the sergeant is looking mighty yummy these days."

"Yummy for somebody else's tummy," I scoffed. "'Cause I ain't the one. Besides, Fanon doesn't take me seriously. And you know my thoughts about what happened to Grandy."

"That someone had reason to off the old geezer? I'm beginning to think so, too."

"Then we're on the same page. And look at this." I handed her Fanon's file of documents and handwritten notes.

Penny riffled through the pages, then whistled. "And hubby said there was nothing to see."

"That's *ex*-hubby, girlfriend. Get it straight." I smoothed out a crumpled page. "This is the list of people I asked him to look into. You can see it's only partially complete."

"I know. These are seven out of maybe a dozen people."

"So, here's what I need you to do. Put that bloodhound nose of yours to work and sniff out what you can find about the folks at the Jasperses' anniversary party. You may as well check up on the funeral-goers, too."

"That might take a minute. Is there somewhere I should begin?"

I thought about it for a minute. "Maybe we should start with the staff."

The next morning I called the number on the business card Fanon had given me. It was for a detective in the Bureau of Investigative Services.

"Hi, I'm trying to reach Detective Emerson Jacobs."

"This is Emerson," came a raspy voice at the other end. "Can I help you?"

I resisted the urge to correct the detective as I'd done my own kids and high school English students. *I don't know if you* can, *but yes, you certainly* may.

"I'm Sapphire Summers. Sergeant Franklin told me to give you a call."

"Which Sergeant Franklin?"

"Well, he said he knows you."

"I know at least three Sergeant Franklins. There's Charlene

Franklin, who is probably not the one since you said *he*. Sergeant Fanon Franklin in Youth Crimes. Sergeant Roger Franklin in Education and Training."

"Yes, it's Fanon. I need to talk to you about someone who died. I'm beginning to think it wasn't an accident."

There was a beat of silence at the other end. I could still hear breathing.

"Hello, sir," I asked. "Are you still there?"

"I am, ma'am. Could you come to the station at eleven a.m. next Wednesday, ma'am?"

"You know that's the day before Thanksgiving, right?"

"I know what day it is," Sergeant Jacobs came back crisply. "Is that a problem for you, ma'am?"

I made the appointment, reminding myself to ask Penny to cover for me that day. I didn't understand why Detective Jacobs kept emphasizing the honorific "ma'am" until I showed up that afternoon. The husky voice on the phone hadn't helped the matter. And Detective Jacobs never bothered to correct me when I'd said "sir."

All those years together on the beat, and Fanon had never told me his partner was a woman.

"I am so very sorry, Detective Jacobs. How silly of me to assume. It's just that your voice is so, um . . ." I considered one, then discarded another adjective. "So distinctive, Detective. Like Rachael Ray or Lauren Bacall. You must hear that all the time."

I felt like a kid called before the principal.

She waved away my apology with stubby nail-bitten fingers. Those hands were the only unpolished thing about her. All else was cool and severe, meticulously pulled together. Detective Emerson Jacobs exuded all the warmth of an igloo. I suppose the chilly reception was because I'd mistaken her for a man on the phone.

Her eyes were a cool gray, her hair a frosty platinum blond. Her lips were a slash of red lipstick in a paper-white face. Even her blouse was a stark snowy shade that blended almost evenly with her skin. It was fall turning winter so she must not be getting very much sun. Especially in a second-floor cubicle without any windows.

"Thanks for seeing me, Detective Jacobs." I paused for an invitation to use her first name, an offer that didn't come. "So here's what I wanted to share with you. Granderson Jaspers died a few weeks ago. He was a longtime acquaintance and a patron of my café."

"Yes. Why should that concern me?"

"An elderly man died in my arms after eating sweet potato pie. It turned out to be a massive heart attack from a Viagra overdose. I think he might have been the victim of foul play. I'm hoping you might open a death investigation."

I handed her the list of contacts. I guess I couldn't really call them suspects. Mattie Jaspers, Shysteen Shackleford, Winnie Mae Welbon, Noble McPherson, Delbert "Do-Right" Dailey, and Annabelle Beasley. "These are some of the people who were around the night before and the day of Grandy's death."

"Alderman Dailey was there?" she asked with a glimmer of interest. "Just how were they connected?"

"As I recall, they were members of the same Masonic lodge, and saw the same cardiologist. I don't know if it went any further than that. It was Alderman Dailey who pushed for the inquest when Grandy's heart attack was ruled natural causes. Another certificate was issued later with a new cause of death."

"Accidental?" she guessed. "Not homicide."

I nodded.

Thin shoulders lifted beneath the white silk blouse. "What do you want me to do?"

Getting Detective Jacobs on board was going to be harder than I thought. Why had Fanon even sent me to this person? She was even more uncooperative than he had been. Before I could stop myself, I heaved a deep, belabored sigh.

She gave me a long stare. "Am I annoying you, Miss Summers?"

"No, not at all. A little frustrated, maybe. I thought you were willing to hear me out."

"Have I told you to stop speaking? Did I ask you to leave?"

I forced myself not to breathe another sigh she might interpret as irritation. I explained all I remembered about Grandy's fiftieth-anniversary event, his demise the next morning at my café, and the funeral that followed a week and a half later. Even to my own ears the details sounded flimsy and insubstantial.

Emerson seemed fixated on Delbert Dailey. My antennae went up. Fanon had hinted Dailey was under some kind of investigation. She underlined his name twice. I could read it upside down from where I sat.

"Was he acting out of character the times that you saw him?" she asked. "Did you observe any strange or unusual behavior?"

Strange and *unusual are synonyms,* I could have told her. Words that essentially mean the same. I hesitated before speaking. "Detective, have you ever met the man?"

"Not personally. I have seen him on the news."

"Well, Delbert is somewhat grandiose, maybe even self-aggrandizing. Some people would call that strange." An image popped into my mind, like a fuzzy snapshot falling from a photo album. "But you know, I did see something at Grandy's funeral that struck me as odd."

Shysteen Shackleford stumbling down the center aisle of the Cathedral of Holy Grace, leaning heavily on his arm.

"Delbert was with Grandy's mistress," I remembered, struggling to process the memory.

"Doing what?"

"Escorting her in the funeral procession. There was something weird about his face."

"His face." Emerson's response was more of a statement than a question.

I tried to explain. "His expression was strange. I guess I'd have to say in retrospect, it was somewhere between a blush and a smirk."

Like the cat that ate the canary and then felt bad about it. Sylvester finally catches Tweety. *I really shouldn't have done it. But damn, it tasted good.*

Somehow it reminded me of Wrigleyville. An ooze of memory, wriggly like a worm. Suddenly I snapped my fingers. The fuzzy snapshot suddenly came into focus.

"I must say," the detective stifled a yawn. "You haven't given me much to go on. Viagra and smirks and funny looks don't really constitute evidence."

I jumped to my feet, startling the woman by reaching out to shake her hand. "I really have to be going. I hope I may call you again."

Detective Jacobs nodded in confusion. "Yes, you can. Of course."

"And, ma'am?" I turned back at the doorway. "You enjoy your Thanksgiving holiday. *Ma'am.*"

One side of the detective's lip quirked, the closest so far that had any resemblance to a smile.

CHAPTER 16

Wrigleyville

I jumped into Red Rover, joined DuSable Lake Shore Drive at 31st Street, and drove twelve miles north. I exited at Belmont, took Clark to Addison then doubled back east past Wrigley Field.

Since seeing Delbert "Do-Right" Dailey at Grandy's funeral, I'd had the oddest, most uneasy sense of déjà vu. As I moved steadily northward, I felt like I was inching closer to the origins of it. I tried to sort out what I was feeling. Tension? A touch of dread?

It was already November and baseball season was over. It wasn't hard finding a spot near the El tracks. I parked my car and set out walking, retracing a route nearly forty years old.

My alma mater is now UIC, which used to be called UICCC. Somewhere along the way a couple of the "C's" went missing, something like they did when SSS-CCC had morphed into Essie's. I had been in my first semester at the University of Illinois, Chicago Circle Campus, which folks abbreviated to "Circle." Later that same year I would meet Charles Merritt Franklin, a high-yella fella with a big floppy Afro and a fetching gap-toothed grin. This same young man would rename himself Fanon.

This was long before I'd become a cougar. Seventeen years old and definitely not legal, I liked older guys back then.

Charles seemed worldly at twenty, already a junior in the Jane Addams School of Social Work and an organizer of the New Black Panther chapter. Eventually he would change his name, begin a career, fall in love, marry me, and join the Chicago Police Department. But none of that had happened yet.

In the company of a girlfriend from high school, I'd taken the Jackson Park Elevated train from the South Side up to Wrigleyville to go reggae-clubbing that night.

It was my first and my only visit to a nightspot whose name I can't recall. We barely had money for the cover charge and carfare home. We were confident there would be men to buy our drinks and we hadn't been mistaken.

With false IDs tucked into our purses, we were itching to get all hot and sweaty, to dance all night like David danced. Swaying close up tight "inna rub-a-dub style" to a real live reggae band instead of the records we usually listened to.

Dry leaves crunching beneath my feet stirred me from my reverie. I realized that particular night in question had also been autumn. I don't know why I couldn't recall the nightclub's name when I clearly remembered what I had on.

My cornrows were plaited close and swept asymmetrically across my head, falling in a cascade of loose braids strung with beads at the ends. I had brought along an album cover to show the braider a photo of Janice Marie Johnson, the bassist. Their *Taste of Honey* LP was the first one I'd bought with my own money. I was a kid when the LP first came out, but Aunt Essie wouldn't let me get cornrows. She said they were too "worldly."

"*Women should adorn themselves in respectable apparel, with modesty and self-control, not with braided hair or gold or pearls or costly clothing,"* she told me. "That's what the Good Book says."

I'd been waiting to get that hairstyle since I was fourteen years old.

My tie-dyed skirt was a wraparound and I'd made the halter top myself from a Vogue Easy Pattern. It was blue on blue with a swirl design that clung to my body like moving water. I wish I still had it, and it still fit me. Whenever I wore it I got so much attention that I started calling it my "man-catching top." I'm pretty sure I had it on the day I caught Fanon Franklin's eye.

About a quarter block away, we spotted a couple leaving the club and walking in our direction. Stumbling might be a better verb. A pool of streetlight splashed across their faces.

My friend leaned toward me and whispered from the side of her mouth. "Some chicks can't hold their liquor."

The "chick" was a curvy Latina in a leopard-print top and tight ruffled skirt. A rose was tucked behind one ear. Shiny black hair piled atop her head was twisted into a sleek topknot. Silver hoop earrings and scarlet lipstick that matched the rose behind her ear made her look like a voluptuous dancer.

They both seemed to be a study in halves. Her eyes were half-closed, her mouth half-open, her body half-collapsed against his. The man she leaned against was half as homely as she was attractive. He half-walked, half-dragged her toward Addison Street.

It all came back to me as if watching through a window-pane. This man was hairy, thick-limbed, and squat, several inches shorter than she. The image of Delbert Dailey at Grandy's funeral pricked at my memory.

Those two only bore a passing resemblance to one an-other. Where one man had been olive-skinned, possibly of

Mediterranean origin, the other was Black with a complexion Penny called "piss-stank yellow." Their facial expressions though were nearly identical.

I'd never forget the look on his face, both shifty and contented. That man from forty years before wore an air of mortification about him, a sour sweet cocktail of satisfied shame. Satisfaction because his date was so hot. Shame because she was wasted. Or so I thought at the time.

I glanced down at their feet. Hers in mid-heeled Mary Janes—a sexy silhouette, yet practical for dancing. His flat brown boots—like tough leather turds—were possibly even uglier than he was. I caught his eye as they came abreast and he quickly looked away. The smirk never left his face.

After that night the image would haunt me, then slowly fade away. How did a woman who took such pains with her appearance let herself go on an evening out? I remembered my Great-Aunt Essie's adage. *God ain't impressed with a pretty face, but he don't like ugly ways.*

I found myself feeling sorry for the homely guy whose pretty girlfriend had gone and gotten so plastered she'd probably embarrassed him in public. Maybe the nightclub asked them to leave even before the band got started. Such a waste of an outfit and a cute hairdo so early on a Friday night.

I wouldn't let that woman be me.

But how had she gotten so sloppy drunk without her upsweep falling? Why hadn't her hair loosened along with her restraint, tumbling around her face? Her flower still looked florist fresh.

Had the woman really been a stumbling drunk? Maybe he was a stranger she'd only just met that night. With enough alcohol in her, he might have looked good enough to go home with. Or had she been roofied maybe by someone she'd only met that night? "Slipping her a mickey" is what they called it back then.

Had we witnessed the prelude to a crime that night? A date rape, a beating, or worse? An accidental overdose, a slow, deliberate death?

Was that man's expression really satisfied shame? Or was it nervous, guilty glee?

If we had known what happened, was there anything we could have done? Confronted the man, tried to rouse the woman, run into the nightclub for help. Mobile devices were not around back then but they did have public phones. We might have found a nearby booth and dialed up 911. Or we could have walked for help. District 19 Police Station was only a few blocks away.

I came to the place where we'd nightclubbed that night, letting men bring us drinks we were lucky weren't drugged. Laughing and dancing "inna rub-a-dub style," or having the rub-a-dub danced on us. Which was basically letting some guy back you to the wall and grind in time to the music.

I couldn't remember the El ride south. Maybe because of how much I'd been drinking. Maybe we'd let some man drive us home. How splendidly naive we were.

Would I ever remember the name of that club? It wasn't on the windows or door. Somewhere in the decades it had become an Italian restaurant, now closed until dinnertime.

I sat on the stoop for a beat, waiting to catch my breath though I hadn't been walking that long. I couldn't stop thinking of a woman I saw back then who easily could have been me.

The memory was overlaid with a newer one. Shysteen Shackleford traipsing down the center aisle of the Cathedral of Holy Grace, half-collapsed against the shoulder of Delbert "Do-Right" Dailey.

His expression crashed back into memory. *A sour sweet cocktail of satisfied shame.* It was plain as the smirk on his face. He was getting away with something he knew he shouldn't have. I didn't know exactly what that "something" was, but "something" was going on.

I got back to Red Rover and cranked up her engine. The Keith Sweat dusty playing on the radio seemed weirdly coincidental and eerily prophetic.

"Something Just Ain't Right."

I'd spent too long in grim reminiscence and now I was running late. Traffic was heavier than usual, people headed for last-minute Thanksgiving shopping or their holiday travels.

I drove west across Irving Park and onto the Edens Expressway, staying on as it merged into Highway 41. As I drove along I mulled over the memory. What did the Wrigleyville memory possibly have in common with an old man's death decades later? There was nothing I could do about the latter. But maybe I could make a difference in the former.

Drugs were theoretically involved in both cases, that and potential overdoses. The other thing was sex. That homely guy at the nightclub may have slipped the woman a mickey. Grandy had taken or been given Viagra, a drug to enhance sexual performance. Both drugs were designed for men who had trouble getting what they wanted in bed.

Then there was that maddening expression the other man had been wearing, a look that Delbert had had, too. A woman leaning against both men, one impaired by drink or drugs, the other by jealous grief.

Maybe Shysteen Shackleford was under the influence, too. If she were actually expecting a child, that would be a terrible idea. Yet she wouldn't have been the first pregnant woman to partake of forbidden substances. If she'd been drugged against her will, it would be even worse.

But what was I missing in the connection between the couple outside of a club decades ago, and another one week before last? It was something I had to think hard on.

I arrived at the Waukegan Courthouse at 4:15 p.m. Unlike Cook County, where I lived, Lake County, Illinois, hadn't gotten around to providing online access to its court records. I was lucky they hadn't closed early, like so many places did the Wednesday before Thanksgiving. I had just forty-five minutes to work with. I hoped it would be enough.

I found the clerk's office on the directory and hightailed it up the stairs.

CHAPTER 17

Remains of the Day

"You went to Waukegan?" Penny squealed. "All the way up there and back in one afternoon?"

"It's the North Shore suburbs," I told her. "Not Outer Mongolia."

"That's no suburb, that's practically out of town. Two more steps and you'd be crossing the Wisconsin border."

"Whatever." I shrugged. "I made it there and back in one piece. How was business today?"

"Deader than the morgue."

I shook my head. "Nobody eats out the day before Thanksgiving."

"No biggie." Penny shrugged. "I got a chance to catch up on my podcasts."

I sighed in frustration, looking around the empty café. "We should have closed today."

"It wasn't a total loss. We had some lunch takeouts from the university, a few big online orders. Did you find what you were looking for up there in the boondocks?"

"It's weird," I said, looking over the legal documents I'd photocopied. "Fanon says there was an order of protection

filed against Tuchman Pfeiffer. Grandy claimed that Pfeiffer
was harassing his wife but his claim was denied. I guess you
can't take out an OP on somebody else's behalf. Incidentally,
there's no record of that lawsuit Grandy was always talking
about, though a motion was filed on his behalf to discover the
extent of Pfeiffer's assets."

"A litigious old goat, wasn't he? I wonder why Grandy had
it in for Tuck?"

"That's the million-dollar question, Penny. No pun intended."

"So why not get it straight from the horse's mouth?" she
suggested.

"Do you mean . . . ?"

"Call him up. And put it on speaker, please. Inquiring
minds want to know."

༄

"Mr. Pfeiffer, it's Savvy Summers. I was up in your neck of
the woods today. I only wish I'd thought of stopping by to . . ."

"Savvy who?"

"Summers, Sapphire Summers."

Either Tuchman Pfeiffer was a master of evasion, or he
was absent-minded in the extreme. "You seem to know me
but I don't know you, Miss . . . What'd you say your name
was?"

"Sapphire Summers, a mutual friend of Mattie and Grandy
Jaspers. I'm the owner and head chef at Essie's Place."

"Oh, right. You catered the anniversary bash and Grandy's
homegoing service. Well, why didn't you say so?"

Penny rolled her eyes and circled an ear with her index
finger.

"That was a marvelous sweet potato pie you served at the party. Why you didn't bring some to the repast?"

It was hard to believe Tuchman hadn't heard the gossip. Maybe it was because he lived thirty-five miles away. My sweet potato pie had nothing to do with Grandy's death, despite opinions to the contrary. If Tuchman didn't know the story, I wasn't going to tell him.

"Mattie decided to go with another dessert option, Mr. Pfeiffer."

"Oh, call me Tuck. We're practically old buddies, right?"

"Are you kidding me?" Forgetting she was supposed to be a silent listener, Penny mumbled the retort.

I gave the "zip your lip" gesture and continued. "Mr. Pfeiffer . . . uh, Tuck. Forgive me for being intrusive but do you have any idea why Grandy thought you were harassing his wife?"

There was a pregnant pause at the other end, then his jovial tone turned suspicious. "Granderson Jaspers was one of my oldest, dearest friends. Why would he say such a thing?"

"He didn't exactly say it, Tuck. He sued it . . . or he tried to."

I explained the futile attempt Grandy made to file an order of protection against him.

"Did Mattie say I was harassing her?"

"Well, no. That's probably why the order was denied."

"I'll have to see it to believe it," Tuck harrumphed.

Penny couldn't restrain herself from blurting out: "So how come your 'oldest, dearest friend' kicked you out of his anniversary party? Riddle me that, Mr. Pfeiffer."

"I already told you, lady. Call me Tuck!"

When the line went dead, I couldn't tell if he had disconnected or the call dropped. I could hazard a guess though.

When I turned to Penny with a lifted eyebrow, she wasn't the least bit apologetic.

"Sorry, not sorry." She shrugged. "That dude was hiding something. Wasn't your lie-dar beeping?"

ᔈ

At forty minutes to closing, the café was still empty. No surprises there.

"Well." I shrugged. "Nobody here but us chickens. We'll close up early. You must have a ton of cooking for the holiday tomorrow."

"I do enough slicing and dicing around this joint. I went over to Stony Island and bought a honey-baked ham. Sergio's making *moqueca* and *feijoada,* and that's about all she wrote."

"What are you doing for dessert?" I asked.

"Taking a couple of these sweet potato pies off your hands."

"You're welcome to them, Penny. No one else seems to want any."

Before we could lock up, the door chime jingled and Delbert "Do-Right" Dailey came breezing in. Actually, it was more like tumbling in. He was noticeably tipsy. His ubiquitous black nicotine lollipop hung from between his lips. The flask that was usually hidden was now in plain view in his front shirt pocket.

"Sweethearts, you're a sight for sore eyes and a balm for an empty belly," he slurred, plopping himself down at Table Two. "I know it's late, but you got a bite for a poor public servant? I could eat a bear tonight."

"We're fresh out of bear meat," I told him, "but let's see what I can find."

Penny gave me an incredulous look and pointed to her smartwatch. I probably should have turned him away, but Delbert Dailey had been on my mind all day. That peculiar expression on his face at Grandy's funeral was still disturbing my spirit. And Fanon, of course, had hinted Dailey was under some investigation. His turning up here seemed propitious.

"You're feeling no pain tonight, Do-Right. Is that sucker spiked?"

"Of course not, sweetheart. I get licorice lollipops custom made from a candy company in Bridgeport. I used them to kick a lifelong smoking habit and now I'm addicted to the damned things." He rubbed his hands together and smacked his lips. "With any luck, a lollipop isn't all I'll be licking tonight."

I decided to ignore his vulgar joke and pretend he was talking about food. I brought out Remains of the Day, a plate of the odds and ends left over at the end of the afternoon. Two squares of cornbread, a smothered chicken drumstick, a cup of chili, and a plate of collard greens. Penny poured him a glass of orange blossom lemonade.

"You two don't mind if I imbibe? I won't tell if you won't tell." Before we could answer he'd fished out the flask and poured some of it into his glass. "Electric lemonade, nectar of the gods. With a little sweet tea, I'd have a John Daly."

"Don't tell me," Penny teased. "Another family member."

Delbert winked broadly. "You're quite the kidder. And not too hard on the eyes, if I say so myself."

As Penny made a gagging motion, Delbert attacked his plate like a death row prisoner on execution day. When that was done, he started gobbling two huge slices of sweet potato pie. Delbert was one of the few customers left who wasn't afraid to eat it.

Did he know something that everyone else didn't? That my sweet potato pie was safe because someone else had poisoned Grandy? A certain someone that might, in fact, be him?

Penny whistled. "That is some impressive consumption, mister. You weren't kidding about eating a bear."

Delbert gave a lusty wink as he shoveled in fork after forkful. "Gotta keep my energy up. The little woman's waiting for me. She'll wear a brother out, I tell you what."

"Delbert," I warned him. "Keep it clean. Nobody wants to hear your bedroom business."

But Penny wasn't above entertaining a bit of off-color pillow talk. "You must be trying to take somebody's title. Grandy the lover used to have a corner on the raunch factor around here."

"Grandy talked a good game." Delbert poured out more vodka. "But my dear brother couldn't deliver. He was an old man with old-school ways. Now me, I'm a youngster with new ideas. I've never had any complaints."

Penny grinned back at him. "A youngster, huh? So that's what they're calling fifty-three these days?"

"Wait a minute, now," I interrupted. "They're saying the fifties are the new thirties."

Delbert turned to leer at me. "Sweetheart, you don't look a day over twenty-five. I like a healthy woman with some meat on her bones."

I was closing out credit card receipts and didn't look up, but I could just feel him ogling my chest. I slipped on a cardigan and held it closed at the neck.

Penny didn't miss a beat. "You really ought to quit it, Delbert Do-Wrong Dailey. You keep that mess up, your butt's going to get Me-Too'd."

Trust Penny to call a spade a spade. I glanced over and studied Delbert's response. The crafty politician seemed at war with the randy player. Embarrassment, brazenness, guilt, and entitlement flitted across his face. Just like they had at Grandy's funeral last weekend.

"I don't know what you're talking about," he finally responded.

"Admit it," Penny prodded. "You're a garden-variety pervert."

"Hey, what can I say? I like BIG BREASTS and I cannot lie." He chanted to the beat of "Baby Got Back." Maybe he was going for comic relief, but it just came off as slimy.

Penny wagged a warning finger at him. "Quit reckless eyeballing my boss."

"The lady knows I meant no harm." He inclined his head toward me. "Sweetheart, get your girl."

"No, Delbert. You get your life." My West Side was rising up, threatening to spill over. "This is my place and you're going to respect me and any other woman up in here. I've let you get away with murder but that ends today. Consider yourself on notice."

Delbert looked chastened but not converted. He lifted his shoulders in an offhand apology. A memory of that sheepish, shit-eating grin flashed back across my brain.

"How's Shysteen Shackleford these days?" I suddenly asked.

He spluttered, choking on his electric lemonade. "Shysteen, you say? Don't believe I know the lady."

"Really?" I pressed on. "You two were looking pretty cozy back there."

He scowled and drained his glass. "Back where?"

"At Grandy's funeral repast," I answered. "Just what do you know about his death?"

"What's to know? The man couldn't keep up with his johnson pills."

"How would you know that's how he died?"

"For Christ's sake," he scoffed. "It's not a state secret. Everyone in Woodlawn knows by now. There's a rule of thumb about Viagras. If you don't know what you're doing, you leave those things alone."

Penny gave him a broad wink. "And you're a man that knows just what you're doing."

"Don't go putting words in my mouth, sweetheart. If I indulge, and I'm not saying I do, I never overdo. What are you two anyway, Cagney and Lacey?"

"Who?" Penny asked.

"Before her time," I explained.

Delbert clicked his tongue in irritation. "Rizzoli and Isles."

His jolly inebriation suddenly evaporated. I'd rarely seen Delbert Dailey this shifty-eyed and nervous. Not even during that embezzlement scandal when a TV news crew caught him on camera trying to crawl from a church basement window.

I blurted out my question before he had a chance to recover. "Do you know who killed Granderson Jaspers?"

Delbert looked at me like I'd grown a tail. "I thought I was tipsy, but you must be on crack. No one but Grandy killed Grandy Jaspers. He fell on his own sword. You seem to forget I'm an attorney and you two are playing the slander game. Cut a dear brother some slack."

"It's not slander if it's the truth," Penny retorted. "We'll cut you some slack when you help get Noble McPherson off our backs. He's been riding us like the Greyhound."

"And while you're at it," I added, "we could use some of those city grants and Title II funds you've been busy hustling up for this ward."

"You can't fight City Hall," Delbert sneered. "That's your problem right there."

"Really? I thought Noble McPherson was my problem. I didn't know City Hall was against me."

An evasive expression flitted across his face as he looked away. "It's just a figure of speech, sweetheart."

"A figure of speech."

Delbert crammed the last bite of pie into his mouth. "It means you can't stop progress. It's like turning around an ocean liner going full steam ahead."

"I don't need clichés, Dailey. I need help."

"There's nothing I can do for you. Not a goddamned thing."

I clicked my tongue. "What kind of alderman are you, anyway?"

"The kind that minds his own business and watches his own ass. And if you know what's good for you, you'll do the same."

He pushed back his chair, grabbed his jacket, and hustled out without a by-your-leave.

"He sounds suspiciously like Noble McPherson," I observed. "I wouldn't be surprised if they were in cahoots, murdering Grandy to ruin my business."

Penny went to the door and locked it behind him. "Noble didn't meet Grandy until the morning he died. And what makes you think Ignoble is on speaking terms with Delbert Dailey? You're sounding kind of paranoid."

"You see what's happening? These fools are driving me crazy."

"Crazy like a fox, Savvy Summers. Did your lie-dar go off? Do-Wrong Dailey was lying about something. And by the way, you let him get away again without paying."

"All he had was Remains of the Day, the stuff we'd be throwing out. He'll pay the next time, I promise."

Penny turned back toward the locked front door. A thoughtful expression spread across her face.

"What's on your mind?" I asked. "I know there's something percolating in there."

"You ever seen Do-Wrong's lady Lynette? She looks like a sucked-out lemon that's been sucking on lemons. It's hard to believe she even has sex, much less with that husband of hers."

"Three sides to every story, Penny. That lemon gave birth to two little limes. Somebody was knocking somebody's boots."

"Yeah, once upon a time. For all we know they did it twice in twenty years." She looked at me with narrowed eyes. "You know he's always staring at your boobs."

"I've noticed," I said. "Don't remind me."

"Something is seriously wrong with that man, always sucking that damned lollipop. He probably wasn't weaned right."

"Oh, well," I protested mildly. "Some guys like it like that."

"He claims that he likes healthy women but Lynette Dailey's skinny as a scarecrow and flat as a board. Shysteen, on the other hand, has boobs for days. She could pass them out on 63rd Street and still have some to spare."

I clicked my tongue in consternation. "Penny, you need to quit it. A great big feminist like yourself should know there's more to a woman than boobs."

"What I'm getting at is this." Penny pointed to the front door. "Delbert bum-rushes this place like a bachelor."

"What do you mean by that?"

"If the wife is so ravenous for her little Do-Wrong, you'd think she'd make him a meal once in a while. I don't think that old drunk was headed home when he left here. I just hope he's not driving."

"You might be right. As Great-Aunt Essie used to say, *He's the kind that wants his pie and pudding both.*"

"Doesn't the saying go, *He wants to have his cake and eat it, too?*"

"That never made much sense to my aunt," I admitted. "What else are you going to do with cake, smear it on your face?"

"I guess old girl had a point. Now, hoarding your pie and pudding both, that's just plain greedy."

We worked in silence for a time, topping off sugar, salt, and pepper shakers. Refilling napkin dispensers, loading and running the dishwasher, compacting trash.

Apropos of nothing, I blurted out: "Why do you suppose Delbert Dailey was dogging Grandy out like that?"

Penny tilted her head and poked out her mouth like Gary Coleman on that old TV show *Diff'rent Strokes.* "'What you talking 'bout, Willis?' Hey, I watch MeTV."

"You heard him talking trash. *My dear brother couldn't deliver. He was an old-school man with old-school ways.* What do you think he meant by that?"

"Just what he said, the dry basics." Penny ticked them off on three fingers. "A little foreplay, standard missionary, very little in the way of variation."

"How would he know what Grandy did in bed, unless he'd been bedding down the same woman? Someone who wasn't shy about kissing and telling."

"Shysteen Shackleford," Penny sneered. "Who else?"

"It might have been Mattie."

"Might have been." She frowned. "But no, I don't think so. Do-Wrong and Mattie, I'm just not seeing it. She strikes me as the kind of woman who might enjoy it slick but doesn't like slimy, if you get my drift."

Busy hands created a fertile mind. Ideas and notions began to bang around my brain. I stopped in the midst of wiping down the stainless-steel island counter. "What if Delbert had something to do with Grandy's death?"

"Well, I don't know. Let's see where you're going with this."

"You just suggested that he might have a thing for Shysteen."

"I did," Penny said. "He's a loser and a lech. But does that make him a murderer?"

I tried to collect the thoughts colliding around like marbles. "I wish I could describe the look on Delbert's face when he was holding up Shysteen at Grandy's funeral procession."

"What was it, Savvy? A guilty conscience?"

"No, it was more like . . ." I turned into my mind's eye, trying to remember that barely suppressed smirk. ". . . It was like he'd hoodwinked someone and overcome the opposition, whether it was the girl's resistance or another man's involvement, and . . ."

"He wound up with the prize," Penny finished for me. "And would probably be taking it to bed."

"Shysteen was Grandy's side chick, but what if Delbert wanted her bad enough to kill for it? He practically admitted to using Viagra, so maybe he had a prescription handy. Maybe he found a way to slip some into Grandy's food or drinks the night before he died."

"That's a lot of mights and maybes," Penny pointed out. "Anybody has access to Viagra, prescription or not. You can buy them on the internet. And I don't think Delbert needed to kill anyone to get Shysteen in the sack."

"Okay, my theory has a few holes in it. But Delbert Dailey somehow strikes me as a guilty man."

Penny shrugged. "Like Donny Hathaway sang in 'The Ghetto,'

everythang is everythang. In the absence of any other evidence, that theory works for me."

Before we left the café, Penny and I sat down in front of my laptop. We decided to create a database of names, motives, and opportunities for possible suspects in Grandy Jaspers's death.

We figured that alibis were moot. Since the exact time of death couldn't be pinpointed, anyone who'd come in contact with him in the last twelve hours before his death might have been in position to administer a Viagra overdose.

"Who's first?" Penny asked, hands poised above the keys. "Cherchez la femme?"

"If you're talking about Mattie, I don't think she's a murderer."

"Just because old girl puts you in the mind of your sainted Aunt Essie doesn't mean she didn't do it."

"I have no idea what you're talking about," I lied.

"Yeah, right," Penny sneered. "You know the spouse is the first one the police look at."

"Why would Mattie kill Grandy? It's just a theoretical question."

"You saw how Mattie went in on him at their anniversary party. Her husband was a tomcat and his death left her a couple hundred grand in the black. Sex and money, the oldest motives in the book."

"Go ahead," I relented. "Put her on the list."

"And don't forget Shysteen Shackleford."

"Is she capable of murder, Penny? Maybe so. But why would she want to kill Grandy? Gold diggers don't usually murder their meal tickets."

Penny's hands clattered across the keys. "Well, duh. Jealousy? Mattie's the wife, Shysteen's the chick on the side."

I shrugged. "I'm not exactly convinced but put her down anyway."

"I already did. Of course, there's Winnie Mae Welbon, since we're talking about women."

"His own daughter, Penny?"

"Didn't you see them going at each other at the anniversary party? I thought they would come to blows. You know patricide goes back to biblical times."

"Arguing with your father isn't a convincing motive for murder unless there's something about the relationship we don't know." I thought about it awhile. "What the hell? Add her to the list."

Penny paused, creasing her forehead. "Why are we only looking at female suspects?"

"You're the one who said, cherchez la femme."

"That's because I'm brainwashed. Why do the detective stories always have a femme fatale, when men commit the majority of homicides? *Cherchez l'homme,* look for the man. That's what I'm talking about."

So much for closing early on Thanksgiving Eve. We continued brainstorming and databasing into the late hours.

CHAPTER 18

The Usual Suspects

**Likely suspects in the death of
Granderson Parker Jaspers**

Name	Relationship	Possible motive	Opportunity
Matilda Jaspers	Wife	Jealousy, financial gain	Could have handled his food and drink at the party and later that night
Tuchman Pfeiffer	Former manager of the Soul Serenaders	Long-standing legal feud; recently charged with harassing Grandy's wife	Could have handled his food and drink at the party (though unlikely)
Shysteen Shackleford	Mistress	Jealousy	Was actually witnessed handling his food at the party; could have given him Viagra later that night
Delbert "Do-Right" Dailey	Family friend, fellow lodge member	Jealousy; may have been dating the the same woman	Could have handled his food at the party

Unlikely suspects in the death of
Granderson Parker Jaspers

Name	Relationship	Possible motive	Opportunity
Winnie Mae Welbon	Daughter	Bad blood between them; other motives to be determined	Could have handled his food at the party
Noble McPherson	Virtual stranger; bought Grandy coffee on the morning of his death	To pin the murder on Savvy and acquire her business	Handled his coffee on the morning he died; could have tampered with the pie samples then absconded with them to cover his trail

Penny looked up from her typing, eyes narrowed in my direction. "I know McPherson is a snake in the grass, but isn't this a little farfetched?"

"I wouldn't put anything past him. Now, who else did we forget?"

"There were all those kids, grandkids, and other relatives at the party."

I shook my head. "None of them jump out at me."

"Well, what about Annabelle Beasley, the stripper turned baker?"

"Now, Penny," I scolded. "There's no proof she was a stripper."

"Then what was she doing at the Pussy Galore forty years ago? Teaching Bible lessons? Mattie and Grandy both knew her. There's some history between the three of them."

I considered it for a moment. "Well, you might have a point. She came to the anniversary party, uninvited, then turned up at the funeral, unexpected . . ."

"... like the guilty party returning to the scene of the crime!"

"The Cathedral of Holy Grace wasn't where Grandy died," I pointed out.

"Maybe she was there to inspect her handiwork, making sure old dude was good and dead. If you're gonna be hard-headed about Noble McPherson, then I'm gonna insist on Annabelle Beasley."

Name	Relationship	Motive	Opportunity
Annabelle Beasley: Owner of Annabelle's Sweet Stuff Bakery	Relationship to the deceased, unknown (though she was obviously acquainted with Grandy's wife)	Professional rivalry; to pin the killing on Savvy and ruin her business	A known baker of sweet potato pie. In the confusion of the anniversary party, could have slipped in and replaced Savvy's pie with a Viagra-laced dessert of her own.

I shook my head. "Now you're just grasping at straws. Have you found out anything about the people who worked the anniversary party?"

"Nothing yet, but I'm still on it. I'll have something for you soon."

Find out more about the staff (names, relationships,
    motives to be discovered)
Photographer/DJ/videographer
Bartender
Caterers ...

"The caterers?" Penny said drily. "Come now, Savvy."

"We can't rule anyone out," I said with mock seriousness. "Didn't I hear you saying that the old man deserved to die?"

"No, I didn't. I quoted that song from the musical *The Civil War*: 'You live or you die by the sword.' What possible motive could I have to kill old Grandy?"

"He always called you 'pennylopes.' That alone is cause for retribution. Then there's having to hear his war stories while you served him his daily coffee and biscuits."

"And never once getting a tip! You're right, Savvy. I'm a prime suspect."

But instead of typing in her own particulars, Penny suddenly collapsed at the desk, burying her head in her hands.

I put an arm around her shoulder. "What's the matter?"

"I swear I didn't kill Grandy," she muttered, her voice muffled behind her hands.

"I know you didn't, girl. I was just joking. Forget I said anything."

Penny lifted a tearstained face. "I didn't kill him, but I sure had a motive. Nobody knows this, Savvy. Nobody but Sergio, and I swore him to secrecy."

Then Penny Porter Lopés, my sous-chef and trusted assistant manager, admitted to borrowing a sum of money from Grandy two weeks before he died.

"You took money from Granderson Jaspers, a man you despised? But why?"

"I was desperate, Savvy. I'd already gotten an advance from you, what? Three times in the last few months."

"Yeah, I've been wondering about that. What was going on?"

"The mortgage was in arrears again, about to go into foreclosure."

I opened my mouth and closed it, trying to figure out a sensitive way to pose my question.

Penny answered before I asked it. "I spent it, Savvy, every red cent. Don't ask me on what, because I don't remember. I've been robbing Peter to pay Paul for almost a year. Finally, it all came crashing down. I'd just gotten that last salary advance from you, but instead of putting it on our bills, I saw Sephora was having a sale . . ."

"You spent it on a cosmetic sale?"

Fresh tears welled in Penny's eyes. "Not all, but most of it. I kept enough in my account to buy a tank of gas. Then that ran out, my fuel gauge was almost on empty . . ."

"You asked Grandy for it?"

Penny nodded. "It's even worse than that. What with keeping a young chick on the side, and his regular expenses . . . well, Grandy never had much money. He was cheap for a reason."

"So where'd he get it?"

"He borrowed it," she told me. "From Mattie's egg and butter money. He knew where she kept it, and took it without telling her, after I swore up and down I'd get it back to him before the anniversary party. And, well. I didn't."

It slowly began to dawn on me. "So that's why they didn't pay the catering bill. Mattie didn't have it."

"Don't make me feel worse than I do," Penny begged. "I already know I'm a crook."

"Borrowing money you can't pay back doesn't make you a criminal."

"No? Well, what about stealing it? Shaking down a dead man."

I shook my head to clear it. "Come again?"

Penny reminded me that after Grandy died, she saw something on the floor beneath Table Two, and put that thing in her pocket.

"His wallet. I checked it when I got home and there wasn't much to speak of. About a hundred dollars in cash."

"Penny, please. You didn't spend that, too?"

She shook her head miserably. "No, but I might have if Sergio hadn't found out. We had the biggest knock-down, drag-out of our entire marriage. I thought he was going to leave me. But then, the next morning he gave me Grandy's wallet back with all the money I had borrowed, and made me promise to give it back. I couldn't face Mattie, so . . ."

The Granderson Parker Jaspers Funeral Fund in a pickle jar! I remembered that it had been Penny's idea all along.

"Penny," I said gently, squeezing her shoulder. "Aunt Essie had a saying. *If you lie, you'll steal, and if you steal, you'll kill.*"

"I told you I didn't kill him. I'd never do such a thing. How could you even think that?"

"I don't. It's just a way of saying an ill-considered deed can be the gateway to more serious offenses. Have you considered counseling . . ."

"*Et tu, Brute?*" Misery turned defensive, Penny held up a restraining hand. "You're sounding just like Sergio. I've already learned my lesson. I don't need anybody's Shopaholics Anonymous to get me straight."

I knew better than to try to force someone to get help they didn't think they needed. "Just let me know if you change your mind."

"I won't. Anyway, here's nothing." She began clattering furiously away at the keyboard. I leaned over her shoulder to read it.

Name	Relationship	Motive	Opportunity
Penny Porter Lopés	Debtor	Owed him a grand	Handled his food at the party and on the morning he died

She looked at me craftily, narrowing her eyes. "Wonder how much old Grandy wound up costing you over the years."

"Meaning what?"

"Eating up your biscuits, drinking up your coffee, hogging Table Two for hours on end, harassing your female clientele."

"Go ahead and put me down. Guilty until proven innocent."

Name	Relationship	Motive	Opportunity
Sapphire Oceal Slidell Summers	Mother Teresa to his beggar	Ridding oneself of a nuisance	Handled his food at the party and on the morning he died

"I think we're about done." I yawned. "It's late and we're getting loopy."

Penny stretched, clacking her knuckles with a sharp crack. "Oh, we're just getting started. What about Parker, the guy's grandson? I always thought that kid was too good-looking to be on the up-and-up."

"Enough with the jokes already."

I flipped the light switch as I left the kitchen. Penny Porter Lopés could sit there typing in the dark for all I cared. I paused at the doorway.

"Just so you know, Penny. I'm putting my money on Delbert Dailey."

"Time will tell," her disembodied voice echoed back at me.

CHAPTER 19

A Bleak Anniversary

I woke up with the uncontrollable urge to bake, but the ground cinnamon in my spice cabinet smelled stale and musty. I went downstairs to get a fresh supply from the café.

As I was about to unlock the front door, I felt someone slip into the doorway behind me. I spun around, keys raised above my head. "Back the hell off!"

"For real, Savvy Summers?" Penny stood silhouetted in sunrise, hands tucked behind her back. "Now you've gone and hurt my feelings."

"Girl, you scared me. Don't ever sneak up on me like that again."

She followed me in as I unlocked the door, relocked it behind us, and headed for the kitchen.

"Did you forget it's a holiday, Penny? No work today. Go home."

"If you're not happy to see me now, you will be in a minute. Can you guess what I have in my hot little hands?"

"No, but I'm sure you'll tell me."

"Come on, Savvy. I'll give you three tries."

I planted both hands on my hips and fixed her with a

murderous glare. "I'm not in the mood to play guessing games on Thanksgiving morning, Ms. Lopés."

"Oh, you're no fun," Penny complained. "Last night you told me to check out the staff from the anniversary party."

"You couldn't have possibly found anything so fast."

"You obviously don't know me." Penny grinned. "How's this for starters?"

She dramatically whipped a hand from behind her back. It held an oversized book bound in white faux leather.

I took the album, flipped it open to a picture at the center page, and was treated to a view of Winnie Mae Welbon's prominent behind poked out in a twerking motion.

"What the hell?"

"The Jasperses' anniversary photo book," Penny explained. "Omar dropped it off to me not twenty minutes ago."

"And Omar would be . . . ?"

She reminded me that Omar Saladin had been the "four-for" photographer/videographer/DJ/MC at the Jaspers anniversary party. Penny had learned "on good authority" that he was a regular open mic performer at a South Loop comedy club. A wannabe comedian, I knew it. Penny had approached him after the set to remind him where they'd met.

"It didn't take much to get the boy to bellyaching," Penny explained. "You weren't the only one Mattie stiffed that night."

"But she did make it up."

"Apparently not to everyone. Remember how Omar ran around the Majestic playing music, snapping pics, taping video footage, and making announcements? The man earned his money's worth, except he never got it."

"None of it?"

"Mattie made a two-hundred-fifty-dollar down payment,

and that's all she wrote. Omar says he's been calling, texting, and emailing. He even went to their house once and slipped an invoice under the door. He's convinced the spat with Grandy that night was just a stunt to stiff him."

"I don't get it, Penny. Why hire the guy in the first place if you're not going to pay him?"

"People do it all the time. Miscalculating, underbudgeting, living that Dom Perignon lifestyle on a Budweiser budget."

"In other words," I narrowed my eyes at her, "being ghetto fabulous?"

"Ap, don't even say it! It's not me we're talking about."

Penny said that Omar still hadn't heard a peep out of Mattie. By now he was fed up and ready to cut his losses.

"I told him that Mattie had been meaning to get back to him," Penny explained, "but got caught up in grief over losing her husband. Omar didn't even know Grandy had passed. So when I offered to settle the bill and deliver the items to Mattie, he was more than happy to turn them over."

"Penny." I shook my head, leafing through the album. "You are something else."

"I know, right?" she preened. "Holler at your girl."

"It wasn't a compliment. This is an invasion of privacy."

"Yet I see you're still looking."

I turned another page. "We should get these things to their rightful owner."

"Yes, we should. So, the question is, when to do the deed?"

"When to take this stuff to Mattie?"

"No, when to crack this open." She fished out a flash drive from her purse.

"I can't believe I'm actually considering going through somebody else's private pictures."

Penny tossed her head in irritation. "Why, thank you, Penny

Lopés. You got mad skills, Penny Lopés. Good work finding new evidence, Penny Lopés!"

"Yes, Penny Lopés," I said between gritted teeth. "Next time try not to break any laws."

"And by the way, you owe me seven hundred and fifty dollars. I wrote Omar a rubber check. I need to hurry up and make it good before it hits the bank."

I CashApped the money into her account, then insisted that Penny handle the login, in case something hit the fan. At least one of us could claim plausible deniability. She sat down to my laptop and inserted the flash drive. The video footage began as a professional-looking production with titles and music. Groups of celebrants arrived at the Majestic in all their finery to the tune of Diana Ross's "I'm Coming Out."

Then Omar had either gotten lazy or was peeved about not being paid. The rest of it was raw, unedited footage. We sat there watching figures move across the screen. The eating and drinking, music and merriment, the dancing and all the drama. Memories of that Friday evening came flooding back. I saw the couples' toast with Mattie and Grandy, this time from a head-on rather than a sidelong perspective.

"Hey, wait a minute," I said at the end of the shot. "Back that up a few seconds, Penny. Yes, right there."

I watched it again, then a third time.

"Well, I'll be damned," I finally said. "Why didn't I notice that before?"

Mattie was being served Fizz 56 by the muscle-bound bartender. As far as I could tell she didn't have a chance to drink it. As they posed for the camera, Grandy had guzzled down four glasses, practically a full bottle.

Then Mattie delivered that embarrassing verbal beatdown of her philandering husband, and quickly left the premises.

Grandy grabbed the remaining bottle and followed her. I was now convinced that sparkling wine was how the overdose of Viagra had been delivered.

Yet in the overall scheme of things, the assumption wasn't all that useful. What's the use in guessing "how" when you still don't know "who" or "why"?

CHAPTER 20

Letter to a Dead Man

There was nothing else suspicious in the remaining two hours of footage. Once we finished watching it, I sent Penny on her way. Then I gathered up fresh cinnamon sticks, put the flash drive in my pocket, tucked the photo album beneath my arm, and made my way back upstairs.

Nobody was there to see me baking and bawling.

On the sad and solemn anniversary of this Thanksgiving, I found myself writing a letter to a man who wasn't there.

My dear, sweet Francis:

Here I am, darling, as you've seen me so many times. The ingredients are measured and sitting on the counter, but I haven't started cooking yet. I sit here writing you a letter that you'll never read—except who really knows what you're doing up there where you are.

I think of you with profound gratitude, and also deep regret. Gratitude because I thought I'd never love again until you came into my life. You were the wiser of us at that point in our lives, even though you were so much younger than I. You had the patience and persistence to keep up the pursuit, even though I tried to push you away.

The regret isn't just because you're not beside me. It's because I wasn't able to save you.

၍

I attacked the food like it had wronged me, mixing up a flurry of flour, honey, nuts, spices, flaxseed meal, almond milk, candied lemon peel, and dried mixed berries. I kept lifting my apron to wipe away tears, but still I forged ahead.

It would be easier if this were a workday in the busy café kitchen and dining room. All the peeling, chopping, seasoning, and roasting would have been welcome distractions. The people coming and going. The pouring, the plating, the serving. The slicing, the eating, the drinking. The bussing, the cleaning, the billing. The café's rhythms were soothing and predictable.

I always closed Essie's for Thanksgiving, and the week between Christmas and New Year's Day. I gave Penny those days off to feed her own family. I wasn't planning on any big holiday cooking myself. I couldn't even think of Thanksgiving without being riven with shock and sadness.

For all my generous curves and a nagging touch of arthritis in my left knee, I was essentially healthy. Francis Summers, on the other hand, had suffered from the triple metabolic threat that afflicts so many Black men—diabetes, high cholesterol, and hypertension combined.

He worked out on a regular basis but took medications only when he felt like it, and never bothered to adjust his diet to his diseases. He insisted on eating whatever he wanted, whenever he wanted, as much as he wanted. Remaining slim and muscular into his forties, Francis mistook physical fitness for internal health. It all came to a head last Thanksgiving, with turkey in the oven, wine chilling in the fridge, and assorted delicacies bubbling on the stovetop.

I never thought for a minute that I'd outlive my second husband. I'd practically been a cradle snatcher.

We'd met under unlikely and inappropriate circumstances. I'd been working my way up the career ladder at the CPS. Divorced already at thirty-three, I'd completed my master's in English lit and had just received a double promotion at Langston Hughes College Prep. I was an assistant principal and director of the English program, thank you kindly.

Francis was just out of college, a fresh-faced recruit in the Science Department. I had actually been on the recruitment committee that interviewed him. A mere babe at twenty-two, he was closer in age to my fourteen-year-old son than he was to me.

With the energy of the newly converted, Francis was always dreaming up new ways to engage the students. He started a science fiction film club and invited me to the first meeting. Sci-fi wasn't really my thing but I didn't admit this to him. In fact, I was more interested in looking at Francis than watching *The Day the Earth Stood Still*.

My ex-husband Fanon was good-looking in his own fashion. But Francis Summers was so beautiful a woman could have eye orgasms just looking at him. The young man had the devil's own eyes, tilted upward with a wicked gleam. He was tall, slender, and full-lipped, with skin as dark as fudge. And twice as sweet, I would discover much to my chagrin.

It didn't take long to fall in lust. Love was some distance behind.

The chasm between us seemed insurmountable, and it wasn't just the eleven-year age difference. We were flagrantly violating CPS regulations on fraternization. We both could have lost our jobs. I didn't want to hear any of the homilies I'd been preaching to others. *The dumbest dodo bird knows better than crapping where it eats,* and *never get your honey where you make your money.*

We carried on our romance in secret. I didn't trust my own happiness and held the relationship at arm's length. I saw no chance of things working out and refused to meet his family. "Why? So they can see the dirty old woman who's been sucking up your youth? Let's not complicate things. We'll keep it light, have fun while it lasts."

I told myself we were "kicking it." I was still holding on to that lie at five, six, seven months pregnant.

Francis tried to shoot down my objections. "So I'm good enough to be your bed buddy but not to be your man. I'm good enough to knock you up but not enough to marry."

You couldn't really call ours a shotgun wedding. It was way too late for that. Nzinga Summers had already arrived. Our flower girl toddled down the aisle clutching a basket to her chest. Despite our rehearsal, she didn't scatter a single rose petal.

When I stepped out for the wedding march, Nzinga broke away from her Grandma Summers, came running up the aisle, and flung herself at my knees. I said wedding vows with my baby on my hip, just like Oprah in *The Color Purple,* when Sofia marries Harpo.

I always felt awkward around my mother-in-law, Jacqueline Summers. What parent wants to see her only child hooked up with a woman closer to her own age than she is to her son's? Then I got to know just how she must have felt.

My son soon paid me back with my own coin. Malik was secretly seeing a college girl who'd been student teaching at his high school. Tiny and childlike at twenty-one, Netanya could have passed for sixteen . . . but wasn't. I hollered statutory rape and threatened to call the law.

"Eighteen years old is legal. They'll laugh you out of court." Malik played the twisted logic of "turnabout is fair play." "That's mad hypocritical, Mom. There's eleven years between you and Francis Summers."

"There *are* eleven years," I corrected him. "If you're going to rub it in my face then try to do it grammatically."

"Whatever. My girl's only three and a half years older than me."

"The difference is, your stepfather and I are responsible adults. You're a teenager still living at home. That woman's your teacher and you're her student . . ."

"If you say one more word about statutory rape, I'm dropping out, running away, and you'll never see me again."

"Okay, fine. We'll just call it a flagrant abuse of power. How about that?"

Francis managed to calm me down. He reminded me that teenage romances typically withered in the bud. In the end I gave up protesting.

Netanya and Malik graduated the same year—she from college, and he from high school. They were wed that same summer. Theirs wasn't even a post-shotgun wedding like mine had been to Francis. There was no baby on the way or already born. Their only son came along several years later. Their marriage has lasted almost two decades, which, given statistics on teenage marriages, exceeded anyone's odds.

In the meantime, Francis and I grew into each other. We were so compatible it sometimes scared me. Although we had our squabbles, we never went to bed angry and rarely without making love. Yet things weren't always perfect. There are challenges to loving someone over a decade younger than you.

We each had different frames of reference. I was born in the era of Civil Rights, the tail end of the Black Power Movement, and Mayor Daley Number One. Francis read about those things in history books. He had come up in the age of Daley Number Two. I listened to jazz and R&B, while he preferred house and hip-hop.

I was married to a young man who played video games with my teenaged son, for God's sake. It's one of the ways they bonded, so it wasn't such a bad thing. Yet seeing them sprawled across the sofa with game controllers in hand sometimes made me feel like I had two kids.

Francis didn't appreciate it when I reminded him to take his meds and watch his carbs. He called it nagging. "I'm a grown man, Savvy. You're my wife, not my mother."

But those were only thorns in the rose garden of our love. The man was as good as his surname. He'd given me twenty-five precious years of summers.

Francis started graying in his thirties, but his face remained smooth and unlined, right up to the end. People marveled how much he looked like himself.

"You know that was a pretty man. He looks just like he's sleeping."

A beautiful corpse was no comfort to me. I would rather have seen him grizzled and gray, spent from a life well lived. By all rights, I should have gone before him. Forty-seven was way too early to die of a stroke. Fifty-eight was too young to be widowed.

How could I bring myself to celebrate Thanksgiving when it had taken the man I loved?

～

My daughter called me at ten o'clock, which was eleven a.m. her time. For Nzinga Summers that was some kind of feat. She had been a night owl since birth. Late to bed, early to rise made a little girl wired at night and groggy in the mornings. Getting her ready and off to school had always been a challenge. Luckily, she now had a job that could accommodate her quirky circadian rhythms.

"I wanted to catch you before you started your day, Mommy." My oldest had started calling me Mom as a teenager. My baby girl still called me Mommy at age twenty-seven. "How are you holding up? Are you okay so far?"

I tried to breeze past the worry in her voice. "Oh, I've been up for ages. I've already made two batches of vegan muffins, lemon poppy seed and blueberry pecan. They turned out pretty well. I wish you were here to taste them."

Nzinga gave a grunt that reminded me for all the world of my Great-Aunt Essie. "*Ump*. I didn't ask what you were cooking, I asked how you were doing."

"I'm always happy when I'm cooking, baby."

"Mommy, you know better. Denial is a river in Egypt. You've got to face your shit."

"Nzinga, language!" I cried. I'd never gotten used to hearing my baby girl cuss.

"Daddy died a year ago today, and these anniversaries are hard. The only way to get through it is to deal with your emotions. Cry if you need to, cuss if you have to. How are you feeling right now?"

I paused to think. "I guess I'd say I'm sad."

"And mad?"

"No, I don't think so."

"It's all right to be mad. I'm angry, too. My father isn't with me, and he won't be for any other holiday. He'll never walk me down the aisle or bounce his grandkids on his knee. And that really sucks."

"Yes, I guess I'm sad and mad." I heaved a ragged sigh. "And none of it is any fun."

CHAPTER 21

A Dose of Good Deeds

When you feed people for a living, holiday dinners can sometimes seem overmuch. I agreed with Penny's philosophy. Let someone else cook for a change.

I took the afternoon to run errands I never had time for on Mondays, my only day off. I drove to Chicago Ridge Mall for a Thanksgiving Day sale, then treated myself to lunch and took in a movie. I thought it would be fun to laugh at a mindless comedy. I hadn't been out to the movies since before Francis died. Sitting alone in the near-empty movie theater made me feel lonelier than ever.

My Great-Aunt Essie always said, *The world's best cure for the blues is a dose of good deeds.* Mine was a holiday visit to the grieving widow.

A bakery box sat on the back seat of the car, tied up with a pretty purple ribbon. It contained two dozen blueberry pecan and lemon poppy seed muffins from the massive batch I'd baked that morning. I'd also stashed the photo album and flash drive in a fancy gift bag. I felt like Little Red Riding Hood on the way to her grandmother's house.

The Jaspers family dwelling was a half mile from the café in a run-down two-flat just west of Cottage Grove. Mattie occupied the first floor, alone now that Grandy was gone. Her grandson lived above her in the second-floor apartment he shared with a young lady, a fellow student and roommate. Mattie was always bragging that Parker, a vocal studies major at Columbia College, would soon be following in Grandy's footsteps.

Thanksgiving Day was in full swing at the Jaspers household. A crowd of relatives milled around watching the game, snacking, and chatting. One of the kids let me in and led me to an overheated kitchen with Mattie's only daughter fully in charge.

Winnie Mae was much more relaxed and domestic than the party animal I'd seen the night of her parents' anniversary party, or the grief-stricken daughter falling apart at her father's funeral. Maybe it was because Grandy wasn't around for her to argue with or grieve over. She wasn't dancing up a storm or crying up a storm; she was cooking up a storm, checking dishes in the oven, stirring pots on the stovetop, and yelling instructions to the older children.

A light sweat shone on her broad beige face. Damp tendrils of wavy hair curled around her forehead. I noticed again how different she appeared from all her other siblings. Winnie looked like a plump golden biscuit. Her older brothers were more like Slim Jim strips of beef jerky. In fact, if I didn't know better, I'd think Winnie Mae was adopted.

"Oh, hey," she greeted me absently. "It's my favorite chef. You staying for dinner? I gotta warn you, we're running way behind."

"I brought a little contribution." I handed her the box of muffins. "But I won't be staying."

I don't know why some think it's okay to sniff the food that other people are going to eat but that's just what she did. Untied the ribbon, flipped the lid open, brought her little pug nose close to the muffins, and inhaled. A flash of the feisty old Winnie emerged.

"Smells good," she grunted. "Ain't no poison in it, is there?"

Lord have mercy on her naked soul!

Look here, I could have told her. *Maybe it was your daddy's tomcatting, Viagra-popping ways that put him six feet under. It certainly wasn't my baked goods, okay?*

I ignored her jab and held my tongue. Thoughts ran several stop signs en route from Winnie's mind to her mouth. She just blurted the first thing that came to mind, without a filter. It wouldn't do to be exchanging barbs with her on the holiday. And I was becoming more suspicious that her father's death was much more complicated than an old man taking too many erectile dysfunction pills.

"I just wanted to have a word with your mother. Is she around?"

Winnie rolled her eyes and sighed, jerking her head toward the dining room. "Mama picked today of all days to go roaming down memory lane. She's been at it for hours, and hasn't cooked a lick. It's all on me. See if you can't bring her back to the land of the living."

Mattie Jaspers's impeccable grooming was nowhere in evidence that afternoon. She sat at the dining table in a shapeless housedress and reading glasses, her bleached blonde tresses tied up in a scarf. She sipped from a juice glass, but it wasn't grape juice. A half-empty bottle of Fizz 56 Sparkling Red sat on the table before her. That setup seemed familiar, and then I remembered why. I'd noticed it earlier when we watched the video footage from her anniversary party.

I looked over her shoulder at family snapshots strewn across the table. Grandy and Mattie were proud of their brood of children. One son owned a barbershop, another was a high school teacher. Two of them lived out of state and worked white-collar jobs. Most had gone to college or trade school. Even Winnie Mae, with her roughness around the edges, had an associate's degree from Malcolm X College and worked as an X-ray tech at Little Company of Mary.

Mattie suddenly slumped, staring at a photo in her hand. It was a younger version of Granderson Jaspers, dressed to the nines in a seersucker suit and panama hat, leaning against a 1980s model Cadillac.

"I never thought he'd leave me like this," Mattie muttered, her voice husky with pain. "I was sure I'd go before him."

"But wasn't Grandy older than you?"

"Yeah, by a good seven years. We both had heart problems, mine much worse than his."

"Yes, Delbert Dailey told me all three of you saw the same cardiologist. What's wrong?"

"I had that heart attack four years ago, probably from having it broken so many times. I'm walking around with a tube inside to keep my blood vessels from collapsing."

"You have to take care of yourself, Mattie."

"You're right about that, Miss Savvy. I'd been meaning for years to sort these pictures. Now's as good a time as any, right?"

"No time like the present," I said gently.

Mattie patted the chair beside her, and I joined her at the table. Together we leafed through decades of Jaspers family memories, from Mattie as a child in Mississippi to her marriage to Grandy, the birth of children, grands and great grandchildren. Christenings, graduations, and weddings were represented. There were also some old performance and publicity shots of Grandy and the Soul Serenaders.

I picked up a sepia headshot of a glamorous 1970s-era diva decked out in a slinky gown.

"Who's this beauty? She's quite the looker."

Mattie gave a short laugh. "Lord, I ain't seen that one in a minute. I used to fancy myself a soul singer back in the day."

I examined the snapshot closely. "Yes, I heard you used to sing."

"I've been writing and singing songs from when I was a child. Tuck Pfeiffer, he was managing R&B artists back then. I met him on one of his Delta tours passing through Hattiesburg, and he convinced me to move to Chicago. He said I could be the next Etta James."

"Why didn't you pursue your singing career?"

A look of bitterness flashed across her face then flitted away. "Grandy happened, that's what. He didn't think it looked right for a gospel artist's wife to be singing those worldly songs, performing in nightclubs where liquor was sold. He called R&B the devil's music. Then the kids started coming, and that was that."

"Well, that's unfortunate." The word seemed weak in the face of her decades of disappointment. "Speaking of Tuchman Pfeiffer, did you know Grandy tried to get an order of protection against him the week before he died?"

"Girl, what you talking?" Mattie exclaimed, hand to her breast. "Protection from what?"

"According to the complaint, Tuck was harassing you."

Mattie burst out laughing. "Harassing me? God, that's a good one."

"So why," I persisted, "did your husband think he was?"

"If I knew half the reasons Grandy did what he did, maybe we'd have had a better marriage." Mattie glanced down at the shopping bag in my lap. "What you got in there?"

"Additions to your memory book."

I took out the photo volume from her fiftieth-anniversary

party and watched her leaf through it, expressions flitting across her face. Smiles, a few chuckles, a peal of laughter. Head shakes, a frown, a "Lord, have mercy."

"Now ain't that something? I've been meaning to get back to that picture-taking fellow. Thanks for picking it up for me."

"It did cost me seven hundred and fifty dollars," I informed her. "Penny paid the guy in full and I reimbursed her. I wouldn't be asking if I didn't have to, but times have been hard."

Mattie held up her hand. "Child, don't even trouble yourself."

She fished around for her pocketbook and wrote me out a check. We heard a baby crying in the living room.

"Is that a new grandchild?"

"Great-grand," she told me. "Winne Mae's middle son went and got some girl pregnant, no wedding plans in sight."

"So how many grandkids is it now, Mattie?"

"The new one makes number fifteen, if you can believe that. Grandy had a son before we married, and Grand Jr. has his two grown kids. My oldest, Joe, has four kids. Benny Lee and Ike have two apiece. Winnie Mae has her three. I doubt if Johnny Rae will have any kids, but you never know."

"How'd you and Grandy come to meet?"

"Soon as Tuck sent my train ticket, I came up to Chicago and stayed with my Auntie Alice and Uncle Leroy. I was so glad to get my singing career started in the big city."

"I bet you had big dreams back then."

"Didn't I, though? Tuck started managing the Soul Serenaders, and that's how I met Grandy. Honey, he was smooth as silk and slick as grease. He may not have been the prettiest, but Grandy seemed like the classiest man in all Chicago. He had a white girlfriend who got pregnant for him. I thought if I gave him a baby, too, I could get him away from her."

"And so you did."

Mattie snorted. "Yeah, well, you see how that worked out."

I handed her the flash drive and asked if she wanted to watch it. Mattie shook her head.

"No, I'll look at it later. I'm weepy enough right now, don't want to start the waterworks again. Dinner should be ready soon. You want to stay and eat? Winnie Mae ain't no Sapphire Summers, but she's a right good little cook when she puts her mind to it."

"No, thanks, Mattie. I've made other plans," I lied. "But I did want to ask you something. I hope it won't offend you. There was a lot going on at your fiftieth-anniversary party."

Mattie grunted. "You sure aren't lying, Miss Savvy."

"Try to think back to that night. Did the wine taste funny?" Mind you, I wasn't even sure that Viagra dissolved in liquid carried any particular taste. I'd have to look into that.

"Not that I can recall. I didn't drink much of it."

"Was there anything strange about the sweet potato pie or any of the food you ate that night?"

Mattie looked at me curiously. "Strange like how?"

"I don't know. A funny taste. Something gritty or powdery in it."

"The food was fine, Savvy. We've been through that already. I know you didn't poison Grandy."

"No, but someone may have given him a lethal dose of Viagra."

"Well, whoever it was," Mattie exclaimed, "they need to be behind bars!"

"I know, and I would like to help put them there. But who'd have wished your husband harm? Do you think Delbert Dailey could be behind it?"

"No, why would he?" Mattie frowned. "But I wouldn't put

it past that little hussy nurse that showed up and showed out at the funeral."

"A nurse was there? Which one was that?"

"Ain't but one Shysteen, I reckon."

I was surprised to hear Shysteen Shackleford was a nurse. She didn't seem like she had that kind of education. "And why would Shysteen kill Grandy?"

"Probably thought she'd be able to get her hands on some money, not that he had any to speak of. That ol' rusty-butt husband of mine stayed as broke as a joke. He's never been able to hold on to a penny. You know the money I had saved up for our fiftieth anniversary? Grandy found that money and spent it, every nickel of it. I reckon he went and gave it to that gal."

He'd given it to a gal all right, but not the one she figured. I did not reveal the truth of it. Whether she would or not, that was Penny's prerogative.

"But it's the wife who inherits when her husband dies. Why would she kill Grandy and expect to get his money?"

"Who knows?" Mattie shrugged. "Shysteen Shackleford ain't the sharpest tack in the toolbox."

"I know the news of her pregnancy must have been shocking to you."

Mattie shook her head. "If the little heifer really is pregnant. Besides, nothing shocks me anymore."

"What happened after you left the ballroom that night?"

"I went home, cut up his clothes, and smashed all his panama hats to bits." She pointed to a fireplace on the opposite wall. "Then I took some lighter fluid and fired them up. Right over there. This room smelled like burnt straw for the longest time."

"I was so shocked to hear your anniversary toast. Not that I blame you. I understand why you didn't want to stick around. I know you don't drive, so how'd you make it home?"

"You can never find a taxi in Woodlawn when you need one. I was planning to walk it. Tuck was still down there when I came out the Majestic Ballroom. He gave me a ride. It's a good thing, too, because those high-heeled shoes were killing me."

"And did Grandy come back home that night?"

"He tried to. I put on the burglar chain so he couldn't get in. He started banging at the upstairs apartment, but Parker and his roommate weren't home. Grandy stood outside the door and cussed a good fifteen minutes, then he left."

"So you never saw him again?" I asked.

Mattie shook her head. Tears welled in her eyes and spilled down her cheeks. Was she weeping from guilt or regret? I hated dredging up painful memories, but I kept on pushing. "Sorry, Mattie. I know it's hard, but please bear with me. Do you know where Grandy spent the rest of that night?"

She raised her hand and angrily dashed the tears away. "Go ask that little ho of his. Me, I'm done talking about it."

Trying to distract Mattie from her sudden gloom, I picked up a formal, sepia-toned portrait of two young people in fancy dress standing stiffly beneath a flowering arbor. "That's a pretty picture. It looks like a work of art."

Mattie leaned over and examined it. "Lord, I wasn't but a baby back then. I'd just graduated grammar school, couldn't be no more than thirteen years old."

"Who's the boy standing next to you? A kind of handsome fella."

"Girl, that ain't nobody but my cousin, Peewee. We graduated the same year. You sure wouldn't have seen me with no boyfriend back then."

"Why not?"

"Mama and Daddy didn't want me courting. That meant getting pregnant, quitting school then having to go work the fields or the white folks' kitchens. They wanted me to make something of myself, so they schooled me off to Hattiesburg."

"Your parents sent you away at thirteen years old?"

"Wasn't no high school for Coloreds in Laurel, Mississippi, where I come from. It was like that in a lot of those Southern towns. You had to move to a city, stay with kinfolks, or find a family you could board with."

"Sounds like a little taste of freedom."

"It was, Miss Savvy. High school was too far away to live at home but close enough to go home on the weekends. But Hattiesburg, Mississippi, wasn't city enough for my dreams."

"What kind of dreams were those?"

"Lord, Miss Savvy. How about electric lights and indoor privies? Ain't gotta be scared of no night riders and Ku Kluxers. Sit down to eat in restaurants and don't have to go around to the back door. When that white man said he would make me a star, I thought I was going to heaven and didn't have to die to get there."

"Do you think you'd ever go back to Mississippi?" I asked her. "Lots of people are moving back south these days. They're calling it the reverse migration."

Mattie shrugged. "I'm walking around with this shunt in my chest. The Lord could take me at any time. Medical care wasn't good down there when I was growing up, especially for the Colored. It might be better now, but I got no reason to go back. All of my people are gone."

"It'd be hard leaving your Chicago family, anyway."

"Yes, it would." Mattie sighed, fitting the portrait into the photo album. "I expect to be here until the Lord takes me home."

I had one last request before I left. "Is Grandy's car still around?"

"It's parked out back behind the house."

"Does anyone drive it?"

Mattie shook her head. "I never learned to drive, and everybody else has wheels. Don't nobody want that old gas-guzzler anyway, though I've been thinking about selling it. Why?"

"I was just wondering if you found anything in it after Grandy died. Anything suspicious or unusual?"

"Nothing but an empty bottle of Fizz." Mattie pointed to the bottle sitting on the table. "That was a surprise since Grandy didn't really like champagne. Yet he must have sat all night in that car, drinking his troubles away."

I hesitated, wondering how to make the request. "Do you mind if I take a look inside? It's hard to believe that Grandy's gone and that old Cadillac . . . well, it just reminds me of him."

Mattie shrugged. She got up from the table and padded into the living room where the family sat around watching football. "Parker, bring the keys to Pawpaw's car. Miss Savvy wants to see it."

Mattie's grandson took me out to the old Cadillac. He stood there shivering in his shirtsleeves, anxious to get out of the cold and back to the game.

"Go on in the house, Parker. I'll bring you back the keys."

The car's interior smelled like Grandy. Sweat, Altoids, and Old Spice. There was also a faint scent of alcohol, like wine soaked into a carpet. I felt around beneath the driver's seat and found a spongy circular object, picked it up and held it up to the moonlight. It was a cork, the mushroom type that pressure-sealed bottles of sparkling wine.

I brought it to my nose and sniffed, smelling wine already drunk or spilled. Then I looked at it more closely. Was that a pinprick in the center? It sure looked like it.

The cork had been sitting under the front seat for nearly a month. Who knows what had happened since then?

CHAPTER 22

Devil's Pie

This season's In Your Face pie toss was a departure from years past.

What was once a fun and funky little fundraiser on the stage of a community theater had now migrated to a downtown soundstage. Costumes and game show elements were added for "entertainment value." In fact, when I arrived with my requisite pies—and a few extras, just in case—they gave me a script, for crying out loud!

In my humble opinion the show's prerecorded theme, a hip-hop takeoff on "Sing a Song of Sixpence" didn't work. "Four and twenty blackbirds baked in a pie" wasn't the most appealing culinary reference. Then, too, a blackbird pie would have been in violation of the "open-faced, bottom-crusted, custard-filled" contest rules.

It was a three-prong competition. First, there was judging by a panel of experts: chefs, restaurant critics, and local bigwigs who deemed themselves too dignified to stand in the firing line of pastry projectiles. Entries in traditional, heirloom, and innovation subcategories were sampled, rated, and scored. While they judged, people browsed the selections and bought themselves slices at $10 a pop. A pretty penny indeed, but all for a good cause.

Then there was the auction of prize-winning pies, to see who would bid the highest for a batch of five. Those who won got five consecutive tries to deck a celebrity in the face.

Corporate sponsors matched each team, dollar for dollar and pie for pie. Contestants played against the celebrities. The more hits, the more money was donated to the contestants' charity of choice. But any time someone could manage to avoid getting splattered, the money went to that celebrity's pet charity.

This represented the "talent" portion of the program. TV weather reporters and socialites arrived at the studio in designer duds and stiletto heels no one would get to see. They were soon suited up in baggy jumpsuits and goggles then set against a canvas backdrop onto which a cartoon pie in boxing gloves was projected. A dialogue bubble above its head taunted, "You want a piece of me?"

Each celebrity judge was expected to sing, karaoke style. The music track started, the teleprompter rolled, the pie-toss contestants got into place. Nervous celebrities began crooning "Bye-bye, Miss American Pie" or "Sugar Pie, Honeybunch" as they watched the pastry missiles flying at them. Eventually, every one of them was slammed at least once. And they had to pretend to be good sports about it.

My new vegan entry swept the sweet potato pie competition to win first place, just as I had hoped. Annabelle Beasley registered a protest, grumbling about "somebody cheating" and "the baker and the talent are acquainted."

Annabelle always got her just dessert, pun absolutely intended. Sweet potato pie wasn't rocket science. I could have told her the simple truth—garbage in, garbage out. Inferior ingredients create an inferior result. The girl put canned potatoes, condensed milk, and margarine in her recipe, okay? There's no way to get a decent pie from all those processed ingredients. Great-Aunt Essie would have had a word with her! In fact, she would have had several.

Whatever she saved in dollars and cents, she lost in common sense was one.

Dime-wise and dollar-stupid was another. Then she would have tied a ribbon on the package with: *The milk that was already spoiled this morning ain't gonna be good this afternoon.*

Annabelle's protest was unsuccessful. She was firmly advised that Alderman Delbert "Do-Right" Dailey had no role in deciding the prize-winning pie. Furthermore, judging was blind, and winning results were final. *Now put that in your oven and bake it, Miss Beasley!*

Little did I know that by the end of it all, I'd be wishing she had won.

Delbert showed up late. Just as my ex-husband announced, he had weaseled his way in as celebrity talent. He may have been a minor celebrity, but the talent part was questionable. It was just my luck—or lack thereof—that Delbert was assigned to my batch of pies, bumping out a local spoken-word artist who'd actually been on time.

Contrary to Fanon's stern advice, I was planning to have a word with "Do-Right" just as soon as I could get him alone. I needed to know just what kind of interest the police had in him. I was determined to get some answers.

No one had ever heard of the charity Delbert designated to receive any money he might win. Knowing "Do-Right," it was a sham operation meant to siphon money into his campaign coffers, if not his own pocket. Since its not-for-profit, tax-exempt status couldn't be verified, the powers-that-be disqualified the group and another legitimate recipient was quickly chosen.

"There are eyes and spies all around us." A disheveled Delbert cornered me in the greenroom, slipping me his ubiquitous flask. "Hold on to that a minute, sweetheart. I'll come back for it later."

I'd seen the alderman tipsy, in fact, just a few days before. Yet that day his voice was uncharacteristically thick, his movements slow and heavy. I shook the flask and found it nearly empty. He must have really tied one on. I tucked it in one of the drawers of the catering cart I'd used to carry in the pies. Returning it to him would be my excuse to have a word with him later. I went out to watch from the studio audience.

Dailey hadn't been on set for run-through that morning, and didn't seem to know what to do. His normally glib persona was very off that day. He was bumbling, clumsy, and confused. He called a production assistant "sweetheart," his all-purpose tag for women. The PA may have worn a ponytail but he also had a full beard.

Delbert perspired under the studio lights, eyes darting and shifting like those of a nervous rabbit. He kept sweating off his makeup and needing to have it retouched. Yes, everyone on camera wears TV makeup, even the male talent.

Thank goodness I'd brought along those extra pies. Every time one was tossed, Delbert would leap off his mark and screw up the shot.

You see, talent was allowed to move their heads, necks, shoulders and torsos, but nothing below the waist. They could twist, bend, and swivel, trying to deflect what was coming at them, yet their feet had to remain on the mark. This wasn't dodgeball, after all, it was In Your Face.

I would've thought "Sweet Potato Pie" with Ray Charles and James Taylor would be more fitting for a musical number. I don't really know who picked Delbert's song selection. To be sure, Rhymefest's chant of truth to power, "Devil's Pie," was a blistering political track. It just wasn't the most appropriate choice for an elected official with a checkered past.

Maybe it was somebody's idea of poetic irony, though Delbert didn't seem to catch it. He kept squinting at the lyrics on the teleprompter as he tried to avoid the pies coming his way. I had to give it to old "Do-Right," though. When he found he couldn't use his feet, he was quick on his head. He kept bobbing and weaving, ducking and dodging, like the hack politician he was.

All he had to do was to make it unscathed through five pie tosses. Then Delbert would have outlasted his competitor, and his charity would take home ten grand.

On the very last toss, right as he chanted, *It's just another slice of the devil's pie, ah. C'mon!* That's when he got clocked full in the face. In a gesture that seemed pure Hollywood, he clutched his chest, staggered backward, and fell out with arms splayed wide. You almost expected him to lift his head and moan, "goodbye, cruel world."

The audience hooted at his antics. A woman behind me hissed, "God, what a ham!"

The floor manager made the "cut" sign, a finger sawed across the neck. "That's a good ad-lib, but the director wants another take. He's going to try it with an overhead shot."

When Delbert "Do-Right" Dailey didn't respond, she knelt over him and nudged his shoulder. "Hey, you don't have to get hit again. Just fall back like you did before."

The man wasn't hearing her. He wasn't hearing anyone. The gag hadn't been meant for comic relief. It wasn't a gag at all.

The stage was quickly cleared of people. Delbert's face was cleared of pie. A nurse in the audience ran up to perform CPR. A team of paramedics arrived quickly and worked efficiently.

Unfortunately, their efforts were neither quick nor efficient enough.

I backed away from the gruesome scene, hand clasped over mouth. Lord, do remember me. This couldn't be happening again!

Delbert Dailey's death made the news that night. "Disgraced politician pie-smacked to death."

CHAPTER 23

Run Toward Fear

Okay, I will admit it. Fanon M. Franklin's career disappointments weren't the only reason our marriage failed.

Great-Aunt Essie always admonished me to *tell the truth and shame the devil.* The truth was, I had my own share of blame to shoulder. In the drama that was Sapphire and Fanon Franklin, we each had our roles to play.

Fanon was the idealistic, disillusioned cop—doomed to be frustrated in work and life. He was always out there fighting windmills. Sometimes he'd miraculously slay one but he never paused to savor his victory. There was always a new battle in the never-ending Fanon's War.

Me, I was the resident shrew. I could take things too hard and sometimes too far. Overreact. Nurse grudges. And yes, I'll admit to the "H" word, too. I could sometimes be hysterical, as I was becoming now.

"You told me to leave it alone, Fanon. Those were your exact words. Let well enough alone. Don't tell me you didn't say it."

"I did say it, Savvy. I'm not denying it."

"Leave police work to the professionals." I paced back and forth, throwing his words back at him. "You're a restaurateur, Savvy, not a detective. Nothing to see here, move along!"

The past few days had been as traumatic as they were bewildering. Right on the heels of Delbert's collapse, the police came to the TV studio. A detective took a statement from me. I told him everything I knew about Grandy's death and its strange similarity to Delbert's. Both of them had died with pie on their face, though I didn't think Dailey had eaten any. The officer assured me there'd be a follow-up and I would be contacted soon.

No one from the CPD ever called. I went down to three different stations and got the royal runaround. Every single last one of them claimed it had happened under another precinct's jurisdiction.

At least now a routine death investigation was underway. The cause of death was all hush-hush, but trust Penny Porter Lopés to ferret it out.

Just like Grandy before him, Delbert "Do-Right" Dailey had died of a heart attack. An overdose of erectile dysfunction medication was implicated in his demise. My vegan sweet potato pie hadn't caused his death. I knew it now as I had known it from the start, even if no one else did.

As troubled as I was with another death so close to home, I was also deeply frustrated. I had convinced myself that Delbert Dailey was a credible suspect in Grandy's death. There was his suspicious behavior with Shysteen at the funeral, that sinister "gotcha" gleam in his eye. And Fanon had all but admitted the man was under some kind of legal scrutiny. There was that husky-voiced Sergeant Jacobs, whose interest in him seemed a great deal more than casual.

Then that cryptic remark Dailey made, urging me to give up my business and move on. Penny said I was being paranoid but I thought there was something strange about the way he said it to me. It wasn't just in anger, it was resignation. Like a deal was already done, a conclusion foregone.

Now that he was dead, unanswered questions about Grandy's demise were no closer to being resolved. In fact, there were more questions now than ever before.

There must be some kind of stigma in a Viagra-related death. An officer at one precinct so much as ordered me to back off. He even had the nerve to scold me for asking too many questions. The deceased wouldn't have wanted all this probing into his private affairs.

"So the gentleman had a little trouble getting it up. How is that a crime? It's not about how he died. It's how the man lived that counts."

Like death had finally bestowed a halo on the politician that everyone knew was crooked. That's when I called my ex and asked him over to the apartment. Well, to tell the truth and shame the devil, I hadn't asked. I'd demanded.

Now Fanon sat calmly on his favorite easy chair, arms folded across his chest. The more worked up I got, the more subdued he became. This, too, had been a part of our pattern.

Back then he would watch me in silence, wary of whatever estrogen-charged rant I was on. Angry tears would often flow from my eyes and accusations from my lips. Fanon sometimes withdrew so deeply into himself he seemed in danger of disappearing. Emotionally, if not physically. Eventually, he did both.

I answered his unspoken accusation. "You don't think I have a right to be upset? Another man's dead and they're blaming it on me."

"No one is blaming you, Savvy."

"The empty tables in my café would kindly beg to differ. Maybe I should go ahead and give Noble McPherson what he wants. I'm practically on the road to bankruptcy. I can still get dimes on the dollar."

Fanon sighed and stood. He hitched up his trousers at the

crotch in that peculiar way men have, reaching down to adjust his junk. Yet he didn't walk away as I expected. Instead Fanon leaned forward and placed his hands upon my shoulders. He gently lowered me back down into the love seat from which the combat impulse had ejected me several minutes before.

"Savvy, let's not do this."

"Let's not do what?"

"You know."

My throat muscles clenched. I had to steel myself against that familiar neck roll. Fanon Franklin was right. I shouldn't be going sister-girl commando on my ex-husband.

I took a deep breath and counted to three. "You're right, Fanon. I'm ranting and raving, you're retreating. It's the same old dance we used to do."

"And I don't want to do it again. Not that particular dance."

"So, what now, Fanon?"

"Well, first an apology's in order."

I sighed. "You're right. I shouldn't have gone off on you like that."

"Not you, sugar dumpling," It'd been ages since I'd heard that old pet name. Decades! "I'm the one who should apologize. You had an intuition about Grandy's death and I didn't pay attention."

"I didn't think the police put much stock in intuition."

"Sure they do," Fanon said. "A veteran cop once told me that our work is blood, sweat, tears, and intuition. Any policeman worth his salt develops a sixth sense about these things."

"Or policewoman worth her salt."

"Indeed. The cop I'm talking about happens to be female." He took a sip from his mug, then frowned and set it down. I'd been talking too much and he'd been listening too long. His tea had gone cold.

Unlike the stereotypical cop on the block, my ex had never been much into coffee and doughnuts. Fanon was more of a tea connoisseur. He shunned tea bags for the whole-leaf variety and drank black for alertness, white for blood pressure, green for antioxidants, rose hip for Vitamin C, red rooibos for head-aches, and peppermint mixed with ginger for indigestion.

I crossed to the open-plan kitchen area and turned on the electric kettle. When the water began boiling, I brought it back to pour over leaves in the bottom of his teapot. A delicate per-fume of chamomile and passionflower rose up from the steam. It was a blend Fanon swore by for relaxation. I knew to let it steep before I poured it out into his mug.

"So, what's going on now with Dailey's case?" I asked him. "Have they noticed how similar it is to Grandy's death?"

"All I know is that he was being investigated for some kind of financial malfeasance. I don't know the details, and it's not going forward. Obviously."

"Swept under the rug, you mean?"

"No, Savvy. That's not what I mean. You can't prosecute someone who is no longer alive. There is a routine death inves-tigation in process, but it hasn't gone to homicide and it may never get there. I don't think anyone's looking to reopen the Jaspers case. Not unless there's some evidence linking the two deaths."

"But it's been almost two months since Grandy died. Would any evidence still be out there?"

"Even if it is, they won't find it if they're not looking. I'm just being honest with you, Savvy. The only reason Delbert's death is getting this attention is because of his notoriety."

"But two men who knew each other died of Viagra over-doses weeks apart," I exclaimed. "That's got to be some kind of huge red flag."

"Not necessarily. People who abuse any kind of drug tend to hang out with those who do the same. Detectives may see it as coincidence, if they see it at all."

I poured out hot tea from the pot and strained it into his cup. "I don't want this matter to keep being ignored."

"Neither do I."

"Then what can we do about it?"

"I can't get involved with any ongoing investigation and neither should you. I'm not a homicide detective so I don't work murder cases. It's my job to protect you."

"Well, that's your motto," I said, trying to temper my sarcasm. *"We serve and protect."*

Fanon leaned forward and took my hands in his.

"You're not just Jane Q. Public. You're the mother of my child. We share a son and a grandson between us. Two people have already lost their lives. I don't want to lose you, too. I'll help however I can, as long as it doesn't put you in harm's way."

I shook my head. "You've done enough. I wouldn't want to jeopardize your career."

Fanon's lips tightened. I had struck a nerve I hadn't intended to. "With my age and background, it's pretty much a moot point. My career, as you call it, has already plateaued. I'm just hanging on until retirement."

It hurt my heart to see him so defeated.

Fanon had been a community organizer turned activist cop, though some saw him as troublemaker and rabble-rouser. For all his years on the police force he stood against racism, sexism, ageism, and all the other "isms" known to exist within the complex bureaucracy of the Chicago Police Department.

Fanon had used his position as one-time president of the Afro American Patrolmen's League to take to task the IAD, the internal affairs division, on police brutality in poor communities, especially against young men of color. He was spurred by the exhortation of his poet friend and mentor Haki Madhubuti, whose challenge was to "run toward fear."

Fanon soon became the go-to guy when his brothers and sisters in blue needed an advocate in their struggles against the powers that be. Sometimes he had support from the rank and file. Sometimes he stood alone. Fanon never had anyone to "clout for him down at da hall." He hadn't learned to play the game of cover your own rear end. His career suffered as a result, and it now seemed irreparable.

Right before our son Malik got married, Fanon was chosen for a special assignment in the Gang Crimes Unit. We were already divorced and I'd remarried by then. It was a temporary tactical operation he thought could be a path of promotion into the Bureau of Detectives. For the first time in his career, Fanon went undercover. He was helping investigate the infamous El Chapo drug ring in Little Village, a Mexican American neighborhood on the city's West Side.

Although he never talked about it, Fanon's racially ambiguous appearance and fluency in Spanish probably helped land him that assignment. There weren't many Latino officers on the force back then. The few that existed were so well known in their communities, most couldn't go deep undercover.

Working near a drug house on Oakley Boulevard, Fanon witnessed two uniformed cops shaking down neighborhood residents. He himself had been solicited. They approached people on the street, demanding to see proof of citizenship. For those who couldn't produce it, the officers demanded cash "fines" to keep them from being reported to Immigration and Naturalization Services, the precursor to Homeland Security.

To intervene would have blown his cover. Fanon brought the matter to his commander, who didn't seem to take it seriously.

Next, he went to the IAD and figured it for a cover-up job when again, no action was taken.

Fanon finally leaked the story to the press. A huge exposé followed, the brass was pressured, and the racist cops were exposed and suspended. One investigative reporter even bagged a Pulitzer Prize. Fanon Franklin was celebrated as a public hero, except within the CPD.

He was charged with insubordination and compromising an ongoing investigation. His censure was a verbal warning and a return to uniform status. That promotion to detective never materialized. When yet another news exposé uncovered the retaliation, Fanon was kicked upstairs to the rank of police sergeant. Eventually, he was assigned to supervise a cadre of officers working out of schools in high-crime areas.

With equal parts admiration and exasperation, I watched him sitting next to me sipping his blended tea. Admiration, because he'd always sacrificed self-interest and ambition for a lofty set of ideals. Exasperation, for much the same reason.

Fanon set down his tea and gazed at me. "Savvy, I'm begging you. Give the process a chance."

"The process?" I asked wearily. "What process?"

"Detective Jacobs wants to see you again."

"Oh, Lord." I couldn't help rolling my eyes. "Not the Ice Maiden again."

"Now why would you call her that?"

"Well, you have to admit it, Fanon. Her demeanor is rather chilly."

He looked at me over his reading glasses. "I don't know what you're talking about. Emmy is real good folks, the salt of the earth."

Really, Fanon? I wanted to ask him. *Are we talking about the same Emerson Jacobs?*

CHAPTER 24

Spin Cycle

Lord have mercy on their naked souls! How long had Channel 6 been dogging my doorstep?

I looked out my second-story window into the pinkening dawn and saw a TV news van parked across the street. The crew milled about on the sidewalk, peering into the darkened window of Essie's, which was still technically named Sapphire Summers Soulfood Café and Catering Company.

I knew what they wanted well enough. They were planning to creep up behind me and catch me off guard. Then they'd quiz me about Delbert Dailey's death in a manner most likely to boost ratings and least likely to yield an articulate response.

They wanted my face on the morning news looking like *America's Most Wanted* meets *Cops*. Preferably my hair would be standing on end, I'd have a few teeth missing up front and spew so much profane ghetto-ese that they'd have to bleep out every other word.

If I didn't respond at all they would chase me down the street as I scurried off like a scared rabbit, a hoodie pulled down over my face. Either way, I'd come off looking guilty as sin.

All I wanted to do was shut my blinds, get undressed, climb back in bed, and leave the café closed for the day.

It had been days since the In Your Face disaster and none of those days were good ones. A catering job scheduled for that weekend was abruptly canceled. Like a hyena slinking up on a dying carcass, Noble McPherson stepped up his campaign of digital harassment.

"In light of recent events," he'd emailed me just yesterday, "perhaps you'll reconsider our generous offer. I think my people have been very patient. They won't wait too much longer for you to come to your senses."

Until Delbert Dailey died, I'd been fool enough to think business was picking up a little. Some of our regulars braved the bad publicity. A precious few patronized the café on a regular basis. Others had simply come to gawk and then left without buying anything. One young woman even had the nerve to order sweet potato pie and sit at the counter taking cell phone photos of it. Then she paid her bill and left it sitting untouched on the plate.

Later in the day Penny showed me her handiwork. The girl had turned that photo into a meme of a pie sniper blasting a submachine gun. She'd posted it to social media, Lord have mercy on her naked soul!

I remembered Delbert Dailey's infamous tangle with a TV news crew. This was during the embezzlement scandal a few years back when he'd been caught trying to sneak away from the offices of the beleaguered Soldiers of the Cross Urban Ministry.

Delbert got stuck at the back side of the church climbing from a basement window. That's where the cameras had cornered him. He had the audacity to hold an interview halfway in and halfway out the window, concocting a story about checking the building's security system. Anyone with eyes and half a brain could tell what he was up to. Giving the devil his due, he managed to play it off.

Even when a person is innocent of any wrongdoing, running from the media with your head down and eyes averted has a way of making you look guilty. I knew I'd have to face the unforgiving eye of the camera. I squared my shoulders, steeled my nerves, and took a deep breath.

At this time of year I usually ran the gauntlet from my second-floor apartment to my storefront café with a sweater or jacket thrown over my shoulders. Today I bundled up in full winter gear—coat, scarf, oversized hat, and gloves.

I'd timed it before. It took all of forty-five seconds for me to lock my front door, scamper downstairs, walk around to the storefront, and unlock the front door. I could move even faster on wintery days like this.

I stepped out into the chilly morning, making sure to keep my head up and a bland expression on my face. I walked around to the front, cursing my bright idea of keeping the back door padlocked from the inside. It worked as a security measure, since we hadn't once been burglarized in our seven years of operation. Still I would have liked, just this once, to be able to slip into the café through my own back door.

A three-person crew breathed steam into the morning cold. They stood chatting amongst themselves, stamping their feet to keep warm. One guy pinched out his cigarette and tossed the butt to the sidewalk.

Ump, ump, ump! Aunt Essie would have grunted. *That boy's got no home training.*

At first, they ignored me as I strolled past. I even glanced back at them with mild curiosity, as any innocent passerby might. It wasn't until I started unlocking the front door that someone figured it out.

"Hey, that's her!" a woman shouted. "Hurry up, she's getting away."

They stampeded to the door, bum-rushing me like a herd of buffalo. Someone pushed a microphone in my face.

"Miss Summers," the reporter shouted, like I wasn't right in front of her. "Alderman Dailey is the second person to die after eating your food. What do you say in your defense?"

I recognized her as Samantha Patterson, dethroned royalty in the kingdom of local TV news. She'd once risen the ranks as a prime-time news anchor. But that was once upon a time. Television can be cruel to aging women even when they've colored their gray, watched their calories, and gone for their regular Botox treatments. Samantha had recently been demoted to location reporting for the morning news.

"Now why would somebody tell a big ol' lie like that?" I asked her mildly. "It's crazy what people will say these days."

"Are you suggesting that Delbert Dailey didn't actually pass away after consuming your pie? Because our sources say otherwise."

Obviously, her sources couldn't line two matchsticks up straight. Either that, or Samantha was telling a bald-faced lie to get an emotional response. Delbert Dailey hadn't eaten my pie the day he died. He'd been hit in the face with it. But debating the matter would only make me look bad on TV. In fact, few people could manage to appear innocent with a microphone stuck in their face.

Instead of arguing I opted for charm. Channeling my Great-Aunt Essie, I softened up and countrified my voice. "Well, look a-here. How long y'all been standing in the freezing cold?"

I held the door open and beckoned them inside. Automatic timers had already turned up the heat, so it was always toasty when I opened up. "Get in here and warm yourselves up. Come on now, I won't bite you."

They gazed at each other in mild panic. *A cooperative victim! What to do, what to do?*

"I'm putting on a fresh pot of coffee. Now, I'm not one to brag, but people say I've got the best coffee in Woodlawn. You can judge for yourself."

The desire for warmth and the need for caffeine finally won out. Samantha Patterson made a beckoning motion. The three-person news crew tramped in after me. The systems were programmed into my smartphone. The cameraman gave a grunt of approval when I turned on the light.

"Nice place you got here." He hoisted the camera onto his shoulder and began taking a panoramic shot of the dining room.

"Why, thank you kindly, young man. Go ahead and relax while I put on the pot. Take pictures of whatever you like, I've got no secrets."

"Don't forget we're on a deadline," the soundman barked, pointing to his wristwatch. He was the same one who'd dropped that cigarette butt outside. "We're slotted for the eight thirty segment."

"Keep your shirt on, Calvin," Samantha retorted. "We've got at least an hour to wrap this package. I don't know about you but I'm dying for a cup of joe."

These people looked like the mocha chocolatta yaya types. I didn't have any fancy flavored blends to offer, so I took extra pains with the brewing. For flavor I added a cardamom pod to the beans before grinding them. Though my Arusha was smooth as silk, I sprinkled in a few grains of salt to eliminate any bitterness.

"Ooh," Samantha moaned minutes later, sipping from the brew. "This is heaven in a mug."

Samantha Patterson's drawn face gave her the look of a

woman forever dieting. Sure enough, she initially turned down my offer of free food. The soundman and the camera operator set down their equipment to gobble their turkey bacon, scrambled eggs, and buttermilk biscuits. They ate like starving men.

I had them literally eating out of my hand. A would-be exposé pivoted into a profile piece. I'd taken the lemon—both literal and figurative—turned it into lemonade, and added essence of orange blossom for an unexpected jolt of flavor. They got shots of me cooking in the kitchen, reminiscing about Great-Aunt Essie and her family recipes. They even took a close-up of her portrait above my work desk, hanging right between Jesus and President Obama.

"Look, Aunt Essie," I whispered. "You're on tee-vee!"

I even persuaded Samantha to do an on-air tasting of grits and salmon croquettes.

"What do you suppose this sets me back?" she asked between shots. "About eight hundred calories, for sure."

I shrugged. "Girl, don't start me to lying."

"Oh, well. An extra hour at the gym tonight." She dug ferociously into her plate of food.

By the time Penny arrived and got over her shock at seeing a camera crew roaming the premises, it didn't take long before she was entertaining them with stories of Delbert Dailey and the dishes he loved to eat. She even did a little impromptu, nondenominational prayer.

"Saint Peter is meeting Alderperson Dailey at the Pearly Gates with a healthy heaping plate of black-eyed peas and cornbread. Hallelujah and amen."

When Samantha tried to bring the conversation back around to the allegedly tainted sweet potato pie, Penny shook her head and tsk, tsk, tsked. "Our beloved Grandy Jaspers and Delbert 'Do-Right' Dailey were huge fans of Essie's food. We were their home away from home, and kitchen away from kitchen. Would the families have us catering the funeral repast if they thought the food was anything less than wholesome?"

It was a rhetorical question, of course. Mattie Jaspers was back on our side, but I wasn't expecting Lynette Dailey to call in any catering orders. I caught Penny's eye and shook my head in warning. *Don't overdo it.* I ducked away from the action when my cell phone rang.

"Why is there a Channel 6 news truck parked in front of your place?" Fanon Franklin wanted to know.

"They're just doing a little piece on Essie's."

"Well, that's a relief. I was afraid you had another dead body on your hands. Look, I'm right outside. She's something of a clock-watcher, so we don't want to keep her waiting."

"Keep who waiting?"

"Don't tell me you forgot our eight a.m. appointment."

"Oh, right," I remembered, shivering involuntarily. "We've got a date with the Ice . . . I mean, Detective Jacobs."

"You did forget, didn't you?"

"Of course not. Hey, Fanon," I asked cautiously. "You didn't come in a police cruiser, did you?"

"Nope, it's my day off. I'm in my Jeep."

"Thank God for Jesus," I breathed.

My carefully finessed effort to spin media attention in my favor would backfire in a Chicago minute with a shot of me climbing into a squad car.

"Give me five minutes to finish up and I'll be right out."

CHAPTER 25

Keystone Kops

The five minutes stretched into fifteen. Still we were only eight minutes late, ten at the absolute most. Fanon sent me in alone while he went to look for parking.

I rapped at the outside wall of her cubicle since it didn't have a door. "Good morning, Sergeant Jacobs. So good to see you again."

The detective pursed her thin lips and glanced up at the wall clock. "Take a seat and let's get started, Miss Summers. I'm on a tight schedule this morning."

I guess Sergeant Jacobs was playing some kind of cat-and-mouse cop game. Instead of getting started like she promised, she opened a file and kept me waiting while she slowly flipped through it page by page. She finally looked up at me, tapping her finger against the desk.

"So-o-o," she breathed out in her husky voice. "How well did you know the deceased?"

I wondered if her oh-so-busy, oh-so-weary attitude was an act or her natural personality. "Well, which deceased are we talking about?"

"Alderman Dailey, of course. Didn't Sergeant Franklin

inform you . . . Oh, hi, there, Fanon." Her voice softened as she looked over my shoulder. "I didn't realize you were coming, too."

With that she broke into such a smile as I'd never seen on the detective's face. You would have thought Santa Claus himself had strolled into her cubicle. Santa Claus, because he inhabits the frozen tundra of the snowcapped . . . Oh, never mind.

Neither Jack Frost nor Old Man Winter had put that smile on Emerson Jacobs's thin little face. It was none other than my personal *was*band, Sergeant Fanon M. Franklin. Jacobs began rising to greet him.

"Sorry to keep you waiting, Emmy," Fanon said. "And please, don't get up."

She was already in the process of leaning across me to give him a tight hug. "It's so good to see you again."

"As always," he grinned back. "You're looking good."

Do you know the woman had the nerve to blush? It probably took all the blood in her system to put that faint flush of pink in her cheeks.

The two officers obviously had an amicable relationship. I found myself wondering if it went any further than that, then shook my head to dislodge the thought. I knew Fanon's tastes in women and didn't think anemic blondes were quite his flavor. Yet Jacobs was attractive in a wan and waify way. Maybe Fanon could actually go for that type. Preferences can change over time. Mine certainly had.

Fanon lowered himself into the seat beside me. "So, tell me, Emmy. Will this make it up to Homicide?"

She shrugged and pointed to the file on her desk. "Doesn't look like it. I thought I'd ask a few last questions and see if your friend here can shed any light on the case."

Fanon had the grace to look surprised. "Savvy's my ex-wife, Emmy. I thought you knew that."

Her thin eyebrow lifted as she glanced at me. "Oh, really? I didn't realize."

"But we're still the very best of friends." I couldn't resist a jab. "How many exes can say that?"

Her expression carefully shifted back to neutral. "You don't say. Any kids?"

Fanon smiled broadly and flipped out his wallet. "That's our son, Malik. He's thirty-nine years old, living out of town, and working as an engineer. And here's our grandson, Gavril. The two of us spoil him rotten whenever we get the chance."

Now why would anyone in her right mind stare at photos of my handsome son and adorable grandson with a worried little pinch between the eyebrows? And she probably didn't even realize she was frowning.

Aunt Essie didn't raise no fool. I couldn't figure out exactly what, but I knew something was up. I wasn't even sure Fanon noticed the effect he had on Emerson Jacobs. He could sometimes be thickheaded that way.

But the Ice Maiden had a thing for him, of that I was convinced. I could practically feel the heat of a low-burning fire. If she wasn't careful, that torch she carried would thaw her frozen exterior. Then she'd melt into a pool of slush like Frosty the Snowman on the first day of spring.

I tossed the ball into Jacobs's court. "Why'd you call me in here, Detective?"

She quickly gathered her wits about her. "You came in earlier to report a hunch about an elderly gentleman's death. What do your instincts tell you about Alderman Dailey's?"

"That they died under similar circumstances," I answered. "Maybe by the same hand."

"And whose hand would that be, Miss Summers?"

I stifled a whiff of irritation. "With all due respect, Detective, isn't it your job to find that out?"

"Surely you must have a theory."

"We came up with a whole list of likely and unlikely suspects. Their relationship, possible motives, and opportunity to kill the deceased."

"Who is *we*?" Jacobs glanced over at Fanon in mild disapproval.

He threw up his hands in protest. "It wasn't me."

"The *we* is me and my assistant manager." I thought back on the spreadsheet Penny and I had created. "The widow, the ex-manager, the mistress. They all had beef with Grandy."

"And what would be their motive to kill Dailey?"

Detective Jacobs had asked a very good question. I had to admit that I didn't know the answer.

She strummed her finger on the desk again. "I see at least one common thread between them."

"And that would be . . . ?"

"You. Or maybe I should say, two common threads. You, and your sweet potato pie." She settled back in her chair to watch my reaction.

Fanon, bless his heart, had my back. Leaning forward in his seat, he said intently, "Now hang on a minute, Emmy. What are you suggesting?"

I answered for her. "She thinks that I'm a plausible suspect. Is that right, Detective Jacobs?"

Jacobs shifted in her chair, glancing over at Fanon. "I have to cover all bases. You know that, Fanon."

"My wife is not a murderer. She wouldn't hurt a fly."

I noticed he conveniently forgot to add "ex" to the "wife."

"For some of you police types, it's guilty until proven innocent," I said. "But what would my motive be for killing two of my most loyal patrons?"

Jacobs shrugged. "You tell me."

"No, you're the detective. *You* tell me." I wasn't afraid of Jacobs. Much.

"Well, for one thing," she theorized, "it's publicity for your restaurant."

"You're right about that. Bad publicity. Business hasn't been this slow in the seven years since I've opened. Okay, what else you got?"

She lifted a fingernail to her lip, then changed her mind and began tapping on the edge of her desk again. "I hear Dailey wasn't easy to get along with. Maybe he got on your bad side."

"He got on a lot of people's bad side. Sometimes he could be a donkey's behind. But if I went around killing off all my obnoxious customers, my business would be in worse shape than it already is."

Fanon raised a finger in warning. "That's enough, Emmy. You asked for Savvy, I brought Savvy. You didn't tell me she was a suspect."

"Not a suspect, Fanon. A person of interest."

Fanon snorted. You didn't have to know cop-speak to understand what that meant. "That's it with the interrogation. Any other questions and we're calling in counsel. Are we done here?"

"For now." Emerson Jacobs looked at him with a wan smile. "What do you say to an after-work drink at Fitzgerald's sometime?"

"Sure." Fanon nodded, then added firmly: "After all this is over."

I couldn't resist adding my two cents. "Me too, Detective. I'd love a drink at Fitzgerald's."

"Well, sure." She looked at me in surprise and managed a wan little smile. "That should be fun."

I'll bet.

We'd shaken hands and were preparing to leave when a thought jumped into my head. "You know, I've been thinking about getting all the suspects together in one place. Maybe invite them all to dinner and ask a few questions. See what comes up."

Detective Jacobs looked amused. "An amateur sleuth playing drawing-room detective gathers the suspects around her. Then lo and behold, one of them confesses. You watch a lot of mystery movies?"

"Now, Emmy," Fanon scolded gently. "No need to get Savvy treated."

"Treated?" she asked in her husky voice. She was clearly confused.

"Treated," I said with feigned patience. "Snapping, cracking, toasting, signifying. Otherwise known as playing the dozens. *Your hair is so nappy because King Kong's your pappy.* That sort of thing."

"I see." She nodded thoughtfully. "A type of urban insult contest, in other words."

"You could call it that." I ignored Fanon, who was trying to steer me out the doorway. "A lot of the dozens are *yo mama* jokes. Yo mama shoots dice with the midnight mice. Yo mama's so fat she gave Dracula diabetes. Yo mama's so white, she made Casper go *da-yum!*"

Now it was Fanon's turn to scold me. "See there, Savvy. That's why I can't take you anywhere. Rain check on that drink, Emmy."

He continued his scolding out in the car. "You really rubbed Emmy the wrong way. What got into you?"

"Into me? She's been giving me the cold shoulder since the day I met her."

Fanon frowned. "I wonder why. I've never seen her act that way around anyone else."

I'll give you one guess, I thought. *And his initials are F.F.*

"Anyway, Savvy, that dinner party thing was a silly idea. Why'd you spring that on her without passing it by me first?"

"I don't know," I admitted. "Just a spur-of-the-moment impulse."

"Well, keep those impulses to yourself. I'll help you out in any way I can but we're not doing anything to compromise an ongoing police investigation.

"What investigation?" I scoffed. "No disrespect, Fanon. Y'all are Keystone Kopping on the real tip."

"No disrespect?" He grinned. "I'm sure you meant Keystone Kops in the finest sense of the term."

"At least I didn't call you the Three Stooges."

"And you better not, or I'll murderize ya. Us Keystone Kops is da best in da country."

"Oh, yeah?" I sneered in my best Brooklyn accent. "Well, how are youse guys in da city?"

We traded Moe, Larry, and Curly gags all the way back to the café.

"Can you believe it?" I said after Fanon dropped me off. "That washed-out blonde was drooling over Fanon so deep I almost drowned in it. I was ready to go find a mop."

Penny peeled potatoes while I snapped string beans for the vegetable side. Business was so slow we'd reduced the lunchtime menu to just one entrée. Today it was mixed salad, smothered chicken, and green beans mixed with white potatoes. Dessert was bread pudding à la mode, the leftovers from yesterday's un-sold biscuits.

"This reminds me of a story." Penny paused, resting the peeler on the counter.

"Can you peel and storytell at the same time? Lunch starts in an hour."

"As I was saying before I was so rudely interrupted, when I was a kid, one of the church mothers would bring stuff in for the rummage sale. When somebody tried to buy one of her discarded items, she'd decide she wanted to keep it, after all. Old girl never got rid of anything. You know what I'm saying?"

"Oh, right," I said accusingly. "I'm so wrong to be suspicious about the Ice Maiden. You went vanilla yourself. How could I expect you to understand?"

"Check yourself before you wreck yourself. I might not have a West Side behind but I was raised in Englewood, the toughest neighborhood in the city. You don't want to meet the ghetto side of Penny Lopés."

"A side I haven't already seen?"

"Yeah, you got jokes. Just remember, Sergio ain't no vanilla. He's a sweet, spicy, melt-in-your-mouth Brazilian *cafezinho* . . ."

"Okay, that's enough." I covered my ears. "TMI. We've es-tablished that Sergio is hot and caramel-flavored."

"Besides," she ignored me, "when it comes to complexion, he's a shade darker than your ex–old man. So, what are you go-ing to do with Fanon? Get back on the saddle and ride, or find another horse?"

"We're almost thirty years divorced, Penny. That ship has already sailed."

"Then let Elvira, Mistress of the Dark, have him. And wish the two of them well."

"I got reasons why I left the man," I insisted. "Stuff you don't even know about."

"Hey, I'm like Mama Lena in *A Raisin in the Sun*." She raised her hands in a surrendering gesture. *"I ain't meddling, child. I ain't meddling."*

"Of course not, Penny. You'd never dream of it. And since those little hands aren't doing any meddling, they're free to do some peeling."

We worked together for a time, seasoning and stewing green beans and potatoes, frying then smothering chicken. Penny stopped suddenly, breaking the silence.

"I wonder," she mused.

"Can't you wonder and work at the same time?"

"I'm not much for multitasking," she admitted.

"Well, spit it out. What are you thinking?"

"I'm wondering if we should cross Delbert Dailey off our suspect list."

"Why?" I asked. "He might still have killed Grandy."

"And then what? Felt guilty about it and downed a bottle of Viagra?"

I mulled it over for a minute.

"Fair enough. I wouldn't consider Delbert a likely candidate for suicide. He was much too vainglorious. And if he didn't kill himself, then he probably didn't kill Grandy. Two Viagra overdoses are too close for coincidence. These deaths have to be connected somehow."

"But I bet you my last dollar," Penny said, and winked, "that if we find out who OD'd Grandy Jaspers, we'll discover who did the same to Delbert Dailey."

CHAPTER 26

Angel on My Shoulder

The first frost of the year breathed death on my container garden out behind the café.

I woke up one morning to find the last bell peppers of the season frozen on the bush. The tomato plants had already borne their last harvest, their stalks bent like thin, broken men. Salad greens withered back into the earth from which they sprang.

Winter had come to Woodlawn overnight.

A fine layer of snow coated my herbs, vegetable pots, and flower beds. I cut back my perennials and covered them in a thick layer of mulch, trusting they'd come back in the spring. I dug the annuals under. Next year I would plant all perennials. It was hard growing things that bloomed for a season, only to die and never return.

I'd seen enough death in my life. Last year had been the hardest of all, though losing both my parents came in a very close second. My Aunt Essie up and died on me not ten years later. Instead of her memory fading away, it was still quite present in my life.

My Great-Aunt Essie had eased the transition after I lost both my parents, but she wasn't there to help me get over losing her. Or maybe, in fact, she was. The thing about it was, I never really mourned because I never let go. When she left this earthly plane over forty years ago, Aunt Essie took up residence inside my head.

I'm an otherwise sane and sensible woman who imagines someone who isn't there as an angel on my shoulder. I never actually see her but I often feel her presence. If people knew that she sometimes whispered in my ear, I'm sure they'd check me into the nearest funny farm.

I put my aunt's portrait on the kitchen island and asked my question point-blank. "Who would want to kill Grandy Jaspers and Delbert Dailey? Why would someone want to pin it on me? And what do I do about it?"

Of course, she was silent.

But that night Great-Aunt Essie visited me in a dream. And like the language of dreams, her answer was cryptic and confusing—a jumble of memories, impressions, and strange events. Maybe even a little prophecy.

Aunt Essie rode shotgun while I drove her ancient jalopy, the one that always seemed one step from the junkyard. Fittingly, it was an Oldsmobile. I'm convinced she held that car together with the power of prayer and sheer determination.

In the dream we were driving north on Lake Shore Drive. I'm not sure where we were headed. When the highway branched away from the water at Hollywood Avenue, we kept on driving. A narrow road appeared before us, running along the strip of beach between the high-rises on the west and Lake Michigan on the east.

The lake began surging, boiling over the shore. Aunt Essie calmly cranked her window shut. The Olds had those old-fashioned roll-up windows. She winked at me. "Takes more than a little water to melt all this sugar."

Soon it was more than a little. The waves began pounding

the car, splashing over the roof. I was afraid we'd be washed into the lake. "Aunt Essie, don't you think we should turn back?"

She firmly shook her head, singing in her cracked, creaky voice. "*Ain't gonna let nobody turn me around.* I'd drink that lake before I let it drown me. Believe that."

We kept pushing northward. Even as the sunny day turned overcast and snow began to fall, the car's interior was warm as summer. Its air conditioner had never worked as far as I knew. I let my windows down to get some fresh air, but couldn't make out my aunt's voice above the wind rushing in.

When I cranked the window back up, Aunt Essie's words had turned into song.

We are climbing Jacob's ladder,
Soldiers of the cross.

"Nothing like a little Jacob's ladder leaf to loosen the tongue." Aunt Essie nudged my elbow and winked. "Mind your lessons, gal, and listen, lest you wind up in Miss Ann's kitchen."

Miss Ann was Southern Black-speak for a bossy white woman. My aunt had been cooking and cleaning for white Southern families since she was eleven years old. She would reach into her store of adages when I was a kid, urging me to pursue my studies so I wouldn't have to do domestic work. I wanted to tell her the message had hit home. I was now a retired career woman with a master's degree. Yet somehow it seemed more important to listen than talk.

"Yes, ma'am, Aunt Essie," I answered, obedient, yet perplexed.

She switched to another spiritual, singing and clapping along. It felt like we were back in church again.

There is a balm in Gilead
To make the wounded whole
There is a balm in Gilead
To heal the sin-sick soul.

She turned again and looked at me intently. "You hear what I'm saying, Savvy?"

"I don't know, ma'am."

"You'll understand it better by and by."

Lake waters drifted skyward like upside-down rain, falling back to the earth as snow.

Aunt Essie got out of the car before I could stop her and went dancing through the snow like a little girl. She moved much faster than I'd ever seen, twirling away from me.

"Wait up, Aunt Essie!" I got out to follow, but saw no signs of her. When I turned back the car had disappeared, too. I was now surrounded by a blizzard of snow, but it wasn't the cold Chicago kind that penetrates your bones. In the secret logic of dreams, this snow was warm to the touch.

I heard someone singing amid the blizzard of hot snow, but I knew it wasn't Aunt Essie. My auntie, bless her heart, was a horrible singer. She sounded just like those caroling monsters in *Gremlins 2: The New Batch*. This song was sung sweetly, high and clear, like the voice of an angel.

I know I've been changed
Because the angel in heaven done
Signed my name.

I woke to the musical alarm on my bedside radio. It was an a cappella rendition of "I Know I've Been Changed," one of those African American spirituals Great-Aunt Essie played all hours of the day.

ↄ

I wondered what my aunt would have made of that dream I had. It was so rich in symbolism—a car, a beach, Lake Michigan, snow, a departed loved one dancing. My aunt deeply believed in the power of dreams to foretell the future and bestow fortune.

She always kept a battered old dream book at her bedside and consulted it the moment she awakened. Whether it was birds or snakes, running water or a woman in white, each dream was prophetic.

The dream book was a dictionary with crude illustrations and cryptic lists of numerals. Anything a person could dream corresponded to a certain numeral. When she dreamt of more than one thing, she'd usually combine the numbers. This guided my aunt in her one and only vice, the playing of policy, that extralegal precursor to today's lottery.

I found Aunt Essie's dream book and began to leaf through it.

Dreams of calm lake waters symbolize inner peace, while turbulent waves represent change.

To dream of snow means change, renewal, and spiritual awakening. The lucky number is 30.

And suddenly I knew what I had to do. An angel from heaven had signed my name.

CHAPTER 27

Murder, She Roasted

"They're the hottest tickets in town, Savvy. See if your baby's daddy can get a couple for me, will you?"

I heard the news first from Penny Porter Lopés, Mouth of the South Side. The Chicago Bears had donated a block of tickets to one of the high schools where Fanon supervised the security detail.

A light bulb went off above my head and I called Fanon immediately. "I hope you haven't given away all those Bears tickets."

"No problem. If you want to come along, I could swing an extra for you."

"Actually," I told him, "I'll probably need two."

There was a stretch of silence at the other end. "Depends on who you're bringing."

"Oh, for crying out loud, Fanon." The nerve of that man! Three decades divorced and still acting like a jealous spouse. "It's not a date or anything."

"Fine." The relief in his voice was audible, even over the phone. "I'll set two tickets aside. May I ask who they're for?"

"You don't even want to know." I hung up before he could

change his mind. The truth was, I couldn't even tell him if I wanted to.

Penny frowned when I told her my idea. "Hey, I thought you were getting those tickets for Sergio and me."

"Don't be selfish, Penny. We've got a menu to plan and a murderer to catch."

∽

The spectral visit by Great-Aunt Essie the other night reminded me what I'd already known. There was an intimate bond between those of us who cooked and the people we served. They entrusted us with their celebrations and woes, the rituals of weddings, birthdays, graduations and funerals. And also their gastronomic safety, which was why so many were avoiding Essie's lately.

Some of our patrons relished their privacy even in a roomful of people. Sometimes our presence slipped so far into the background that they seemed to forget we were there. You'd have to gauge the right moment to bring a menu or take an order, or you might preempt a marriage proposal or interrupt a pregnancy announcement.

People also chose these moments to deliver less-than-happy news, be it an admission of adultery or demand for a divorce. More than once a jealous loved one had burst into the café to confront a significant other in an intimate tête-à-tête with the other man or woman.

At other times our involvement was requested and desired. We'd be asked to bring out a cake blazing with candles, or join in the singing of the birthday song. When patrons came in alone and sat at the counter, it was often a signal that they wanted a listening ear along with their meal. Some had no one else to talk to. For others it was easier unburdening to a stranger. It was almost like the relationship people had with their therapist, bartender, or hairstylist.

Saddest of all were the aged, the poor, and the unhoused people coming in with the coins they'd saved or hustled to treat themselves to coffee and a slice of pie. Then there were latchkey kids eating alone, waiting for a parent to get back from work.

So many souls out there needed to be unburdened.

You do your best listening at mealtimes, 'cause that's when people do their best talking.

I really owed Aunt Essie, though I couldn't repay the debt. That dream had suggested a creative way to pick a few brains over circumstances surrounding Grandy's and Delbert's deaths.

Thanks to Fanon's largesse, though probably not his approval, I could lure them in with the chance at a pair of playoff tickets. I would wine them and dine them with food and drink a-plenty. I didn't have a liquor license but that was fine. I wouldn't be selling any booze, I'd be giving it away.

Then I'd swoop in with some carefully worded questions and a hidden sound recorder. Those folks would never know what hit them.

Back during the days when we were still married, Fanon had been part of a sting that netted the CPD hundreds of arrests. The targets were mostly male suspects charged with violent crimes from aggravated battery to armed robbery.

Their plan was deceptively simple. In secret cooperation with the Chicago Police Department, the NBA Central Division sent out notices to people with outstanding warrants, notifying them they'd been entered to win a pair of Chicago Bulls Championship Final tickets. Meanwhile, the police department rented out the banquet hall of a Loop hotel and waited for the droves to come pouring in.

This was back when Michael Jordan was still here and the Bulls were the winningest team in the NBA. Everyone followed them without fail—including, apparently, the criminal element. Playoff tickets were hard to come by. Everybody wanted them, and few could afford them.

When the targets turned up in person to try their luck, a couple of plainclothes officers registered them at the door, checked their IDs, handed out ticket stubs, and sent them through portable metal detectors. Anyone with hidden weapons was instructed to check them. Then they were escorted into the banquet hall.

"Don't tell me," I interjected. "A bunch of cops were waiting to pounce on them and haul them off to the pokey."

"Yeah, but not right away. We still had to hold the drawing," Fanon explained. "Otherwise we'd be committing fraud and none of those arrests would stick."

Once a critical mass had been assembled, a festive atmosphere filled the room as a ticket stub was pulled. Some lucky loser won a pair of tickets they'd probably never get to use. The fateful announcement came as uniformed officers flooded the room. The cheering quickly turned to jeering, with the music turned up high to disguise the sounds of protest.

"You are under arrest. Drop to your knees and place your hands behind your head."

The detainees were handcuffed, lined up, and escorted out a side door to waiting paddy wagons. Then the space was freed up for the next batch of alleged perpetrators. Cook County Jail was bursting at the seams that day.

At the time I'd felt sorry for those guys, betrayed by their loyalty to a beloved home team. Now I was ready to take a page from the same playbook.

I got busy in the week before the football game. I put up announcements all over the café. I set out a slotted jar to collect the entries. Two prizes would be awarded.

The second prize was a free Monday-night raffle party. Those winners would also be entered into a drawing for the grand prize—a pair of Bears playoff tickets. I made the rules very clear. *Contestants must be present to win!*

I realized how suspicious it would seem if the only people in attendance were those who knew the victims. So, half of the invitees would be randomly chosen from the contest entries I'd collected. The others were those who'd made our lists of likely and unlikely suspects.

I began plotting a devious yet delicious plan.

I'd already discovered what Aunt Essie called "Jacob's ladder leaf" was the herbal sedative valerian. I figured her reference to "a balm in Gilead" was lemon balm, which I found at a health food store on 53rd Street. I already knew about passionflower and chamomile from Fanon's tea-drinking rituals. I even re-searched a few other ingredients like lavender and skullcap. I tested out recipes and discovered that some herbs had strong flavors that needed to be disguised. Others were quite palat-able, delicious, in fact.

Catnip, for instance, wasn't just crack for kitties. It was ed-ible for humans, too. While it made cats go stir-crazy, it had quite the opposite effect on people. Brewed in a tea or cooked into food it mellowed you out nicely without actually making you high.

I tested out a new menu that was a bit more epicurean than my usual café offerings:

"Tranquility" herbed whitefish
Wild and brown rice "peaceful" pilaf
"Calming" green beans almandine
"Stress-busting" mixed salad
"Serenity" shortcake
Assorted "unwinding" beverages

I marinated the fish in catnip, olive oil, and sea salt. I concocted a chamomile cream to layer with mixed berries between slabs of lavender-scented shortcake. I muddled lemon balm into dressing and shaved valerian root over romaine, red onion, and grape tomatoes.

Then there were the beverages.

For imbibers, my ginger hot toddy was guaranteed to warm bones and loosen inhibitions. I'd also serve a reputable though fairly inexpensive Spanish sparkling wine. No headache champagne for this occasion.

For teetotalers, I found a hot chocolate recipe made with valerian leaf, lemon balm, and lavender. It was perfectly delicious and superbly relaxing! To further the calming effects, I mixed tinctures of skullcap and passionflower into my regular lemonade and added extra orange blossom essence and honey to disguise the flavor.

I secretly called it my Truth Serum buffet.

Penny, making lemonade in the café beverage station, heartily disapproved. "How you gonna invite people for food then drug the hell out of them? Especially when you've been accused of poisoning people."

"Not drugs," I insisted. "Calming herbs, straight from Mother Earth. Some of the ones we've been using all along have powerful medicinal properties, too."

"Yeah, right," she grumbled. "Tell it to the judge."

"But it's true. Sage has both astringent and relaxing benefits. Basil calms the nerves and the stomach. Black pepper relaxes the body and relieves the common cold. And licorice treats everything from stress to athlete's foot."

"And the last time you cooked with licorice was . . . ?"

"Well, never," I admitted. "But I'm looking into it."

Penny shook her head and squeezed her lemons. "I never knew you were so conniving."

"I wouldn't call it conniving, but my nickname is *Savvy*, after all. I'm not tricking people into eating something they don't want. I'll tell them what's in the food, I always do. I just want them calm, relaxed, and ready to unburden their souls."

Penny doffed an imaginary hat. "Jessica Fletcher ain't got nothing on you, boss."

"Who's Jessica Fletcher?"

"You know, the mystery writer and amateur detective on that old TV series. *Murder, She Wrote*. Except in your case, it's Murder, She *Roasted*."

CHAPTER 28

A Warriors' Ballet

Penny and I spent the next few days working out the logistics of the event. This is how we figured it all would happen.

We'd invite an equal number of suspects and civilians culled from the entry jar. Invitees could bring a plus-one, but only one. We would insist that everyone RSVP. And since our people were notorious scofflaws, we'd follow up by phone.

We'd segregate the suspects from other guests by assigning them to prearranged seating. Although we'd be working the event, Penny and I would casually mingle, asking questions here and there. Our reinforcements would pick up the slack.

The last part of the plan was the most challenging. Questioning some six to eight suspects would be nearly impossible for Penny and me to manage alone. I called up my ex-husband.

As I might have predicted, Fanon required some persuading. To tell the truth and shame the devil, he wanted no part of the plan. In fact, he wanted us out of it, too. "I'm not going to do this and neither are you."

"But, Fanon, we've got it all figured out."

"You're not inviting a potential killer to dinner, someone who may have taken two men's lives. What if the person brings a weapon and decides to shoot up the place?"

"That's not the MO," I insisted. "This person is a poisoner, not a shooter."

"That's perfect, Miss CSI. Smothered chicken with a side of Viagra."

"And a whole lot of happy, horny customers," I joked. "At least the men will be. I don't think Viagra works on women."

"It does if someone doesn't care who they overdose. Your guests could all wind up in the ER, men and women alike. The perfect end to a perfect party, am I right?"

"Of course not, Fanon."

"Then how about the morgue?"

I'd begged, cajoled, and finally appealed to his sense of gallantry. "If you don't want justice for Grandy and Dailey, don't you care about my safety?"

His voice was gruff with equal parts worry and frustration. "I'm begging you, Savvy. Call this thing off."

"It's too late. The invitations already went out."

"Okay, you win. But after this, you've got to stop playing amateur sleuth. I need you to promise me, Savvy."

"I will. I swear on my auntie's grave."

Forgive me, Great-Aunt Essie.

"Dang, what happened in here?" Winnie Mae Welbon stepped through the door and suddenly stopped in her tracks.

Henpecked Henry bringing up the rear bumped smack into her ample backside. "I don't know, baby. It sure looks different, don't it?"

Essie's was suitably transformed for the evening. It wasn't just the tastes, textures, and tranquility of the beautifully laid out Truth Serum buffet. Carefully curated sights, sounds, and smells contributed to the ambiance.

Crisp white cloths topped each table. Iced champagne—well, its Spanish cousin—reclined in gleaming silver buckets. The overhead lights were dimmed and candles bathed the room in a warm amber glow. The buffet centerpiece was a lush floral arrangement in winter whites—roses, hydrangeas, paperwhites, and sprigs of baby's breath.

Every table held a single long-stemmed white rose in a crystal vase. The aromatherapy diffuser puffed soothing scents of jasmine into the air. Ella Fitzgerald's lilting voice crooning over the sound system encouraged guests to relax "In a Mellow Tone."

With sound turned off on the flat screen TV, even prerecorded videos of crushing replays from vintage Chicago Bears vs. Packers games seemed like a ballet of bulky warriors.

Jazz music segued into soft rock. The Young Rascals' "Groovin.'"

The guests drifted in on CPT, Colored People's Time. We were prepared for it.

"Hors d'oeuvres?" Penny proffered a tray of crudités and mini quiches.

Parker circulated through the dining room with champagne and hot chocolate.

I collected coats and outerwear and stashed them in a portable coat check, then directed people to their assigned seats. The turnout was a minor success. Everyone from the list of suspects was in attendance except Mattie Jaspers and Tuchman Pfeiffer.

Even my nemesis from Sweet Stuff Bakery showed up. She must have recovered from her customary defeat at In Your Face. Either that, or she was relishing the way tragedy overshadowed my winning streak. In which case, she was there to gloat.

Annabelle waltzed in wearing a threadbare fur she absolutely refused to part with. It rested on the back of her chair all evening, except when she went to answer the call of nature. Then the tatty little fur went into the ladies' room with her.

"She actually thinks somebody wants that thing?" I whispered to Penny. "Annabelle couldn't pay anyone to steal that pile of rabbit pelts."

"Rabbits? I would have thought their long-tailed cousins."

"Squirrels?"

"Nope." She grinned. "The other ones."

"Ugh." I shuddered. "Gross."

We worked the room just as we planned. I took Tables One and Two. Under the guise of topping off drinks and filling out tickets for the prize drawing, I served Winnie's table.

Penny worked Tables Three and Four. Despite that he was assigned to sit elsewhere, the guy who tended bar at the Jasperses' anniversary party turned up late and joined Shysteen at Table Three. He wore a red and black Bulls starter jacket. Like Annabelle Beasley, he declined to check it and draped it over his seat back. The young man's name, we had discovered, was Evrian King—like the bottled water with an extra "r."

Fanon was assigned Table Four, where he had the pleasure of waiting on Annabelle Beasley. He went to introduce himself and offered her a handshake. She stood up and gave him a bear hug. "Blessings, brother! Ain't no strangers here. Any friend of Safflower is a personal friend of mine."

I wondered if that worked with enemies, too.

Annabelle continued to simper. "What did you say your name was, honey?"

"Fanon Franklin, ma'am. And you are . . . ?"

"Annabelle Beasley, bless your heart." I could have sworn the woman winked at him. "Can I pray for you tonight?"

I'd have to get Fanon into the café more often. It didn't hurt to have law enforcement around with a murderer on the loose. And that hunk allure he exuded wouldn't hurt my business, either.

No, I wasn't above pimping out my ex-husband's sex appeal. So? What's it to you? You want I should go out of business?

Fanon also got to work Table Five. Noble McPherson had come clad in Green Bay Packers sports gear, right down—or *up,* I guess—to a silly cheese-head cap.

Chicagoans were clannish as street gangs about their sports teams, especially when pitted against old rivals. Emotions were known to run high during football season. Most Packers fans knew better than to sport green, white, and gold in enemy territory. I guess Ignoble didn't get the memo.

Penny shook her head at the spectacle he presented. "The brother, and I use the term loosely, must like to live dangerously. People have been beaten on the streets and fired from their jobs for sins of lesser magnitude."

We circulated through the dining room, homing in on our designated tables. The guests were happy, loose, and loquacious. Which didn't surprise me at all. Aunt Essie was right. People talked more when they were relaxed, comfortable, and just a bit tipsy. We let the food, drink, and atmosphere do their work.

With a roundabout line of questioning and subtle eavesdropping, I'd come across several interesting tidbits of information I couldn't wait to mull over later with Penny and Fanon.

CHAPTER 29

The Ultimate Party Pooper

Yet the plan did not go off without a hitch. Two separate incidents pooped on the mellow mood of the party, one of them at the start of the evening and the other at the finish.

There was a ruckus at Table Five. I heard a loud, indignant bellow and looked over to see Noble McPherson pointing a finger in Fanon's face. His voice carried clear across the dining room. "Back off, buddy. That's none of your business!"

"Hey, my bad," Fanon tried to mollify him. "I just asked a question. No harm intended."

And no harm taken. That was the gracious way to respond when a man swallowed his pride and conceded his blunder. McPherson was nothing if not *un*gracious.

He stood there glowering like an overgrown trick-or-treater in his ridiculous cheese head. "Don't mess with me, homey. I'm a dangerous man."

"Calm down." Fanon laid a hand on his shoulder. "No need to get riled up, brother."

"I am not your brother!" Noble hollered. "And take your hands off me! Don't make me get the law on you."

I could see Fanon trying to stifle a grin. "Oh, we wouldn't want that, would we?"

"Yeah, I'll bet. How many times have you been to jail? I'll bet you've got warrants coming out of your . . ."

"Okay, that's enough."

My ex was quite nonconfrontational for a Chicago police officer. He'd never had that chest-thumping brand of braggadocio that some cops were known for. In fact, he preferred to call himself a peace officer rather than a policeman. This probably came from his lifelong discipline to tai chi and other martial arts.

Love your enemy and you drive them crazy, was one of Fanon's mantras. *What you are will show in what you do,* was another.

But I could tell that Noble's pestering was sorely trying his patience.

"People are trying to enjoy themselves." Fanon's words were said so softly I barely heard him. "I'm sure you don't want to disturb them, so I think it's time you left."

Parker scurried over with Noble's coat. Fanon made a sweeping gesture toward the door. Noble looked around indignantly, like he expected someone to come to his defense. When no one did, he hustled out, swearing just loud enough to be overheard. Several curious glances followed him out the door.

"No worries, folks." Fanon mimed a chug-a-lug motion. "I think our friend tied on one too many."

The playlist segued back into jazz. John Coltrane's instrumental rendition of "My Favorite Things" happened to be one of my favorite things.

Noble's interruption seemed to sour the atmosphere. People began shifting restlessly in their seats. I signaled Penny discreetly. It was time to get the raffle underway.

"Ladies and gentlemen, may I have your attention?" She

clapped her hands to silence the chatter. "The lucky winner of this pair of tickets will be escorted to the pre-season game of the Bears—*yay!*—versus Packers—*boo!*—in the luxury of a chauffeur-driven limousine. Put your hands together for Lopés Livery, which so kindly donated the ride."

She winked at her husband Sergio, the one-man owner/ driver of the limo service. "Please stand so everyone can see you, Mr. Lopés. And for anyone with transportation needs from weddings to proms, birthdays to that special night on the town . . ."

"Thank you, Penny," I interrupted the shameless infomercial. "We have business cards for anyone who'd like to patronize Lopés Livery. Fanon, will you also do the honors?"

I lowered the music, the Impressions' "We're a Winner," and held out the bowl of ticket stubs. Fanon closed his eyes, reached into it, and fished one out.

He smiled his famous gap-toothed grin, pausing for effect. "Courtesy of the Bears and Chicago Police Department, I'm pleased to announce the winner of two pre-season tickets is . . ."

He paused, looking teasingly around the room. "Are you ready?"

It went so quiet you could hear a man belch.

"Henry!" Winnie Mae scolded. "That's nasty."

"Sorry, baby."

". . . Shysteen Shackleford!"

The woman uttered a muffled scream. She scampered forward in stiletto heels and a very low-cut maternity dress. Her abundant bosoms jiggled and jounced with every movement. She grabbed Fanon and kissed him full on the mouth. And she'd only met him that very evening! Maybe I'd have to rethink that idea of installing my ex as resident chick magnet.

"Thank you, Jesus." Shysteen's feet did a little holy dance. Her boobs did a dance of their own. "I never won nothing before in my life. The Lord has truly blessed me, hallelujah!"

"Amen," I said, taking her by the elbow and steering her back to her table.

Shysteen had seemed about to start speaking in tongues, which wasn't in the plan for this evening. And then there was the matter of that smack on the lips. Fanon was no longer my boo and I had no claims on his affections. I still didn't appreciate that young hussy smooching him on the mouth like that. Respect the ex, that's all I'm saying!

When Shysteen got back to her table, Evrian the bartender leapt to his feet and crushed her in a bear hug. "Yo, babe. We goin' to the game!"

Shysteen twisted away from him, patting her hair and clothing back into place.

"Who says you're coming?" she hissed, sneaking a furtive glance back at Fanon.

I made a mental note. *Shysteen and Evrian, do the two of them know each other? If so, how well? Get on it, ASAP. And tell Fanon to steer clear of that man-eating hussy.*

The sound system was playing Bobby McFerrin's "Don't Worry, Be Happy." Though the prize tickets had already been awarded, no one seemed in a hurry to leave. The music played and people chatted, lingering over dessert, coffee, and hot chocolate.

When the playlist segued into Tony! Toni! Toné!'s "(Lay Your Head on My) Pillow," Winnie Mae and Henry Welbon got up to slow dance on the patch of floor near the counter.

Meanwhile, Penny, Fanon, and I gathered in the kitchen doorway to compare notes.

"Well, what did you find out?" I looked back and forth between them. "Come on now, cough it up. Who's going first?"

Fanon raised his hand like a schoolkid. "Let me get this over with, then I'm out of here. You know I didn't want to be involved with this mess in the first place."

"You see that tall drink of water?" Penny pointed to Sergio, dozing at Table Six. "The poor guy is dead on his feet. He's been on the road since seven in the morning and he's right back at it tomorrow. I'm pulling rank on you, pardner."

Yet she perched on a counter stool, stretching out her legs, cracking her knuckles, and spinning her tale. If Penny hadn't been so in love with her own voice, then maybe we could have avoided the last party pooper.

"I had to cut Shysteen off after her second glass of wine. For someone supposedly pregnant, she sure loves to knock them back."

"Can you cut to the chase?" I pleaded. "Your husband's over there nodding like a jack-in-the-box. Did Shysteen Shackleford do or say anything important?"

"When I mentioned Grandy Jaspers to her, she almost started crying. They were oh, so very much in love, according to her. When I asked how she was taking Delbert Dailey's death, Shysteen clicked her tongue. 'Child, I don't know nothing about that old freak.'"

"That old freak," Fanon repeated. "Her exact words?"

Penny nodded. "Now, what did she mean by that? If that's her way of saying he was a weirdo, she wouldn't be telling a lie."

Fanon barked a humorless laugh. "Penny, please. Don't act like you just fell off the turnip truck. You know what it means to call somebody a freak. It's a person of certain proclivities and not the vanilla kind."

Penny smirked and snapped her fingers. "My thoughts exactly."

I had to admit that they may have had a point. Was Shysteen's opinion of a man she didn't "know nothing about" unintentionally revealing? Was she privy to his bedroom business because she'd been in there with him?

"Evrian King was sitting right there, listening to every word," Penny continued. "And didn't he give a little grunt, like he agreed with her assessment of Delbert Dailey? Something just doesn't add up. Fanon, what part of a woman do you like?"

My ex-husband was taken aback by Penny's sudden non sequitur. "I don't know what you're getting at. I like all the parts."

She shook her head insistently. "No, what kind of body man are you? My Sergio's a leg man. I first met him one day when he followed me to the parking lot. I had on shorts and he'd seen my gams half a block away. I was ready to deck him one then I heard that cute little accent."

"So what, Penny? You got good legs." Fanon studiously avoided looking down at them. "Where are you going with this?"

"Since you were married to Savvy, I figured you for a breast man." Penny gestured in the general direction of my chest. "And you've got to admit, she's got the bomb boobs."

This time he did take a good look. "Yeah, she does. Although she wasn't quite so well-endowed back when we were together."

"How did my breasts become a topic of conversation?"

Penny ignored my protest. "Savvy dresses way more modestly than Shysteen, so she doesn't show them off like that. But if the two of them were in a race for mayor of Tittytown, it would probably end in a runoff. Don't you think so?"

Two pairs of eyes focused on my chest.

"Savvy's probably a bigger cup size," Fanon theorized. "But then, she's a bigger girl."

"Yoo-hoo, everybody. My eyes are up here." I pointed to them. "And what does my cup size have to do with the matter at hand?"

"Fanon is a boobaholic, just like Dailey was."

Fanon shook his head. "How could you possibly know that, Penny Porter Lopés?"

"You think because I'm chairman of the Itty-Bitty Titty Committee, I don't know the score. But it wasn't my girls he was salivating over. Do-Wrong was in here like white on rice, staring at Savvy's chesticles. He even tried to grab them one day, right after Francis died."

"Did what?" Fanon half-rose from his seat. "He put his slimy hands on you? Son of a . . ."

Penny was the only one I'd told that story. I had never intended her to share it with anyone else, leastwise any ex-husband of mine.

"Back off, you caveman," Penny ordered. "You can't go and kill him because he's already dead. Besides, Delbert Dailey got his just deserts that day. Savvy socked him so hard it fractured a bone in her finger."

Fanon sat back down and placed his arm around my shoulder. "So that's why you were wearing a sling at Francis's funeral. Why didn't somebody tell me?"

"For what?" Penny frowned. "So you could turn it into a slugfest? The two of you duking it out right over the casket?"

I raised a warning hand and directed her back to the matter at hand.

"Speaking of funerals, Savvy got an eyeful of Dailey at Grandy's services. Shysteen was sprawled all over him. Sure, maybe he was just comforting a devastated young thing who just lost her sugar daddy. A devastated young thing with the porn star proportions he clearly admired. But was this a man known for his compassion? Or was he the type that did for others only when they did for him? I think you know the answer."

I thought about the last time he'd been here in the café, drunk as a skunk and horny as a toad. He'd been badmouthing Grandy, a man twenty years older and six feet under.

My dear brother was old-school, he had boasted. *Now me, I'm a youngster with new ideas. I never had any complaints.*

He had claimed to have a hot date later that evening, but if that were true, I don't think it was with his wife. Could it have been Shysteen? I was about to share this theory with my partners in crime, or rather criminal inquiry, when the front door flung open wide again. A blast of wind blew through the room, icy enough to extinguish several candles. A woman strode in on an early winter gust, heels clicking sharply against the wooden floors. Even plain-clothed in trench coat and leather boots, she had "cop" written all over her.

The music on the system was, ironically, the Isley Brothers' version of "Summer Breeze." But the wind whipping through the dining room did not seem to make anyone feel fine. Nothing but cold air went blowing through the jasmine in their minds.

Detective Sergeant Emerson Jacobs was a one-woman party pooper.

. . . and a Packers Fan, to Boot!

People stopped in midsentence, eyeballing at the newcomer. Evrian King jumped up, grabbed his jacket, and bolted for the door.

Note to self: have Fanon check to see if the young man has a criminal record.

When I rushed forward to find her a seat, Detective Jacobs waved a hand in dismissal. She parked herself at the counter and swiveled around to watch the party disassemble.

People bid their goodbyes, pulled on boots and coats, and streamed out the door. A remaining few had the nerve to request to-go containers to carry home the leftovers.

"My people, my people," Penny lectured. "None of you ordered a meal you didn't get to finish. You don't doggie bag no free buffet. That's just tacky."

All the good vibrations went out of the evening. The buffet was reduced to crumbs, the tablecloth beneath it hopelessly soiled. Shysteen darted away with the floral centerpiece tucked beneath her armpit before anyone could stop her.

"Well, group," I told my staff. "This mess isn't going to clean itself."

"Actually," Detective Jacobs called out in her gruff voice.

"I'd rather you hold off on cleanup. May I please have a moment of your time?"

She posed it as a question, but I knew a command when I heard one. I put Penny and Fanon on cleanup detail then went over and stood across the counter from Jacobs.

She stared back with a stern expression.

I smiled uneasily. "To what do I owe the, um ... pleasure of this visit?"

God help me for choking on that one word. Some fibs are just hard to spit out. I was definitely headed for hell, with all the lies I'd been telling lately. Great-Aunt Essie always said that lying led to greater sins.

Drumming a finger against the countertop, Jacobs pinned me with an icy gaze. "Miss Summers, are you acquainted with a Mr. Noble McPherson?"

"Unfortunately, I am. He flounced out of here in a hissy fit not half an hour ago."

"What do you mean?" Jacobs seemed taken aback. "McPherson was here?"

"First, he was eating, drinking, and socializing like everyone else. Fanon came over to chat with him and suddenly he got all bent out of shape. Words were exchanged and he was asked to leave. I guess he didn't know Fanon was five-oh or he wouldn't have threatened to call the cops on him."

Jacobs sighed in irritation. "I'm surprised that man had the nerve to show up here. Your guy is keeping us busy, that's for sure."

"My guy? Are you talking about Fanon or Noble?"

"I meant McPherson. Why? Is Fanon your guy?"

I decided not to dignify the question. "So, Detective. What's this all about?"

She explained to me that Noble McPherson had filed a

complaint against me. According to him, I had assaulted him here in the café then threatened him with poisoned sweet potato pie.

"Lord have mercy on his naked soul," I sighed. "Just when I thought it couldn't get worse, the man takes wrongdoing to new depths."

Jacobs regarded me quizzically. "And that's not all he had to say. He also warned me to keep an eye on you as a possible suspect in the Jaspers and Dailey deaths. Is it true you were a defendant in a wrongful-death lawsuit?"

"*Were* is the operative word, Detective. This happened over a month ago and it was all a big mistake. Mattie Jaspers withdrew the lawsuit not even a week after filing it."

"McPherson says the family was pressured into dropping charges. He said money exchanged hands, something about a catering contract. Is there any truth to this, Miss Summers?"

"Let me tell you one thing about McPherson." I lifted a hand to beckon Fanon over. "As my Great-Aunt Essie used to say, *If his lips are moving, he's lying.*"

"Who's lying?" Fanon came around the counter and stood beside me. "And what are you doing here, Emmy?"

"She just stopped by for a friendly visit. Oh, and to let me know that Noble McPherson has filed a complaint against me for assault and . . . what's the other charge?"

Jacobs looked up at Fanon. "Terroristic threat, actually."

"Terroristic threat," I repeated. "Apparently I beat Noble within an inch of his life then threatened to force-feed him poisoned pie."

Jacobs glanced at Fanon with a lifted eyebrow. "And you said she wouldn't hurt a fly."

If that was her attempt at a joke, Fanon didn't seem to be amused. "I don't believe you came here to deliver a message,

Emmy. Are you here to serve a warrant? Are you going to arrest her?"

"Of course not," she retorted. "I'm investigating a citizen's complaint. The alleged incident happened back in October. Frankly, it seems suspicious that he would wait so long to report a crime then turn up at the very place he claimed he'd been attacked."

I heard the slide of soft-soled shoes across the floor and smelled the scent of Obsession. Penny suddenly appeared at my other side. I was now fully flanked by my peeps.

"I'll tell you why Noble McPherson does what he does," Penny declared. "Because he's a liar and the truth ain't in him. He's nothing but a bully, a big ol' pain in the butt . . . and a Packers fan, to boot!"

Jacobs turned to look at me. "Which still doesn't explain why he filed that complaint."

"Hold on, Detective," I ordered. "I'll show you a thing or two."

I went to get my tablet, pulled up an email thread, and pushed the screen across the counter to her. "If anyone has a complaint, then I'm the one who should be filing charges."

Jacobs scrolled through the harassing emails Noble had sent trying to buy me out.

"I've got a slew of voicemails and text messages, too. He desperately wants to buy and I'm not selling. That's why he's making those charges against me. Terroristic threat? Please! He's the one terrorizing, and now he's trying to weaponize the police to help him do it."

"Damn," Jacobs muttered under her breath. I'd never heard her cuss before. "And if Dailey hadn't died when he did, then he'd probably . . ."

"Probably what?" My ears pricked up immediately. Delbert

"Do-Right" Dailey had been under some kind of investigation. What did this have to do with Noble McPherson?

The detective promptly clammed up. "Nothing. I misspoke."

"If he ever gets this property, you know what's going to happen," Fanon explained. "He claims he wants to franchise the business but I think it's the real estate he's after."

"We'll be gone the way of the dinosaur," Penny said, "which would really, really suck."

"I guess it would," Jacobs agreed. "I hear the food here is pretty good."

I slapped my forehead. "Lord, where are my manners? Let me get you something to snack on. The main dishes and sides are pretty well demolished, but we still have a little dessert."

"What do you want to wash it down?" Penny offered. "There's orange blossom lemonade and sparkling wine. Or I could offer you some herbal hot chocolate."

"Would a cup of black coffee be too much trouble?"

"Coming right up."

Fanon held up a finger. "Make that two. I'll take mine with honey, if you have it."

"Coffee, Fanon?" I sliced a generous serving from the remaining lavender berry shortcake and slid it into place on the counter. "You never drink coffee. You always said it gave you insomnia."

"It does. But something tells me I'm going to be up way past my bedtime."

And wouldn't you know, he was right.

CHAPTER 31

Lie-dar and Lay-dar

Only the five of us remained in the café's dining room. Sergio snored like a lawnmower at Table Six, head nestled in his folded arms. I stood behind the counter with Fanon and Penny. Sergeant Jacobs sat before us, an awkward silence settling on us like dust.

Jacobs's fork speared the last crumbs of shortcake. It had been a popular dessert choice. "I didn't mean to interrupt your conversation. Carry on as you were."

"What conversation, Detective Jacobs?" I lied. "We were just straightening up."

At the rate this was going, we'd be on cleanup detail deep into the night.

Penny bumped my hip with hers. "Don't be letting her guilt-trip you. We've got nothing to hide. Right, Fanon?"

He cleared his throat in warning, grabbed the empty dessert plate, and took it over to the bussing stand. When Jacobs tilted her mug toward him, he sighed loud enough to be heard but went to get the coffeepot.

"I tell it like I smell it, Detective," Penny continued, "and something was stinking to high heaven around here this evening."

Jacobs looked around and sniffed, like the odor was in the post-party wreckage.

"You know, Savvy has that lie-dar," Penny told her.

"Really? What's that?"

"She can sense lies like a polygraph. My secret power is lay-dar. Give me a whiff and I can tell, just like Aretha sang, *who's zooming who*. I'll bet my bottom dollar that Delbert Dailey and Grandy Jaspers were bedding the same woman."

"Yeah," I agreed. "I was thinking that, too."

Penny leaned forward and stared at Jacobs. "You don't find it at all suspicious that both of them wound up dead from exactly the same causes?"

Fanon set down Jacobs's coffee with a sigh. "You're digging your own grave, Penny Lopés."

She deliberately ignored him. "Just think about it. Shysteen seemed genuinely upset about Grandy's death, and I don't think she was pretending. She's not that good of an actor. She might not have been in it for the love, but maybe for the loot. Grandy went around telling people he'd be worth millions once his lawsuit paid off.

"What lawsuit?" Jacobs asked.

"He claimed to be suing his former manager," I explained, "for songwriting credits stolen way back during his showbiz days. Maybe he expected a payday. Maybe it was just a line to reel the women in."

"And our girl Shystie was dumb enough to bite," Penny snickered. "Or greedy enough. If you look up *gold digger* in the dictionary, it's got her picture right next to it."

Jacobs looked back and forth between us. "Go ahead. Continue."

"Shysteen wasn't even married to Grandy," Fanon protested. "Unless his will says otherwise, no way she's getting a penny."

Penny didn't snap her fingers like normal people did. She probably learned the trick from Sergio. Flicking her right hand sharply, she clacked index and middle fingers together. Jacobs flinched at the sudden sound. It was like light-gauge gunfire.

"That's exactly why I don't think she would have killed him," Penny insisted. "If anything, she'd wait until they were married to bump him off. When Grandy died Shysteen didn't even get condolences. Maybe when that baby's born she can sue on the kid's behalf."

Fanon faked a big yawn. "Let's call it an evening. We all have work in the morning."

Jacobs held up a nail-bitten hand. "Not so fast, Fanon. I want to hear this."

"So, here's the part I don't get," Penny went on. "Shysteen admitted Grandy came to see her two hours after the anniversary party, begging to spend the night. They talked for half an hour, had harsh words, and she put him out. She says they weren't intimate that night, so why would he be taking Viagra? I asked her if she knew where Grandy slept that night. *Probably in his car,* she said. *It was parked out front of my building until early the next morning.*"

"He turned up here twenty minutes to eight," I remembered. "So Shysteen could have handled Grandy's drinks or tampered with his food anytime the night before. In fact, I saw her take him and Mattie some sweet potato pie when the party was still going on. And I did find that champagne cork in his car with a puncture mark in the middle."

"That's evidence," Jacob said sharply, "that you should have shared with the police."

"You made it clear you weren't investigating Grandy's death. I thought you wouldn't be interested."

She held out her hand to me. "I certainly am."

"You don't think I have it on me now, do you? I'll turn it over as soon as I put my hands on it."

Jacobs nodded grimly. "Please see that you do."

"So the gist of it," Penny summed up, "is Shysteen had the means, but probably not the motive. I could see her wilding out in a fit of jealous rage. But poisoning is more of a premeditated act. Wouldn't you say so, Detective?"

Jacobs shrugged and sipped coffee, her gray eyes watching us above the mug.

"Don't forget that bartender from Grandy's anniversary party," I added.

Although he'd been trying to shut us up, Fanon raised an inquiring eyebrow. "Evrian King. What about him?"

"He was assigned to another table," Penny explained. "They didn't come in together so I'm not sure why he went to sit with Shysteen. At first, they didn't have much to say to each other. Evrian was looking real close when Shysteen ran up to get her prize tickets."

"He couldn't help himself," Fanon retorted. "She was jiggling like jelly."

Hm. So he had been looking.

"Evrian was excited as a bushelful of clams," Penny added. "He seemed to think he'd get to be Shysteen's plus-one, though she didn't seem on board with it."

I chuckled at the memory. "She was probably hoping Fanon would be her date."

"Me? I don't know that little girl," he protested. "She's got to be what? Around Malik's age."

"At least a decade younger," I teased. "She obviously likes her menfolk on the geezerly side."

"Yeah, Savvy. I got your geezer."

Jacobs blinked and shook her head. She seemed to be having

trouble following our code-switching between Standard and Black English.

"Evrian has a physique on him but he's nobody's Neil deGrasse Tyson," Penny observed. "If he and Shysteen have something going on, they're a matched set. Dumb and dumber. I'd be worried about any kids coming out of that union."

"Do you think Evrian could have killed Grandy?" I asked. "He didn't handle his food at the anniversary party, but he definitely had access to everybody's liquor."

"And get this," Penny announced. "Oh, you're going to love it! When I asked what he thought about two old men dying from a Viagra overdose, he made the stupidest remark on record. *Viagra? Man, that's the greatest pill ever!*"

So Evrian was no stranger to erectile dysfunction meds. Interesting.

Penny continued her report. "When Shysteen went up to collect her winnings, I had a chance to ask Evrian what he thought of her. He took his sweet time looking her up and down."

"Then what happened?" I demanded when Penny paused for dramatic effect.

"*Aw, she thick,* is exactly what the genius told me. *She got that* badonkadonk *booty and them big ol' bresses.* Please don't ask me to translate *badonkadonk,* Detective. And yes, he pronounced breasts in two separate syllables. Not the most eloquent brother on the block. In fact, you couldn't use the words *articulate* and *Evrian* in the same sentence."

"He made a pass at a pregnant woman?" Jacobs was aghast. "What a scumbag!"

"I don't know about a pass but he sure seemed interested. Then Evrian said something that didn't make much sense. *She working that DNA, working it hard. I like that in a female.*

Then he looked kind of guilty and mumbled, *I ain't mean nothing by it.*"

"DNA?" Jacobs mused. "Is it one of those urban expressions, something men say when they like how you look? Working that DNA, as in her genetic traits are lining up nicely."

"Well, maybe." Penny seemed skeptical. "If so, it's an expression I never heard before. I asked Evrian King one last question. *Do you think Grandy and Delbert were deliberately killed?* He gave an idiotic grin and told me, *everyone knows it's her.*"

We looked down at Penny's index finger. It was pointed straight at me.

"So that's the lowdown on Shysteen and Evrian. *Lowdown* being the operative term. It's been real, but I'm about to turn into a pumpkin before your very eyes. Let me get our coats."

While she did, Fanon went over to rouse Sergio from his sleeping position at Table Six.

"Penny Porter Lopés has left the building," she called on her way out the door.

CHAPTER 32

Drawing-Room Detective

We hung our heads like juvenile delinquents in the principal's office. With hands primly folded on the counter, Emerson Jacobs looked back and forth between us.

"Anyway," I tried to change the subject. "What should I do about this complaint McPherson filed against me?"

"Those charges he filed seem frivolous. They probably won't stick. But as far as this other matter." She pointed toward my tablet. "I'd get myself a lawyer."

"Anything else, Emmy?" Fanon asked. "We've had a busy evening."

That was Fanon's diplomatic way of saying, *I want to go home and get some sleep.* Jacobs ignored the hint. Her skinny little finger went to tapping on the countertop.

"When I walked up to your door I noticed a sign," she said. *"Closed for a private event."*

"We're always closed on Mondays," I informed her. "I just didn't want anyone walking in off the street."

Jacobs looked down at her raggedy nails like they were a snack. I rolled my eyes and jerked my head in her direction. I didn't have to say it for Fanon to see it. *In off the street like this one here.*

Tap, tap, tap went the finger on the counter. A beat of silence followed before Jacobs continued. "So . . . just what kind of private party did I walk in on?"

The two of us exchanged nervous glances. It was official now. We'd been busted.

"You once asked me if I liked mystery movies," I explained. "To tell the truth, I don't."

"Then you're a *CSI* fan," Jacobs guessed. "You watch a lot of *Law & Order*."

"No, not really."

Fanon just had to drop his two cents in. "Murder mysteries, Emmy. She reads them by the truckload."

"This isn't drawing-room detecting," I objected. "It's a technique that's been tried and proven over generations. My Great-Aunt Essie knew from personal experience. I've learned it myself from running a café. You do your best listening at mealtimes because that's when people do their talking. That insight comes from centuries of servitude, not Agatha Christie novels."

Jacobs turned to me and clucked her teeth impatiently. "What does that even mean? Explain yourself, Ms. Summers."

Fanon shook his head at me. He made a sawing motion across his neck. *Don't go there.*

"You're right, Detective," I conceded. "It's drawing-room detecting, just like you said."

Jacobs frowned in irritation. "Crimes are solved by police work, not fiction and fantasy. I'm surprised you went along with this, Fanon."

"It was all my idea all along," I insisted. "Fanon had nothing to do with it. He just happened to stop by this evening."

"I don't need you to cover for me, Savvy. Emmy is my colleague, not my commanding officer." He turned to Jacobs.

"Two men have died under suspicious circumstances, and nothing so far has been done. Savvy's become a bit frustrated and I have a few concerns myself."

"Every suspicious death is not a homicide. You know that as well as I do, Fanon. The death investigation is closed on Delbert Dailey. We never had one on the other gentleman."

"And frankly, that worries me," he admitted. "We wanted to see what we could find so we invited a few people over for dinner. What's the problem?"

"You interrogated them. Conducted an investigation without authorization."

"We didn't have to interrogate them," I said defensively. "We treated them to a free dinner, a few cocktails, the chance to win a nice prize. Some mellow music and relaxing ambiance would have even you singing like a bird, Detective."

Jacobs smirked. "Now there's an idea. Maybe we should start serving champagne in the interrogation room."

"So, smacking the perps around with a rubber hose. How's that working out for you?"

"Now, Savvy," Fanon scolded. "That was uncalled for."

"You guys could learn from our technique," I stubbornly insisted. "It worked, Fanon. You know it did."

"So, other people were questioned?" Jacobs wondered. "What did they have to say?"

"You really want to know?"

"I asked you, didn't I?"

It was beginning to seem like we were the criminals here, two piteous perps found guilty until proven innocent. I wondered if Fanon was feeling the same way.

You're accused of hosting a free buffet and raffle. Hands in the air and up against the wall. You have the right to tell us anything and everything you overheard.

I took a deep breath. "Okay, Detective Jacobs. I had my smartphone in the pocket of my apron and a wireless microphone clipped onto my bra strap. I didn't want to trust anything to memory."

"It's not illegal to record your own conversation," Jacobs said. "Illinois is a one-party consent state."

"Yes, I know that. What I didn't want was to blow my cover and make it obvious I was snooping. I just hoped that the target in my sights was relaxed and lubricated. Winnie Mae Welbon, by the way, is Grandy's youngest child."

"Did she get along with her father?" Jacobs asked.

"Like Biggie and Tupac. Kanye and the rest of the world. You do know who they are?"

"Don't be cute, Miss Summers."

Though they had been dancing awfully slow, Winnie Mae was flushed and breathless with exertion. Henry Lee whipped out a handkerchief from his breast pocket and dabbed the sweat from his ladylove's brow.

"Will you look at that," I teased. "The last of the old-fashioned gentlemen."

Henry doffed an imaginary cap. "Why, thank you kindly, Miss Savvy."

"When you got yourself a lady," Winnie boasted, "you know how to treat one. Right, Henry?"

"You're right about that one, baby."

I hesitated for a beat, trying to think of how to approach Winnie Mae. Luckily, she gave me the opening I was looking for.

"Too bad Mama didn't feel like coming." She glanced around the room. "She likes fancy parties like this."

"And if Grandy was still around, the two of them would have been slow dancing, just like you and Henry Lee."

"Have you met my father?" Winnie frowned and shook her head. "Daddy didn't have a romantic bone in his body. He would have dumped Mama in a corner and gone limping off to mack on some other female."

Since I'd seen the man in action, I could hardly disagree.

"I know he was a flirt, but I believe he really loved your mother."

"Oh, he was fond of Mama in his way. He just didn't treat her right. Besides that, Daddy's precious sons could do no wrong. But me, the only daughter he had in the world? That's a whole 'nother story."

"Now, baby," Henry murmured. "Don't get yourself worked up."

"You know it's true, Henry Lee. Me and my daddy were oil and water. We always clashed, back from the time I was a little bitty girl. I remember standing in the front room practicing my middle school graduation song. It was 'Optimistic,' by Sounds of Blackness, and I had a solo. Daddy came in the room and stood there frowning at me."

"Don't do it," Henry soothed, rubbing her arm. "You'll fool around, make yourself cry."

It was too late. Fat tears welled in Winnie's eyes and rolled down her cheeks. She grabbed my hand and squeezed it. "You'd have never done your flesh and blood the way my Daddy did me. I know you wouldn't, Miss Savvy."

"What way?" I wondered. All kinds of horrible thoughts flooded my mind, making me wonder what kind of monster Grandy really was. "What did your daddy do to you?"

Winnie Mae was beyond speaking at this point. She buried her face in her husband's chest, sobbing like her heart was broken.

"She gets like this sometimes, Miss Savvy. Grandy dying like he did, it brings up old feelings."

"Oh, no," I whispered. "Please don't tell me that Grandy . . ."

People turned to stare when Winnie raised her tearstained face and bellowed. "*Girl, you can't carry a tune in a tin bucket. That's just what he said to me. You must not be no child of mine.*"

In the face of Winnie's devastation, I was careful not to show my relief. "I'm sure he didn't mean anything by it. It's that old-school child-rearing our people carried up from the countryside."

"Tough love," Henry agreed. "I know I used to get it."

"Me, too," I told them. "I wasn't a bad kid but I was a nosy one. *Always got your nose in grown folks' business,* my mother used to complain."

Winnie Mae sniffled, wiping her tears. "Did she, now, Miss Savvy?"

I remembered my mother's soft southern accent, which could deliver the most devastating blows. "*I don't know where you come from, Sapphire Slidell, but I suspect you are the devil's child. If you don't straighten up your fast little tail, you'll be going down there to live with him.*"

Winnie grabbed her husband's handkerchief and blew her nose with it. The waterworks seemed to have dried up.

I smiled ruefully. "I really used to wonder if the devil was my real daddy."

Winnie Mae managed a dry chuckle. "No, you didn't, either."

"Sometimes I did. I know my mother loved me, though sometimes she had a funny way of showing it."

"Old school," Henry repeated. "Good thing we don't raise the kids like that nowadays."

"A to the men!" The feisty side of Winnie Mae resurfaced. Smokey Robinson's "Cruisin'" started on the sound system.

"You gonna have to excuse us, Miss Savvy. This is my sho 'nuff jam."

She stood and grabbed her husband's hand. Henry followed her dutifully across the floor. I watched them shuffling around their square yard of dance space. His arms were wrapped protectively around her shoulders, her face snuggled contentedly against his chest.

"And you know," I told Fanon and Jacobs. "I have a bone to pick with Penny about that nickname. Henry isn't henpecked at all. He's water to Winnie's fire, earth to her air."

"What do you mean by that?" Jacobs asked.

"He knows how to handle the live wire he married."

"And what's your reading of Winnie?" Fanon asked. "Did she strike you as a suspect?"

"Winnie Mae and her father had their differences, but is family resentment a motive for murder? Winnie says she didn't know Dailey and I'm convinced those deaths are connected."

Jacobs turned to Fanon. "What do you have to say for yourself, old partner?"

My ex-husband squirmed under her chilly gaze. Maybe it was the prospect of 'fessing up to off-the-books police work.

"Unlike Penny and Savvy, I didn't compile a dossier on my group of . . ." He paused, fishing for a word.

"Suspects?" I asked.

"Let's call them persons of interest, shall we?"

Sergeant Jacobs nodded. "That works for me."

CHAPTER 33

Report from Table Five

Fanon gave a fulsome sigh. "So first, here's my disclaimer. My report won't be quite so detailed as Penny's and Savvy's. For one thing, the ladies are acquainted with these people and this was my first time meeting most of them. For another, I did make something of a blunder."

"That's hard for me to believe." Jacobs's smooth brow pleated in a frown. "What kind of blunder could that be?"

Fanon held up a cautionary hand. "Just hear me out, okay? I wasn't about to tell anyone I was an off-duty cop. I thought I'd keep my history with Savvy on the down-low, too. People might speak more freely if they saw me as just another member of the waitstaff."

Jacobs eyes widened. "You were working as a server?"

"Just bringing folks their drinks. People got up and helped themselves to the buffet. I'll have to admit, I let Annabelle Beasley get to me. She's as irritating as a tick and as phony as a three-dollar bill."

Detective Jacobs frowned. "Who's Annabelle Beasley?"

I rolled my eyes. "She runs a bakery and imagines herself my rival."

"Oh, I see. A friend of yours."

I couldn't help making a face. "Didn't you hear what I just said? It's like I'm talking to myself."

Fanon tried to defuse the sudden tension. "Annabelle's envy of Savvy was pretty obvious. She talked about how nice a gathering this was but every compliment had a sharp edge. And she couldn't pronounce Sapphire to save her life. The woman kept calling her *Safflower*."

That one seemed to tickle Jacobs's flimsy funny bone. "Safflower Summers. That's rich."

"As soon as I showed her to Table Five, Annabelle Beasley started gossiping about Savvy and her 'sweet potato crimes.'" Then she went after the fancy buffet, though it didn't stop her from eating it. According to her, it was 'putting on airs.'"

Fanon was one of those Black folks who visibly blushed when he was embarrassed. "Annabelle got a little bent out of shape when she found out we used to be married."

"Why would that upset her?" Sergeant Jacobs asked.

"I guess she'd been doing a little lightweight flirting."

"I knew Annabelle would be trying to mack," I joked, patting Jacobs's hand. "I'm sure it didn't sit well when she found out she was trying to sop up my sloppy seconds."

Lord have mercy on her naked soul! You would have thought I had slapped her. Jacobs flinched at my touch, glancing down at the place where my hand had grazed her. She didn't even ask me to define the term "mack." Maybe the detective had been trying to do a little macking and sopping herself.

"You shouldn't have let that woman get you rattled like that," Jacobs admonished, just like I hadn't rattled her. "I guess it's hard to remain detached when it involves a member of your own family. Or former family."

"Yeah, I know. You don't have to rub it in," Fanon said

evenly. "And Savvy will always be family. We have a son and grandson together."

He went on with his report.

"Noble McPherson was seated near Annabelle, so he heard everything we'd said. He'd been ordering me around all evening. *If I might interrupt your socializing, bro-ham, could I trouble you to refill my champagne? And bring it to me in a fresh glass.* Sitting up there in his Packers gear with a great big cheese head on top, getting all snooty with me."

Noble told him he didn't realize I had an ex-husband, but maybe Fanon could talk some sense into "that hardheaded woman." Yes, that's what he called me. And then launched into his favorite rant about me holding up progress on a lucrative business prospect.

"Annabelle had both ears cocked, a sly little smirk on her face," Fanon remembered. *"You want me to have a word with her, mister? We're very close, you know."*

"Of course, that woman had no intention of helping me!" I fumed. "She wanted McPherson to give her something to nibble and regurgitate later."

"My goodness," Jacobs blinked. "You make her sound like a dairy cow."

Fanon had taken Noble aside and explained that I liked to keep my business private. Not only that, but maybe he should just take "no" for an answer. Noble didn't take kindly to his suggestion. He grumbled, *I don't see how it's any business of yours,* just like he hadn't tried to get Fanon to talk some sense into *that hardheaded woman.*

"I'd never met this man before but I knew he was a snake after Savvy asked me to look into his business dealings. His investment group already owns options on all the vacant land on this half-block. Savvy and another apartment building owner are the last holdouts. So now he's pulling strings to have both properties condemned."

At some point Jacobs fished out a tablet from her purse. Her fingers danced across the screen as she took notes.

"Under what concept is he going for condemnation?" She glanced around the café. "It can't possibly be substandard conditions. I don't know about the other building but this place has obviously been kept up."

No one but my deceased husband Francis had actually known the truth. Against the advice of my financial advisor I'd cashed out my IRA when I retired from CPS. I had sunk most of it into buying and rehabbing the building. The rest went toward furnishing and equipping the café.

"It's eminent domain," Fanon explained. "They had an all-cash contract for a quick closing on the apartment building down the street. There's some kind of mechanic's lien on the property so the closing was delayed. If not for that, he'd own the place by now."

"So, he's gotten his hands on this entire half-block?" I asked. "Everything except these last two properties?"

"I haven't researched all the vacant lots but if they're tax delinquent he'll have to wait two years before he can claim the property. Since you're not rolling with his program, it's easier for him to go eminent domain, seize all the properties including yours, get a judge to assign fair value, and pay everybody off in one fell swoop."

"But why?" I wondered. "What's he going to do with half a city block?"

Jacobs answered for him. "A strip mall, university expansion, condo development. You're on a busy thoroughfare, just half a mile south of Hyde Park. Woodlawn is very up and coming these days. You're sitting on a valuable piece of property here."

"Much too valuable for a simple little soul food café," Fanon added. "In the eyes of Noble McPherson and his people. His limited liability corporation seems to be a dummy company. The true identity of his partners hasn't yet come to light."

I took a deep breath. "McPherson and the outfit he's working with just want to get their hands on my building. All that stuff about franchising my name, that was just a pretense."

Fanon got up to empty the last of the coffeepot into his and Jacobs's cups. It was the most I'd ever seen him drink in all the time I'd known him.

"It's some kind of strategy to buy you off cheap. If you knew a big development was coming down the pike, you'd be in a better position to negotiate."

Emerson Jacobs turned to me with a condescending eye. "Let me explain the concept of eminent domain. The government seizes a property and establishes a fair price for it. Then it can be exploited for the greater public good. Without it we wouldn't have many of our public works—our roads, parks, public libraries."

"Thanks for the white-splanation," I scoffed. "What are people's homes and small shops when you can build a strip mall full of payday loan stores and fast-food joints? Or maybe another big box store to drive all the mom-and-pop shops out of business."

Detective Jacobs turned off the screen on her iPad. "I think we're done here."

Fanon threw her a careful glance. "So here's the way I see it. An old guy overdoses on Viagra and nobody cares. Then some corporate hustler tightens the screws on a small business owner and a hack politician also winds up dead. This is way too close for coincidence."

"If there's anything to this," Jacobs answered carefully, "and I'm not saying there is, I wouldn't be at liberty to discuss it. I can only tell you this. Politics and corporate greed make a deadly cocktail. You guys have blundered into a high-stakes poker game. It might be time to fold your hand, cut your losses, and call it a day."

"Leave well enough alone, huh? You're sounding exactly like Delbert Dailey."

"Bad guys can sometimes give good advice." Jacobs stood, smoothing down her skirt and pulling on her coat. "You don't want any bombs going off prematurely. It just might blow up in somebody's face."

It sounded like an ominous warning. Or maybe more like a threat.

CHAPTER 34

The Mountain to Mohammed

The drive up north was pleasant this Monday afternoon in mid-December. No need to race up the Edens in rush hour traffic, like that Thanksgiving Eve drive to the Lake County Courthouse a month ago. Now I had time to take the scenic route.

I turned off North Lake Shore Drive and joined Sheridan Road at Hollywood Avenue, winding through Rogers Park and past the Calvary Cemetery that separated Evanston from Chicago.

I had entered the North Shore, where some of the most affluent communities in the nation hugged Lake Michigan's western shoreline. It was the same lake I splashed in most summers at 63rd Street or the beach at South Shore Cultural Center. But oh, what a difference the miles made.

The drifting snow flurries and winding road forced me to move at a leisurely pace. I saw details of the passing landscape that I would have missed at faster speeds.

I passed the sprawling Northwestern University campus with its mix of nineteenth-century and modern architecture. A few miles up the road I came upon the towering Bahá'í House of Worship with its latticed white stonework and glittering dome. On a route that veered away then turned back toward the lake, sprawling mansions sat back from the road on luxurious estates that could have held several city blocks. Behind tall iron gates were park-like grounds with bare-branched trees and tall evergreens dusted in white.

As I drove through Wilmette and past Winnetka the scenery changed from wealthy residential and business districts to wooded groves, shallow ravines, and steep shoreline bluffs. The meandering ride cleared my mind and strengthened my resolve for the mission ahead.

Sergeant Jacobs had once again ordered me to back off. She even warned that failing to do so might have dangerous consequences. Yet there seemed no sign that the police were making any headway in the strikingly similar deaths of two men. No one had been arrested, no one named, no one had been charged. Had anyone even been questioned? I had my doubts.

Not only were the deaths of Granderson Jaspers and Delbert Dailey still unresolved, my business situation remained precarious. We were still limping along on poor turnout and limited income. I didn't know how much longer I could hold out. Scrooge McPherson and his coterie of cronies could be pulling strings that very moment to condemn my entire stretch of city block and close my business in time for Christmas.

Detective Jacobs said I had stumbled into a high-stakes poker game. Yet I'd been shuffling through the deck and two wild cards kept turning up. If I told Jacobs I was still mulling over a remark I overheard at a funeral two months ago, what would she have to say? Probably nothing.

As I considered the suspects, those who'd been hiding at the bottom were shifting to the top of the deck. I'd discovered next to nothing about them, which made them seem even more suspicious.

There was bartender Evrian King, whom I had deemed the Jack of Spades. Instead of a fool's cap and harlequin suit, I imagined the Joker in dentures and a shiny black toupee.

Of those who'd been invited to the playoff raffle, Mattie Jaspers and Tuchman Pfeiffer were the only no-shows. Mattie, I had seen on Thanksgiving Day. Other than that abortive Thanksgiving's Eve phone call, Tuck, on the other hand, was scarcer than hen's teeth. He hadn't responded to the multiple messages I'd left by text and voicemail. It didn't help that he lived twenty-five miles beyond Chicago Police Department jurisdiction. Would anyone take the effort to drive up there and question him? I didn't think so.

I mulled over the remarks that had sent me out in search of Grandy's former music manager. *The man had a vocal talent you can't deny, but he must have been smoking funny cigarettes. We both know who wrote those songs and it certainly wasn't Grandy.*

And then there was his insistence that he and the deceased were dear old friends, when Grandy had unceremoniously kicked him out of the fiftieth-anniversary celebration.

Why had Tuck shown up to Grandy's anniversary party and funeral in the first place when it seemed obvious the man detested him? Why was Grandy suing Tuck for copyright infringement? And why had he charged him with harassing his wife and tried to have a protective order taken out against him? All these questions went begging for an answer.

Mohammed wouldn't come to the mountain, so I was bringing the mountain to Mohammed. I would use the element of surprise in my favor, though I didn't know whether I'd be welcomed or turned away. I wasn't even sure I'd find him at home, but I was prepared for whatever surprises or disappointments the day might bring.

In Glencoe I turned away from the lakefront and drove a half mile inland. The GPS led me to an address on tree-lined Elder Court. Unlike some of the mini-mansions I passed along the way, this was a sprawling but modest split-level with a brick and frame facade. Yet compared to homes in my corner of Woodlawn, Tuchman Pfeiffer's home was palatial.

I pulled into the driveway and parked between a late-model Prius and dilapidated Cherokee. This was good news so far. At least someone was at home. I paused for a moment with the driver's-side door ajar. A dog was barking somewhere in the distance. I feared it might emerge and come bounding up before I made it to the front door.

When I saw the coast was clear I rang the doorbell, waiting for Tuck to answer. Preparing to explain my unexpected presence, I was therefore surprised when a handsome young man opened the door.

"Happy Hanukkah to you, Miss Savvy." He grinned. This was a smile I was quite familiar with. The boy had a mouthful of metal. I was so gobsmacked to be greeted by Grandy's grandson, it took me a beat to respond.

"Why, thank you, Parker. Happy Hanukkah to you, too."

"Grammy didn't say you were coming." He stepped aside and held the door open wide. "Come on in. We're all in the music room."

The "we" were Tuchman Pfeiffer with a yarmulke perched atop his toupee and two elderly women who were smaller, female versions of him. Another young woman was a trim beige beauty who could have been modeling the glass of wine she held. She looked rather like a young Tyra Banks.

If anyone seemed surprised to see me, it was "Grammy." Mattie Jaspers sat in a wingback chair holding a glass of wine.

Elegant in pearls and burgundy silk, she fixed me with a penetrating stare.

"Look who's here, Grammy," the young man announced. "It's . . ."

"Yes, Parker. I can see who it is. Afternoon, Miss Savvy."

"Afternoon yourself, Miss Mattie," I replied awkwardly. "And Happy Hanukkah, one and all."

"Well, look who the cat dragged in." Tuck grinned, showing off his ill-fitting dentures. He rushed over to pump my hand. "It's Miss Sweet Potato Pie."

"Sapphire Summers, actually. Call me Savvy."

He held up an imaginary mic and crooned into it off-key the lyrics to Stevie Nicks's "Bombay Sapphires." "I know who you are. We're practically old buddies. You catered the Granderson Jaspers funeral. Good old Grandy, may he rest in peace, not pieces. He's singing in the heavenly choir."

Parker burst into sudden song, his voice a much more melodious treat after hearing Tuck's. "When I die/Hallelujah, by and by/I'll fly away . . ."

Tuck broke into a stiff-legged holy dance. "Praise the Lord, sho 'nuff."

"Now, Tuck," Mattie scolded from across the room. "Don't blaspheme the Lord on Hanukkah."

Tuck halted his spastic movements, adjusting the yarmulke-topped toupee that had slid to one side. "That's my workout for the week."

If only I had realized that Tuck was Jewish, I'd have known he'd be keeping the holiday.

"This wine isn't kosher, Brother," one of the ladies complained in a quavery, peevish voice. She gulped it down anyway.

"Chloe, you know better." The other older woman reached

over and smacked her wrist. "It's bad manners to drink before the toast."

"What would you say to a Hanukkah toast?" Tuck asked. "I hope you like prosecco, the poor man's champagne."

I nodded my assent, though the surroundings I stood in seemed anything but poor. Tuck beckoned the young beauty seated on the love seat next to Parker. "Lani, would you do the honors?"

The supermodel lookalike nodded graciously. Her voice was as manicured as her sculptured nails. "Anything else you need, Mr. Pfeiffer?"

"Another place at the dining table. After the toast, of course." Tuck raised his glass. "*L'chayim,* to life. I ask not for a lighter burden but for broader shoulders, the better to carry my check to the bank."

∽

I bided my time through the holiday toast, the prosecco and the prayers, the first candle lit on the menorah.

Although I tried to decline the invitation, the taller, sturdier of the women bullied me into staying. She quoted a text from the Torah. "As Leviticus 19:34 tells us: *the stranger that dwells with you shall be to you as the home-born among you, and you shall love him as yourself.*"

Tuck led us into a formal dining room where I worked my way through a heavy luncheon of artichoke latkes and sour cream, a well-seasoned brisket of beef, kugel noodles, and a golden challah shaped into a Star of David.

Tuck was proud to tell everyone around the table he'd prepared the meal "with my own little lily-white hands." The only dishes not made from scratch were the challah bread and dessert pastries from a kosher bakery in Highland Park.

"Brother made the brisket?" Chloe looked around in confusion. She seemed dazed and slightly confused. "I thought his Colored girlfriend cooked it."

"For shame," Edith shouted. The elder sister was sprightly but seemed hard of hearing. "You're being such a not-nice racist."

Chloe blinked behind her thick-lensed glasses. "But Colored people cook really good. The nursing home kitchen is full of them."

Tuck blushed a fiery red and turned to Mattie, murmuring. "Sorry, Miss Matt. Chloe's Old Timer's seems to be acting up."

Mattie seemed unruffled. Pointedly ignoring Tuck's apology, she passed Chloe the platter of latkes.

"That's nice of you to say, Miss Chloe. But I'm no kind of chef. Miss Savvy's the real professional." She turned and looked me in the eye. "Her sweet potato pie is to die for."

CHAPTER 35

Mattie Walked Out on a Frozen Night

I swallowed my patience, along with the coffee and cream. A dessert assortment of rugelach, mini doughnuts, and cookies were served from platters on a sideboard.

We were back in the music room again. We sat facing a massive picture window, looking out across a snow-covered ravine. I wondered how sunset would look filtering through the denuded trees. The scenery here was so different from Chicago's flat, featureless landscape.

"Oh, look at the deer!" Lani exclaimed as a doe and fawn appeared at the crest of the ridge. They edged cautiously toward the house, sniffing at snow-covered hedges. "Aren't they cute?"

"There's nothing cute about those creatures," Tuck huffed. "They gobbled my Black Beauties, thorns and all."

"Mother planted that rosebush when I was nine," Chloe suddenly recalled. "The year after Father came back from Korea."

"Betty had Black Beauties in her wedding bouquet, too," Edith added. "Remember that?"

Chloe frowned. "Who's Betty?"

"How can you forget Betty Bloomberg, your best friend

since grade school? Brother married her in 1959, right here in the music room."

"I miss my little Betty Boop," Tuck murmured, serious for once.

I mulled over the quality of memory, its pains and pleasures as delicate as the scent of faded flowers. A wife had died and the roses were gone but another Black Beauty sat in an armchair across the room, toying with her pearls and watching me closely.

With its comfortable seating and soft lighting, the music room held low bookshelves, polished brass bowls full of flowers, thick Persian carpets, and a baby grand piano. Framed vintage record albums adorned the farthest wall.

Tuck tickled the ivories as Parker crooned a holiday medley—"Dreidl," "Hanukkah, Oh Hanukkah," and "Light One Candle." How had a college kid from the South Side learned those kinds of songs?

"Put on your yarmulke/It's time for Hanukkah . . ." Going again for comic relief, Tuck bleated the lyrics of Adam Sandler's "The Chanukah Song." Then he tried an ad-lib, MC-style. How did Tuck not know how painfully corny his shtick was?

I moved for a closer look at the artists Tuck had managed over the years. Disco tuxes with sequined lapels had apparently been the cat's meow back in the seventies. Several of the LP covers featured extravagantly outfitted younger versions of James Blumenthal, who quit the group in the eighties at the height of their popularity; Junebug Clemons and Theobald James, who'd died a few years back; and Grandy Jaspers who'd recently gone to join the other two.

The single lit candle was flickering low, the Hanukkah

luncheon nearly over. Questions crowded my head, the ones I had come with and the new ones taking shape.

What was up with this long-standing feud between Tuck and Grandy? Could a wealthy North Shore resident have actually written those hardscrabble Southern gospel hits? Or was it true, as Grandy had charged, that Tuck had stolen his songwriting credits?

It wouldn't be the first time such a thing had happened. Little Richard, Muddy Waters, Chuck Berry, Marvin Gaye. The list of Black musicians ripped off by unscrupulous record companies, handlers, and even fellow musicians was long and tattered. Would Grandy have eventually prevailed had he lived to see his day in court? And since he hadn't, would his survivors carry on the fight?

Had Tuck committed murder to protect his wealth and reputation? Why had Grandy accused the man of harassing his wife and filed for a protective order the week before he died? Could Mattie still be in some kind of danger? And if so, why was she nibbling pumpkin spice doughnuts in the culprit's own music room?

What was a Missionary Baptist like Mattie Jaspers, along with her grandson and his dazzling, live-in girlfriend—Parker wasn't fooling anybody with that "roommate" business—doing at a Hanukkah dinner? And why were they celebrating with Grandy's nemesis and his elderly sisters?

Was Tuck wining and dining them in an effort to talk them out of pursuing the copyright infringement lawsuit Grandy never got around to filing? Might he have also colluded with a certain deceased alderman? If Tuck murdered Grandy, had he also killed Delbert Dailey? And why would he have done so?

However much he had skirted the law in some of his political dealings, Dailey was also a licensed attorney. Maybe Noble had some help in convincing Mattie to file that frivolous lawsuit against me when Grandy died back in October. Did she also consult Delbert about the legal case against Pfeiffer? Had this somehow led to his death?

What was this unexpected connection between Mattie and Tuck? Was romantic rivalry behind her husband's demise? Did the two of them collaborate to commit double murder? Questions, so many questions.

I could practically hear Penny scolding me. "That's an awful lot of mights and maybes."

If I could have ten minutes alone with Tuchman Pfeiffer then *maybe* I *might* get some answers.

The opportunity soon presented itself. Tuck began clearing the dessert dishes.

"Don't anyone move. I'm just taking a few things out to the kitchen."

Ignoring his instructions, I gathered up coffee cups and saucers, carried them in after him, and began loading the dishwasher.

"Don't mess up your manicure now, Savvy."

"I'm more than happy to help with cleanup," I said. "I don't often get to enjoy other people's cooking."

"And I don't often cook for professional chefs. I hope it wasn't slop."

"Of course not. Your late wife was lucky to have you in the kitchen."

Scraping dishes at the kitchen sink, Tuck gave a low chuckle. "Oh, I was second cook at best. My wife was the super chef around here. She could've been a restaurateur, just like you. Betty Boop's Kitchen—all kosher, all the time."

"Did your children enjoy her cooking, too?"

Tuck paused at his task, shaking his head. "My wife and I were childless."

"Oh, I'm sorry," I blurted. "I didn't mean to . . ."

"You didn't mean to what?" Mattie interrupted, entering the kitchen.

"Miss Summers asked if I had any children."

"She did?" Mattie placed hands on her shapely hips, looking back and forth between us. She obviously knew the answer to that question. "Tuck, it's time for me to get going."

"So soon, Matt?"

"It's late and there's a long drive ahead."

Oh, good, I thought. *I'll have some uninterrupted time with Tuck.*

"It was good seeing you, Mattie," I told her. "Let's catch up sometime soon."

Mattie lifted an arched eyebrow. "We can catch up right now. Parker and Lani want to stop off on the North Side for some kind of hip-hop show. Me, I'm not into all that boomp-de-boomp. I'll ride back to the city with you, if that's all right."

So much for getting Tuck alone to pump him for information.

"I don't suppose one of Tuck's sisters . . . ?" I stopped, realizing how desperate I sounded. "It's just that I promised to help with the dishes."

"The ladies have already said their goodbyes," Mattie explained. "Edith doesn't live anywhere near our side of the city. She's taking Chloe back to her nursing home then heading home to Skokie. So, it looks like it's me and you, Miss Savvy. Ready to roll?"

"Ready when you are, Mattie." What else could I say?

It could've just been my imagination, but as Tuck helped us

into our coats at the front door I thought I saw a meaningful glance pass between the two of them. Tuck pecked my cheek then leaned toward Mattie. She ducked her head and deftly slid away from his kiss.

"So long, Tuck." She waved him a breezy goodbye. "Catch you later."

"Mattie walked out on a frozen night," Tuck's cracked voice serenaded us out the door. He switched tunes as we walked toward the car. *"It's like Bombay Sapphires/Hey, I can take you higher."*

"Lord, help us." I winced. "What is that?"

"I guess it's supposed to be singing."

Secrets on the Edens

I decided to head back on Highway 41. The December days were growing steadily shorter. With so many twists and turns on Sheridan Road, I didn't relish the prospect of driving it after dark.

"That Tuck sure is a funny guy. He could've been a stand-up comic."

I had just thrown out my third conversational gambit, but Mattie Jaspers wasn't biting. She all but ignored me, responding to my chatter in grunts and monosyllables. She was clearly upset and finally let me know why.

"You know, I figured you for a better class of woman."

"I beg your pardon?"

"Crashing in on somebody else's party. That's not like you, Miss Savvy."

"I didn't know a party was going on. I apologize for barging in."

"Umph. Maybe it *is* like you, after all." Mattie resettled herself in the passenger seat as we merged onto I-90. "You do have a way of just showing up at holidays. That's a long drive and a lot of trouble just to track me down."

"I wasn't trying to track you down. It was Tuchman I came to see."

"Tuck?" Mattie's voice rose half an octave. "What on earth would you want with Tuck?"

Did I detect jealousy in that flash of side-eye?

"Mattie," I said as gently as possible. "Is there something you want to tell me?"

"This is a pure-dee mess." She clicked her tongue in exasperation, gesturing toward the clogged traffic on the Edens Expressway. "They got rush hour coming and going these days."

I decided to give her a dose of her own medicine. The silent treatment. I waited until Mattie finally broke the silence. "So what did Tuck say to you about his kid?"

"He told me he was childless."

"Well, that's not true," Mattie harrumphed. "We're both of us liars. Liars and cheaters, too."

On the hour's drive back into the city, secrets unraveled like a skein of tangled yarn. Two winged creatures flew out of Pandora's box, one of them a biggie.

Sometime back in the 1980s, Mattie found out that Grandy had taken up with one of his old flames. The white woman who'd given birth to his oldest son had recently moved back to Chicago from Arkansas. Instead of denying the affair like he usually did, Grandy freely admitted to it.

"You know what my fool husband said, Miss Savvy? That the woman's father had finally kicked the bucket."

"How's that any excuse for cheating?"

"Grandy always had me thinking that he left Gloria Jean for me. What really happened, her folks down south found out she was with a Black man. Her father sent news from Harrison, Arkansas. If Grandy didn't leave that gal alone, there was a hanging tree with his name on it."

"He threatened to kill him?"

"I don't know how the man was gonna lynch somebody long distance. Still, it was enough to put the fear of God into Grandy. Gloria Jean went back to Arkansas, had her baby, and let her Klansman daddy help raise it."

"Talk about poetic irony. I wonder how that turned out."

"All I know is, Grandy zoomed back to her like a rock in a slingshot once her daddy was gone. To make matters worse, Gloria Jean was nothing to write home about. I may not be no Miss America, but that hillbilly chick was ugly as sin."

"The rebound, Miss Mattie. Men always want what they can't have."

Her face tightened with remembered pain. "*This ain't but for a minute, Mattie.* That's what he said when he packed his things, those panama hats and polyester leisure suits. *Just some unfinished business to get out of my system.*"

"So, he left you?"

"He bought his slut a high-rise condo and left me at home with six little boys. It wasn't just my hurt feelings. Grandy was messing with my pride. He had always done his dirt behind closed doors. Now he was right out in the open, shacking up with it on South Shore Drive."

Heartbroken over Grandy's flagrant cheating, Mattie cried on his manager's shoulder. Tuck had recently lost his wife to breast cancer. Mattie was hurt and lonely. One thing led to another.

"I was never in love with nobody but Grandy. Tuck and me, we were like two cracked vases propped up together, trying to hold each other up. We just tried to comfort each other in our brokenhearted suffering."

Their affair resulted in a pregnancy and the birth of a daughter, Winnie Mae.

"So that's why your girl looks so different from her brothers. I always wondered about that."

"He left Gloria Jean when I got pregnant, don't know if that was the reason why. The Soul Serenaders were on their last leg by then and so was Grandy's money. He couldn't buy new Cadillacs every few years like he always used to. He had to make that '88 Bonneville last for the rest of his life."

"You think his mistress put him out?"

"Used him up," Mattie sniffed, "and sent his broke ass packing. Like a fool, I took him back. It's what I always did."

I refrained from sharing a Great-Aunt Essie nugget of wisdom. *If you let a man walk all over you, don't be surprised when he calls you a carpet.* Mattie's years of being a doormat were in the past, the man who wiped his feet on her was gone. What was the use of pointing it out?

We crawled along in silence for a few congested miles.

"Does Winnie know Tuck is her biological father?" I asked.

Mattie shook her head firmly. "She doesn't know and she doesn't need to know. Nobody knows but me and Tuck, you, and the great God Almighty."

"I wouldn't tell a soul, you know that. But what about Tuchman's sisters? They don't know anything about the relationship?"

"Chloe's got that Alzheimer's, so a lot of things just pass her by. If Edith suspects, she never lets on. They only met Parker the year before last. When he got serious about his music, Tuck took him under his wing. He's putting the boy through college, you know."

"With the money from Grandy's songwriting credits?"

"What songwriting credits? Grandy never wrote any songs."

"You mean to tell me it was Tuck after all? I find that hard to believe."

"Miss Savvy, you heard him trying to sing. The man can't carry a tune in a tin bucket."

"You don't really have to sing to be a songwriter."

"Tuck is not a songwriter," Mattie insisted. "If you must know the truth, I'm the one who wrote those songs."

"You?"

"Every single last one of them."

"You wrote all those Soul Serenaders hits, then what?" I shook my head in confusion. "You sold him your publishing rights? That's how he came to own them?"

"Tuck doesn't own my catalog. It's registered to the Tuchman Pfeiffer Heritage Trust. We set it up like that in the beginning, everything nice and legal."

"But I don't understand . . ."

"I had to protect myself and my kids. Grandy wasn't just a cheater, he spent money like water. Seemed like he wasn't happy until his last penny was rolling out the door."

"Great-Aunt Essie would have said, *That man had a hole in both his pockets.*"

"And tried to turn my pockets inside out, too. Do you know how long I'd been saving for that fiftieth-anniversary party? I wanted to wear a pretty dress, drink champagne, eat my cake, and have friends and family around me. Me and Grandy never really had a real wedding."

"You got married in a civil ceremony?"

"Shotgun in the basement of City Hall by somebody who looked like he was drunk. Afterward we walked over to State Street and ate lunch at the Woolworth's counter. Then Grandy went to his second-shift job over at the foundry. I rode the El back home. No reception, no gifts, no guests, no cake."

"I'm sure that was disappointing." I merged into the express lanes that would take me through to downtown. "Every woman dreams of a perfect wedding."

"Grandy said he would make it up to me when he could afford a wedding ring. Then it was after the baby was born. Then when the second one came along. After we paid off our mortgage. I always thought our problems started with those broken promises."

"It's like Aunt Essie always said. *The milk that was already spoiled this morning ain't hardly gone be good this afternoon.*"

"If it was too late for a beautiful wedding, at least I could have a nice fiftieth-anniversary party. I didn't want to ask my kids for help. They have their own families, their mortgages and bills. I pinched off my egg and butter money for over a year and hid it away in Parker's apartment."

"Don't tell me, Mattie. I already know. Grandy found the money and spent it."

"By then he had met that young skank, Shysteen. She was working at the nursing home where Grandy went after his hip replacement. He was feeling low because he couldn't hardly walk after the surgery. He went into rehab lame but sane, came out of it walking and crazy. It didn't take the little hussy long to dig her claws in."

"Sex and money, the reasons most marriages break up."

"My marriage wasn't breaking up, Miss Savvy. We had been through trouble so many times. But then I heard that hussy had a brand-new engagement ring. I figured my fiftieth-anniversary nest egg had bought it. I been with him for fifty years and didn't even get a wedding band."

"I always wondered why you never wore one."

"I know I said I was leaving him. I said it loud and clear and hard, in front of everybody. I just wanted to bring him low like I had been brought. I wanted him to hurt like I was hurting."

"It couldn't be easy living with that betrayal. I don't blame you for putting your foot down."

"Don't even try it, Miss Savvy." Mattie wagged a finger in warning. "I can tell how your mind is moving. No, I did not murder my husband behind some gold-digging female. She wouldn't have lasted, they never do. If I wanted my husband dead, I'd have killed him fifteen women ago."

"Why didn't you cancel the anniversary party when the money went missing? How would you have paid for it if not for Grandy's life insurance?"

"Since we weren't taking anniversary gifts, we set out a money tree so people could give whatever they wanted. That was Grandy's big idea. He thought it would pay back the money he wasted."

"And did it?" I asked.

Mattie shook her head. "We got maybe a couple hundred dollars from it. It didn't matter, though. I get paid when I'm eating, sleeping, or using the bathroom. A few cents here, a dollar there when one of my songs gets remade or played on the radio. I've even had one on the soundtrack of a movie. And trust me, Miss Savvy. It adds up."

"But you just said everything was held in trust."

"No, the publishing rights are in trust. The income goes into an investment account in the name of a secret company. Tuck set it up so Grandy wouldn't know about it."

"A limited liability corporation?" After learning of Noble McPherson's shady dealings, I knew some of the ways people shielded their income and identities.

"The Win-Mattuck LLC," Mattie said proudly. "I thought that up myself."

"Win for Winnie, Matt for Mattie, and Tuck for Tuchman?"

"You got it, Miss Savvy. Whenever I was hard up, Tuck transferred a little cash into my account, not so much that my husband would notice. It's what I always did when Grandy messed up the money, which was often. You know how many times our building's been in foreclosure?"

I knew about the last one from Fanon's investigation. "I would have thought your mortgage had been fully paid off by now."

"Paid off and remortgaged, two or three different times. Hiding from our creditors, going through bankruptcy, folks coming out to cut off my lights. I've been through it all. If it hadn't been for Tuck, Grandy would have got his hands on all that money and it would be long gone. Lord knows I loved him, but I had to protect myself."

I pulled up to her tumbledown, over-mortgaged two-flat on East 64th Street.

"I don't know if you remember this, Miss Mattie. It happened at Grandy's funeral repast. Annabelle Beasley had you cornered . . ."

Mattie clicked her tongue in sympathy. "Poor thing. I really feel for her."

"You feel sorry for Annabelle? But why?"

"I know she gets on people's nerves, claiming to be bornagain and acting like a hellion. She's still trying to find her way into God's grace, bless her heart."

"I couldn't help overhearing something she told you," I reminded her. "*This could ruin me, Mattie. I need to know, just what did Grandy tell you?* What was she talking about?"

"That's not for me to say."

"Does it have anything to do with her time at a certain gentlemen's club in Yazoo City?"

"Why're you asking if you already know? It's a place Grandy used to frequent back in the day, long before he met me."

"Your friend must be so afraid of people finding out."

"I wouldn't exactly call her a friend," Mattie explained. "She's a person I've known for a long time. Annabelle tries to deny what she was by being something she's not. So she used to dance near-naked some forty years ago? It ain't that bad a sin nor big of a secret."

"What's the story with the cake she made you?"

"When I asked if she could give me a discount on a wedding cake, she said she'd do it for free, so long as Grandy and I knew how to keep our mouths closed. I should have known that cake would go crashing to the ground, like everything else in our marriage."

"So in reality, what Annabelle was offering was a bribe."

"Look." Mattie heaved a fulsome sigh. "We all got our crosses to bear, but if you can't bear no crosses then you can't wear no crowns. Annabelle Beasley needs to own up to her past and claim her redemption, like Mary Magdalene in the Bible. *Let he who is without sin cast the first stone.*"

"How far do you think she'd go to keep her secret?"

"Girl, you need to quit it!" Mattie surprised me by bursting out laughing. "If Annabelle Beasley was killing people to hush them up, Grandy wouldn't be the only one to be gotten rid of. There's a whole line of people behind him, including me. And I reckon you, too."

Mattie's commentary was interrupted by the ringing of her mobile phone.

"Saved by the bell," I joked. "Do you need to get that?"

She looked down at the phone, then deleted the call. "It's just Tuck checking to see that I got home safe. I'll call him when I get inside."

Throwing all caution to the wind, I asked my last question. "So, what's the deal? Are you and he back together?"

Mattie gave a half-shouldered shrug, reaching across to unlatch her seat belt. "It's decades since our little fling, but Tuck says he never stopped loving me. Maybe I'll give it a try and see if lightning strikes again."

"Second chances don't come every day."

"But I could never feel for him like I did my husband. For all his cheating, trifling ways, I loved me some Grandy Jaspers. Yes, I did. Just couldn't help myself."

CHAPTER 37

The Soft Overcomes the Hard

"Why are you so down in the dumps?" Penny asked. "You ruled out an innocent person. That only narrows the field of suspects. Now you're free to find the real culprit."

"It muddies the waters, is all," I sighed. "Now I don't know what to think or who to blame. But then, I never did."

The breakfast rush was over, if you could call two dine-ins and five take-out orders a rush. In the hour's downtime between breakfast and lunch we prepared our Tuesday special—mixed greens with smoked turkey, deep-fried lemon pepper perch, broccoli coleslaw, and cornbread. Dessert was pecan bread pudding with bourbon sauce.

"No, it clears up the waters." Penny briskly stirred a bowl of cornbread batter. "I always thought Grandy's story was questionable. If Tuck had really stolen his music, it wouldn't have taken so long to sue him."

I seasoned the perch fillets with sea salt, lemon pepper, and paprika. "He must have gotten wind of Mattie's role in writing all those Soul Serenaders hits. Why else would he accuse Tuck of harassing his wife? He wanted to throw a monkey wrench in the works."

"It's hard to believe Mattie had to hide money from her

husband. How many old Cadillacs and polyester suits does one man need?"

"Womanizing isn't cheap these days. Especially when you're on the wrong side of seventy-five."

"Well, he sure wasn't Daddy Warbucking up in here. In fact, he was a downright Ebenezer Scrooge with his two miserable biscuits and bottomless cups of coffee."

I dipped the fillets in egg wash then dredged them in a seasoned cornmeal. "That's classic addictive behavior. You spend on your wants and get others to invest in your needs."

"A greedy, grimy old player," Penny pronounced. "It wasn't about suing Tuck. He was following a paper trail that led to Mattie's money. Grandy was probably going to divorce her and take half the marital assets. Then he could start over with Shysteen and that brat she's about to drop."

"It wouldn't be the first time he'd left her for another woman." I took out the tin of sunflower oil and heated up the deep fryer. "Poor old Mattie. Look at all she's been through."

"Poor old Mattie, nothing. You still don't think she had a motive for murder? Tuck, too, when I think of it. Don't cross either one off your list."

"You think?"

Penny snapped her fingers. "So, Mattie had a secret stash to protect her from a spendthrift husband. And maybe Tuck didn't profit from Grandy's death, but it gave him a chance with a woman he's been wanting for forty years. Money and booty, the oldest motives in the book."

"Except for one thing," I reminded her. "If the two deaths are related, then why would either of them kill Delbert Dailey?"

Penny sighed. "You got me there. It's a puzzlement for sure. What's so is so, what's not is not."

"Girl, you're on those movie musicals again, aren't you?"

"Guilty as charged." Penny lifted the batter-covered spoon. "I stand accused of binge-watching *The King and I*."

"I figured as much. Which version?"

"All three. The original with Yul Brynner, that Russian guy in yellowface. Then I watched the film version of the Broadway show with that Ken Watanabe. He's Japanese, not Siamese but I'll let him slide since he's fine as hell."

I took out two cast-iron skillets sized for baking cornbread the old country way. I still used the cookware Aunt Essie brought with her from Mississippi by way of Memphis. Over a century's worth of good food had been prepared in those pots.

"And the third one? You said you watched all three films."

Penny seemed embarrassed to admit it. "Disney made an animated version in the 1990s. Don't judge."

"A kiddie cartoon? You're pitiful, Penny."

She poured out the cornbread batter and shimmied the skillets to settle the contents. "I'm a movie musicaholic. What do you want from me?"

"You can put that cornbread in the oven and start chopping the greens," I told her. "And speaking of *The King and I,* don't forget Fanon's tai chi lesson on Monday."

Penny clicked her tongue in irritation as she slid skillets into the preheated oven. "I don't even have time for all that."

"He insists. With people dropping left and right, he wants us to know a little self-defense. It'll be me and you. Upstairs in my apartment, four p.m. sharp."

Penny turned the collard, turnip, and mustard green mix from the rinse water into an industrial-sized colander. "What does this have to do with *The King and I*?"

"Siam is now Thailand," I told her. "And tai chi is a Chinese martial art."

"I'm not getting the connect. The two nations don't even share a border."

"*Thai*land, *tai* chi? Duh!"

Penny set about chopping with a vengeance. "So, I'm the pitiful one? Tai chi and *The King and I* have nothing to do with one another. That Tuck's disease must be catching."

"Tuck's disease. What's that?"

"You seem to be competing with him for the title of corniest pun ever uttered."

Penny had helped me push the furniture against the wall, grumbling all the while. Then we rolled up area rugs and stacked them beneath the dining table. Now that the great room floor was clear, we lounged in our sweats at the kitchen island waiting for a pot of masala chai to brew. Fanon buzzed the downstairs doorbell.

"You'll have to wait until afterward," he warned, bringing a whiff of winter chill in with him. "Tai chi is best practiced on an empty stomach."

"But the tea is already made," I grumbled. "You could have told me before."

Fanon's eagle eye roamed the room, landing on a metal flask lying forgotten on a bookshelf. "What's that?"

"Oh, for Christ's sake." I told him. "It's Delbert Dailey's. I forgot all about it. He told me to hold on to it, then passed away before I could return it."

Fanon watched me with a critical eye. "That's evidence, you know."

"Evidence for what?" I scoffed. "Jacobs already told me there wouldn't be a death investigation."

"I'm not going to argue with you, Savvy. Turn that in to the police."

～

I knew Fanon had been practicing for years but this was the first time I'd taken a lesson.

"The art of tai chi is all about circles," he told us, "just like the shape of the yin and yang symbol. You see what I mean?"

He went through a series of slow movements with rotating arms, swooping and swaying, dipping and swan diving on dry land. He explained the poses as he went along then asked us to follow him.

"Hold up a minute." I stopped him. "You mean to say this is martial arts? It looks more like dancing to me."

He gave a gap-toothed grin then bowed deeply. "It's good to talk about tai chi. It's even better to practice it."

I shook my head doubtfully. "I don't know, Fanon. Maybe I should sit this one out. All that dipping and bending is probably going to aggravate my bum knee."

Even Penny, who originally hadn't wanted to be there, either, sang her two cents. "*Clear the decks, clear the tracks/You've got nothing to do but relax.*"

"Everything might be coming up roses for you," I scoffed. "The jury's still out on me."

Maybe I was just jinxing myself, but I swear before God, it turned out to be true. Tai chi just wasn't my thing.

"Straighten your head, Savvy," Fanon instructed. "A neck held erect focuses your mind."

I didn't glide into "striking the wild horse's mane," I lurched into it.

"Coordinate your movements," my ex demanded. "Move your upper and lower body as a single unit."

When I tried to "step back and repulse monkey," I heard an ominous cracking in my left knee. Come tomorrow morning that was bound to be sore. Fanon kept up his coaching. "Use the mind instead of force. The soft overcomes the hard, like the gentle but persistent flow of water that wears stone into sand."

"Yes, Fanon," I protested. "But doesn't that take thousands of years?"

"Patience is something that can't be rushed."

"Well, I don't have a thousand years to learn this exercise."

"It's not an exercise, Savvy. It's a discipline."

Penny took to tai chi like fish to water. Fanon lavished her with so many kudos and compliments I got a twinge of resentment. I felt like an elephant on roller skates.

At the end of the hour's lesson I was tired, frustrated, and cranky. Yet the next morning my knee wasn't stiff and sore like I expected. In fact, the joint was looser, more flexible than before. I still wasn't convinced that "waving hands like clouds" would keep me safe on the streets of the Chi but maybe it would help with my arthritis.

My long work hours at the café didn't give me much time for a workout regimen. The stationary bike in my bedroom was gathering a thick layer of dust. I decided I would keep up the tai chi, if for nothing other than the workout.

I never actually thought that the discipline would come in handy one day.

CHAPTER 38

Savvy on the Stakeout

I was overcome by the insatiable desire to see where those who had known Grandy Jaspers and Delbert Dailey lived.

The same week I began studying tai chi was also the week I started following people. I didn't tell anyone about it, not even Penny. I wouldn't be able to explain what I was doing because I didn't quite know myself. I wasn't very good at it, especially at the beginning.

I drove over to Shysteen Shackleford's place, although I didn't like hanging out there too long. She lived in one of the infamous Chicago Housing Authority complexes, The Projects, aka The Jets. With visible drug traffic right out in the open, I felt wary parked on her street. I'd stick around for a few minutes then drive away to return later. The third day I struck pay dirt.

One evening as I was about to pull off, I saw Evrian King leaving the building. His bulky physique was instantly recognizable. His Bulls starter jacket seemed insufficient against the winter cold. He bundled it around himself, stuck his bare hands in his pockets, hunched his shoulders against the wind, and strode off down the street. I slowly tailed him several blocks and watched him disappear into the Green Line El station on Ashland Avenue.

I had already discovered that Evrian lived in Roseland, far out near the city's southern border. I found his address and haunted him there. What was he doing fifteen miles away in Shysteen's West Side apartment building? It seemed an unlikely coincidence. Something had to be going on.

Early one morning in the midst of a snowstorm, I saw Shysteen leave her building and take off down the street. She slogged through accumulating drifts of snow, tugging at a small person's hand. I couldn't determine the gender of the child bundled up in cap, mittens, boots, and a lime-green snowsuit. Was this soon-to-be mother already a mother?

As they came abreast of the car I lowered the window slightly. Shysteen pulled the child along with her, fussing all the way.

"Riley, you better keep up with me," she nagged. "You're going to be late for school and make me late for work again."

"Mama, I'm cold!" Riley wailed piteously. "I wanna go back home."

"You can't stay at home all by yourself."

"Yes, I can. I'm old enough."

As the two of them passed the car I impulsively called out. "Shysteen, it's Sapphire Summers. Can I give you a lift somewhere?"

"Oh hell, yes," she hollered, mixing the profane with the sacred. "Lord, thank you, Jesus."

She bundled the child into the back and climbed into the front seat beside me. "You got any tissues, Savvy?"

I handed her some from the pack in the center console,

wondering about her home training. She could at least have addressed me as "Miss Savvy."

Shysteen handed the wad of tissues to the child in the back seat. "Blow that nose, little girl. You ain't going into school all snotty like that."

So much for the mystery of Riley's gender.

"Where can I take you, Shysteen?" I asked her.

"Riley goes to Skinner over on Adams and Racine."

When I pulled up in front of the school, Shysteen wiped Riley's nose one last time.

"Can't you take me inside, Mama?"

Shysteen huffed in irritation. "Girl, I ain't got time. You want me to fool around and lose my job? You're always saying you're big enough. Get in there by yourself."

The shock I felt must have showed on my face.

"I usually go inside with her," she explained as we pulled away. "But I'm running late for work and they already wrote me up twice. I don't know what I'd have done if you hadn't turned up when you did. Can you drop me off at the El?"

"How far are you going?"

"You know the Harbor View Nursing Home out there on Harper?"

"That's not that far from me. In fact, I'm headed to Woodlawn now. Do you want a ride?"

"Hallelujah!" Shysteen cried. "I'm living large today."

Shysteen was living large and I was living in luck. Whether it was sheer gratitude or mere indifference, she hadn't even bothered with the obvious question. What was I doing out near her place, so far away from my own?

Rush hour was beginning and traffic was slow in these near-blizzard conditions. I knew I'd have at least forty-five minutes to question her. And luckily for me, Shysteen wasn't shy about talking, at least not in the beginning.

It was becoming a routine, this questioning of people while driving in a car. There was something about the closed-in intimacy of a vehicle moving through traffic. It was ideal for the act of unburdening secrets.

CHAPTER 39

Working That DNA

Shysteen unfastened the seat belt, loosened her coat, and slipped out of it. Her rounded belly strained against pink scrubs emblazoned with red interlocking hearts.

"Damn, Savvy. Can you cut down that heat? I'm sweating all through my clothes. I forgot how crazy pregnancy is. Either you're freezing or you're boiling."

She removed her gloves and fanned her forehead with them, an ostentatious diamond in a princess cut gleaming on her left ring finger. Would this be the ring that Mattie believed her egg and butter money went to buy? Though I knew better. Penny had been the unfortunate beneficiary of an ill-advised loan, but who knows? Maybe Grandy had "borrowed" enough from his wife to take care of both women.

"I never knew you had a child, Shysteen. How old is little Riley?"

"Almost nine years old. She's in the third grade at Skinner. If I had her a few months earlier, she would have been in fourth grade by now."

"You don't seem old enough to have a child that age. You must have had her young."

Shysteen continued to fan herself. "I was in my sophomore

year in high school, fifteen going on sixteen. My mother said I was making my bed hard but I didn't listen to her. If I had known what it was to raise a kid, I definitely would have waited."

I gestured toward her abdomen. "Now that you're older and more experienced, you must be looking forward to this one."

An odd expression wrinkled her brow before she shrugged it off. "I guess so. He asked me to have a baby for him and promised he'd take care of it. When he came into his money he was gonna divorce old girl, wife me up, and sit me down."

"What do you mean, sit you down?"

"He said he didn't want no wife of his working. I could quit my job and stay home with the kids, just like old girl did."

"And who is he?"

"It's Grandy, who do you think it is? You trying to call me a ho? I know who my baby daddy is."

"Of course you do, Shysteen. I was only asking." Her heated reaction seemed over the top. Was she upset at what I thought or what she already knew?

I asked if she had any regrets about dating a married man.

"They didn't really have no kind of marriage. Grandy didn't love her and she didn't love him back. You heard what she said at that party."

"People say things when their feelings are hurt. Sometimes they don't really mean them."

"She meant every word of it," Shysteen sneered. "Miserable old bitch."

"Other than being married to Grandy, why are you so mad at Mattie?"

"It's all her fault." She seemed genuinely distressed, almost near tears. "She's the reason Grandy died."

"Are you saying that Mattie killed her husband?" How

strange that both of Grandy's women were flinging the same accusations at each other.

"I don't want to talk about it no more." She grabbed a cell phone from her purse and began furiously texting away.

I decided to take southbound Lake Shore Drive. The view of the snowy lakefront was far more pleasant than the concrete expanse of the Dan Ryan. The extra time on the slower route would give us more opportunity to talk.

I waited until Shysteen put away her phone before I spoke again. "I didn't mean to upset you. I'm a mother myself. I can't imagine how hard it must be raising children on your own."

"Damn right it's hard," she complained. "I can't even afford a car. When Grandy was alive he would pick up me and Riley most days."

"That made life a lot easier, I guess."

"It sure did. Now I got to wake up before day just to get my kid to school and myself off to work. When the weather's bad it can take two hours. Then on holidays when she's out of school I've got to struggle to find somebody to watch her. I've been trying to get some home health care jobs on the side, just to bring in a little extra money."

"It hasn't worked out for you so far?"

"I got into a little trouble at work. When people find out about it nobody wants me."

"Yes, I heard about that. Something about elder abuse."

"I didn't financially and sexually abuse no old man. It was all a goddamned lie!"

"Was this about Granderson Jaspers?"

"No, it was somebody else. Those charges didn't stick and they had to give me my job back."

"Why would someone say such a terrible thing about you?"

Her response reinforced my belief that those charges might

have merit. "Those old dudes ain't got no money and most of them can't do nothing but a little licking and lapping."

"Okay. Well then." I tried not to show my shock. "I guess this went for Grandy, too?"

She gave a little shiver as if reliving past pleasures. "Baby, he could do it all. When that man was on his pills, he could really work the sheets."

"Is that so? Because Delbert Dailey described him as an old man with old ideas. I think he was describing his lovemaking skills."

"Alder Dailey was rank and rotten. How would he even know what Grandy did in bed?"

"I wondered the same thing myself. The only way he'd know is if he'd slept with Grandy himself," I answered, then added: "Or you said something to him about it."

A look of guilt flashed across her face. Then she set her mouth in a straight, stubborn line. "Don't care what nobody said about Grandy. I like-ded it. And I like-ded him."

I had to admit a grudging respect for a woman who knew what she wanted and went after it. What I couldn't respect was that she wanted another woman's husband.

At the same time, I found myself wondering what a man in his seventies could possibly do that a twenty-four-year-old had like-ded. Maybe it was something outside of the bedroom— the attention, the flattery, the expensive gifts he nearly bankrupted his household to lavish upon her. The promises he made of a future free from financial worries.

I found myself wondering exactly who'd been using whom in that situation. Shysteen for going after an elderly man and the little bit of money he had, expecting more to come? Grandy, a dirty old man bedding down a woman young enough to be his granddaughter?

Was anyone really clean in this whole situation? Or had they both been using each other?

"Disarm aggression with surrender," Fanon urged us. "When you meet inflexible hardness with yielding softness, the opponent's strength disappears."

Yeah, right, I thought. Like I believed any of that. If that was the case then Olive Oyl would be heavyweight defender of the world and the Pillsbury Doughboy a WWF champion.

If I seemed bitter at this point, it was because it was already the third tai chi lesson and I wasn't much better than I'd been at the beginning. I didn't like doing things if I couldn't do them well. It's why I'd dropped golf and stopped going to my tango classes. I was tempted to do the same with tai chi. Although I couldn't grin about it, I gritted my teeth and bore it.

When the uncomfortable ordeal was over and Fanon had left, Penny and I pushed the furniture back into place and picked up around the apartment. I told her about the conversation I'd had with Shysteen the other day.

"Men seem to go for the aggressive type," Penny explained. "I don't know why that is."

"Well, you're no shrinking violet yourself. And sometimes men like naive young things, so they can lord it over them."

"I wouldn't use *naive* and *Shysteen* in the same sentence, Savvy. She may be no Michelle Obama but the girl is plenty shrewd. If there are two things that woman knows, it's her money and her men."

"I guess you're right." I unrolled a kilim area rug into place. "If Grandy Jaspers had stayed alive, she figured she'd be sitting pretty by the time their baby came."

"If it is his baby. You're the one who saw Evrian King creeping from her crib in the dead of night."

I had finally admitted to Penny my clandestine stealth activities. "Who knows how long they've been kicking it. Maybe it's Evrian's kid."

"Or Do-Wrong Dailey's, don't forget."

"No, that connection came after she got knocked up," I insisted. "Shysteen said she only met Delbert the night of the anniversary party."

"And you believed that? I guess you're the one that's naïve. Maybe you should change your name from Savvy to Gullible Summers."

"Shysteen is nobody's Girl Scout but she's not that good of a liar. She said she first met Evrian at the anniversary party, but I could tell it wasn't true. She looked off into nowhere and started tugging at her wig."

Penny picked up a pillow and pointed it like a weapon. "My point exactly. Once a liar, twice a liar."

"What would be the point of lying about when she met Delbert Dailey?"

"I could ask the same question about Evrian King." Penny huffed.

I shook my head in frustration. "You saw yourself how Shysteen avoided Evrian at the playoff raffle."

"Spurned him would be a better word."

"She didn't interact with him at the anniversary party, either. There's something about Evrian she wants to keep hidden. But she was all open and notorious with Dailey at Grandy's funeral. Whatever it was between him and Shysteen, I think it started after Grandy died."

Penny fluffed the sofa pillows and patted them into place. "If you say so, Savvy."

"And can you imagine," I continued, "a woman who seems to have absolutely nothing going on for herself was juggling three different men? Some of us can't even find one."

"There's a perfectly decent one in front of you, Savvy. And you wouldn't be stealing anyone's stuff, just taking back what you returned."

"If you're talking about Fanon Franklin, that's not an option. It's over and done with, water under the bridge, and all those clichés."

"You're sure about that?"

"Positive," I told her. "And even if I wanted Fanon, and I'm not saying I do, he hasn't shown a bit of interest in me. In fact, I'm beginning to wonder what's going on with him and Sergeant Jacobs."

"Here we go again. Look, Savvy. I tell it like I smell it and I'm smelling nothing there. Whatever's up with Emerson and Fanon, I doubt if it's romantic. In fact, she seems to focus more on you than the ex-hubby."

"That's because she hates my guts. She thinks there's something going on between me and Fanon."

"Well . . . is there?"

"What about *it's over with* don't you understand, Penny Lopés?"

"How do they know each other anyway, the hottie with the body and the mouse that roared? They seem an unlikely pair."

"They were partners back when Emmy was a rookie cop just out of the academy. He basically showed her the ropes. I knew he had a partner but he never mentioned she was female. He probably thought I'd be jealous, and maybe I would have been."

"You think they were going at it hot and heavy back then?"

"Who knows?" I shrugged. "I'm sure it didn't sit right with him when someone he trained surpassed him."

"Surpassed him? Wait, aren't they both police sergeants?"

"Yes, but she's a detective sergeant. She's right where Fanon wants to be."

"So, if you can't beat them, join them?" Penny made a circle with one hand and a rude gesture with the opposite forefinger.

"They do say the bond between police partners is something like a marriage."

"Yeah, all those long hours together on the beat."

"Penny, you know better than that. Cops don't walk a beat anymore. But being closed up in a squad car is probably even more intimate than being out on the street. You might be spending more time with your partner than your own family. You look out for each other in dangerous situations. Then add in the chemistry between a man and a woman. She may look wan and wasted, but the detective isn't ugly."

"Yeah," Penny joked. "She's working that DNA."

I paused, startled. "What did you just say?"

"You know. What Evrian said about Shysteen. *She working that DNA, working it hard. I like that in a female.*"

"Hm. I wonder what he meant."

A hunch began shifting and taking shape. I picked up my phone, looked up the number, and called the Harbor View Nursing Home. I asked for human resources, pretending to be a potential employer.

When I was transferred to Eloise Carmichael, the executive manager, I slid into my professional voice. "Hello. What can you tell me about Shysteen Shackleford?"

Ms. Carmichael was all business, too—crisp, cool, and careful. "All I can divulge is that Shysteen Marie Shackleford has been employed with Harbor View for the last two and a half years."

"Can you tell me at least what her job title is?"

"All I can say," Miss Carmichael repeated, "is that she works here. Good day to you, ma'am."

She disconnected without saying goodbye.

I got up and reached for my coat.

"Where are you running to all of a sudden?" Penny asked. "Clue a sister in."

"Wait right here. I'll tell you when I get back."

I wondered why they called it Harbor View when there was no water in sight. Beyond East Woodlawn and Jackson Park, Lake Michigan couldn't even be seen with binoculars.

I pulled up to the nursing home and parked out front, scoping out the premises. On a bench outside the building, two young women sat smoking in the freezing cold. I locked the car and walked over to them. "Sorry to interrupt your break. Would either of you know a Shysteen Shackleford?"

"Yeah, we know her," the one with braids replied. "Who's asking?"

I extended my hand for a shake. "Forgive me, ladies. The name is, uh . . . Emerson Jacobs."

They introduced themselves in turn. Camilla was thin with braids and the longest fingernails I'd ever seen. Laquita was plump with a pleasant smile and a short Afro.

"I've been looking into home health care for my father," I lied. "Ms. Shackleford came to my attention. I know she works here but Ms. Carmichael won't tell me anything about her."

"I know I shouldn't be saying it." Laquita lowered her voice. "But I wouldn't hire her to look after my dog. Shysteen sucks as a CNA and she's known for crossing the line with patients."

Camilla shook her head. "You talk too much, Laquita."

"So she's a CNA? A certified nursing assistant, not a nurse?" I clarified.

Camilla, the one who told Laquita she talked too much, snickered. "Who, her? An RN, that's rich."

"You need to have at least an associate's degree and then pass the boards to become a registered nurse. Shysteen hasn't been in the vicinity of anyone's college. I'm surprised she got through her licensing course."

Camilla blew smoke circles above her head. "If the teacher was a man I can tell you how."

"Oh, my." I began backing away. "Shysteen may not be the best choice for Daddy, after all. Well, thank you, ladies. I appreciate your honesty."

Laquita got up and walked me to my car. "What did you say your name was, Miss?"

"Oh, uh," I panicked then remembered. "It's Emerson Jacobs. But you can call me Emmy."

"If you need someone for your father, I'm a CNA, too. I'm also studying for my BSN, the bachelor of science in nursing. I work second shift here but I'm available mornings when I don't have classes. And I'm very good at what I do."

"Really, Laquita? That's great to hear. We ought to keep in touch."

As Laquita took my cell phone to input her contact information, I recalled the odd comment Penny heard at the playoff raffle. *She working that DNA . . . I like that in a female.* It all made sense to me now. Brainiac that he was, Evrian had been pronouncing *CNA* as DNA. If he knew what Shysteen did for a living then he must have known her all along.

"Have you met Shysteen's boyfriend?" I asked Laquita.

She wrinkled her nose in distaste. "He worked in the kitchen up until last summer when they fired his sorry behind. Evrian was caught stealing meat and selling it on the side. Chicken, pork chops, hot dogs, you name it. What kind of loser steals food from old people? I don't know what Shysteen sees in that man."

"You have to admit he's a good-looking fella."

"What looks good to you, ain't always good for you." Laquita could have been channeling my Great-Aunt Essie.

"So they were together, what? Four or five months ago? And Shysteen is five months pregnant now."

"It makes you feel for the baby, doesn't it? Poor kid doesn't know what it's in for. Oops, you got a call coming in."

The Hall & Oates song "Private Eyes" sang out. It was Penny's ringtone.

"Don't worry," I answered. "I'll get it later."

"So, I put in my phone number and email address, too. If you call and I don't answer just leave a message or shoot me an email. I promise I'll get right back to you, Emmy."

I almost looked around to see if Sergeant Jacobs was behind me. Aunt Essie always said that lies were like roaches. *Shine a little light and they scramble off in all directions.* My lies were clearly getting away from me.

I took my phone back, excited at what I'd learned but guilty at how I'd learned it. Laquita seemed a nice girl and I felt like a lying fraud. I imagined all the roaches that were scampering away.

But I was a lying fraud who knew something now that I definitely hadn't known before. In fact, I had learned several somethings. I couldn't wait to tell Penny all about it.

CHAPTER 40

Private Eyes

No sooner had I pulled away from Harbor View than "Private Eyes" sounded again. Penny was at it, calling me again.

"Quit blowing up my phone," I barked. "I'm on my way back home."

Knowing Nosy Lopés as I did, I guessed she had grown impatient sitting there alone, not knowing what was happening. I decided not to tell her on the phone. I'd wait until I could see the startled whites of her eyes. When I heard "Private Eyes" a third time, I sent the call straight to voicemail.

Instead of parking in the customary spot behind my building, I pulled into a space on Ellis Avenue and walked back around front, pondering what I'd discovered. I rounded the corner of the building into a disturbing déjà vu.

People waited at the entrance to my apartment, nearly blocking the doorway. I almost ran smack into Samantha Patterson, the Channel 6 reporter who'd tried to ambush me when Delbert Dailey died. She must have gotten kicked back upstairs because this was the prime-time news hour and not the morning report she'd been demoted to.

It wasn't like before, when an advance sighting prepared me for the sneak attack. This time I was caught completely off guard. A crew trailed behind Samantha as she rushed toward me with microphone upraised.

"Ms. Summers, Ms. Summers. Can you comment on the news?"

"What news? I don't know what you're talking about."

"The Delbert 'Do-Right' Dailey case. It was just announced."

I paused for a moment, taking it in. "Did Evrian King have anything to do with it?"

Samantha shook her head. "Who's Evrian King? A Wisconsin real estate investor named Noble McPherson is said to have masterminded the plot. The indictment just came down today."

"You're kidding me!" I exclaimed. "That snake in the . . . pardon me, the gentleman in question has been hounding me for a very long time, trying to get me to sell out. I knew he had it in him, I just can't believe he did it."

"What does this mean for the neighborhood you call home?"

"This is not just a victory for Woodlawn, it's a victory for justice. It's about time someone paid for murdering two men in cold blood."

Samantha's eyes nearly bugged out of their sockets. She blinked in confusion before regaining her aplomb. "Did you say that two men were murdered? Elaborate, Ms. Summers."

"It's fairly obvious. Grandy Jaspers and Delbert Dailey both overdosed on Viagra. I believe he crushed it up and put it in their drinks. But certainly, you must know this by now."

"Now let me get this straight. In addition to these other charges, you're claiming that Noble McPherson is also responsible for two men's deaths? Dailey's and another person's?"

Now it was my turn to be confused. "What other charges? Murder wasn't what he was indicted for?"

"In collusion with the late Alderman Dailey, Noble McPherson has been charged with an influence-peddling scheme to condemn and acquire properties here in Woodlawn and in other South Side neighborhoods. Now what details can you give me on these alleged murders?"

I edged warily toward the door that led to my upstairs living quarters. "Sorry, I misspoke. Forget what I just said."

"Did McPherson have help?" Samantha persisted. "What was the other person's role in this? His name again was ... ?"

I maneuvered around her, extracting my key to unlock the door.

The soundman removed his headphones and whispered. "I think she said Evian King."

"Evian King!" Samantha shouted as I darted inside and shut the door. I peered through the window and saw her turn sideways to the camera, an eager expression on her drawn, perfect face. "In addition to an illegal land grab scheme, a witness suggests that Noble McPherson and a possible accomplice, Evian King, may be responsible for the deaths of two men. You heard it here first. Samantha Patterson, the five o'clock Channel 6 Evening News."

I ran upstairs, unlocked my front door and collapsed against it, panting like I'd run the marathon. Penny sat on the sofa with cell phone in hand, a stricken expression on her face.

"Why didn't you tell me a news crew was out there?"

"I tried to warn you, Savvy. You should have answered your phone."

Mary rode a donkey, shout for joy
Joseph walked beside her, shout for joy

A loop of carols and holiday songs serenaded the diners. Christmas week brought new customers into the café. We sorely needed the revenue.

But things weren't all rosy here at the ranch. Noble McPherson had already hit me with a defamation of character lawsuit for the remark I'd inadvertently made on the news about him being a murderer. My business lawyer told me it wasn't her field of expertise. She referred me to a criminal defense attorney who charged nearly four times her rate. Two steps forward, one step back seemed to be my theme song. I held my breath for the next few days, hoping the worst was over.

We were usually open from early morning breakfast to late afternoon lunch. We stayed open late on Christmas Eve, accommodating last-minute shoppers and the curiosity seekers who'd seen me on the evening news.

"Whew, what a day!" Penny sighed when the last customer left at 10 p.m. "With any luck we'll be cleaned up and in our beds by midnight."

"You go on home to Sergio," I told her. "I'll handle it here."

"No, Savvy. I can't leave this on you. I bet you haven't even started wrapping your Christmas presents."

"Everything's under control," I told her. "My son and his family don't celebrate Christmas. And I'm flying to New York in a few days to spend the holiday with my daughter. We'll have a belated dinner and gift reveal."

"Well," Penny said reluctantly, pulling on her coat and boots. "If you're sure about it."

"Positive."

Instead of heading for cleanup in the kitchen, I poured myself a steaming cup of hot chocolate. I kicked off my shoes beneath Table Two, where I sat to rest my body, mind, and spirit. In the days that had followed the Harbor View visit and the Channel

6 News ambush, I hadn't had much time to reflect. Though I knew more than I had before, I didn't have all the answers I needed.

Yes, Shysteen Shackleford had concealed a secret romantic relationship with Evrian King. She may even have lied about her unborn child's paternity in an attempt to trick Grandy Jaspers into marrying her. But would Shysteen actually murder the man who had promised to "sit her down"? And then kill Delbert Dailey, who'd probably been her bed partner too? If so, then why?

The obnoxious criminal conspiracy defendant Noble McPherson was a much more attractive candidate for murder. He'd ruthlessly pursued his aims by hook or by crook, going so far as to involve Delbert Dailey. Some of the details of their larceny had finally come to light.

As a secret partner in the Jonesboro-Lee dummy corporation, Dailey had long been in cahoots with McPherson, its sole proprietor. Delbert had been helping him evade the law to acquire land in gentrifying Woodlawn at bargain-basement rates. When all was said and done he'd resell the land at high market rates to those clamoring to develop it.

Dailey stood to make a killing in McPherson's plot to acquire my property and my neighbor's three-flat, as well as the adjoining vacant lots. His untimely death had undoubtedly slowed progress on the scheme and thwarted an investigation that had been ongoing for months.

But was he responsible for those murders?

White-collar crime was one thing; murder was another. Had McPherson actually killed two men for financial gain? Did Grandy somehow get in the way, or was killing him a ploy to cast blame on me and ruin my business? Noble had proven himself to be quite the schemer, but then so was Delbert Daily.

Had Dailey tried to swindle his business partner and paid the price with his life? It was all so confusing. Too many suspects, too many motives, and no conclusive answers.

The media had a field day with the murder scandal but the police weren't taking it seriously, as far as I could tell. I'd gotten a phone call from Sergeant Jacobs, scolding me for withholding evidence and instructing me to turn over Grandy's pinpricked champagne cork and Delbert's vodka flask. I didn't know for sure who had told her about this evidence, but who else could it be? Fanon was the only one who knew about the vodka flask. I'm sure he was trying to save me from myself.

I'd actually promised to bring the evidence down to the station that morning, but in the Christmas Eve rush, I hadn't been able to leave the café.

I was worn out, depressed, and nothing was making sense.

I hauled myself to my feet, took the keys, and went over to lock the front door and lower the blinds. I looked outside through the crackle-paned window. Business had been good for such a chilly day. The evening was clear but biting cold with a below zero wind chill factor. It wouldn't be a white Christmas this year but it would be a frigid one.

The distorted shape of a night service #63 bus pulled up and discharged passengers at the bus stop across the street. Several people alighted, loaded down with packages. Zero-hour shoppers clutched their last-minute shopping bags and trudged into the side streets, bent forward against the biting wind.

When the bus pulled away, three people remained. Through the fissured glass I could barely make out two adults with a child between them, each of them holding a little one's hand. They didn't move toward the residential streets but stood there watching my lighted storefront.

Why on earth would people be out with a child at this time

of night? Did they really expect me to be open at 11:30 p.m. on Christmas Eve? I had already flipped the "Open" sign to "Closed" and was tempted to turn out the light.

I imagined Aunt Essie asking, "What would Jesus do?" A family was hungry on the holiday, like that homeless couple that rode into town on a donkey two thousand years ago.

I sighed and opened the door. As I watched the figures come into shape, the two adults pulling the child along, I heard a shrill and familiar voice. "Mama, I'm cold! I wanna go ho-o-o-me!"

CHAPTER 41

Room at the Inn

Under the halo of a streetlight, Evrian King, Shysteen Shackleford, and her daughter Riley came into focus. Before I could react, they had crossed the street and pushed past me into the café.

"See, she *is* still open," Shysteen cried, stamping her feet. "Lord, it's nice and warm in here. Oh, look at that pretty Christmas tree, Riley. You by yourself tonight, Savvy?"

"Yes, I'm cleaning up, but . . ."

"What you got to eat?"

"Actually, we're closed. I'm sorry to disappoint you after coming so far."

Riley tugged her mother's sleeve. She drew one word into three pitiful syllables. "I'm ho-on-gree!"

"All right, have a seat," I said wearily.

The threatened tears magically disappeared. Riley gave a snaggletoothed grin. "I want chicken nuggets, macaroni and cheese, and I do not like vegetables."

"Now that I can't promise," I warned. "But let's see what I can pull together."

I scraped the pot of black-eyed peas and rice, julienned and stir-fried the last collard greens, and made a quick batch of hot water cornbread, frying it flapjack style on the griddle. I carried the Remains of the Day out to their table and served it to them family style.

"We're closed until after the New Year," I explained, "so the cupboard is pretty bare. That's why I'm not going to charge you for this food. I sure hope you folks enjoy it."

Evrian grabbed his fork and dug in. Shysteen took the cornbread with her bare hands and tore it into thirds. She gave one piece to her child and one to Evrian and took another herself. Not a "thank you" passed anyone's lips, Lord have mercy on their naked souls.

"How's the food?" I asked. "Does it hit the spot?"

Shysteen grunted. "It's all right, but I wish you had put some meat on the table."

"Bring me something to drink," Riley demanded. The child had no manners to speak of, but there was obviously no one to teach her.

I brought out the carafe of hot chocolate and poured it into three mugs. Then I sat back down at Table Two, pointedly waiting for them to finish. It wouldn't do for them to get too comfortable and linger for hours.

Evrian took his fork and pointed it at the half-empty cup sitting before me. He said his first words of the evening. "What, you ain't drinking yours?"

I lifted the cup to my lips then put it back down. "It's not hot chocolate if it isn't hot."

"It ain't polite to let your guests eat alone," Evrian said coldly.

If that wasn't snowman calling the marshmallow pale! The rudest man in the city of Chicago was lecturing me on etiquette.

"This isn't a dinner party," I said, heading for the kitchen.

"People who run cafés don't usually sit down and eat with their customers. I don't mean to rush it, but you need to finish up."

When I went to the sink to pour out the cold chocolate, a sludge stuck to the bottom of the mug. I hated lumps in my hot chocolate so I never used cocoa powder. I melted 85% dark chocolate chips in a pan, whisked in hot milk, added honey and a drop of peppermint oil and poured it into a carafe to keep warm. It always went down silky smooth. My guests had been raving about it all holiday season.

I probed the residue and found it slightly lumpy. My fingernail touched a tiny chunk of something white. A chill of dread started in my chest and spread down to my gut. Had someone been tampering with my drink?

I picked up my phone and dialed Sergeant Jacobs's number. It shouldn't have surprised me that it went straight to voicemail. It was Christmas Eve, after all. Before I could even leave a message, I sensed the bulk of Evrian filling the kitchen doorway, blocking out the available light.

He stood there in his impractical starter jacket, staring directly at me. "What you doing back here?"

"Oh, nothing." I dropped the cell phone into my apron pocket. "Just cleaning up for the night."

"Well, we about ready to go."

My sense of relief was palpable. I trailed him to the dining room where Shysteen sat with her coat on, tying a scarf around Riley's neck. A bell sounded faintly from the Catholic Church.

"It's midnight," I announced weakly. "Merry Christmas, everyone."

Shysteen's response was a derisive snort and inexplicable warning. "Merry Christmas your own damned self. Next time stay out of my business."

Evrian gave a humorless laugh. "Won't be no next time, Shysteen."

The chill that came on me in the kitchen returned tenfold. My knees shook so badly that I had to sit down to keep them from buckling.

"I don't want to leave, Mama," Riley complained as Shysteen pulled her toward the door. "It's cold outside and warm in here."

Evrian pulled on a pair of tight gloves. He followed the two of them to the door, but didn't accompany them through it.

Shysteen turned back to Evrian. "You hurry it up. It's cold on that bus stop."

"Y'all go on back home," he instructed. "I'll catch up with you later."

I ran forward and tried to duck out behind them. Evrian grabbed my arm and yanked me back inside. Riley spotted the move and whirled on him with fury. She aimed a kick at Evrian's shin. "You leave her alone, she's nice!"

I appreciated the gratitude, however late-coming and ineffective. Evrian pushed Riley and Shysteen out, locked the door behind them, and extracted the keys from the dead-bolt lock. Dragging me along by the arm, he surveyed the dining room walls.

My curiosity edged past my apprehension. "What are you looking for?"

"Where the lights at?"

I felt for the cell phone in my apron pocket but didn't take it out. I could have turned them off with my smartphone but I wasn't divulging that. "They flip on and off in the kitchen."

He pushed and shoved me through the kitchen doorway. "Hit those lights, lady."

I opened the door to the circuit box, then flipped off the dining room lights and those in the kitchen, too. Without a single window in it, the kitchen was plunged into total darkness.

"What the . . . ?"

I heard him stumble toward me and bump into the center island. The back door presented a possible escape. I snatched the keys from Evrian's hand and ran to unlock the padlocked exit. I struggled to unwind the chain that held the lock in place and threw my weight against the door. It was swollen in the frame and didn't budge an inch.

"Where the hell you at? Cut them lights back on!"

I heard Evrian moving closer. I knew this kitchen like I knew my own face, even in the dark. I darted past him, the chained padlock still in hand. I opened sliding cabinet drawers into his path and could hear him cursing as he crashed into them.

I ran to the front door to insert the key. I got it in but wasn't fast enough to turn it. Evrian caught up with me. He yanked me back, delivering a stinging slap to the side of my face. When the chained padlock dropped from my hand, he picked it up and tugged both ends, testing the strength of the metal.

"See, I was trying to take it easy on you. Now you're going to get what you deserve."

I spoke without thinking. "Well, I don't deserve this."

Holding the chain in one hand, Evrian grabbed my arm with the other. He pulled me toward the counter that ran the far length of the dining room. I stopped struggling and dropped to the floor. Evrian was strong but not that strong. He tried but couldn't lift my deadweight.

"Get up and walk," he ordered. "Don't make me hurt you, lady."

"No, I think I'll stay like this. You'll hurt me either way."

I curled onto my side and glanced at the ceiling. The ornate, painted-over metal tiles were part of the vintage charm that had convinced me to buy this place. Maybe after I got back from New York while we were still closed for the holidays I'd have them stripped and polished down to their original copper glow.

In tai chi you must remain calm. Be loose, not limp. Focused, not tense.

I lay there admiring the ceiling tiles, a circular design interlaced with flowers, remembering the mantra of a man I once loved. Still loved in my fashion. *The art of tai chi is all about circles.* I looked over to the portrait of Great-Aunt Essie barely visible in the dark.

It's not your time to go, I could almost hear her saying. *So don't you give up now!*

When Evrian started kicking to get me moving, I curled my body into a compact circle, drawing knees to chest and tucking my head. Not resisting but not yielding.

Evrian tried to shove me to my feet. Then he grabbed at my clothing and began dragging me toward the counter. Grunting and cursing and panting hard, he had to keep stopping to readjust the bundle that was my body.

Evrian's afraid of being seen, I suddenly realized. *He wants me out of sight, behind the counter.* I never had a chance to close the blinds above the picture window. It was dark in there but someone could still peek through the window and see something.

As he pushed and dragged me across the hardwood floor, I tried not to feel the bumps and blows. I talked to stall him, trying to satisfy the curiosity that itched below my panic.

"Oomph. It was you who gave Shysteen that shiner she was wearing at Grandy's funeral, wasn't it?"

"Damn straight," Evrian growled, taking off his red starter jacket and hanging it on the back of a chair. In the near darkness I could see him wiping sweat from his brow. I went on all fours and began crawling rapidly toward the door, dropping back into the fetal position when Evrian turned back toward me.

"But why'd you hit your girlfriend, Evrian?"

"She was freaking off with that Delbert Dailey. When Grandy passed, Shysteen went to see if he could help her get some of Grandy's money. She was just supposed to talk to him, not let him jump her bones. I went to kiss Shysteen one night and it tasted like nicotine and sugar."

"But what about Grandy? She was sleeping with him, too."

"That was different," he insisted. "We wouldn't have to wait long before old dude checked out. Then we could get back together afterward."

"Afterward? So Granderson Jaspers was going to die sooner or later. You'd kill him after he married Shysteen and she inherited his money. It was Mattie who was meant to die that night. Argh! Then Grandy would be free to remarry without paying spousal support."

"Shysteen messed that one up, too. Stupid chick can't do nothing right. She stole a big needle from work to shoot Viagra into old girl's wine bottles. Grandy wound up getting it instead."

"You were counting on the fact that Grandy only drank beer. But it was a toast. Mattie sipped from Grandy's bottle and he drank champagne from her glass. A lot of champagne, as it turned out. He got the overdose that was meant for her. You and Shysteen knew that Mattie's heart was bad and a massive dose of Viagra would probably kill her, like it did Grandy and later, Delbert Dailey."

"If anybody had it coming, Dailey was the one," he sneered. "That trick was threatening to sell us out. First, he promised to help Shysteen get that money. So, she told him the truth, that it might not be Grandy's baby. He was supposed to keep that on the QT."

I'd snort with laughter if I hadn't been hurting so bad. "A man like Delbert would hardly respect attorney-client privilege. Ow! That hurts."

"Then he flipped the script and said he wanted a cut, otherwise he'd tell everybody the baby wasn't Grandy's. He was on them Viagras anyway, so it didn't take much to put him down. He came to the Jets to see her one night, too damned cheap to get a hotel. I slipped some in his vodka while he slept it off."

"I know you tried to OD me, too. You put something in my cocoa when I was cooking your food. I don't have heart problems, so I doubt it would have killed me. But you're too stupid to know that. Even if it did, no one would think the Viagra in my system was an accident. You aren't going to get away with this, Evrian."

"You talk too much, bitch. See, that's your problem. Sticking your nose in other folks' business. Going on TV and calling out my name. Ain't nothing worse than a snitch."

With a mighty heave, Evrian pulled me halfway to my feet and propped me against the counter. He pinned me there with his shoulder and raised the chain in his other hand.

The softness that cradles hardness, a needle within a ball of cotton.

I wasn't a woman anymore, I was a fluff of cotton blown by a hard wind. Instead of bracing for the blow, I fell away from it. The length of chain hit the counter hard, followed by Evrian's fist. He roared with pain, cradling his hand against his chest.

I scrambled to my feet and ran to the front door. This time I managed to unlock it before Evrian reached me. He drew back his head to butt mine, a move I'd seen roughnecks do on the West Side.

Movement springs from supreme stillness, opening then closing.

I threw my arms open, as if to hug him. Evrian's head moved toward mine and I fell into the pose "strumming the lute." My head sank forward into the curve of my body.

Instead of crashing against me, Evrian connected headfirst with the pane of crackled glass. I heard a sickening thud like a watermelon hitting concrete. He tumbled over backward and lay sprawled on the floor. Evrian King was out for the count.

I couldn't believe what had happened, the smear of blood running down the window. The bloody gash blooming on his forehead. I looked down, stunned at the bulk of Evrian. I had felled my opponent without touching him.

Evrian was knocked out but he might not stay like that. I grabbed the chain and looped it several times around his neck. I thought I could fasten it to the door's overhead transom, the only thing within reach that might hold him. Once I had him secured, I could call 911. I threw one end over the metal transom but I wasn't quite tall enough to pull it down and padlock it to the other end.

By the time I dragged over a chair, Evrian was groaning and twisting. The loose chain fell from the transom and hit him on top of the head. He yelped with pain but still tried to rise. The length of chain around his neck rattled like the Ghost of Christmas past.

It now seemed that my only hope would be escaping while he was still slow and groggy. I pushed past him for the unlocked door, but it began opening inward. Someone outside was coming in. Another vicious accomplice? Shysteen returning to make sure the job was done?

"Stop right there!" I ordered with a force I didn't feel. "Don't come any farther or you'll get what he got."

Whoever it was ignored me. The overhead chime sounded and the door fully opened, letting in a blast of frigid air. Detective Emerson Jacobs stepped into the room. She looked down at Evrian struggling to his knees. That irritatingly husky voice of hers was never more welcome than now.

"What on earth is going on?"

"This man is trying to kill me, is what's going on. Look, he's getting away."

Weaving on unsteady feet, Evrian King lurched toward the door.

"Hold on," Jacobs growled. "Not so fast."

When Evrian weakly ordered her to get the hell out of his way, she drew her revolver and aimed it at his head. "You're already bleeding from a head wound, buddy. I don't think you want a matching one. Now lie face down with your hands behind your neck."

Evrian groaned but complied, collapsing to his knees and rolling onto his belly. Jacobs knelt beside him and fastened on the handcuffs.

"You have the right to remain silent. Anything you say can and will be used against you in a court of law. You have the right to an attorney . . ."

CHAPTER 42

To Live For

My left eye was blooming like a bloodshot tomato. Tomorrow I'd have a shiner for sure. Evrian King liked to give women purple eyes, it seemed. I gingerly placed a pack of frozen corn over it.

"Girl, wrap that thing up before you get freezer burn." Penny folded a dish towel around the package. "Raw steak works better than frozen vegetables. It'll draw down all that swelling."

"You know we're fresh out of steak." I leaned sideways against Fanon's broad chest. His arms were wrapped around me like he'd never let go. I had to admit it felt good.

"Who told you to be a hero, Savvy? I'd never forgive you if something more serious happened." He leaned in to kiss the top of my head. "And I'd never forgive myself."

Penny shook a reprimanding finger. "You should have locked this place up and called the police. Why the hell did you let those people in?"

"They had a child with them. It was Christmas Eve and the kid was hungry."

"If I've told you once, I've told you twice," Penny lectured. "That bleeding heart of yours will sink your ship one day."

I explained how they had conspired to murder Mattie so

her husband would be free to marry Shysteen. The bumbling duo wound up accidentally killing Grandy instead. With their golden goose expired, the two of them came up with a plan to get their hands on the money he had, or would soon be getting. That unborn child Shysteen was carrying would be their golden ticket.

"She was Billie Jeaning the poor old fool," Penny sang. *"The kid is not my son."*

Consulting the alderman for legal advice backfired when Dailey seduced Shysteen—or she seduced him—then demanded in on the plan. Evrian had been willing to lend her out when he thought she'd be raking in the cash. When there was nothing in it for him, the guy wasn't willing to share.

"In other words," Penny decided, "Evrian's a pimp."

I tilted my head in consideration. "Maybe more like a gigolo."

"Get to the point," Fanon demanded. "Why'd they come here after you?"

I explained that Evrian became enraged when I accidentally blurted out his name on the Channel 6 TV Evening News. They thought I was getting close to the truth and came here to shut my mouth for good.

Outside, the blinking blue police lights bounced and strobed in the crackled window. I was glad to see it still intact after Evrian's misdirected headbutt. It would take more than one hardheaded thug to shatter that thick pane of glass.

Detective Jacobs had been outside the café, directing the uniformed cops. The front door opened and she breezed back in, brisk with officious energy. When she saw me in the loose circle of Fanon's arms she stopped stock-still, frowning.

"That was a foolhardy move, Ms. Summers, taking on a reprobate like Evrian King. You're lucky a black eye is all you got out of the deal."

I could feel Fanon tense beside me. "Emmy, this is hardly the time..."

"She's just as worried as you two," I interrupted. "Sergeant Jacobs may have saved my life. Cut the woman some slack."

Her expression softened as she came to join us at Table Two. "I must admit I am relieved. This could have been so much worse."

"But it wasn't," Penny pointed out. "Savvy took down a murderer all by herself, which is more than can be said for you coppers."

"He was just one out of two accomplices," I sighed. "Shysteen Shackleford is on the run. I sure hope she doesn't get away."

Sergeant Jacobs accepted the mug of hot chocolate Penny handed her, frowning into the steaming liquid. "I'd rather have a coffee, if it's the same to you."

"Not a chance, it's all packed away. Beggars can't be choosers."

As the three of us sat sipping hot chocolate, Sergeant Jacobs announced that Shysteen had been collared. She and her child had walked to the bus turnaround on Stony Island. The uniforms caught them patiently sitting on a westbound #63 about to pull off.

"Now that's a new low, even for her!" Penny exclaimed. "Who brings a kid to a homicide?"

Sergeant Jacobs stirred her cocoa with a teaspoon. "She said she couldn't find a babysitter. As if double homicide and attempted murder weren't enough, she'll now be charged with child endangerment and neglect. The daughter's in the hands of DCFS now."

"Where is Shysteen?" I asked, readjusting the cold pack over my eye.

"Both the perps are bagged and tagged. We don't have many

cars out on Christmas morning so we had to put them in together." Sergeant Jacobs's brow wrinkled in disgust. "Even with handcuffs on they were going at it hot and heavy in the back of the squad car."

"You're kidding." Fanon shook his head. "Getting it on in a police cruiser? In all my years on the force, I never heard of anything like that."

"It didn't get as far as that. I broke up their little make-out session and tried to get across the seriousness of the situation. Shysteen had the nerve to say, and I quote: 'Ain't no telling how long before I get some again.'"

"Damn, that girl is high-natured." Penny seemed almost impressed. "Knocking the boots on the way to the pokey, a regular Bonnie and Clyde."

"She's more like a textbook sociopath," Sergeant Jacobs said. "Lack of conscience and sense of consequences, narcissistic in the extreme. Though she may not actually do the deed, she's good at getting susceptible men to give her what she wants."

"I knew she had a criminal past," I said. "But I never suspected her of murder."

Sergeant Jacobs drained her cup. "Homicide has had an eye on those two. Certain things came to light during the Dailey investigation that I wasn't at liberty to share. We were gathering evidence but had some interference. If only you had been more patient."

I shrugged tiredly. "Well, it's over and done with now. I'll sleep better with those two behind bars. Thank God you turned up when you did. How did you know I was in trouble?"

Jacobs said that even off duty, she regularly listens to voice-mails. "And you left a very long one."

"I did?"

"You didn't disconnect after you called. When I listened

and heard what was going on, I jumped in the car and rushed over."

"It sure took you a while."

"I had to come from Canaryville and I called in backup. The uniformed officers were on their way. I'm surprised I beat them here."

Penny removed the ice pack from my eye, gathered our mugs and took them into the kitchen.

I yawned convulsively. "What time is it now?"

Sergeant Jacobs checked her wristwatch. "Almost three a.m. I know you've been through an ordeal. A homicide detective is coming to take your statement. When that's done you can get some rest. Fanon, we've got it under control. You can go home now, if you like."

"If it's all the same, I'll stick around," he volunteered.

Sergeant Jacobs shrugged. "As you wish."

"I still can't get over it." Fanon shook his head. "Arrested on suspicion of attempted murder, with a pending double homicide. And Shysteen's first thought is trying to get some. I'm sure some of those hard-legged sisters in the Cook County Jail will be happy to oblige."

"Fanon!" Detective Jacobs stared him down. "'Hard-legged sisters?' I had no idea you were so homophobic."

"You know I didn't mean anything by it, Emmy. Just some levity in a grim situation."

Her thin lips tightened. "Well, it's not the least bit funny."

Fanon gave a sigh of exasperation. "Come on, lighten up."

She gave him a sister girl wag of the head. "I'm as light as I'm ever going to get."

"You're what?" I couldn't tell if she was serious until she turned to me and winked.

"I'm so white I made Casper go da-yum. And I also happen

to be one of those hard-legged sisters you speak of. So check yourself before you wreck yourself, Fanon Franklin. And Ms. Summers, when you decide to drop this zero, there's a hero for you right here."

She pointed to herself with both her thumbs then spun on her high-heeled boot and clicked out the door. Somebody must have given her a dictionary of Black English.

Fanon blinked in disbelief. "I've known Emerson Jacobs for decades. How did I not know this?"

Penny emerged triumphantly from the kitchen with a new ice pack for my eye. "I told you, Savvy Summers. It's you she's been macking on, not Fanon. My laydar never lies."

The groundbreaking ceremony went off without a hitch. Bundled up like Nanook of the North, I struck my shovel futilely against frozen ground while cameras clicked and news cams hovered. There was even a drone circling the sky above us, though I wasn't sure who it belonged to.

The developer posed for more photos with me and Sophia Valdez-Johnson, the new alderperson of our ward. But when Channel 6 newswoman Samantha Patterson thrust a mic in my face and asked for a statement, I held up a restraining hand.

"It's twenty below zero out here and I can't feel my hands anymore. If you really want a statement, then meet me inside."

The small crowd followed me into the fragrant warmth of Essie's Place. Some headed directly for hot coffee at the beverage station against the far wall. A buffet spread of light refreshments waited out of sight on the kitchen island: collard green quiches, salmon croquettes, curried tuna mushroom caps, vegetable crudités, and for dessert, sweet potato tarts, pineapple upside-down cupcakes, and the berry lavender shortcake with chamomile cream that had gone down so well at the playoff raffle party.

"Let's hear it for the hostess with the mostest," Penny shouted, leading the crowd in a verse of "For She's a Jolly Good Fellow."

I finally accepted the mic. "Thanks for those kind words. I hope to live up to all that fulsome praise, for now and in the future."

At least fifty guests were gathered for the groundbreaking of Woodlawn Plaza. It was purely a ceremonial occasion, as no ground had actually been broken, not yet anyway. Building of the new shopping center wouldn't begin until the summer.

We had an all-male serving staff that day. Fanon passed around flutes of champagne while Parker circulated through the room with trays and passed hors d'oeuvres. Penny and I got to be guests for a change. A few familiar faces were in attendance that afternoon.

Sergeant Jacobs wore a white winter woolen pantsuit so stark she almost disappeared in it. When she winked at me, I waved weakly and edged a little closer to Penny.

"What's the matter, Savvy?" she asked.

"I ain't afraid of no ghosts."

Still, Emmy's newfound persona was growing on me. Though I was in no position to reciprocate, it was reassuring to learn she was a woman of passion. It seemed the Ice Maiden wasn't quite so icy after all.

Mattie and Tuck openly held hands, stealing shy glances at one another. Winnie Mae stared at them in amazement, nudging Henpecked Henry and pointing.

I could even imagine the dearly departed gathered to help celebrate the next phase of my life: my parents and grandparents,

Great-Aunt Essie, Francis Summers, Grandy Jaspers, and even that rascal Delbert Dailey who'd loved my food so much.

"My building will eventually be razed to build a shopping center," I announced. Collective gasps went out among the crowd. "But never fear. The deal we struck was more than fair. Most importantly, there's a guarantee that once Woodlawn Plaza opens the year after next, one of the flagship businesses will be Essie's 2.0."

It was the first time I'd publicly announced the bittersweet news about the café's imminent closing. I'd be shutting down by the middle of the following year. In the meantime, I was looking for a commercial kitchen from which to operate my catering business, as well as somewhere else to live. I'd be waiting at least a couple of years to reopen in the new space.

In the downtime I planned to work on the cookbook project, *Aunt Essie's Table*. Maybe I'd get to travel a little. I'd just spent a week with Nzinga in Brooklyn, but I was long overdue for a nice long visit to my son and his family. I'd always known when things weren't right with Malik. And I could tell by his voice on recent phone calls that something was definitely wrong.

The new location for Essie's wouldn't have the charm of my vintage storefront. No copper ceiling tiles or gorgeous hardwood floors. No gray stone facade at street level or second-floor living quarters. On the other hand, it would be three times the size of the original with all the amenities of new construction, not to mention plenty of free parking for my customers, and walk-in traffic from other businesses in the strip mall.

In the political fallout over the McPherson/Dailey scandal, the new developer had bent over backward to make things right with me. The price I was able to negotiate could have given me a comfortable income for many years to come, if I actually planned to retire again. Which I didn't. I was happy to host a groundbreaking ceremony this windswept winter morning. It wasn't just my blessing for the upcoming project. It was also a strategic opportunity to publicize Essie's, the present version and what was to come.

Who knew that sweet potato pie would bring so many mixed blessings?

"Certain others have called my food *to die for.*" I gave Mattie Jaspers a nod of recognition and she nodded right back. "We're on a mission to make soul food as elevated as it is delicious. Our motto comes from my Great-Aunt Essie, who cooked her food with *a pinch of bacon grease and a pound of love.* The bacon grease is metaphorical, but the love is for real."

"A to the men!" Winnie shouted. As usual, she'd been frequenting the champagne bar.

"And that's not to die for," I continued. "It's to live for and live well. You don't have to go to heaven when you can taste it here on earth."

I gave a little bow, shook off the applause, and returned to my seat. My ex-husband Fanon, looking dapper in black and a white apron with the new Essie's logo, reached over and squeezed my hand.

"Well done, sugar dumpling," he whispered to me. "Well done, indeed."

I dipped into a light curtsy, ignoring the cracking in my left knee. "Why, thank you kindly, sir."

Great-Aunt Essie's Epithets

Lord have mercy on their naked souls.
(Only God can forgive such outrageous behavior.)

*There were three sides to every story: her side, his side, and
    the dad-gum truth.*
(Self-explanatory.)

The world's best cure for the blues is a dose of good deeds.
(When you're really down in the dumps, helping someone
    else can make you feel better.)

*God ain't impressed with a pretty face, but he don't like ugly
    ways.*
(Self-explanatory.)

*You do your best listening at mealtimes, 'cause that's when
    people do their best talking.*
(People let their guard down when they're enjoying their
    food and drink.)

Fish stank starts from the head on down.
(If something is wrong at the bottom then look at the top
    for the cause of it.)

If his lips are moving, he's lying.
(Nearly every word this person speaks is likely to be
    untrue.)

If you lie, you'll steal, and if you steal, you'll kill.
(Lying is a gateway offense to much more serious
   crimes.)

Child, he went running out of here like a scalded haint.
(He left here in an awful hurry. A "haint" is a ghost in
   Southern vernacular.)

*Lies are just like roaches. Shine a little light on them and
   they scramble off in all directions.*
(When you tell too many lies, they can easily get away
   from you; nor do they hold up well to light.)

Nice-nasty.
(A person of ill intent who pretends to be virtuous.)

*The crumb you throw away today might fill you up
   tomorrow.*
(Waste not, want not.)

Dime-wise and dollar-stupid.
(Spending a dollar to save a dime; penny-wise and pound-
   foolish.)

*Whatever she saved in dollars and cents, she lost in common
   sense.*
(See previous line.)

Trouble comes in threes.
(When something bad happens, two other things are
   waiting to go wrong.)

The milk that was already spoiled this morning ain't hardly gone be good this afternoon.
(When something starts out wrong, it's hard to make it right.)

That man is some kind of twisted mess. I bet his bowels ain't regular.
(He acts up because he's constipated. Aunt Essie thought this malady was at the root of most ills.)

Tell the truth and shame the devil.
(Truthfulness is a victory over evil.)

A pinch of bacon grease and a pound of love.
(The best meals are made from humble ingredients and a loving heart.)

Mind your lessons, gal, and listen, lest you wind up in Miss Ann's kitchen.
(Get your education so you won't have to work as a domestic.)

You've got to give some to get some.
(Though generosity is its own reward, it is often rewarded in kind.)

If you let a man walk all over you, don't be surprised when he calls you a carpet.
(If you allow a man to mistreat you, it will only get worse as time goes on.)

The devil you know is better than the angel you don't.
(You're better off taking chances with a questionable
  character you know than with a seemingly virtuous one
  you don't.)

Don't get my Mississippi up!
(Fool around and find out!)

He's the kind that wants his pie and pudding both.
(He always tries to get more than he deserves.)

That man had a hole in both his pockets.
(He was beyond broke.)

Aunt Essie's Table

୧

BEVERAGES

Great-Aunt Essie sometimes flavored her lemonade with home-made magnolia syrup, which isn't that easy to come by these days. I adapted her recipe with orange blossom water, available online or at food stores serving the Middle Eastern market.

ORANGE BLOSSOM LEMONADE

(serves 4)

½ cup honey or simple syrup
1 cup very hot water
2½ cups cold water
Juice from 3–4 lemons (approximately ½–¾ cup)
3 teaspoons orange blossom water
Sparkling water
Lemon slices (optional)
Mint sprigs (optional)

Use your mixing cup to add the sweetener into hot water. Whisk until fully dissolved. Pour into a quart-sized pitcher and briskly stir in cold water, lemon juice, and orange blossom water until well mixed. Chill in the refrigerator for at least an hour, then serve over ice cubes with a splash of sparkling water, a slice of lemon, and a sprig of fresh mint. It's a refreshing summer beverage to enjoy any time of year.

Like that infamous scamp, Delbert "Do-Right" Dailey, you can make the drink "electric" by replacing ½ cup of cold water with an equal measure of vodka and switching out the orange blossom water for an orange liqueur like triple sec, curaçao, or

Aperol. For a John Daly aka "Dirty Arnold Palmer" variation, add ¾ cup of cold iced tea.

PEPPERMINT HONEY HOT CHOCOLATE

(serves 2)

> *2 cups milk**
> *¼ cup honey*
> *4 oz dark or semi-sweet chocolate chips*
> *2 drops peppermint oil or ½ teaspoon peppermint extract*
> *Pinch of salt*
> *Freshly whipped cream (optional)*
> *Peppermint candy canes (optional)*

In a medium saucepan, bring milk to a simmer over medium heat. Once simmering, whisk in honey until dissolved. Remove pan from the burner and add the chocolate chips. Let chips soften, then whisk until completely melted and mixed. Add peppermint oil and salt. Serve in a mug with a dollop of whipped cream and a candy-cane garnish. If you like adult beverages, add ¼ cup of peppermint schnapps.

*You may substitute dairy milk for any plant-based milk like soy, almond, oat, or coconut.

DESSERTS

These pies serve 6–8 people, depending on how you slice it. Why not double the recipe to make one for your guests and save one for yourself? You'll thank me later.

AUNT ESSIE'S SWEET POTATO PIE

One pie shell (store-bought or homemade)
3 large or 4 medium sweet potatoes
2 eggs
½ stick butter, softened
1 cup granulated sugar
1 cup whipping cream (½ cup reserved for garnish)
1 tablespoon lemon juice, freshly squeezed
1 tablespoon vanilla flavoring
1 tablespoon nutmeg
1 tablespoon cinnamon
Vanilla ice cream (optional)
Freshly whipped cream or vanilla ice cream (optional)

Aunt Essie's full-bodied, Southern-style pie has all the rich, traditional flavors. Prick the dough with airholes, then blind bake the pie shell in a 350° oven for 8–10 minutes, then set aside. Puncture the sweet potatoes all over with a fork, then roast at 375° for 45–50 minutes, until fork-tender. After the potatoes have cooled, peel and mash them with a large fork or potato masher. The mash shouldn't be lumpy, but should still have a little texture. Beat the eggs slightly, then add to the mixture. Stir in butter, sugar, ½ cup cream, lemon juice, vanilla, and spices. Transfer to prebaked shell and shimmy slightly to settle. Bake at 350° for 40–45 minutes until set. Let cool for 20–30 minutes, then slice and serve with a dollop of freshly whipped cream or vanilla ice cream.

SAVVY'S "IN YOUR FACE" PRIZE-WINNING VEGAN SWEET POTATO PIE

One vegan pie shell, store-bought or homemade
3 large or 4 medium sweet potatoes
13.5-oz can of full-fat coconut milk
½ cup each: brown sugar and honey*
4 tablespoons vegan butter, softened
2 tablespoons freshly squeezed lemon juice (approximately one small lemon)
1 teaspoon nutmeg
1 teaspoon cinnamon
1 teaspoon ginger
1 teaspoon allspice
1 teaspoon vanilla
1 teaspoon cornstarch or arrowroot
Pinch of salt
Nondairy whipped cream or vanilla ice cream (optional)

My lighter, spicier version is made without any animal products. Prick the dough with airholes, then blind bake the pie shell in a 350° oven for 8–10 minutes, then set aside. Perforate the raw sweet potatoes with a fork, then roast at 375° for 45–50 minutes until fork-tender. After the potatoes have cooled, peel and mash them with a large fork or potato masher. The mash shouldn't be lumpy, but should still have a little texture. Stir in coconut milk, then thoroughly mix in the other ingredients. Transfer to prebaked shell and shimmy slightly to settle. Bake at 350° for 45–50 minutes until set. Let cool for 20–30 minutes, then slice and serve with a dollop of nondairy whipped cream or a scoop of vegan vanilla ice cream.

*You may substitute the honey with maple syrup or agave.

STARTERS/ENTREES

Enjoy this updated version of West African *akaras* as an appetizer with a variety of dipping sauces, a vegan entrée, or tucked into a bun with all the fixings as a veggie burger.

BLACK-EYED PEA FRITTERS*

(makes 5–10 patties, depending on size)

2 cups of raw black-eyed peas, soaked for 5–6 hours (preferably overnight)
½ carrot, roughly chopped
½ zucchini, roughly chopped
1 small chopped onion
2 cloves minced garlic
Salt to taste
*Old Bay seasoning to taste***
2 tablespoons vegetable oil

Mix all ingredients except the vegetable oil in a blender or food processor at medium speed. The veggies provide their own moisture but feel free to add a little water if the mixture is too crumbly. Shape into patties and fry in hot oil, four minutes on each side.

*Courtesy of Chef Tsadakeeyah of Majani Soulful Vegan Cuisine in Chicago's South Shore

**For a spicier version, add ½ teaspoon cayenne pepper.

LEMON PEPPER AIR-FRIED PERCH

(serves 4)

> *8 perch fillets**
> *2 eggs, beaten*
> *Seasoned cornmeal coating, mix together:*
> > *1 cup of cornmeal*
> > *1 teaspoon salt*
> > *1 teaspoon lemon pepper*
> > *1 teaspoon garlic powder*
> > *1 teaspoon paprika*
> *Lemon wedges (optional)*

An easier and healthier approach to deep-fried fish is air frying your fillets. Dip fillets individually in the egg bath, let drain, then roll in the cornmeal mixture. Set coated fillets on a paper towel–covered plate or wire rack to hydrate for 5–10 minutes. Place the fillets in the air fryer basket, making sure they're not crowded. Depending on the size of your appliance, you may have to cook in batches. Cook at 375° for 10 minutes, then flip the fillets over and cook for an additional 5–7 minutes.

Serve with a lemon wedge and your choice of sauces. Tartar sauce is a fan favorite, though I'm a hot sauce girl myself.

*You may substitute any mild, flaky whitefish like cod, sole, tilapia, or halibut.

Soulfully yours,
Savvy Oceal Slidell Summers

Acknowledgments

Writing this novel was a long and arduous journey some ten years in the making. My background has primarily been as a literary and historical fiction writer. I've read mystery novels for most of my life but had never attempted to write one unless you count that failed PI procedural of thirty years ago. I thought the title was oh-so-clever, but couldn't think of a single case for *Freddy, Willie, and Able* to solve.

Novelist and folklorist Zora Neale Hurston said: "You've got to go there to know there." *Savvy Summers and the Sweet Potato Crimes* has been an exercise in "going there"—trying to learn what I didn't know and unlearn some things I did. I've worked through various revisions and drafts trying to master the voice, characters, and genre conventions while also tentatively testing some of those boundaries.

The most satisfying works for me are true to the worlds they portray. As a reader, I love to immerse myself in the particularities of an experience, whether it's an Irish hamlet, a Napa Valley vineyard, a New England bakery, or an urban ethnic restaurant.

I'm a second-generation Southern migrant whose family connections on both sides extend to Mississippi. While this novel may not look like the conventional cozy, it tries to remain faithful to the people and experiences I was raised with, and the places from which they originated.

People talk so much about how "it takes a village," that the expression has almost become a cliché. I want to recapture that Igbo and Yoruba West African proverb and restore it to its original context. Many hands make light(er) work, and multiple hands have touched this project.

Lucille Freeman may not remember this, but the idea emerged (so far as I remember) from a late-night conversation at an informal writer's retreat in New Buffalo, Michigan. I told her about my great-aunt Oceal, who ran a boardinghouse out of her apartment, cooked and sold meals from her kitchen, and operated several soul-food diners on the west side of Chicago. Lucille believed Aunt 'Ceal's experiences would make a good story, so I sat down and started writing. The mystery came later.

A village of trusted readers gave constructive feedback on early drafts: Lucille Freeman, Lou Macaluso, Lydia Barnes, Kalisha Buckhanon, Kellye Garrett, and Mia Manansala. Fellow members of FLOW (For Love of Writing) also offered comments and suggestions at various stages of the work: Lydia Barnes, Tina Jenkins Bell, Felisha Madlock, April Gary, Heather Byrd, Chiskira Caillouet, and Janice Tuck Lively. Other alpha readers include Sarah Cypher, Lorraine Harrell, Kimberley Nightingale Cornwell, Kia Dennis, Manju Soni, Abby Vandiver, and Zoe Wallbrook.

I also appreciate the logistical support provided by Carolyn Haines, Kalisha Buckhanon, Kallie E. Benjamin, Valerie Burns, Valerie Wilson Wesley, Raquel Reyes, Abby Collette, Chef Tsadakeeyah Ben Emmanuel, Chef Carla Hall, Kellye Garrett, Mia Manansala, Esme Addison, Lori Rader Day, Tracy Clark, Chef Maya-Camille Broussard, Susanna Calkins, and my Torch Literary Retreat Fellows Deborah "Deep" Moten, Ifesinachi Okonkwo, Liz Brown, Destiny Hemphill, m. mick powell, Meredith King, and DW McKinney.

My tribe at Crime Writers of Color, Sisters in Crime-National, and Sisters in Crime-Chicago, have been incredibly supportive, with special thanks to Lori Rader Day, Susanna Calkins, and the Sisters in Crime selection committee that awarded me a grant to research multicultural cozy mysteries.

I've received valuable institutional support for this and other literary endeavors. Artist retreats and residencies have been immensely supportive—those remarkable communities to which artists run away from home in order to rest, reflect, and work. At the very beginning, Larry S. Reiner loaned out his Michigan cottage for the FLOW Writers Retreat at which this novel was born. Somewhere toward the midpoint, Write On, Door County, provided a cozy corner to develop the work over two weeks. Jerod Santek even brought me on board to speak at a WODC mystery writing conference when I had but a single crime-writing publishing credit to my name.

Near the end of the process, with book contract in hand, Story-knife Writers Retreat awarded me the Joan Perry Barnes Crime Writers Fellowship where I worked on second-round edits. A million thanks to Dana Stabenow for her generous support and largesse. I am also grateful to Esme Addison for her useful Zoom course, "How to Write a Cozy Mystery," with special appreciation to classmates Rebecca Harrison for her continued support and Cristilisa "Missy" Gilmore for professional recipe testing.

I'm deeply inspired by literary novelists who've branched off into crime writing. Sherman Alexie, Rudolfo Anaya, Rita Mae Brown, Joyce Carol Oates, and Valerie Wilson Wesley have provided solid examples of how to flex the bounds of genre with consummate style and grace.

Much gratitude to my first cousin Don Jackson for being an exemplar of family excellence, and for introducing me to the world of gospel music. Grandy Jaspers is by no means a representation of that experience, but a character of many contradictions, excesses, and comic relief.

Other people's stories sometimes drift into our work, so be careful what you say, or even think, around writers. We might put it into a story! I trust that Michael West won't mind my sharing a certain family member's "romantic mathematics." My sister, Sheryl Jackson Osinowo, has always warned against the perils and pitfalls of "headache champagne." Bits and pieces of David Lemieux's intriguing professional life have also seeped into the story. Fanon Franklin, I'm looking at you!

Law enforcement is an intrinsic element of crime writing, with figures of the valorous public servant and the tortured, traumatized police officer becoming staples of the genre. There are also tropes aplenty of the bumbling small-town constable and corrupt big-city cop.

I wanted to examine an underexplored element, that of law enforcement activism. I'm inspired by the cadre of "culture cops" working for social change. These men and women began entering the field on the heels of the Civil Rights and Black Power movements and assassinations of Black leaders. I am tremendously indebted to David Lemieux, former Black Panther and retired Chicago police detective, for his insight into CPD policies, politics, and culture. Thanks also to Abby Vandiver for offering the benefit of her legal experience. Any legal or procedural errors that arise are mine, and mine alone.

It's hard to believe it's been twenty-five years since my last novel was published. My agent, Regina Brooks, has been a marvel in guiding me through this new landscape and shepherding my career. The editorial and marketing teams at Minotaur Books have been such a pleasure to work with: Maddie Alsup, Sarah Beth Haring, and Hector DeJean. We went back and forth on the cover design but finally came together on striking book jacket art by Vi-An Nguyen.

The sensible and sensitive Hannah O'Grady had been looking for a cozy mystery set on Chicago's South Side, and lo and behold, found my manuscript in the slush pile of a writing competition. The story wasn't quite ready, but she helped me get it there. I couldn't have asked for a better editor.

I've had a fascinating journey with Malice Domestic, the mystery-writing fan convention that cosponsored the competition I won with my then-unpublished manuscript. If we ever get a chance to meet, buy me a drink and maybe I'll tell you the story. I was especially gratified to attend their 2023 convention and receive the Malice Minotaur Award for Best First Traditional Mystery Novel.

I would be remiss if I didn't mention the Circle of Confusion Writers Fellowship, the cohort, staff, and my mentor, Antonio D'Intino, who all helped me to adapt this project into a television series. I believe the opportunity still awaits, and as Brook Benton prophetically sang: "It's Just a Matter of Time." My daughter, Adjoa Opoku, has both been a helpmeet and a cheerleader on this project.

I salute the ranks of amateur and professional chefs who honor our culinary heritage. As Chef Tsadakeeyah of Chicago's Majani Soulful Vegan Cuisine says, "We're treading on sacred ground."

My forebears have been whispering in my ear all the while. My great-aunt, Oceal Patterson, upon whom Aunt Essie is partially based; my grandmother Ella Mary ("Muh Dear") Ingram, who helped raise me and my three siblings; my late cousin-aunts Beatrice Woodson and Estella Whitney, who came up with my mother as best friends and twelve-year first cousins on the Great Migration journey from Mississippi and Memphis; and Doris Lee Jackson, who mothered the four of us through the sunshine and storms of a challenging life.

Meda wo ase! Praise be to the ancestors.

Michael Brandt

Sandra Jackson-Opoku is the author of the award-winning novel *The River Where Blood Is Born* and *Hot Johnny (and the Women Who Loved Him)*, an *Essence* magazine bestseller in hardcover fiction. She also coedited the anthology *Revise the Psalm: Work Celebrating the Writing of Gwendolyn Brooks*. Her fiction, nonfiction, and dramatic works are widely published and produced in *Adi Magazine*, *midnight & indigo*, *Aunt Chloe*, *Africa Risen: A New Era of Speculative Fiction*, *New Daughters of Africa*, *Obsidian*, *Another Chicago Magazine*, *storySouth*, Lifeline Theatre, the Chicago Humanities Festival, and others. Professional recognition includes a Plentitudes Journal Prize, the Hearst Foundation James Baldwin Fellowship at MacDowell Arts, a National Endowment for the Arts Fiction Fellowship, an American Library Association Black Caucus Award, a City of Chicago Esteemed Artist Award, the Iceland Writers Retreat Alumni Award, a Globe Soup Story Award, the Joan Perry Barnes Fellowship in Crime Writing at Storyknife Writers Retreat, and a Pushcart Prize nomination.